ENVOY

DON'T MISS THESE OTHER THRILLING STORIES IN THE WORLDS OF

HALO

ENVOY

TOBIAS S. BUCKELL

BASED ON THE BESTSELLING XBOX® VIDEO GAMES

GALLERY BOOKS
New York | London | Toronto | Sydney | New Delhi

G

Gallery Books
An Imprint of Simon & Schuster, Inc.
1230 Avenue of the Americas
New York, NY 10020

First Gallery Books trade paperback edition April 2017

GALLERY BOOKS and colophon are registered trademarks of Simon & Schuster, Inc.

For information about special discounts for bulk purchases, please contact Simon & Schuster Special Sales at 1-866-506-1949 or business@simonandschuster.com.

The Simon & Schuster Speakers Bureau can bring authors to your live event. For more information or to book an event contact the Simon & Schuster Speakers Bureau at 1-866-248-3049 or visit our website at www.simonspeakers.com.

Manufactured in the United States of America

10 9 8 7 6 5 4 3 2

Library of Congress Cataloging-in-Publication Data is available.

ISBN 978-1-5011-0687-3
ISBN 978-1-5011-0688-0 (ebook)

This is for all the Halo fans who've loved Gray Team as much as I have. Thank you for giving me the chance to tell another one of their stories.

Thars's ships' crash site

Unwavering Discipline debris field

Gray Team crash site

Rak

Astlehich River

Masov Oasis

Sandholm

Carrow (Rakoi) "The Uldt Desert"

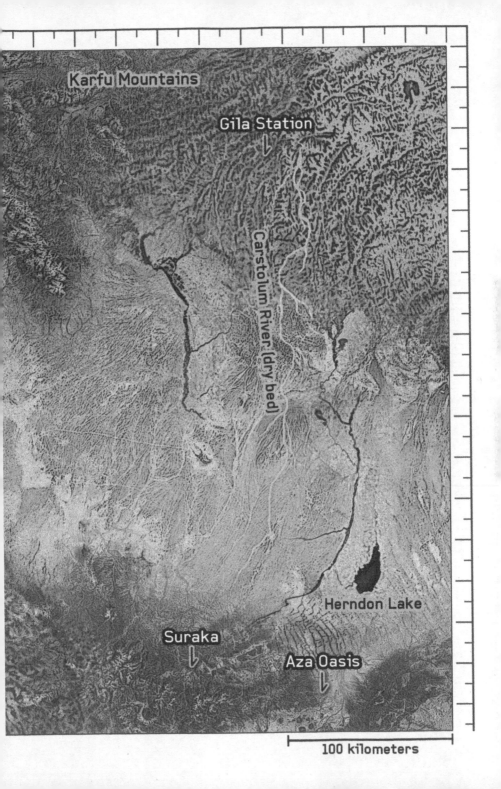

CHAPTER 1

Melody Azikiwe watched a Sangheili heavy destroyer die a slow, fiery death above the planet Carrow's upper atmosphere. Even from kilometers away, she could see the iridescent purple hull shimmer as the destroyer's thinner, almost waspish waist broke apart. The rear finlike structures spun off in a series of explosions, though the bulbous prow remained intact and still moved forward.

She was grateful to be standing inside a protected bay on the *Unwavering Discipline*, a former Covenant capital ship and sturdy heavy cruiser, in these final hours of what had become a bloody Sangheili civil war over Carrow's skies.

Melody watched plasma fire whip through the space between the vessels to carve up the remaining part of the other ship. Lights guttered out and what was left of the destroyer slowly fell through the upper atmosphere, blazing white-hot as the speed of reentry turned it into a stretched-out cloud of glowing debris.

From where she stood in the bay with her three Diplomatic Corps staff members, Melody could see the rest of the naval battle in the dark by the lines of plasma bolts dancing across empty space as Sangheili ships exchanged constant fire. A sudden blast of energy lanced out directly toward her and she flinched. The massive, vaulted hangar shuddered. The shield opening shivered as it dissipated the energy.

Adam Hsein, one of the three secretaries who made up Melody's staff for this diplomatic mission, glanced over at the hangar's open mouth. They all wore functional gray uniforms. Diplomatic Corps utilitarian clothing—not quite military, but clearly not civilian. Though Jens Forsburg had a yellow scarf around his neck, Jens never being one for regulations.

"How long do you think the *Discipline*'s shields can hold?" Adam asked nervously.

"This ship is really getting the crap beat out of it," Victoria Weaver agreed.

Another shuddering impact knocked them off their feet.

Melody staggered back up as Adam grabbed her arm. "You okay?" he asked.

Melody nodded. Victoria and Jens huddled protectively around her.

"*Unwavering Discipline* is a heavy cruiser," Melody reminded them, not for the first time since the fighting between the Sangheili had broken out in Carrow's orbit. It was an old vessel with an equally archaic, zealously Sangheili name. But that only meant it had survived many an encounter. "The shielding is strong. It'll take more than a few hits to knock it out. The fleetmaster knows what he's doing."

Victoria looked dubious. "I think he's losing."

Jens looked absolutely terrified that she'd said that out loud.

"We're not the experts on Sangheili fleet engagements," Melody remarked, glaring at Adam. He'd started this whole train of thought among the staff.

Adam shrugged in response but then nodded that he understood. They didn't need to be thinking about shield strength or who was winning the battle right this second. The two of them had always worked well together, half their communication being the nonverbal subtleties needed in the Diplomatic Corps.

"We should keep moving," Adam said, and pushed at their shoulders.

They walked past a row of teardrop-shaped Seraph fighters and three Spirit dropships. Despite the nature of the job, Melody was uncomfortable around the dropships in the gloom of a hangar. She was used to seeing them above the mountains, swooping down and bringing death. They looked like massive, flying tuning forks, the long forward-pointing arms vomiting Covenant soldiers out on the ground when they landed.

Six years ago they were the enemy. Now she could speak their language.

Things changed so fast. But it was still sometimes hard to shake the bad memories away. Even as an envoy. Even if the Spirits were empty and just being used for spare parts.

"Here we go." Melody stopped in front of the ship's Ren, a small and boxy specialized utility shuttle capable of quick, short-range travel thanks to its four impulse drives. "Victoria, get down to the coordinates I gave you. That's the safest possible area from all this mess. Don't head for Suraka."

They'd just seen hours earlier what Fleetmaster Rojka 'Kasaan's enemies had done to the city of Suraka from orbit. A vicious, pre-planned attack that had neutered human defenses in a matter of hours. Any ships with slipspace drives destroyed, on the ground or in orbit. An action destroying any chance of the peace that Melody had come to negotiate. And it had been followed by the Sangheili all turning on each other. It was a raw, ungloved Sangheili fight for the future of this world, with Melody caught in the middle.

Victoria looked across the hangar, back out through the Sangheili shields toward the battle. "You've got to be kidding me. I've only ever flown through a combat situation in a simulator, back on Earth. And that was only as part of standard training."

"And this kind of situation is what that training was for," Melody said. She squeezed Victoria's shoulder in reassurance. "You can do this. I have no doubt."

Melody tapped the control pad and the shuttle's door dropped open. Adam and Jens slipped past and inside to strap in. Victoria stayed put and grabbed Melody's hand. Her own hand was pale against Melody's skin, even in the strange Sangheili light. "You can't stay here."

"I have to," Melody replied.

"We'll be stranding you. Why are you staying? You can't stop any of this. You need to come with us. Your mission is over."

Melody projected calm and confidence for her staff. "Just get everyone down safely to Carrow. I can't talk about what's going on any further."

Victoria glanced around and lowered her voice. "You realize you're sending us to the middle of the desert. There's nothing there."

"You'll be all right. Trust me," Melody said.

"Does all this have something to do with the Office of Naval Intelligence?" Victoria had always been very curious about Melody's ad hoc ONI training sessions just before taking this mission. Not that Melody could have disclosed anything about that particular situation even if she wanted to.

"It's a safe place," Melody said. "Now, I'm ordering you: go!" There wasn't much time left.

At this point, Melody wasn't sure how long *Unwavering Discipline*'s shields would *really* hold. Her staff knew it; she knew it.

Melody Azikiwe wasn't a naval officer, but it seemed to her that *Unwavering Discipline* was now outgunned. At first, Fleetmaster Rojka 'Kasaan's fleet had been evenly matched against the other attacking Sangheili ships. But a Jiralhanae fleet had inexplicably since joined in, and the tide had clearly turned.

Melody had already seen two of Rojka's light destroyers obliterated while shielding the *Unwavering Discipline*. The fleetmaster had pulled in frigates to replace them. But that was all he had now—each of his heavy destroyers was burning in Carrow's upper atmosphere, ambushed by the Jiralhanae and unable to fall back to help him. Her staff's judgment had been correct: this was clearly the end of the battle.

Melody pushed Victoria in and closed the shuttle door. "Go!" She banged on it and backed away.

It sat there for another long minute.

Finally, the engines kicked on. The shuttle shot awkwardly across the hangar floor, wobbling in the air. Once outside the hangar, it seemed to pause for a second, until the engines lit up to fling it away from the ship just as another plasma assault struck the shields. Melody staggered back at the impact and smacked her ribs against a stack of stripped-down Sangheili engine parts, slicing an area of her palm on a jagged metal edge.

She hissed in pain. Then she grabbed her side and jogged her way back through the hangar. The direct hits to *Unwavering Discipline* increased as she moved. Apparently she'd gotten her staff off the ship just in time.

Melody pulled a strip of cloth out of her hair. It had grown out of regulation length and right up into frizzy chaos while on board the Sangheili ship. She hadn't had time to cut it herself, and there weren't exactly any Sangheili hairdressers on board. She wound the strip around her hand and then kept it clenched in a fist to hide the cut. This had less to do with protecting her injury and more to do with the fact that the Sangheili believed spilled blood to be shameful.

The fleetmaster stood waiting for her in a nearby corridor. Rojka 'Kasaan was surrounded by two of his trusted commanders and five guards who waited just behind them. Rojka himself towered over Melody, all two and a half meters of gray, saurian alien. He had a full weapons harness on, which was ominous—it meant he expected to be fighting hand-to-hand at any moment. Rojka's upper and lower mandible armor shifted as he spoke to her.

"Your staff has finished dishonoring themselves?" he asked in Sangheili as he began to walk. Melody had to hurry after him and his retinue as their long backward-joined legs strode rapidly down the corridors of his ship. "I see that the shuttle flees for the surface of Rakoi."

Rakoi. That was what the Sangheili who had taken residence on Carrow called the planet, ignoring the already existing human name. Rojka had explained to Melody that the Sangheili chose the different naming convention to honor the devastated human city of Suraka, somehow. And the Sangheili had built their own city, across the Uldt desert from the remains of Suraka, and called it Rak. All in memory of the human place they had once destroyed, never realizing that humans who had originally fled would actually ever try to come back to Carrow.

"This battle is not my staff's to fight," Melody replied, slightly out of breath as she struggled to keep up. It was hard to switch her mind to the alien language. She'd only been speaking it for a few years after being accepted into an accelerated immersion language program in the Diplomatic Corps. Though the last two months speaking Sangheili with warriors on this ship had *really* accelerated her abilities.

"Yet *you* stay aboard with us," Rojka observed.

"Yes. How does the *Unwavering Discipline* fare, Fleetmaster?"

The Sangheili's head, almost snakelike, twisted to look down at her. *Looking down: that comes so easily to them,* Melody thought. She wondered if it was their height that had given them their natural haughtiness toward other species.

"I have eliminated many of the enemy's destroyers and frigates," Rojka told her.

"But you're still outnumbered," Melody said. "And taking direct fire. That can't be a good sign, Fleetmaster."

Rojka slowed his loping walk. "You are correct," he said, thoughtfully. "Soon, Thars will send his best warriors for me when he disables this vessel. We have stopped maneuvering and are preparing to be boarded. My understanding, Envoy, is that you do not have extensive training in combat. Would you like to be honorably executed by my hand so that you are not captured alive?"

Melody instinctively pulled back. Then she stopped herself and remembered her cross-species training. "I thank you for your offer, Fleetmaster." Because it *was* a genuine and sincere offer from a Sangheili. "But I will not choose death by your hand."

"You understand that because you have made cause with me, Thars will not grant you a quick death. Or an honorable one. He cares little for humans."

"I stayed for another reason," Melody said, quickly shifting to get out in front of Rojka and half jogging backward. She lowered her voice so that only Rojka could hear what came next. "I want to wake the Spartans."

Rojka stopped in his tracks and roared, armored mandibles flying fully open in rage. Melody backed off, despite having steeled herself for just this reaction. "No! Their fate is sealed—sealed by actions they took long ago! Consider this their judgment. You tried your best, Envoy, but they were dead. Dead to begin with."

She had to make a martial argument. Something that a skilled fleetmaster would understand. "They can fight your enemies, they are an asset—" Melody started to say.

The Sangheili stepped forward and lowered his face down to hers, his wide, unblinking alien eyes staring deep into her own. "The only good thing about dying here is knowing that they will perish along with me."

He walked past. His soldiers moved with him, pushing Melody aside as they hissed at her.

Rojka craned his head around. "I have posted guards on what you seek," he said, "in case you have other thoughts about this matter."

Melody gritted her teeth. *Damn it.*

Rojka 'Kasaan stalked his way into *Unwavering Discipline*'s command bridge. Here, in the raised central platform of the cavernous room buried deep inside the heavy cruiser, he could see the situation at a glance by looking at any of the many holographic projections feeding him information about the battle and his ship's status.

Daga 'Rathum, one his most trusted field commanders, looked over at him. "We have lost *Retribution's Promise*," he announced.

That was Rojka's last escort. Their throat was now exposed to Thars 'Sarov. Rojka had fought like a trapped animal and managed to eliminate two of the enemy's heavy destroyers, along with four light destroyers and a frigate. But Thars was still coming for Rojka with four damaged frigates and his own heavy cruiser.

Rojka could have annihilated those too, were it not for the other fleet.

The Jiralhanae. Rojka cursed them. Two of their heavy cruisers and two heavy destroyers also advanced, patched together and pushed with engines underpowered due to the sheer amount of extra armoring the Jiralhanae added to the vessels. What a strange way to do battle: to purposely put your ships into the middle of fire and not even try to evade it. To just sit there and merely take the damage while firing back.

Rojka and Thars had both come to this world to create a new one together. To start over after the war took everything. Now it was clear that, while Thars might share an uncle with him, the only blood Thars now cared about was Rojka's: spilled on the ground of combat. And sadly, he was about to get that.

But why had Thars allied with the contemptible Jiralhanae? Why would they even be here after the result of the Great Schism they had set into motion years earlier? The Covenant had failed, obliterated under the weight of many lies; as a result, the Sangheili did not make common cause with Jiralhanae anymore, at least not as equals. No, this was strange. Thars was apparently so consumed with a desire for power and a hatred of the humans that he preferred to turn to the Jiralhanae and buy their loyalty rather than to Rojka, one of his own bloodline.

What did we call the Jiralhanae? Brutes. Rojka always thought it low and insulting. Yet he also found a certain fondness for the accuracy of the term. They were, indeed, Brutes.

Rojka had fiercely damaged his enemies, to be sure, but the inevitable was clear: he had lost this fight.

A part of Rojka looked forward to defining how the battle poems of his descendants would remember this moment. How he would die against great odds. He'd vanquished more ships than he'd lost. And when he was boarded, he would kill many traitorous Sangheili before he fell.

But another part of Rojka mourned the sheer waste.

"A weak kaidon should be attacked," he said to Daga, "but face-to-face, or with assassins. This fight between evenly matched fleets will only weaken Thars when he attempts to take Rakoi for his own. He will not even be able to fight the humans on this world as he wishes, despite the blow he struck them before embarking on this coup."

"Rakoi will not be able to stand as an independent colony," Daga said. "Everything we risked, everything we fought for, Thars now throws away."

"Such a fool I have never met. We were barely keeping our ships repaired and in good order," Rojka said. "Now we have lost most of them in this pointless battle among ourselves." Keeping a proper fleet maintained since the Great Schism and the breaking of the Covenant was difficult. Since the San'Shyuum Prophets and Jiralhanae betrayed the Sangheili, forsaking the Covenant's thousands of years of seeming invincible unity, they had all been making do by stripping parts off older vessels to keep any working ships running. Being a part of the Covenant had once meant access to great shipyards, great wealth, and even greater power. Now it was only a memory.

"He does not make us strong. He weakens us," Daga agreed.

Rojka missed the order and certainty of days past, longing for the knowledge of exactly what was to be done. He yearned for Sanghelios, his species' cradle world, though he knew he would never see it again. And of course, it was best not to think about Glyke, Rojka's own homeworld.

But to consider all he had lost right now would be to make himself weak before he needed to be his strongest.

He should never have let humans on his ship to begin with. Ever since he had first heard of the species, things had been falling apart.

Pesky, pesky things, these humans.

Rojka checked the holographic images on the projectors. A wave of enemy dropships flung themselves out into the space between the fighting vessels. *Unwavering Discipline* had lost most of its ability to fire back. But Rojka wasn't about to give the order to run. "If I am to die, so be it—whether it is in opposing rebellion by Thars, a sneak attack by the Jiralhanae he makes cause with, or anything else. I have fought well. I will die well."

"We die by your side, glorious and honorably!" a warrior called out from one of the entrances to the command bridge.

"Indeed," Rojka said, turning and looking down the main corridor from where his death might approach.

He fervently hoped Thars himself would lead the attack.

CHAPTER 2

Melody ran through the high, almost cathedral-like arched corridors of the *Unwavering Discipline.* The walls of the alien ship swirled with dark reds and purples unlike any of the neutral, gray materials Melody knew from her time on UNSC vessels. The first time she'd boarded a Sangheili ship, Melody had surreptitiously knocked on a wall to make sure it was solid, not some fleshy substance, as if she were standing inside some living thing. A giant whale.

Right now she was deep in the belly of the beast. *Inside* a Covenant ship.

No, not Covenant anymore, Melody corrected herself, as she skidded around another bend. This was a *Sangheili* ship. The Covenant had mostly collapsed during what the Sangheili often referred to as the Great Schism. And they were still trying to figure out how to thrive in this new post-Covenant era. That included a splinter group of Sangheili swooping down on what had once been a human colony world on the edge of the Joint Occupied Zone. A world this splinter group of Sangheili had believed was abandoned.

And it had been, to be fair to the Sangheili, until those who'd been forced to leave it during the war finally managed to come back.

The human refugees who had narrowly survived the Covenant's vicious attack on their world returned to Carrow's surface, moving in to rebuild the abandoned city of Suraka, and they immediately found the Sangheili already several months into building their *own* keeps on the far side of the desert that separated them.

Go broker a peace between the Sangheili and Surakans on Carrow, Melody had been told. *Fighting's already breaking out in the Uldt desert. Talk to Fleetmaster Rojka 'Kasaan. Find a solution that everyone can live with, because we can't let this blossom into a local war on Carrow that drags the UNSC into an all-out conflict over the JOZ with the Sangheili.*

But understand that it will all be a cover for a much more important mission—

"Watch yourself, *nishum*!" A Sangheili foot soldier shoved Melody aside as he bounded around a turn. She dodged just in time to avoid being slammed against the wall by another just behind him.

Nishum: the name of an intestinal parasite, used as a pejorative for *human*. Melody watched him disappear, then kept moving.

After the Covenant first showed up a generation ago, there'd been a brief, exciting moment across a number of military-contracted scientific communities on Earth where they debated what it truly meant to make contact with not just one but multiple alien species for the first time. Surely the initial attacks in the Outer Colonies had been the result of some sort of communication breakdown, a misunderstanding.

Melody guessed that, at the first notice of the Covenant's existence, it had been thrilling to know that humanity was not alone. For several days, the universe would have had stopped seeming so vast and sterile. There was suddenly the promise of teeming civilizations and incredible discoveries humankind had yet to stumble across.

Any feelings humanity would have had like that were quickly strangled and murdered, as reports and vids of planets that had been glassed by Covenant ships trickled back to those same communities. The Covenant's leadership—the Prophets—wrapped their atrocious actions in a religious fervor that burned inexorably from world to world. It was like a horrific story from the pages of some history book. It hadn't been a dream come true to find out that there were other thinking creatures out there in the void of space—it had been a damn nightmare.

The Covenant implacably destroyed human outposts and colonies no matter what was done to stop them . . . until the threat finally made it to Earth itself, to the coastal megacity of New Mombasa—the one place on Earth that she called home. Melody had stopped thinking about the future, back then. There had only been survival.

After the war, Melody faced her fears, however, and became an envoy to some of the very aliens that had laid siege to New Mombasa, those who had destroyed everything she'd once loved and held dear. It was almost impossible to stop thinking of them as part of a merciless enemy force and start considering them as individuals. Individuals made up of different political groups and tribes. Especially since they had stratified and splintered after the war into different ideologies. And different levels of threat.

Some of her colleagues still referred to the Sangheili as the Covenant, but it was an incorrect shorthand. As an official envoy, a diplomatic representative of the Unified Earth Government, she knew better. There were countless different Sangheili groups, all with distinct ideologies and agendas. Some looked very much like the former Covenant, but others were the exact opposite.

Again, these were *Sangheili*. Not the faceless foes of the past thirty years. She'd spent two months embedded here in their culture, on their ship, as she had tried to negotiate peace.

But that had clearly failed, and now Melody was back to where she'd been as a civilian in New Mombasa: once again focused on surviving minute to minute.

Another brutal impact rocked the *Unwavering Discipline*. She slammed against the nearby wall and caught her breath. Melody wondered if she could have tried harder to urge Rojka to attack his enemies when they began destroying human ships that could get out to call for help. *It would make us look weak*, she knew Rojka would have told her. *You must always show your power when negotiating with Sangheili*, Melody had been taught.

She summoned all her strength at hand. This next step was going to be hard.

Melody turned the corner and passed through the door of one of the ship's armories. A massive Sangheili weapons master looked her up and down with all the studied displeasure of a creature finding something foul on its doorstep. Other Sangheili browsed the racks of Covenant weaponry stretched behind the alien, and there was a studied hush in the air, as if they all stood inside a library.

Melody mustered up a reservoir of calm. "I am here for weapons," she said with all the affectation of a general who expected everyone to jump at the sound of her voice.

The towering guard looked haughtily back down at her. "A weapons master cannot equip you," he growled with a deep rumble. "You are not a fighter."

In charge of this armory, the Sangheili guard was the closest thing to a quartermaster Melody had encountered aboard the ship. "How will I prove my honor when your vessel is boarded?" she snapped at him. Several warriors perusing racks of weaponry in the far back paused to look over at her. "Will you strip that from me by your refusal to give me a weapon?"

The Sangheili seemed agitated. "You are a weaponless negotiator. A human. You were not permitted to bring weapons aboard to begin with."

"That was before," Melody said. "But now I'm forced to stand with you. I *will* fight. I *must* fight."

"This I understand," he replied. "But . . ."

"But yet you still refuse me."

That finally got his attention. He reared back and balefully regarded her. "You have no rights here. You are not Sangheili."

"I have the right to fight with honor! Summon your fleetmaster. Refuse Rojka 'Kasaan to his face. But I—" Melody gambled and hoped that Sangheili were unsure about other species' emotions, as she was sure her fear showed on her face right now. "I *will* be armed."

Now she mentally crossed her fingers and shoved past him, leaning her shoulder in hard so that when she struck him, it would actually move the alien ever so slightly out of her way.

He's going to cut off my head, she thought.

The weapons master was visibly furious. But the thought of hailing the fleetmaster for something so seemingly trivial was clearly not a palatable option, and the strike she half expected from behind never came. Melody didn't dare turn around or show weakness. She walked over to the nearest row of weapons.

With a slightly trembling hand, ignoring the murderous stares of the Sangheili further down the stacks, she grabbed three plasma grenades. One for each of the pockets in her uniform.

But then there was the most important thing. On a tour of the armory two months ago, she'd noticed something almost discarded in a corner. *Was it still here?* Melody stalked around the shelf. Yes, there it was: a dusty Kig-Yar point defense shield. She strapped it on her forearm and tested it. The transparent concave shield of energy flared into existence.

She quickly turned it off and grabbed a plasma pistol. Type-25 Directed Energy Pistol—she remembered that from ONI training. It was one of the smallest weapons in the Covenant arsenal, yet in her human hands it looked massive and bulky.

"A tiny weapon for a tiny creature," one of the warriors standing nearby spat as she left, still working on cultivating an air of confidence aimed in their direction.

The guard growled as she left but made no move to stop her or confiscate her ordnance.

As soon as she was out of the armory, Melody let out yet another breath she hadn't realized she'd been holding and then started to jog. She'd been walking the innards of this ship for weeks now. It had taken her all of that time to persuade Fleetmaster Rojka to agree to a meeting with the leadership of Carrow's human contingent over the future of the joint occupation of the planet by their two species. It had been the first formal meeting since they'd both settled into Rak and Suraka on their different sides of the Uldt.

She'd even hoped that maybe, when it was all over, they could sit down over coffee and perhaps even settle on the same damn name for the planet.

Then the real fighting started. It had sprung from Rojka's own ranks, once-loyal allies that had become enemies, possibly seeing his willingness to negotiate as weakness. Many Sangheili down on the planet and in the fleet had been expecting to force the humans into a treaty of the Sangheili's choosing. Words like *compromise* and *negotiate* weren't an active part of their lexicon.

Melody would have put money on Rojka winning this little civil war until the Jiralhanae had arrived. ONI reports indicated that the Brute fleet's leader had even more seasoned warriors behind him, and was a far more skilled commander than the Sangheili estimated.

None of this was going as planned. She'd expected to have much more time to figure out how to negotiate both a planetary peace and the other mission—the critical handover back to ONI of the Spartans locked away in individual cryotubes. ONI wanted their property back and Melody was supposed to get it for them.

Instead, she was now risking her life at the last minute to try and get at the Spartans while the world fell apart around her.

What a mess. What a damn mess.

These ships are too old, Rojka 'Kasaan thought. The deckplates creaked. The engines struggled; there were not enough trained Sangheili throughout to maintain them. Barely enough to crew them. In fact, these aging cruisers had not been flown for some time. Rojka had been bitter about being forced to watch over the ill-repaired reserve fleets during the Great Schism.

But when it had come time to assemble a small fleet of his own out of those ships, and flee to create a new life, he had been fortunate to have that ability. Other kaidons did not have such a luxury, landlocked to their own worlds and whatever fates they held.

Now, to watch these same ships he had nursed and rebuilt over the years burn—that tore something deep inside him.

Khoto 'Gaaran, one of his trusted commanders, hailed Rojka

from the still-surviving frigate *Vengeful Deed*. "I will not be able to join your side," Khoto said. "The Jiralhanae fleet divides us too effectively."

"I thought you were already gone to us," Rojka said. And then after a moment: "Khoto, you have fought as well as any fleetmaster could expect. I would not fault you for turning back for Sanghelios. Leave Rakoi in your wake; there is nothing more for us here on this world, I fear—"

"I think I can severely damage the lead Jiralhanae cruiser," Khoto interrupted. "It has turned from battle and is heading down to the planet's surface."

An interesting development, Rojka thought. *Where is it going?* The daylong battle in orbit had changed from feinting and dancing around each other into the locked embrace that was currently the final showdown. He hadn't had an opportunity to scan the planet's surface since his enemies had closed in on him.

"It is finished," Rojka said. "There is only death here now. Leave, my friend."

"I have no plans to leave," Khoto said. "And there is nothing for me on our people's homeworld. I came here of my own volition. And now it has been spoiled for me. First by the humans, and now by our traitorous own. But I am closing in. The Jiralhanae will know our vengeance."

Khoto's small and barely shielded frigate would last minutes, if that.

Rojka watched the holographic projections of the battlespace as the Jiralhanae cruisers responded to the *Vengeful Deed*'s sudden swoop toward their leading warship. They lumbered about, trying to catch it. The space between the vessels quickly filled with a barrage of plasma fire from the Jiralhanae craft as they gave up on the chase and simply started shooting.

Within seconds, the debris of Khoto's ship spread out in a fading cloud. Rojka closed his eyes for a brief moment and allowed himself to silently mourn his friend.

"Fleetmaster, the traitor hails us," a communications officer called out. Rojka's eyes snapped open, watching the Jiralhanae cruiser continue to make its way for Rakoi's surface.

Rojka turned his attention to the command bridge, incredulous. "Thars himself wants to speak, *now*?"

"Yes, Fleetmaster," the officer replied.

"Put him through, then."

Thars 'Sarov appeared in a hologram before them all, and it took everything for Rojka to hold on to the reins of his rage. He would remain calm, not show his emotions to an upstart that still licked the shell of his own afterbirth off his face. An upstart that Rojka had sheltered, given ships to, and even elevated to the rank of shipmaster itself!

Cousin. Traitor. Worm.

"So . . . you will be trying to board my ship soon," said Rojka. "I wonder if you will come to face me yourself? Or will you wait until others have risked all?"

Thars did not allow himself to be baited. The younger Sangheili appeared to gloat instead, enjoying a moment of triumph from afar.

"Surrender now, and I will let your lineage and what few supporters you have among the keeps of Rak live," Thars said. "Tell them all to cooperate and not seek revenge."

Ah. Thars was worried about holding on to power. A confident leader would move forward and not try to cut a deal. He would face the challenges and dissenters after a moment of grasping for control, and do this head-on. Rojka decided to prod this deficiency.

"Do you see the Jiralhanae headed for the surface?" Rojka

asked. "What reserve ships have you set to protect the keeps of Rak? Fool! The Jiralhanae are now moving against you."

"Rak does not need protection, cousin," Thars rumbled. "The Jiralhanae are not headed for our colony. They are landing their packs in the human city. I knew they would do this."

"Was that their price?" Rojka said. "If you'd stood by my side, we could have had all that we wanted from the humans."

"Yet you *negotiate* with the creatures that destroyed our own *homeworld*!" Thars shouted. "Or do you not remember Glyke? Have you forgotten the strong rivers and thundering winds of the world that we were born to? And all the Sangheili who burned with it? The humans will give us nothing that we cannot take! But you? We all know you would let them leash you, and that your human master walks the halls of your ship."

As Rojka had watched the human ships burn, he had kept thinking of ways to work with the envoy to keep war from obliterating yet another world. There had been so much death already. And Glyke . . .

He pushed that from his mind and squeezed his fist tight to speak. "You did not destroy the human fleet—you dealt it a blow that gave us a solid ground with which to negotiate."

"An act you would never have had the courage to begin."

"But many of those ships in the attack fled to regroup," Rojka continued. "That is how the humans fight. You cannot swat a cloud of flies and declare them dead. They are still hiding out in the system, waiting for their best chance to strike back. A bargain with the humans would have—"

"Left us bowed before an inferior species. The humans here on this world will know our strength. When I am done, they will even cease to call it their home."

Rojka forced himself not to howl with rage. What strength did the Sangheili have left here after fighting each other and destroying so many of their own ships? Thars had made them weak. And now he had invited another enemy into the fray. "Thars. The Jiralhanae will betray you."

"After they take care of the humans for us?" Thars said. "Then they will have served their purpose. I will come from behind and slit their throats, one by one. And then I will occupy the city such that when the human military arrives, I will explain that their colonists needed protection from the Jiralhanae. I will not have to beg them for anything—they will be indebted to me."

Rojka digested that. The plan, though overly complex, did have merit. "I must admit that you are cunning, like the humans."

The satisfied look on Thars's face faded. "While you played steward to a dusty, mothballed fleet around Sanghelios, I watched Glyke burn with my own eyes. Our homeworld, cousin, brought to utter and complete ruin even after the war with the humans had come to an end. A cowardly assassination by cowardly creatures. Do not compare me to the vermin. I will have Rakoi as payment. Tell me only if you want your name to be added to your clan's battle poem. Or if I should merely bury it in the rubble I shall make of your family, along with the keep you have built on the desert's edge."

"History will never hear that Rojka 'Kasaan surrendered."

"Then I will make sure you die ignobly."

"You will fail." Rojka cut the communications link. He looked around his control bridge. "Prepare for boarding."

Governor Ellis Gass held on to the side of the door as the scarred old Warthog hopped a curb and plunged down into a parking bay under the Wulandari Building, where the Surakan Stock Exchange had its offices. The Exchange had been shut down for the last month. Since then, no one had rung the old brass ship's bell that had flown through slipspace all the way from Luna to be mounted in the pit's ceremonial balcony.

She wondered if anyone had removed the bell to store it away for safety.

"Stay down, Governor!" her driver shouted.

Behind them, a Jiralhanae Prowler burned on the street, riddled with holes from the extraordinarily loud and heavy machine gun mounted just centimeters over Ellis's head. The sled-like Prowler had been rushing to block them when the militia volunteer manning the Warthog's main gun opened fire. And then her driver had just rammed the alien vehicle before Ellis realized what was happening. Thankfully, the Prowler had sustained enough damage from the Warthog's mounted weapon that a broadside collision was enough to finish it off.

She brushed dust and dirt from her suit as the Warthog rattled down one more level of the parking bay. It stopped in front of a large, gray concrete wall. The words EXECUTIVE PARKING had been sprayed on the wall in red stenciled letters.

On the street outside, the sound of something flying between the buildings shook the floor.

Distant explosions thudded. From the direction of the residential districts, Ellis realized.

"Authorization?" the driver loudly asked. He was now talking to Militia Volunteer Command-and-Control on one of the Warthog's comm units. He'd asked Ellis something already. She'd been distracted. Still in shock.

Ellis struggled to remember the code, to tell the driver, but couldn't. She clambered out of the Warthog and then unceremoniously threw up all over the ground. She hung on to one of the tire's deep treads, her fingers digging into the mud and grit there as she heaved.

The gunner, barely eighteen, was lying strangely against the side of the bed-mounted weapon. He hadn't said anything since the driver had hurtled them into the dark safety here. Ellis looked into the boy's glassy eyes. Dead. There was a charred black hole in his chest that she could see straight through.

"Oh, no," Ellis whispered, raising her hand.

The driver was done talking to Command-and-Control and scrambled to the back of the Warthog. "Dizzy!" He was an older man with graying hair, calm and pragmatic in the middle of what felt like a mad dash to get here. But now he wiped his eyes as he grabbed the gunner in a hug around the shoulders. "You Brute bastards . . ."

A loud engine roar echoed through the bay's caverns, bouncing off the walls and startling Ellis.

The driver pulled Dizzy's body down, set it on the ground, and then took his place at the heavy mounted gun, spinning it quickly around to face the incoming vehicle.

It was another Warthog roaring up to them. The driver relaxed.

Lamar Edwards, her vice-governor, dropped out of the arriving vehicle. "Ellis, are you okay?" he asked.

She staggered forward and grabbed his shoulder, utterly relieved to see him. "Lamar, I . . . I can't remember the codes to get us down," Ellis said, her voice cracking.

"It's okay," he muttered, but not unkindly. Then he said to the driver, "Call in that the governor and vice-governor are coming down. Authorization whiskey-papa-tango-five-nine-eight-six-four."

"Yes, sir," the driver said, climbing back into the front of the Warthog.

Ellis and Lamar stood in silence for a second. The dead gunner was called Dizzy, but she had no idea who the driver was. Yet they'd both saved her life. Her bodyguards had rushed her out and handed her over to the militia volunteers during the initial bombing. No time for names or introductions.

Yesterday she'd been planning to attend a potentially historic summit between the Sangheili leadership, her administration, and the Unified Earth Government's own envoy. Now she was in the middle of a war.

Lamar looked over at the body. "I don't know my driver's name," Ellis said in a low voice.

"The SMV didn't have time to get name patches on some of the new uniforms," he replied.

SMV—Surakan Militia Volunteers. She hadn't focused much on the SMV, considering she'd inherited it when she took office. With the Covenant a thing of the past and the UNSC fighting off in the distance, it shouldn't have been needed. As far as Ellis had been concerned, the war was over.

The parking garage floor jolted and began to descend into the ground. Lamar didn't stumble but easily moved with the disruption. As he would. The EXECUTIVE PARKING stencils rose slowly as they moved down into the earth. Slabs of concrete, stained with tire marks and fluid leaks, swung closed into place over her head with a *clang*. Lights flickered on around them as they rumbled down the massive elevator shaft.

"This is a mess, Lamar," Ellis said. She looked down at the scars on the brown, weathered backs of his hands, then back up at his green eyes and the military-short haircut he preferred. Lamar had been an ODST in the UNSC Marine Corps—what they had referred to as a Helljumper. He never talked about what he'd done back in the war, but he'd agreed to run with her for office. She'd needed to prove to the Carrow refugees that her administration had the expertise to keep them all safe. She'd resented that necessity at the time. But now she'd never been happier to see the man. "I mean, I was working on high-volume pump design improvements and infrastructure logistics when I ran for office. Now I'm making decisions that leave people dead."

Lamar gave her a look. She'd known this wouldn't be easy when they left the relative comforts of the UEG refugee reserve created for them on Mars and returned to rebuild Suraka. "We all took the risk to come back here," he said.

"Too big a risk. We should never have trusted the Sangheili. We should've known our peoples couldn't coexist, that they'd want this whole world for themselves." History would judge her poorly. All that money going toward keeping a security fleet in orbit; Ellis had thought reducing it would help pay for the civil engineering projects Suraka desperately needed. Five years ago, they'd returned to Carrow and started rebuilding. But Ellis had always felt they could address the neighboring Sangheili settlement after Suraka had been fully restored from the damage it had suffered during the war. After all, they were separated by the vast, lifeless Uldt desert: why would the Sangheili ever cross it?

"A lot of people believed in you. They still do." Almost a million, all refugees from early Carrow and other colonies still uninhabitable due to the Covenant's thirty years of unhindered destruction, had come to Suraka in various stages over the last five years. So many hopes and dreams were embedded in this small, ruined city. Suraka had been suddenly evacuated when the Covenant continued their rampage through the Outer Colonies in 2531. It had lain fallow for twenty-two years, ignored by all. And now it was unbelievably the center of a new conflict, five years into rebuilding.

Ellis wiped her cheek with a shaking palm. "People trusting me may have made the gravest mistake, Lamar."

"You have to dream of a future. Or all the hard decisions we'll need to make next, they won't *be* for anything. And it has to be for something."

Lamar should have been governor, Ellis thought. She would have been better off remaining a civil engineer or project manager.

"No one could have stopped the Sangheili from attacking the city," Lamar said.

"We could have worked harder to stop people from settling outside of Suraka. Those smaller settlements out in the Uldt. They spooked the Sangheili." A large brown line passed by. They were now ten stories down, Ellis estimated. Halfway there. She thought the pistons sounded a bit under-oiled. "I could have built those people better oases. They wouldn't listen. All they had to do was wait."

"It's hard to tell people who have lost everything to keep living in temporary housing," Lamar said. "Hard to tell them that the independence we promised them would take time."

"I should have been firmer." Ellis wrapped her arms around herself. A couple hundred thousand Sangheili versus a million humans, and growing. The Sangheili in their sprawled-out keeps and holdings. Feudal, fortified, and strategic.

"You didn't provoke the Sangheili into this," Lamar said. "You can't own that."

Ellis had woken up today to the sound of explosions. The ground thudding. Arms grabbing her, hustling her into a Pelican to get her clear of the new governor's house on the edge of Suraka. An SMV commander gave her a hurried briefing as the Pelican barreled inward toward the city. Human ships with slipspace ability in orbit and on the ground had been obliterated by Sangheili destroyers. She'd been planning to fly out tomorrow to meet the UEG envoy and the kaidon—Rojka 'Kasaan, leader of the Sangheili here on Carrow—on one of those ships.

Utterly stunned, Ellis learned that communications back to Earth had been targeted and taken out in seconds, before anyone in Suraka had even realized what was happening. The ferocity of the Sangheili attack was overwhelming. In a matter of seconds, Carrow was completely cut off, isolated, and vulnerable.

Then, according to some very confusing reports, the Sangheili seemed to have turned on each other just as viciously as they had struck Suraka. The SMV had ordered any surviving ships to flee and hide, as those on the ground scrambled to secure the city against further attack.

Ellis had hoped for a lull here as the Sangheili fought among themselves. Instead, out of nowhere, the Jiralhanae had dropped from orbit to land in Suraka, wreaking havoc on a scale she had only read about in fiction. They plowed through everything that crossed their path, and left few survivors.

Right here in *her* city.

And then there was the matter of her son.

"Lamar . . . Jeff's in the militia. I haven't heard from him. I've been asking everyone since I was picked up. No one has anything to tell me."

"I'll ask around when we get inside," Lamar said softly. Then added, "I didn't know he joined."

"I didn't want to advertise it. He always thought it would come to this. He didn't think making concessions to aliens that were never supposed to even be here—who drove us off Carrow to begin with—was right, or tenable for that matter. I didn't want my opponents using him against me. I let him sign up under his father's name."

Her husband, Senj, had died three years ago. Jeff shared his father's opinion of all things alien. Neither of them had easily forgotten their time as refugees, so he'd joined the militia. Senj would have been proud.

Spending so much time on the rebuilding efforts, Ellis had barely seen Jeff in the last year. She tried hard to remember the last thing she'd said to him, but it wouldn't come back to her right now. That should have bothered her more than it did at the moment, but she felt unmoored, numb, and fuzzy.

The elevator ground to a slow halt in front of large hangar doors. Ellis might not have been a soldier, but she *was* an engineer. She'd been a part of building these backups during the previous administration, in the first four years since returning to Suraka. They'd drilled down deep into the rock below the city and hollowed out impregnable spaces to shield the citizenry and militia—on the remote chance that anything like this would ever happen. Many of these underground facilities were interconnected with heavily fortified armories at strategic intervals.

Ellis had protested the investment of resources and time but had served the previous governor well, getting everything done in record time and under budget so that they could move to bigger and (so she had thought) better projects for Suraka's second age. It was *because* of these defenses that she'd run against her predecessor on a platform of reorientation: expanding Suraka to take in even more people than it could currently hold.

She might be out of her element at the moment, but she was still home under her own city. *I'm the one who built this underworld*, she thought. That gave her strength and let her summon a measure of focus now that imminent danger had been removed.

And from here, she would rebuild Suraka again.

"It's time to start fighting back," Ellis said. "We've lost a lot of people with the first wave of Brutes. But it's going to be tough for anything to reach us down here. We'll need to regroup."

"No other choice," Lamar said.

The fortified doors at the bottom of the shaft opened, revealing the large storage facilities and bays filled with militia activity.

"Carrow is *our* world," Ellis said. "We won't let them take it from us."

CHAPTER 3

*U*nwavering Discipline's shields flickered under the latest barrage of plasma and then dissipated as its systems finally gave out. Rojka sat in his command chair, following the chain of breakdowns throughout the ship on his diagnostic sensors. Some instinctive part of him wanted to shout at the crew to start working on repairs. But that was a foolish act, dragging out just a little more time before the inevitable.

"Dropships and boarding craft are almost here," Daga reported to Rojka.

Soon dozens, possibly hundreds, of Sangheili would come boiling through holes punched in the hull. Thars might even have the Unggoy aboard his ship, which he would use in a suicidal first wave to soften up Rojka's fighters.

That was the real reason Rojka didn't want any of his crew trying to fix the shields or keep *Unwavering Discipline*'s engines running for maneuvers. The moment those craft surrounded the hull, Rojka would note their locations and move his crew to create killing avenues and choke points for the incoming boarders.

Thars was going to pay a tremendous price for this vessel.

"This fight will be remembered for generations," Daga announced.

Certainly Thars would never forget it. Rojka let a wave of satisfaction pass over him. "If Thars dares set foot anywhere on this ship, he will die."

To perish facing one's enemy was all that a true Sangheili could ask for.

Daga turned away from a projection console. "The weapons master needs a moment of your attention, Fleetmaster."

"What is it?" Rojka asked. The timing was distracting. He broke away from staring at the boarding craft falling toward the hull.

"He says the human envoy demanded ordnance." Daga sounded surprised and somewhat impressed. So was Rojka. He pulled at his own weapons harness and mulled that over for a moment.

"The envoy is merely a negotiator. Can a human like that even use our weapons?" Rojka asked. "Are they trained?"

Daga cocked his head. "When I fought on the world they called Reach, the civilians usually fled before us without fighting, or perished well before I arrived. I had assumed not."

Rojka checked the lines of boarding craft on the hull's visual sensors again. Their large, armor-cracking maws loomed larger. Not long now. He checked his thigh for his energy sword. It was there. Ready to soak in the blood of his enemies.

"Human or Sangheili, it should be any creature's right to die in face-to-face combat," Rojka said. "Let her keep what she has taken. The envoy will perhaps enjoy a good death by our side. Where does she make her stand?"

Daga conferred with the ship's limited battlenet array. "The envoy is now deep in the storage holds. I have a designation . . ."

Rojka was thunderstruck. He stood up and shouted, "She makes no stand and plans no fight!"

Daga recoiled at the sudden outburst. "Fleetmaster?"

"She makes a fool of me!" Rojka hissed. "Disregards my direct orders!"

The understanding then dawned on Daga. He looked around and lowered his voice. "She is trying to release the Demon Three? But they are guarded by warriors you trust."

"Which is why she has armed herself." Rojka stalked toward an exit.

"We are abandoning the command bridge?" Daga said, alarmed. "What of Thars?"

"After what the Demon Three have done, would you die well knowing that they might at last manage to escape?"

Daga still wasn't convinced. "There are the guards."

"The envoy has deceived us. I should never have taken her aboard."

"We were not strong enough to defy the human government," Daga said. "We had to negotiate. We had to make certain the allies of Thel 'Vadam did not view our presence here as a threat."

Daga was right, of course. But Thars had nonetheless used the presence of the human envoy on *Unwavering Discipline* to claim that Rojka was nothing but an Earth puppet. Even among Rojka's crew, there were many Sangheili who had little love for the humans.

Now the envoy was attempting to release the Spartans. It was, for Rojka, the killing cut to his patience with having her aboard his ship. "I doubt the envoy ever came aboard to build peace alone. I think she also came here precisely to free the Demon Three. This was always her mission. Send one of your best warriors with me. We need to find and stop her."

Two of Rojka's senior warriors guarded the doors to a hangar deep on the lower decks of the *Unwavering Discipline*, plasma rifles tight up next to the armored harnesses. Either one of them could rip Melody apart faster than she could sneeze.

They looked up as she hurried toward them. "Quick!" Melody shouted. "A boarding team has breached the hull behind me!"

The plasma grenade she'd just stuck on the wall further up the corridor should go off any second—

The explosion—in the compressed air pressure of the ship— roared in her ears with an intensity she had not expected. The guards hesitated for a second, and Melody wondered if she had found the only two Sangheili on the ship not interested in proving their worth as fighters.

"There are Unggoy in the breach!" Melody shouted.

The promise of an easy foe proved to be too much of a draw. The two guards ran up the gently curved corridor toward the de- struction.

Melody waited a moment, then, once they were out of sight, shot the door lock with the plasma pistol.

Nothing.

"Damn it."

Melted metal from the control pad she'd shot dripped slowly toward the floor.

"The human lies! There are no Unggoy here!" shouted one of the guards from the distance.

Melody dropped her second plasma grenade up against the crack in the doors. No time to get clear. She fired up the Kig-Yar point defense shield and huddled behind it.

The blast from the grenade knocked her clear back against the other wall. Quickly recovering, Melody turned the shield off and scrabbled toward the small hole she'd created with the grenade.

Glowing hot edges seared her back and sides as she wriggled into the dark cavern of a room just as the two furious guards reached the door.

Melody held the deactivated Kig-Yar gauntlet against the hole and turned it on. The edges spat solid energy against the floor and forced the shield up into the soft, heated metal, where they fused together, effectively blocking the only way into the room. The frustrated guards kicked and pulled at it, but the energy shield remained firmly wedged in place.

In the dim light of the hangar, she could just make out the three hulking cryo-chambers stacked against the wall by the door.

She hit the light panel. The rest of the room revealed itself to be an entire storage bay crammed with spare parts. Half-stripped Spirit dropships with disturbingly rib-like skeletons gleamed in the harsh light, their engines ripped out. Cut-up Banshees and Vampire fighters were held down by metallic straps. Rows and rows of rounded buckets with Sangheili script denoted dirty salvage for every imaginable kind of ex-Covenant craft.

She'd known the Sangheili fleets were ghosts of their former selves and that Rojka had limped his own fleet to Carrow on chewing gum and spit. This confirmed it. The proud fleetmaster had never shown her *this* particular area when touring her around his vessel.

Melody turned back to the cryo-chambers.

With the lights on, she could now see that each of them indeed contained a Spartan.

They looked like statues in there, she thought. Statues roughly two meters tall and wearing half a ton of armor. Just waiting. They didn't know it, but the Spartan trio had been sealed up for almost six years while drifting deep in former Covenant space.

Adriana-111, the muscle behind the three. A deadly sniper and a chaotic influence on the group. She was not one for protocol, and she had little patience for leadership. But she had proven herself against tremendous odds repeatedly, according to the files Melody had read.

Michael-120. The technical expert who could fly, shoot, or hack pretty much anything after watching it being used. Known for jury-rigging deadly weapons out of spare parts. And breaking through any security thrown his way. He was also their pilot.

And Jai-006, their leader. ONI records indicated that without Jai, the team would simply not hold. It was his will that drove them forward. Kept them focused. An indomitable fighter, even among other Spartans.

This was Gray Team.

Now they stood in front of her, frozen in place.

Melody tapped out codes on the chamber readouts and started cycling them awake. She was doing this faster than was safe, but they didn't have much time.

She took a closer look at their armor now that she had a spare moment. This was the first time she'd seen Spartans up this close. It was one thing to see vid or images and quite another to stare up at the massive bulk right in front of your fingertips. *Living history*, she thought, with no small amount of awe. But she frowned as she leaned forward.

This team was battered to hell. Deep furrows left by plasma fire scarred almost every element of the Mjolnir armor. Large, irregular dents in their chest plates caught the shadows. Jai-006's slightly crooked helmet had a visor at the top that had curled downward from some incredible impact.

Melody couldn't see anything behind the silvered faceplate. Just her own tired face looked back at her, curiously warped by the curve.

"Come on," she whispered, checking the readouts.

"Envoy!" shouted a familiar, guttural voice from the other side of the doors. Rojka, projecting the kind of anger that was universal.

Melody glanced at the readouts one last time. She took a deep breath and walked over to the doors. "Yes, Fleetmaster Rojka?"

"You wake the dead."

"They offer you a chance to fight back against your cousin."

"No, they do not! The Demon Three must pay for their sins!" Rojka replied. "What you are doing is unacceptable. But . . . I shall grant you one opportunity. Know that you will join in their fate if you do not turn this shield off so we can enter."

"I'm sorry, Rojka," Melody said. "I can't do that."

"I was indeed foolish to let you aboard my ship. Tell me, was it ever your true intent to negotiate peace between my people and the humans, or was this all just an opportunity to liberate the Demon Three?"

"I wanted peace," she said.

Yes, her primary job *was* to restore peace between humans and the Sangheili, but ONI had recruited her discreetly to pass on any recon about Gray Team's condition while she was aboard the Sangheili ship and, if possible, negotiate a release. As part of their normal function, the UNSC had also trained Melody and her staff to use Covenant technology and weapons.

Even more enigmatic, during her ONI sessions Melody had received extra training from one Commander Ivrin Yarick on how to rapidly cycle a cryo-chamber without irreparably damaging its contents. Just in case, he'd noted.

Just in case what? she'd asked. *It's not like I can smuggle three Spartans out of a ship full of Sangheili. That can't be my real mission . . . can it?*

Yarick had looked at her, his expression inscrutable. *It's just in case*, he repeated. *We told you what's down on that planet. We're covering every conceivable eventuality.*

Maybe the Spartans will smuggle you out of the ship, he said with a grim seriousness.

Now the bottom chunk of the door leading into the hangar blew apart. The Kig-Yar shield flew forward and smacked Melody's legs. She pitched face-forward to the floor, slamming her cheek. Her vision blurred as she lay there and tried to get her thinking straight again.

"Grant me entrance!" Rojka shouted from what now seemed like a long distance away, his entrance blocked by the partially sealed door. There were other angry words. Focusing on Sangheili language with her head spinning this fast took too much effort.

An energy sword burst through the door. It sizzled and spat, cutting down slowly as the Sangheili on the other side strained to shove the shaped plasma through solid metal. Melody could see thick, alien feet through the hole in the bottom.

Hands shaking, blood dripping off her chin down onto her arms, Melody took out her third plasma grenade, armed it, and heaved it ever so gently through the missing chunk of door.

"Wort wort wort!" the Sangheili shouted, feet thudding as they leapt for safety. She knew what that meant, but her brain was too fuzzy to translate after exerting the energy it took to steady herself and throw the grenade.

The plasma grenade's explosion sucked the breath out of Melody, yanking the air out through the hole. She dropped to her knees and fired the acquired plasma pistol three times through the opening.

She couldn't focus on the door. It waved and wobbled in front of her.

She glanced down to see the floor covered in blood around her feet. Too much blood. A strangely shaped piece of metal on the side of her stomach stuck out of her uniform. Melody tried to reach for it, puzzled. She didn't remember getting hurt, but it was clearly a jagged sliver of the door that had speared her.

Right now, rather than continue to stand and fight back the Sangheili, it felt a lot more important to sit down and shove her back up against the nearby cryo-chamber. She'd already lost too much blood.

Melody strained against the pain, propped the plasma pistol on her knee, and kept it aimed at the doors.

Whenever she saw so much as a shadow, she fired.

But the shadows didn't just appear near the doors. They spun around her, lifting the room up and whipping it around her in looping, wobbly circles until she closed her eyes.

"Rojka! It's about more than just the Spartans . . ." She tried to shout, but her voice faded away as if she stood at the far end of a tunnel. "It's . . . something bigger."

The tunnel door slammed shut. The sounds faded. Everything fell away from her.

Melody tightened her finger on the trigger. The last thing she felt was the recoil of the plasma pistol firing, firing, firing.

The Jiralhanae chieftain Hekabe jumped from one of the arms of a siegework gunship and landed on the ground with a satisfied grunt. The gunship itself, a machine sometimes called a "grave-maker," was a rugged, nest-shaped gun platform, crudely fused together and plated over with heavy armor shielding, struggled to get back into the air. Its weight seemed to momentarily overpower the sputtering blast and roar of its cluster of downward-facing engines, before it climbed back up into the sky. Hekabe felt satisfaction watching the tanklike craft providing Jiralhanae on the ground with substantial firepower from its array of heavy-grade spike autocannons, now that it had deployed him and his warriors to the surface.

A blast of hot air hit Hekabe's face from a building on fire nearby. He watched with interest as the oddly rectangular metal and glass structure succumbed and collapsed to the street in an explosion of debris. A rolling cloud of noxious dust struck him and his eyes narrowed. Above it all, his extensively armored cruiser, the *Foebane*, hung in the air, an immeasurable shadow blocking out the city's sky. More grave-makers bristling with vicious firepower fell rapidly from its belly, delivering packs and hordes of Jiralhanae. Several of the ships skittered off between the human buildings, dipping and weaving, opening fire at anything that moved below.

Hekabe breathed in the stench of burned rubble as he shifted his massive gravity hammer—Oath of Fury—from his hands and slung it over his shoulder. War hammers traditionally passed through a long line of elders through the customs of his people. But this one he had pried from the hands of an enemy in combat, then used it to finish him off.

"Look at our might!" Hekabe shouted into the hot wind. The chieftain wore a large, rugged combat harness from the Jiralhanae's time within the Covenant: black-crimson armor masked with ornate linework. He raised Oath of Fury over his helmet. A single crest dominated the helmet, with two flanking plates that swung backward to either side, and a fearsome horn that jutted from above his snout—a design that paid homage to Doisac's native *degaeorth*, a giant predatory beast that stalked the planet's dense forests. "Their structures are weak! *They* are weak!"

Hekabe's captains surrounded him. Their own armor also came from the old era of Covenant service, though most had made dramatic modifications, cobbling together features from the Jiralhanae heritage and trophies recovered from conquered foes— even the remains of the foes themselves.

"I think I could bring their buildings down with a single strike of my hammer," Hekabe gloated.

"They do build puny things, Chieftain!" Vikus shouted over another wave of gunships kicking up dirt as they released rows and rows of Jiralhanae warriors onto the outskirts of the human city. "We did not have to worry about them interfering with our efforts."

Hekabe bared his teeth at Vikus. "And who was worried?"

Vikus, who shaved his face raw and kept his head mane in a pair of tall strips along the top, looked directly down at the ground. "There were some," he growled. "But they were wrong to doubt you, Chieftain."

"The infestation of the weak does not affect our plans," Hekabe said. "It offers us a chance to harden our warriors to battle."

"Yes, Chieftain. You are correct. The humans have fled from here. They do not disturb us." From the corner of his eye, Hekabe watched Vikus take several steps back. The Jiralhanae captain clenched his jaw, as if fighting to say something else but keeping it in check. Vikus, it seemed, had been one of those concerned about the large number of humans at the site but wisely now said nothing.

Good. Hekabe wouldn't be forced to kill him then. This was just another in a long series of doubts expressed by the Jiralhanae horde-captain in the past several months. Clearly Vikus wanted the chieftainship—Hekabe could see it on his face whenever he looked at him. But Vikus evidently favored life more than an uncertain chance at power. There were many Jiralhanae of the clan who had assumed Vikus would be the one to have killed the former chieftain Remarus—Hekabe's great-uncle—and taken his title. But to the surprise of many, it had been Hekabe who seized the opportunity and slit the old warrior's throat.

There hadn't been any other option at the time. Hekabe could have either moved against Remarus from the shadows to save them all from the peril he had placed them in, or waited only to see everything lost. The master packs, or skeins, feuding on Doisac had consumed so much of their world that the only way some packs could even get supplies was to raid the Sangheili frontier, stealing from the race that previously had oppressed their people within the Covenant. The global Jiralhanae civil war went far back in time: the two enormous skeins of Jiralhanae had battled each other on Doisac before the Covenant ever came along. They had destroyed each other—their civilization, their lands, and their people—with nuclear weapons, setting all Jiralhanae back hundreds of years.

Some thought it had made them feeble, but Hekabe thought it had tempered his people. Made them stronger in the long run.

The Rh'tol skein now gloried in the piracy against the former Covenant. It let them show their true strength to the very face of the Sangheili species that had so poorly treated them. The Vheiloth skein saw such looting and destruction as an unfortunate necessity. But Hekabe believed it all to be simple weakness.

It was time for Jiralhanae to stop scavenging for scraps.

Many chieftains disagreed with him. To take these ships to help a Sangheili faction in a minor civil war was—for their part—utter madness. The Sangheili had lorded over the Jiralhanae in the

Covenant for decades. They openly despised the Jiralhanae and had torn apart the Covenant in open war the very moment the Jiralhanae became favored by the Prophets. The Great Schism, as most Jiralhanae knew, had shown the truth of the Elite–Brute relationship—the Sangheili were arrogant and cruel slavers. For Hekabe to offer assistance to an Elite showed incredible vulnerability and poor character, as far as his opposition was concerned.

Hekabe had to kill many doubters in order to get his pack to this world that Sangheili and humans squabbled over.

He knew there were still skeptics, like Vikus, lurking among his warriors. And so it wasn't angry Jiralhanae back on Doisac that Hekabe had feared, and that he had been forced to silence or outmaneuver. Those who had questioned Hekabe's plans and desired to see him dead had been easy to spot. It was the quiet ones—who would betray and kill him in the dark as Hekabe himself had done to Remarus—who troubled him. Though he would never speak of this.

Destiny was now within his grasp. "Are the Sangheili ships still fighting above us?"

"Yes," Vikus said.

Jiralhanae autocannon platforms flew patterns over the city's skyline, black smoke chugging from their engines as they unloaded a barrage of white-hot metal into enemy fortifications. Knifelike Prowler and Marauder groundcraft roared around the human streets, heavily armored warriors hanging off their plating. The cruelly shaped Jiralhanae vehicles looked as though they had been cobbled together from raw pieces of steel, optimized for bone-crushing speed and unforgiving firepower. "Excellent. The longer the Sangheili remain distracted, the better."

"They are trying to board their kaidon's ship."

Their honor, Hekabe thought, prevented them from just

destroying it from a distance. Well, it was good for him. The Sang-heili would battle each other for some useless reason or another for many hours yet before they understood why Hekabe had *really* landed planetside.

That was all the time he needed.

Hekabe projected a map into the air from a holotank sitting on the ground. "Destroy any buildings in this zone," he ordered, initating a perimeter-like designation in the hologram. With the vast section of the human city spread before them, a precise area was carved out for Hekabe's operation. This was not going to be indiscriminate destruction: he had a plan. "Then we will bring the Unggoy down from the *Foebane*."

He glanced at the desert in the distance. When he was fin-ished here, the Sangheili would rue the day they had ever heard his name.

As would the humans.

CHAPTER 4

ai-006 dimly heard the sound of repeating plasma pistol fire. He raised an armored hand and pushed against the glass of the cryo-chamber. His skin under the Mjolnir armor blazed with frozen itch. He wanted to dig his fingernails in under the surface and just rip it all off to get it to stop.

There was a woman—likely the source of the pistol fire—slumped over onto the floor. The walls in this place under the emergency lighting looked smooth, organic, with flowing bulkheads swooping down from the tall ceilings. In the distance to his side was a large cavernous hangar bay, filled with rows of Covenant vehicles and machinery. Jai kicked the protective glass to shatter it. He yanked free of hoses plugged into his armor and stepped out of the chamber.

A wave of extreme sickness dizzied him. He forced himself to stand still for a second and let it pass.

"Where are we?" Adriana-111 asked inside his helmet. "Can you let me out?"

Jai crouched next to the fallen woman. She wore a gray uniform he didn't recognize. Blood splattered the collar and torso. A lot of it came from the wound in her right side, where there was a jagged piece of metal sticking out from under the fabric. Her nose and busted lips dripped more blood down off her chin. "We're inside a Covenant ship."

"Agreed," Mike-120 now also chimed in over Jai's helmet. "You don't get interior design like this from a standard Martian shipyard."

"Any idea who your new friend there is?" Adriana asked.

"A civilian, or some kind of civil-service type," Jai replied. "Wounded. I know I heard plasma fire when coming to."

"Me too." More glass shattered and armored boots hit the deck as Adriana stopped waiting for Jai to free her and took matters into her own hands. "Someone must have opened my cryo-chamber and removed my weapons at some point," she reported, sounding annoyed.

"Looks like we got picked up by the Covenant." Mike mulled that over for a second. "But we're still alive. That can't be good."

"The woman, why is she aboard a Covenant ship?" Adriana asked. "Mike . . . my hands are shaking. I can barely control them."

Jai looked back and saw Mike free himself and lean over his cryo-chamber's readouts. "This wasn't a good thaw," Jai said. "Keep your helmets on—stay alert. Mike, any more information about our situation?"

"Yeah: we got unfrozen on an emergency cycle. Done on purpose," Mike reported. "We're going to be grumpy and miserable for a while. Feels like they poured a million fire ants into my suit. Major cryo-itch."

"How big of a nap did we end up taking?" Jai asked.

"It says . . . Military Standard Time has us on the first of September in the year 2558? That's five years, eight months. That . . . that can't be right."

All three of them stood quietly for a second, digesting the

information. *Almost six years*, Jai thought. They'd gone under the last day of 2552.

No time for this. "Okay. Sitrep," said Jai. "We'll figure out exactly what happened to us later. Right now, though, we're apparently locked up in a Covenant ship of some kind and have been unfrozen rapidly. There is a badly injured civilian present—possibly the one who thawed us—and she's armed with a Covenant weapon. Thoughts?"

"Look at that door damage," Adriana said.

Yes, there it was. He should have seen that sooner. This unfreezing had affected him a bit more than he realized. It was extremely hard to focus. "You think she came in through that?"

"Burns on the back of her clothes?" Adriana asked.

Jai gently moved around the woman on the floor for a better look at the singed cloth of her uniform. "Yes, she's got 'em."

"Biofoam," Mike called out. He'd been rummaging around his cryo-chamber and now threw a canister toward Jai, who was busy ripping the woman's uniform open around the stomach. He held her down and yanked the metal out from just above her hip.

The civilian's eyes snapped open, the pain jerking her out of unconsciousness with a startled moan. Her eyes were brown and matched her skin underneath all that fresh blood on her face. She hissed with pain but controlled it and looked around nervously.

"You're hurt. I'm trying to help you," Jai told her.

"Sharks," she muttered, grabbing his armored forearm. Her fingertips scraped across the alloy plates. "Rojka too. Coming." She scrabbled around for the plasma pistol and tried to pick it up.

"Shhh." Jai jammed the tip of the biofoam canister under her torn skin. She grunted and dropped the weapon, eyes rolling up into her head. "I'm sorry."

She passed out but was now packed with biofoam to stabilize the bleeding.

"We have no weapons," Adriana said. Jai kicked the plasma pistol over to her. She stopped it with her boot and leaned over to pick it up. "This is a very *small* weapon." Her tone suggested she didn't even really think of it as a weapon at all.

"All we have for now," Jai said, checking the unconscious woman for identification of any kind. "Mike? Any further ideas on where we are exactly or what's going on?"

"Based on the size and layout of this room, I'd say we're in a storage cavity of a late-war Covenant cruiser, probably ORS-class. Give me some time and space, I'll get into their systems and pull out the info we need." Mike ripped a cover off a nearby console and began pulling out strips of wire to connect Covenant information systems into his Mjolnir armor's inputs.

"Something tried to kick this door in," Adriana observed. "Look at the plasma burns. They cut through a large piece of it already. Why'd they stop?"

A trickle of blood dribbled out of Jai's nose and down his lips, salty and sweet with cryochemicals. He took a deep breath and focused hard on ignoring the bonfire of pain slowly burning through his skin. He should be screaming and tearing at himself. Instead he drew on his training. "Adriana, stay by the door."

Adriana posted up in front of it, plasma pistol drawn. Mike shifted around the console to keep the door in sight in case things went bad fast. Jai, meanwhile, pulled the unconscious civilian out of the pool of blood surrounding her. He dragged her toward the cover of what seemed to be the disassembled remains of a Seraph fighter.

"Yeah, someone's mopping up down the corridor," Adriana

said, checking the pistol. "Maybe Unggoy? I heard one scream. Hang on—we've got something approaching now."

An energy sword suddenly popped through their side of the door and slid down toward the deck, finishing the cut already present. Part of the door shivered and then flew forward as it was kicked in. As the debris bounced across the floor, Jai crouched in front of the civilian to protect her. The alien metal struck his raised forearms and knocked him back a few centimeters.

Jai stood as two Sangheili warriors burst in. They paused as they sized up the Spartans. Then they attacked.

Adriana opened fire on the nearest one, its back half-turned to her as it almost walked by where she stood up against the door. It spun just in time for her to smack into it. They both rolled across the ground, its energy sword slapping into the floor's metal and skidding about. Adriana kept firing the plasma pistol point-blank up into its chin until it stopped moving, scorched pieces of its head oozing from between the helmet plates.

The second Sangheili ran straight into Jai and knocked him back into the Seraph. Parts scattered and Jai scrambled to get back on his feet, throwing a chunk of hull aside as he stood. The Sangheili raised its energy sword and slashed at him. Jai jumped back from the blade, trying to draw the enemy away and distract it, but the alien didn't bite.

It paused and looked back, just in time to get tackled by Adriana. She'd since taken the energy sword away from the dead Sangheili by the door. She slashed at the alien, but it rolled to the side, parrying the blow before tossing her clear.

"Catch," she called out to Jai as she landed on her feet.

Jai grabbed the plasma pistol that Adriana casually threw at him. Then she leapt again into the air and pressed her attack on the Sangheili.

The enemy creature scrambled to one side a split second before Adriana crashed onto the deck and dented the floor. She crouched, ready to spring once more, the energy sword casting a pool of blue light around her as she waited for the next move.

Jai opened fire. The Elite's armor flared, and it scurried off in between the rows of dismantled Covenant vehicles lining the hangar.

The two Spartans moved closer together, back to armored back against the gloom, waiting. Adriana faced the hangar, Jai the light of the open door, anticipating that more Sangheili would pour through at any moment.

"It didn't try to finish us off. Have you ever seen that happen?" Adriana asked.

"Dangerous fighter," Jai said. "High rank. Naval commander of some sort."

"Yeah, as strategy goes, three on one is not a good match," Adriana replied. "It's going to either call for reinforcements or try to take us out individually. Once it gets its breath back. I hit it pretty hard."

Mike interrupted them. "I've gotten into their systems. Apparently—and I'm trusting that the translation software we had half a decade ago is still functional now—we're on the Covenant cruiser *Unwavering Discipline.*" He paused. "It's under attack and in the process of being boarded."

"By . . . ?" Jai asked.

"I think . . . more Covenant?" Mike replied. "Some of the ID signs have changed—I'm not too sure what I'm looking at. It's not normal Covenant designation info. I mean, we're almost six years out of date, so—"

"So, no idea who exactly we're dealing with," Jai said.

"No." Mike yanked the wires free of the panel now that he'd gotten what he needed. "And no UNSC here either. The ship battles are Sangheili on Sangheili, according to the sensor data I could snag. However, their systems are monitoring some human chatter from down on a planet that we're orbiting. Not sure what exactly we're in the middle of here."

"Planetside is maybe where this civilian came from," Jai said. "How do we get out of here?"

Mike waved a hand at the strange boneyard of stripped-out, half-built Covenant vehicles. "Give me enough time, maybe I could cobble something together. But you want the truth? Those boarders aren't going to give us time."

"Internal Covenant politics of some kind," Jai said. "But if they're hovering around a human world, we need to see what we can do to help. That should be clear to figure out, yes?"

He waited for a second, then Mike said, "Yes."

"Yes," Adriana agreed.

A consensus. Jai was relieved.

The vessel shook under their feet. Something big had hit it. Another series of thumps sounded across the hull. Jai looked around just as the eerie lighting above the cryo-chambers flickered and died. "Think that's the boarding party?" Jai asked.

"Yes," Mike agreed. "Second wave. Whoever's defending this ship already absorbed a few boarding parties while we were defrosting."

"Any particular way to get off the ship that you think we should focus on?"

"We look for something flightworthy in this mess while trying not to get shot?" Mike offered.

"If they had our cryo-chambers, then they probably have our lifeboat as well," Adriana said. "If it's still intact, that is."

Jai tossed the plasma pistol to Mike, then bent down and picked up the civilian. "Let's fan out and try to find it."

"So that our new friend can snipe us one by one as we wander around its hangar?" Adriana asked.

"I said fan out, not split up. Stay within eyesight," Jai said.

"With pleasure."

Adriana seemed satisfied. They spread out and began walking through the shadows—the mangled skeletons of ruined Covenant craft.

Governor Ellis Gass and Vice-Governor Lamar Edwards walked past the consoles and screens of the underground command center. Surakan militia in beige uniforms hustled around, murmuring urgently to each other as officers conferred.

The lights in the command bunker flickered and died. A second later the emergency power kicked in, bathing everyone in dim red light. "It'll take a half minute for them to switch over to the backup source," Lamar said.

Backup energy came from a small reactor powered by a stolen and partially disassembled Havok thermonuclear device—one of the things Ellis had been briefed on the moment she became governor. No one felt it necessary to tell civilians there was an active nuclear device lying deep under their city. And Suraka had more than just the one highly powerful weapon. During the war, the planet's former colonists had managed to fake documents and take advantage of the confusion of battle to obtain more than a dozen thermobaric bombs, which had been carefully smuggled to Carrow right under the UNSC's nose.

And that didn't include what the New Colonial Alliance had provided them during the early months of their resettlement: a fleet of ex-UNSC ground and air vehicles, as well as weapons and munitions, presently stored in a series of underground bunkers on the far side of the city. So far, the Surakans had only tapped into a small reserve of their supply. Ellis was confident that would change in the coming hours.

Lights blazed back on and the gentle, constant background hum of machinery shoved the sudden silence away.

"We need to meet with the military brass," said Lamar.

"Who's here?" Ellis asked.

"Grace, Aru, and Kapoor." Lamar pulled Ellis aside into a nearby conference room, where three older, dour-looking militia officers waited around a table for Ellis and Lamar to join them. She recognized Kapoor and Grace. Ellis had been on a committee at some point about Surakan militia staffing levels. But right now, she couldn't recall any of the details. At the time, she'd been more focused on getting the sewer systems repaired. Right now, storm water runoff didn't seem quite so pressing.

Red stripes on the shoulders indicated they were officers. Three buttons over the stripes indicated that Ellis was standing in front of generals. Kapoor had been promoted since they'd last met.

"Generals," Ellis said, nodding to them.

"We don't have time for a fancy briefing with much in the way of visuals," Lamar said. He leaned in close to Ellis and all but whispered, "I'm here to translate any concepts. Take a deep breath—you look like you're about to topple over."

Lamar leaned back and swiped through messages and updates on a screen he'd pulled up on the surface of the table.

Ellis looked directly at her generals. "Okay," she began. "What are we looking at?"

"Bottom line: we are screwed," General Kapoor said, each word snapped out crisp and distinct. "Ground-based long-range anti-aircraft and surface-to-space capabilities were all targeted in the first strike. Every single ship capable of jumping to slip-space on the ground or in orbit has been destroyed. We have thirteen non-slipspace-capable ships that retreated to the far side of Kiriken. But they're just hiding in the moon's shadow. If the Sangheili really want to ferret them out, it'd be easy enough."

"I thought they'd scattered further away," Ellis said.

"Fuel, Governor. They need to conserve energy if we're to have the ability to strike back," Kapoor said.

"And *all* our communications are destroyed," Ellis said. "Is that still true?"

"We are working to rebuild the least damaged station." General Grace delivered that. She wasn't dour, Ellis noted, revising her earlier impression of the general, but simply exhausted. The general had yanked her hair back into a quick ponytail. Her red eyes and puffy pale face hinted at stress and lack of sleep.

For some reason, that helped. Ellis relaxed slightly and put her mind toward unpacking the situation in front of her. "We've lost the high ground to the Sangheili, and we've lost the surface to the Jiralhanae. We're unable to call for help. We have thirteen ships at our disposal for local use only. And we have the militia, most of whom took to the ground under the city."

"Civilians have evacuated to the unoccupied side of the city, Sector 31. Many of those are in shelters and bunkers where we can safely house them," General Aru added. "More still are heading into the sewers."

Ellis nodded. "Then dispatch militia with water and thermal blankets to the civilians we know went below and get them out. Relocate them all to Sector 31, if it's secure."

"I'll issue the orders," General Aru said.

"How much of the city do the Jiralhanae have, and have the Sangheili landed yet?" Ellis asked.

Lamar shifted in his seat. "We don't know what exactly is going on between the Sangheili factions and the Jiralhanae who landed. So far, they're razing the residential districts at the edge of the desert and have set up a perimeter. But they've left the financial center alone, as well as industrial and shopping—most of Suraka seems to still be relatively intact. Any response we make, we need to make sure we don't antagonize Sangheili that are potentially willing to reopen talks. Fleetmaster 'Kasaan's people, in particular."

" 'Kasaan's fleet has been destroyed," General Kapoor said. "From what we can tell by eavesdropping through our orbital relays, his flagship is being boarded even as we speak."

That took Lamar down a peg. He looked at the table, shaken. He swiped his screens closed, unable to multitask between administration and what was happening in the room. Even though he'd been military, on the campaign trail last year both he and Ellis had deeply shared a vision of peace with the Sangheili and a focus on rebuilding Suraka. "I can't believe it."

"Okay, then. 'Kasaan isn't a player anymore. We can assume the Sangheili are, once again, our enemy," Ellis said. "Our dream of peace with them is dead, Lamar. Think about it—most likely this was something they planned long ago. They found all our communications stations, every ship with slipspace ability, including commercial vehicles on the ground, and then attacked in synchrony. They've been studying us with a mind for a killing blow like this for some time, even as they asked for meetings. Generals, our options?"

They began to lay out scenarios. Some surprises were up their sleeves. Like four or five asteroids in a stable orbit, already prepped to be mined, that could be used to threaten the city of Rak or even to take out a Sangheili ship—that is, if they weren't spotted and destroyed on the way in by enemy defenses. But they weren't enough to do anything against whole fleets.

Out of the corner of her eye, Ellis watched Lamar wincing. "We cannot slug it out punch for punch," he said. "We've run the simulations. The Sangheili may have fewer numbers, but their ships dominate what we've cobbled together. Our vessels are colonial leftovers and donations toward the dream of an independent planet out here. And let's be honest: we've gotten away with autonomy because the UNSC chooses to look the other way. They can't project strength this far out, especially since we occupy their selective blind spot in the JOZ."

"Are you saying we should have sacrificed freedom and sovereignty to sit inside the embrace of those tyrants?" General Grace snapped. She was old-school, very pro–colonial autonomy even from before the Covenant War. Some rumors said she had worked with Colonel Robert Watts himself.

Lamar held up his hands, a placating gesture. "No. I'm saying we're staring death in the face, and we've led almost a million human beings here to share our fate. I'm concerned with the very real possibility that we've all made a horrific mistake by severing all infrastructure ties with the UNSC."

The generals collectively bristled at that.

Ellis leaned forward. "Look, we can't change what we've done, whether it's a mistake or not. We have to work with what the reality is now. So let's focus first on the Jiralhanae. We still don't know what they're trying to do here, but it doesn't seem like they're out to take the entire city. So let's start observing them and encircling them. Probe their defenses. Keep me briefed on everything we learn. In the meantime, let's get the civilians as far from the Brutes as we can. Sector 31 needs to be as secured as our militia numbers allow. And contingency plans: I want three varying ones simulated and studied by the morning. I want options for getting communications back, getting civilians off-world in case massive destruction is on its way, and all our options for fighting back. Nothing's off the table or too out of the box."

Aru, Kapoor, and Grace nodded, reenergized. They stood up and filed out of the conference room.

As they left, Ellis leaned over and grabbed Lamar's shoulder. "You okay?"

Lamar stared into space for a long moment, then took a deep breath. "In the war, as an officer . . . I sent a lot of people to die with the hope that those who survived would see peace someday."

Ellis rubbed his upper arm. "You know, we had the meeting scheduled for tomorrow morning with the UEG envoy and the Sangheili. The governor's shuttle they were set to use had a slipspace drive."

"You can't think about that," Lamar said.

"I feel I have to. I'm not going anywhere, Lamar. But you served in two wars," Ellis said. "You're a soldier. Yet you still argue for some kind of peace here?"

Lamar leaned back in his chair and raised an eyebrow. "It's *because* I'm a soldier I'll argue for peace. I know the value of peace more than the average civilian ever will. I know it's worth doing everything you can to secure it."

"So is that going to be a problem for us?" Ellis asked. Even though she outranked Lamar, he technically had more authority than she did during a combat scenario like the one they now faced. As Surakan vice-governor, he actually had veto power over civil security and defense decisions in the event that the city was threatened. And the militia looked up to him. At one point, she'd been worried he'd run against her based on his service record.

"It won't be a problem," Lamar said. "Because doing anything for peace sometimes includes fighting for it, once everything else has been tried. I just want to make sure we've tried everything else first."

"The Jiralhanae are in our city. Killing our people. We tried everything, Lamar. I think it's time to fight." She'd caught her breath, surveyed the field. It was crystal clear, Ellis felt.

She stood up to leave, but Lamar put a hand on her forearm. "One more thing: during the meeting, I checked up on Jeff for you. I got a message that he's safe. He checked in per protocol. He's with a patrol monitoring the Jiralhanae Prowler movements just outside the Rughet Factories. He's sending some useful intel via drones they're patching through and his patrol's own sightings."

Ellis took his hand. "Thank you, Lamar. I mean it. Thank you."

"You must be proud of him," Lamar said. "He's very brave, volunteering to stay put."

Ellis blinked back tears. "Yeah, that's what I'm afraid of."

"I got to know him when we were campaigning together. He's *smart* brave, like his mother," Lamar said with a smile. "That kind of brave keeps you alive in places like where he is. So you do well by him, okay?"

Ellis smiled back, let go, and wiped her eyes. "I'll try, Lamar. Thanks again."

The Demon Three moved through Rojka's ship with impunity.

The rage that this could be happening built up inside the fleetmaster to a point where he feared it would overwhelm his very senses. He'd lost a strong fighter, Mrata, to their hands. That needed to be repaid, among many other debts.

He moved through the gloom with his active camouflage on, studying the Spartans so that he could decide just how to pick them off.

One Spartan he could face alone. But three meant he needed a careful strategy. The one hiding by the door that killed Mrata had hit Rojka hard enough that he still ached. He would kill that Spartan last.

Their apparent leader was quick on his feet as well, but unarmed and carrying the envoy's body. That would be the first one to die.

"Fleetmaster." Daga's voice came to Rojka through an apparatus wirelessly connected to his armor and embedded in his earpore. "Where are you?"

"I hunt the Demon Three," Rojka whispered.

"The second wave of boarders approach. We need you with us," Daga hissed. "We struggled with the first wave already. Let the Demons go. It is time for a different fight."

Let them go? Perhaps Rojka could have looked past his hatred and traded the Spartans to the more powerful kaidons of Sanghelios in return for promises of supplies, weapons, and additional warriors to fully secure the keeps of Rak. Perhaps . . .

Rojka clenched the hilt of his powered-down energy sword in frustration and anger. Maybe he could even have traded them back to the humans' government, who apparently wanted them so badly, in exchange for some manner of permanent peace.

But truly, deep inside, he wanted the trio to pay for their crimes.

The Demon Three should not be permitted to live. Not when they'd taken so many Sangheili lives. He had been dwelling on what he should do since he had picked up that human shuttle among the debris of Glyke.

"Everything has been ripped from us," Rojka said.

"Perhaps all that remains is choosing the honorable death," Daga replied.

"I should have killed the Demon Three when I found them. I thought it *clever* to think like a human for once and use them as currency," Rojka spat. "Now I pay the ultimate price."

The old ways—no diplomacy, no negotiations, no contact. Just grievances aired in the fighting pit, the hot sand beneath your feet, a sword in hand, and your enemy a pace away.

Like the battle Thars now brought to him.

"Fleetmaster . . . know that we are taking a last stand in the command bridge," Daga said. "We need to be at each other's side if these are to be our remaining moments."

Rojka nodded at the wisdom. It was time for him to leave. The Demon Three would die soon enough, along with the rest of his ship. He would have to comfort himself with that.

Unwavering Discipline shivered as more boarding craft struck the side of the bay. Molten metal sparked and lit up the hangar as the circular boring maw of one of the attack shuttles—a vicious and unrelenting breaching vessel known as the Tick—burst through the weak shielding holding back the vacuum of space and opened a corridor to give infantry access to the interior. Enemy Sangheili warriors poured into the area.

"The fight has come to me, it appears," Rojka said. "Send additional warriors to my location, Daga."

Rojka turned off his active camouflage. His energy sword flared on, covering him in a blue light that burned back the shadows.

CHAPTER 5

Hekabe listened to the staccato pops of the humans' gunfire. There was a crudity to their ordnance and chemical charges that he found appealing. Throwing metal out of a barrel: it was so effective and destructive when the pieces struck. Like a spike rifle, but with smaller ammunition—an aspect of warfare the Jiralhanae had in common with these skittering pests.

But the humans tended to scurry around, popping up here and there. They had no *spirit*.

Hekabe's warriors had done well. They had taken a large circular section on the border of the human city and secured it. Streets had been barricaded at the edges Hekabe designated, and gun platforms rocketed overhead to provide full fire support.

Meanwhile, his massive cruiser had started demolishing the buildings and the ground with its plasma batteries, while thousands of Unggoy thralls toiled with machines—heavy excavation platforms like Scarabs, Locusts, and even their own bare hands—to push rubble toward the edges of the now-occupied Jiralhanae areas of the city.

Hekabe stood on the crater's rim, towering above the site on the piles of rubble at the perimeter, and watched the massive destruction of the city with eager satisfaction.

But the crack of human weapons kept distracting him. The gunfire was getting closer.

"Kritus! Anexus!" Hekabe shouted. "What are the humans trying to do beyond the barricades? Is this their counterattack?" Judging by the sounds of the melee from the buildings near the occupied rim, just a couple of streets away from Hekabe, it seemed like a small one indeed.

"It might be only a first wave," Anexus said. "We can call the ship to our aid or fall back to our artillery."

Hekabe stared at Anexus. What foolishness was Anexus talking about? "The ship continues to blast the ground for the slaves and their overseers. You want to divert it for a smattering of humans?"

Anexus thought about that for a moment. "They should not stop digging?"

Hekabe considered killing Anexus on the spot. "No, they should not stop. No matter how many humans worm back out of their hiding places!"

"But there are many humans in this city," Anexus said.

Hekabe laughed and picked up Oath of Fury, his gravity hammer. "Then let us go and cull their numbers so that they are not such a burden for you, Anexus. Follow me, if you are a true Jiralhanae and not frightened of these weak little aliens."

Kritus roared in response and grabbed his weapons. Less enthusiastically, Anexus followed.

Hearing the battle cry, Jiralhanae warriors turned and saw the three of them running down the pile of rubble and toward the barricades. They joined the rush behind the wedge that Hekabe, Kritus, and Anexus now made.

The enemy gunfire increased, bullets pinging against nearby walls. Hekabe could see glimpses of human squads in the alleyways across the roads from the barricades. They were sneaking around, trying to snipe at the Jiralhanae emplacements.

"Get across there and destroy them," Hekabe ordered as he clambered over one of the barricades made of rubble. Across the intersection, the humans maneuvered to keep a steady stream of fire on small groups of lesser Jiralhanae. Several of them shifted around with a larger machine gun on a tripod and opened fire, the heavy weapon chattering as it turned.

Ah. This is more like it, Hekabe thought.

Warriors just behind Hekabe fell, the salvo enough to wound or slow them down. But Hekabe continued forward into the shadows between two buildings where the humans hid, ignoring the metal slugs slapping off his armor.

The Jiralhanae chieftain burst into the humans' midst. He was energized to see their small alien eyes open wide with fear as he appeared. From Hekabe's experience, humans seemed to expect their enemies to shoot back and find cover. They were always shocked by a charge into direct fire.

They scattered before him, and rightfully so.

Hekabe raised Oath of Fury and slammed it hard into the street. The sound of the hammer's impact echoed from every flat surface nearby, its gravitic energies expending violently in every direction. All around him, the bodies flew away and bounced off the building walls and ground when they landed. Many immediately perished, so close were they to the hammer's strike.

There was a large splash of blood on Hekabe's shins. These so-called human fighters didn't even have real armor. They depended on their numbers and running away.

Such easy prey.

There, another one darted behind a toppled pillar the hammer had knocked over. The human was scrambling for safety. Just like the barn rodents on Doisac.

Hekabe dropped the hammer on it and was pleased to witness a pair of bloody legs soar into the air and a head carom down the crumbling wall facades.

His lips curled. This wasn't a full attack. This was barely a pack's worth of humans. He would have to discipline Anexus later for his panic. If Hekabe didn't beat some sense into his subordinates, they would continue making mistakes.

Being a leader was tiring work.

Hekabe looked around. Dozens of humans dead. The sound of their weapons had ceased.

One of them, a male, remarkably still lived. Blood streamed from its nostrils as it crawled slowly toward a fallen rifle. As the human grabbed it, Hekabe knocked the weapon out of its hands and picked it up by the throat. They were so tiny and inconsequential that he could hold this vermin up with one arm.

"You will know my name before you die, human. I am Hekabe . . . and you are nothing to me," he growled at it.

The human did not understand his words but kept struggling against his hold. It spat at Hekabe.

"Yes. That's good. I admire that. Fighting until the end. At the end of the Great Schism, when the human and Sangheili vessels attacked the ship where my pack's little ones huddled in the corner, I am told they called out for me and begged for mercy. Understand, they were too young yet to know the concepts of dying well as we do, human warrior. They did not know how to stand firm in the face of death. So, they begged. Do *you* beg?" he asked, grinning in satisfaction. "I do not understand your language, but you don't look like you are begging."

Hekabe increased the pressure on the human's spindly neck and listened to its angry sounds.

"Do any of you understand the human language?" Hekabe asked of the other Jiralhanae now gathering around him. Unlike the Sangheili, who thought it warranted to use translation devices to learn of the enemy's schemes, Hekabe had no plans on making any conversation with the aliens. Just killing them.

"It tells you its lineage," a warrior remarked. "And its name. It calls itself *Jaff.* Of this world's chieftain."

Hekabe lowered his voice. "I see. And yet, even though I should be proud of the fact that *my* pack's little ones died in battle, all I can do is think about how frightened they must have been. Whether they hoped I could still save them. Of their despair. It should not haunt me. But it does."

The human struggled to dig its hands into Hekabe's arm. It gasped for air.

"There are no other chieftains of this world now," Hekabe announced, louder now. "There is only Hekabe!"

And no more of his pack would ever again die at alien hands.

Hekabe squeezed until the human's neck audibly snapped and the body slumped in his hand. He casually tossed the body into the rubble.

"Back to the dig," Hekabe ordered.

The outcome of this skirmish would certainly be enough of a message to the humans to leave the Jiralhanae alone to their work.

Through his heads-up display, Jai looked at the incoming Sangheili spreading out through the hangar. The first wave of boarders had breached the ship's armored hull and were now opening its bay doors from the inside, giving dropships and other craft easy access to its energy-shielded interior. They hadn't spotted the Spartans yet, as they were standing still among the cover provided by the rows and rows of disused and partially stripped Covenant craft. Jai shifted the civilian's body in his arms slightly. They'd staunched the worst of her bleeding, but she needed real medical assistance soon. "We need to fall back."

"No," Adriana said. Her recovered energy sword flared to life. "Let's take that boarding vessel."

Jai could see from his cover at the end of one of the giant stacks of stripped Covenant parts that a ship-to-ship battle was taking place outside the hangar in the darkness of space, as brilliant flashes of distant light winked on and off. Point defenses of the Covenant ship they were on were still firing, stabbing plasma at the waves of Tick boarding craft looking to attach to its hull and bore their way in. Chunks of debris from destroyed Covenant fighters and unlucky dropships tumbled about with every explosion.

"Mike?" Jai asked, a small note of frustration creeping into his voice.

"There's a whole ship full of Sangheili on the other side of the hangar doors," Mike said. "There are only twenty or thirty in this area. I think our odds are better here. I should be able to fly one of these Ticks—if we can clear the hangar and get aboard."

They were ignoring Jai's orders. He fought his annoyance as he ducked plasma fire, turning his back to it to protect the civilian, and huddled up behind a Covenant Phantom that seemed to be completely sawed in half.

"They've spotted us. What are we doing?" Mike asked.

Jai's armored boots crunched the mechanical guts of the Phantom that had been ripped out from under the dropship's armored skin, making it look as if it had been disemboweled, frayed cables trailing out from the body on the nearby floor like grimy entrails. This area was more like a junkyard packed high with spare parts than a smoothly polished Covenant war machine. Another puzzle to shelve away for later.

"You said you *should* be able to fly the Tick? I don't like *should*," Jai said. "I like *can*." And Adriana had sounded determined, but not confident, about taking the boarding craft to begin with. They were throwing dice here. This was also a Tick breaching vessel. It wasn't exactly made for precise exfiltration maneuvers in a battle-space. It was designed like a torpedo with a siege-bore, specifically for launching at enemy ships, impaling their armor, and then burning them open for boarding actions.

"*Should*'s better than *dead*," Mike replied.

"We're taking it," Adriana repeated as she clambered over a nearby stack of dismembered wings. "They'll put up a fight, but we can make it." The two Sangheili who'd turned a nearby corner looked up as she dropped onto them, the enemy shooting wildly into the air at where she had been a split second earlier.

She beheaded one of them with the energy sword. The other hit her with its shoulder, slamming them both into the hull of a decommissioned Seraph fighter. Adriana rolled out of the dent she'd made in the Seraph's hull as the Elite tried to fire its weapon point-blank into her helmet. Melted alloy splashed back onto them both as the plasma bolt missed and hit the Seraph's undercarriage just a centimeter to the right of where Adriana's head had just been.

Adriana spun around the Sangheili and climbed up its back, grabbed its neck with her free hand, and forced it hard to the ground under her. The energy sword flashed as the alien hit the floor while she simultaneously impaled it. It wriggled, screaming as Adriana leaned all her weight into the sword, the weapon burning slowly through its chest and down into the deck plating.

Jai heard heavy footsteps adjusting course in the hangar. "Well, we have their attention now," he said. "We take the Tick."

A Sangheili rounded the corner of several large engine pods stacked together. Adriana turned to look at it as Jai tensed. There was no way she could get out of the way in time before it fired on her.

A wave of plasma fire hit it first. Mike advanced calmly with the carbine he'd acquired from the headless Sangheili.

Adriana kicked the plasma rifle from the other dead Elite over toward Jai. "Okay then. The Tick," she said.

Jai picked the rifle up, then carefully adjusted the unconscious civilian so that she rested over his shoulder. "I'll cover."

Mike fell back with him. Adriana ripped the bay door off a Covenant Phantom to their side, encircled by stacks of equipment. They stepped inside after her.

Jai glanced around at the gutted interior. "Is the ship we're on some kind of recycling barge?" He looked at a jagged hole in the opposite side, the result of an explosion that clearly had occurred long before they'd arrived.

"Hold on," Mike said, coming in after Adriana. "Check out your three o'clock."

"Well, hello, old friend," Adriana murmured. "Jai, it's Whiskey Tango Foxtrot One."

"The one and only," Mike said. It was their designation. Self-assigned. Not protocol.

Jai followed them back out of the Phantom chassis, being careful not to hit the civilian's head on the side of the hull. He glanced slightly right and saw what they were referring to: Whiskey Tango Foxtrot One was a battered UNSC Bumblebee.

The Class-5 Heavy Lifeboat had burn marks all the way down the left side, but was otherwise intact. For Jai, it felt like it had only been a few foggy, confusing hours ago that they'd dragged the cryo-chambers and latched them to the inside of the escape transport. He could remember half-daydreamed snippets of doing that . . . somewhere in a murky past life. The tension as they'd struggled to get away from a dying ship above the surface of a doomed alien world. A feeling that it was a long-shot chance at survival, as he waited to be frozen. And then confusion when they'd suddenly woken. Apparently almost six years had passed like a bad dream, and now they were getting back aboard this death trap of an escape pod. Déjà vu all over again. "We all on the same page then?" he asked.

"If we can get it up and running, there should be enough fuel for round two," Mike said. "The airbrakes haven't been triggered yet either. We just used it to get off the *Vacuna*, not go planetside."

"I count four Elites between us and the Bumblebee," Adriana said.

"We're going to be launching this thing out into the middle of a Covenant naval battle," Mike said. "But it'll pop out of here like a bat out of hell. I think we might be able to dodge the worst of it. The armor looks like it can still take a beating, as long as nothing too big gets slung at us. It'll certainly be safer for reentry and planetfall than the Tick. Hopefully they haven't been stripping it apart like everything else in here."

"Okay, let me swing around to flank the long-necked assholes over there," Adriana muttered. "Then we move. Run and gun until we get inside and close the door."

"It's a plan," Jai said, as Adriana leapt over a nearby pile of tubing and Covenant engine parts.

"Okay," Adriana said. Now she actually sounded merry to go

along with her determination and, yes, in this case, confidence. A better combination, Jai thought. "Charge them."

Jai held the civilian's head to his shoulder with an armored gauntlet, trying his best to protect her as he shot the gap. He followed Mike out into the open, running as fast he could for the Bumblebee. His thighs screamed in protest, skin still searing with cryo-itch as his feet dug hard into the floor. When the half ton of Spartan got up to speed, he leapt up to clear the remains of a Banshee fighter and started firing at the first Sangheili he spotted.

It gaped for a second, then dove for cover as its armor shielding flared. Mike and Jai both focused their fire on it until it ran for safety.

Plasma fire exploded nearby, kicking up spare parts and sending debris scattering. "Take out the farthest one—he's more accurate," Jai said.

Mike crossed in front of Jai as Adriana slammed her way out from behind a pile of discarded ship-mounted weapons and hit the closest Sangheili with enough force to throw him fifty meters back. The limp alien slid across the deck plating.

A nearby Sangheili started shooting at Adriana. The shielding on her Mjolnir armor flared but held together as she rushed to meet it.

"Don't chase them—get to the lifeboat!" Mike shouted as Adriana rounded a large stack of scrap metal and disappeared.

Jai slammed into the side of the Bumblebee as Mike tapped on a control pad. The rear airlock door opened, drawing from the vessel's reserve power. Mike scrambled inside as Jai covered the open airlock door with his plasma rifle. "Adriana! Where are you?"

Lights flickered on and a familiar hum filled the interior of the Bumblebee as Mike climbed into the pilot's chair and started the ready sequence. Something heavy clanged on the top of the Bumblebee.

Still holding the civilian, Jai crouched, aimed up, and stepped back.

"It's me." Adriana dropped down and jumped into the Bumblebee. "Spotted one of them with a plasma launcher. Thought I'd save us some trouble before he got us in his sights."

Jai followed her into the lifeboat. Mike glanced back, and once he was given the all-clear, the thick airlock door thudded shut and hissed.

Outside, the sound of plasma fire plinked against the hull as two Sangheili ran toward the craft. More would be gathering around them shortly.

Jai set the civilian into the chair next to him and pulled the harness down over her shoulders. She stirred but didn't wake. He glanced out through the narrow airlock windows at the approaching Sangheili. The reinforced glass scorched as more plasma fire hit it.

"Our buddy with the plasma launcher had a friend. So I borrowed their weapons," Adriana held two plasma rifles up as she shoved her legs against the far side of the wall, just as Jai had done. The harnesses in here couldn't be pulled down over their bulky armor; they were designed for a small crew of average-sized humans, with a large rear bay capable of carrying things like a heavy weapons cache or a slipspace drive—or a trio of Spartan-laden cryotubes.

Mike looked back at them. "Ready?"

One of the Elites that had reached the Bumblebee was now battering an energy sword against the airlock door in the back, attempting to tear his way inside.

"Go!" Jai said.

The lifeboat's thrusters kicked on and blew the Sangheili standing behind it across the hangar deck. The Bumblebee screamed and screeched its way across the hangar floor, metal grinding hard.

"Mike?"

Mike tapped at controls to his sides, ignoring his teammates. The lifeboat bounced and then slapped the deck again. The scraping sound intensified.

"We won't have any hull left if you don't stop doing that!" Adriana shouted.

"Don't interrupt the pilot—he's busy," Mike muttered. The Bumblebee bounced again, then stayed in the air just in time to clear the carcass of a Covenant Phantom. Jai noted that Mike was trying to stay low so that the Spirit dropship now breaching the atmosphere shielding at the front of the hangar didn't shoot them with the massive cannon hanging off its undercarriage.

They wobbled again.

"Hold on," Mike said. The thrusters punched. The Bumblebee flung itself out of the hangar and past the Spirit. "And cross your fingers."

Bumblebees were fast, tiny, and hard to track—but they weren't invincible. If one shot from a capital ship connected, they'd be a haze of glowing dust before they even realized they'd been hit. Covenant plasma fire crisscrossed the vacuum around them. Mike jammed the thrusters, changing their speed and course randomly, tumbling through space as he deftly navigated the dense field of enemy fire.

For several moments, Jai waited tensely for a final explosion of heat as Mike skillfully piloted them through fields of dying Covenant ships, hulls carved apart and spewing debris and alien bodies out into the vacuum. He was using the chaos of battle to shield them, deliberately moving through the smoldering remains so that they could hide among deorbiting junk.

"I'm trying to home in on a beacon down on the planet," Mike finally announced, his voice ragged. "Hang on, I've got a readout here. We're above an Outer Colony world: Carrow. The origin point of the beacon is a city called Suraka. It might be a leftover ping from before the battle up here started; it probably got hit hard by the Covenant, so we're definitely really far behind enemy lines. It's automated. Wait . . . someone's actually down there . . . I'm getting some chatter, but a lot of it is encrypted and it's not standard UNSC. I think there are definitely people hiding out down there."

"That sounds better than nothing," Jai said. He wondered if this was why the Covenant was here, to wipe out whatever human population remained planetside.

There had been entire worlds where that had happened. The Covenant usually got around to finishing the job. The last message Gray Team had received from the UNSC indicated that Covenant forces had reached Sol and begun the occupation of Earth. Extinction was imminent. Jai wondered if humanity had somehow survived, or were they above the last pocket of human civilization right now? Six years was a long time to be out of the loop.

But here the Sangheili had clearly been fighting each other. What had that been all about?

"I'm not even sure if I can get us there. We're on a bad trajectory," Mike said. "Steep. But I don't want anything following us. We're going to take a real beating on the way in."

The air around the lifeboat glowed red with heat from reentry. Curtains of flame crept up around them to hide the ocean and clouds of the planet below.

Rojka watched the small human transport explode out of *Unwavering Discipline*'s hangar as he thrust his energy sword into one of Thars's warriors. The dead Sangheili slumped to the ground. The Spartans had killed another eight or nine on their way out. Rojka another four. The remaining enemy had fallen back to their dropships and boarding vessels to regroup.

Cowards.

Seeing so many of his foes' bodies around the hangar pleased Rojka. But it was shameful to see that so many of them had been killed by the Spartans, denying the fleetmaster and his crew the glory they deserved. And the Spartans' seemingly successful escape was a humiliating capstone atop the whole affair.

Earlier Rojka had anticipated certain death fighting the boarders. He had hoped differently, but somewhere deep inside he knew there was no chance Thars himself would ever board *Unwavering Discipline* until Rojka was dead.

So be it. But he would go down fighting just the same, as would Rojka's trusted inner circle. And while undermanned for a cruiser, the rest of Rojka's thousand-strong crew aboard the *Unwavering Discipline*—the last ship standing of Rojka's once-great fleet—were committed to battling Thars to the bitter end.

Still, the escape of the Demon Three chewed at the back of his mind, pulling his attention away from the honor of a last stand.

Before they managed to escape, he had come close to the human lifeboat but was unable to stop it. He had only enough time to toss a malakost tracker onto the transport before he was attacked by enemy Sangheili. The tracker would tenaciously cling to the vehicle's hull exterior, no matter the duress. It would even survive reentry.

So once more, the Demon Three roamed free. *Gray Team*, the

envoy had called them when she tried to open negotiations to acquire them.

Rojka had mostly stopped calling the humans *nishum* somewhere near the close of the war. It had been a hard adjustment. He had been taught to follow the teachings of the Prophets and the Path of the Great Journey by his elders since learning how to walk and hold a practice weapon. He had been a devout warrior from the earliest of ages.

It had all fallen apart so quickly. When Rojka learned that the San'Shyuum had betrayed their union with the Sangheili, stirring up a coup by the hands of the Jiralhanae, it felt like his world had been cracked apart: everything he had once put his faith in was ripped away. Rojka was demoted by the newly appointed Jiralhanae leadership, stripped of his fleet, and sent to the shipyards to take care of the old, damaged vessels, in that brief window of time when the Sangheili were thrown from the halls of power and the Jiralhanae took their place.

Shortly after that shift in power, the Arbiter and his allies led a rebellion that turned into a full-blown civil war—the Great Schism—resulting in the end of the Covenant's campaign against the humans. Stranded in a band of ship debris being repaired around the Sangheili homeworld, Rojka had still *believed*. He still held to the Prophets' words, hoping this whole controversy would pass like a bad dream. After all, this was their sacred calling, the cleansing war, their destiny—it was *everything* to them.

But the Covenant had really been torn asunder, and it was gone. Forever.

Now everyone was still trying to find their own way in the aftermath. A *new* way, as the Arbiter Thel 'Vadam had pointed out in his pleas for all Sangheili to stand with him and make peace with humans. The universe held so much uncertainty, so much chaos. Rojka had welcomed the new leadership, even if he still longed for the old ways.

Despite the lies of the Prophets, the humans were just an intelligent species. Another civilization. That was it.

Yet that trio of Spartans? They would always be vermin to Rojka. Most Sangheili, no matter their allegiance or creed, could put aside all differences to see these Spartan wretches killed. For they were indeed demons.

Humans, Rojka found, he could make alliances with. Once you really dealt with them, you discovered that they were cunning and resourceful, even if they lacked honor and resiliency. The Sangheili actually stood stronger with their new human allies by their side. But he had been utterly imprudent to leave the Demon Three alive in stasis, as if they were some kind of bargaining piece to be traded, looted off the remains of something he had once plundered in space.

That was Kig-Yar thinking.

A true Sangheili would have killed the Demon Three the moment the intel came in confirming their location and he found them floating in deep space, frozen and smug, helpless in the face of their own atrocities.

Rojka had lost *his world*. He had lost his fleet. And within moments, he might likely lose his ship and his life. These things, he could barely make peace with. But seeing the Demon Three escape burned away at him with an indescribable rage.

His plan to die here would have to be postponed for the time being, Rojka realized. This could not stand.

He contacted the command bridge. "Armed engineering teams to the shield generators," he ordered. "Restart the engines. I am returning to the command bridge."

Ancients, judge me, he pleaded. But he had decided to forgo glory. What Rojka desperately wanted instead was vengeance. Fiery and pure.

He would do this for all Sangheili.

He was going to hunt down the Demon Three. *For Glyke,* he thought.

He would kill them all where they stood.

CHAPTER 6

An aide appeared at the door of Ellis's temporary office in the bunkers deep under Suraka. "Governor?" He fidgeted for a second when he got no response. He pushed the door further open and tried again. "Governor?"

Ellis pulled the stim patch off her forearm, crumpled it up, and threw it into the trash can by the plastic desk. "Just a moment."

She leaned back in the chair, waiting as she rubbed her tired eyes. Then the warming sensation prickled the roots of her hair. Her heart sped up a beat and a flush crept up her face. Wakefulness returned.

"Okay,"—Ellis glanced at the aide's name tag—"Cameron. Let's go."

Cameron led her out through the command center and to the meeting rooms. *We're in the middle of a war,* Ellis thought, *and somehow I'm spending more time in conferences and sitting around than I ever have before in my entire administration.*

That seemed ludicrous. Surely she should be standing next to a commander near a field of battle, right?

But no, there were the endless planning sessions, documents, and decisions that had to be made from the bunker. Lots of decisions. And Ellis needed to be there for each one. She had to *know* what was happening. Because she was responsible, in the end, for everything that happened to Suraka. That's what the people had elected her for. Trusted her to do.

Inside the meeting room, Ellis looked around the conference table, frowning. She seemed to be missing two generals. "Okay, General Grace, I'm ready. Where are Aru and Kapoor?"

General Grace looked up from reading documents on a datapad in front of her. "They're resting. They were coordinating during the attack and never had a moment to stop."

"Oh."

Grace nodded curtly at the documents. "We now have a better idea of the Jiralhanae strength and how far they're willing to press forward."

One of Grace's aides had mounted a paper map of the city on the wall—this is how they had done this sort of thing hundreds of years ago. Paper on a wall in an underground facility. It seemed incredibly inefficient and impractical to Ellis, but it was all they had right now. Someone had used a marker to shade areas showing the Jiralhanae-controlled sections of Suraka, isolated on the border of the city and the vast Uldt desert. "The rough headcount is about three hundred Jiralhanae on the ground, judging by the dropship intervals and spotter counts," the aide said. "They're demolishing the buildings and using heavy equipment—large, heavily weaponized excavation platforms, like the ones we saw during the war. Now that they've secured the area and airspace, they're using a legion of Unggoy to push the rubble toward the city. It may be some kind of barricade. We're not sure. We don't have any eyes in the sky at the moment, but some reports indicate they're leveling all the buildings in that zone of the city as well."

General Grace added, "They stopped our incursions, reacting

very negatively whenever units passed the financial district and approached the residential areas. They did not pursue during retreat but kept to the occupied areas marked off on the map. For Jiralhanae, they were very organized about it. Usually you can lure them out with a three-person team—decoy squads designed to break up pack numbers. Two for firepower, and someone posing as bait. They never took it. Step past the demarcation point, though, and they attack en masse and with extreme prejudice."

Two hints in one statement about Jiralhanae brutality, Ellis realized. "How . . . many people did we lose testing their defenses?"

"Twenty percent casualties on units sent in before withdrawal," Grace said, grimacing. "We're still sorting out the casualty lists, lots of possible MIAs, others deserters. Some of them are pretty shaken up after seeing these aliens face-to-face, and seeing what they're capable of. They certainly earn the name Brutes."

Ellis knew that General Grace had been offered a career track in the UNSC and could have continued a life back on Mars, in the UEG's population dispersal effort. Grace had no love for the UNSC, but many found a way to bury that in exchange for stability. Most people here in Suraka had considered building new lives back in Earth's solar system after becoming refugees, living on the Martian reserve for the first few years after the war. Any citizen here could have continued down that safe, comfortable path.

But they'd come to Carrow. Many with children. So far from the UNSC, out here in the Joint Occupied Zone where so many glassed worlds existed. They'd wanted a place of their own. Freedom from the wars of the past, from the UNSC's overextended control. Some believed the UNSC would eventually use the

Covenant as an excuse to gain full military control of the colonies—all of them, including Carrow. Conspiracy theory crap, but Ellis had heard it often enough when campaigning for governor.

Ellis constantly reminded voters of the fact that she'd grown up on Carrow and was eighteen when she'd fled Suraka with her entire family before the Covenant fleet could arrive. She'd been forty when she returned here. Jeff had been born on the UEG's reserve, a network strewn across the southern dunes of Terra Cimmeria on Mars. Her husband, another refugee, had hailed from Arcadia. She'd met him in the camps.

Her delayed engineering degrees, something she'd fought to get even as the war crept closer and closer to Earth, had been a defiant victory. Her return to Carrow, yet another.

"How many casualties will we take if we try a full assault?" Ellis sat down in one of the conference chairs. "We have four thousand in the militia and three or four thousand volunteers, right?"

Grace nodded, hesitant. "We don't have any orbital support with our ships hiding out past the moon. If we tried anything of that nature, the overwhelming probability is that we'd be destroyed by the Jiralhanae or Sangheili ships in orbit. It would be suicide."

"And if the enemy didn't have the high ground?" Assuming some miracle, or that everyone aboard the Surakan ships laid their lives down to give everyone on the ground a chance.

"Hundreds of Jiralhanae against our militia, and them armed to the teeth with fully weaponized ground and aircraft?" Grace shook her head. "I can't condone any manner of frontal assault at this time, even assuming the remote possibility the other ships could provide some support. The risk is simply too high."

Ellis sank further back into her chair. She'd browbeaten and shepherded so many toward her platform of reinvestment and ambassadorship. She'd worked hard to get negotiations between the Sangheili here on Carrow with the UEG as a mediator. All things the prior governor, Kait Adelie, had chosen to delay in order to first make sure the militia was built, the bunkers were dug, and Suraka was fully prepared for the worst. The Sangheili only had tens of thousands in the keeps of Rak, banding those together into something like what humans would call a city. Humanity outnumbered them by a million in Suraka. But the Sangheili were vicious fighters.

Ellis had viewed a potential war as tremendously wasteful. Yes, the Sangheili had landed six years ago and started building in the Uldt, thinking Carrow abandoned, only months before humans returned to reestablish Suraka. And yes, they were very territorial. But the UNSC hadn't protested the Sangheili colony, and in fact, some suggested that Carrow was offered to the Arbiter's people by the UNSC to assuage their Sangheili allies in light of some unspeakable crime. What was more likely was that the UEG hadn't even had eyes on the planet at all since the Covenant attack years earlier, but once they found it, it would have only strained the tense postwar relations to demand that the Arbiter and his leadership uproot tens of thousands of determined warriors. So they didn't.

And the first few years had been so quiet, Ellis thought. You could even pretend that there weren't aliens living on the other side of the Uldt. Imagine that, somehow, a sandy, impassable border protected them. Sure, people here grumbled. But it was reiterated by their advocates over and over that the Sangheili weren't like the rest of the Covenant. Their naval fleets had actually turned on humanity's enemies and fought side by side with people.

Then, as time went on, more and more "incidents" had happened at the edge of the desert.

Conflicts between human settlers and Sangheili. Maybe war *was* inevitable. If that was to come, she had thought then, let it be after humanity had grown in numbers and in manufacturing ability. Infrastructure. Resource allocation. Trade. Everything that came along with a burgeoning human economy.

She'd had the figures, damn it. Three more years, and the Sangheili here on Carrow would have been utterly unable to face them in any kind of context.

Maybe that was why they had attacked now.

"Governor?"

Now people were throwing their lives away in "probing defenses" so that they could ascertain the strength of this sudden Jiralhanae occupation? And Ellis herself had been the one who said they needed to probe those defenses, hadn't she?

Ellis flipped through the notes her aide had taken of orders she'd given, looking for written confirmation that she had actually suggested they do this. A few days earlier, she was working through plans to solve runoff issues at the base of Arduu Ridge; now she was sending soldiers into a meat grinder to test enemy defenses. *What could ever prepare one to be a wartime leader?* she wondered. Nothing—it was a constant roller coaster ride of emotions, guilt, and fear.

"Governor, are you okay?" Grace asked, concerned.

There. There it was, on paper. She'd clearly ordered this disaster. It had just been words, though. Things that she'd known would be expected of her. *Probe their defenses*, she'd ordered. *Figure out what's going on up there.*

But now the blood was on her hands.

This was all too messy. Ellis couldn't see a way around it—people would die, no matter what choices she made. And if she choked, people would still die. There were only less-bad decisions here.

Ellis looked up at the general and her aide, who were both staring at her. "I . . . I just want them off our world," she whispered. Not just the Jiralhanae—she meant *all* of them. "I want them to go away."

No matter which way Ellis pushed the pieces around, they would not click into place. Not this time. Her entire life, she'd been able to visualize a project and make it all line up. Now there was just unstructured chaos and those haunting less-bad choices in her head.

The general glanced at the aide and back to Ellis. "We're trying to come up with solutions, Governor. Really, we're trying."

"Then we have to try harder, General. We have to *push* harder. We owe it to the people who took this journey with us to Carrow and who gave everything of themselves."

General Grace rubbed her temples, letting her guard down for a second to show how tired she also was. "I know, Governor. Believe me, I'm feeling the weight of it all as well."

From the *Unwavering Discipline*'s command bridge, Rojka 'Kasaan watched his enemies scatter before him as his heavy cruiser accelerated, shields suddenly back up. Thars's boarding craft and dropships sloughed off the hull, then spun and darted about fruitlessly as the fleetmaster shouted commands to ignore them.

Daga had followed his orders to get the shields online. Loyal

Sangheili had bled the decks slick, defending repair parties throughout the ship. Lives had been spent. Even now, his crew kept fighting hundreds of intruders throughout its many corridors as the cruiser moved.

And, Rojka swore to himself, it would be for a worthy cause.

"Is this a final attack on Thars?" Daga asked. He had not questioned any of Rojka's demands. No one had. The energy Rojka had returned to the command bridge with had galvanized all his officers. Something was afoot—the crew knew their fleetmaster and their kaidon. Possibilities seemed to brim as they murmured to each other of Rojka's gambit: perhaps ramming the vessel into the traitor, or even going back to Sanghelios itself to return here with a greater fleet.

"No," Rojka said to his second in command. "Thars is now beside the point. He does not matter."

Three enemy frigates turned and raked *Unwavering Discipline*'s sides. Shields sputtered out once again. Rojka gave commands to spin the ship, spreading the damage out. Occasional bursts of plasma fire ripped through the hull. But Rojka was quicker. The belly he turned to his enemy's spear was always the fat, never the muscle. Let them pierce his decks, but leave his engines intact.

"Fire back!" Rojka shouted. "Do not stand and gape at me, or I will strike you down myself to preserve your own honor!"

"If we are not attacking Thars, then what are we doing?" Daga asked. Fear colored his voice. "Are we running from him?"

Rojka gave Daga a hard look. "*Running?* I am Rojka 'Kasaan. I will not be tainted by cowardice. I want *vengeance*."

Rojka paused and looked out at the bridge crew. Only his most trusted officers knew about the Demon Three. He was sure many of his crew had been curious about why he had posted armed guards at that particular hangar bay. The quarantine held, however, and the existence of living human Spartans had remained a secret for most on *Discipline*.

"I would talk to all my crew," Rojka said, tapping at controls to initiate a shipwide message.

The ship shivered, struck again, as Rojka nodded and began speaking. "Some time ago, many of you wondered why I took this ship back to the ruins of Glyke—the world most of you had considered home. For six years now, since its destruction, I have left many probes in the system—watching, waiting, reporting everything. They found a signal: a human signal. On the borders of the debris field, a single human escape craft was found, and aboard, three stasis chambers. Inside them, we found the Demon Three, a team of what the humans call 'Spartans.' They were held captive in secret on *Discipline* for a time, as I pondered how to exact their punishment."

One of the lower-ranking officers on the bridge gasped, eyes widening.

Rojka continued. "We do not run from Thars. We chase the Demon Three now, as they have escaped this ship during battle, and with the human envoy's help. Thars's attack and the envoy have stopped us from bringing the Demon Three to proper justice for what they did to Glyke, and I will not let them slip from our grasp again. Will any of you?"

Now they all understood. Their eyes collectively gleamed.

Rojka looked at a single pip on one of his holoprojectors. "We are tracking them. We *will* catch them. We *will* kill them. Only then will we again turn our attention to Thars. *This* is why I ask you to fight the boarders. *This* is why you must hold the engine rooms and shield generators."

The command bridge erupted in delighted roars of assent.

Daga looked overcome for a moment. "I am with you, Fleetmaster and Kaidon. I pledge myself to this. I am sorry I doubted you. The demons will pay for the horrors they unleashed."

More hits. Damage reports rolled in across projectors faster than Rojka could even understand them. "Is the slipstream drive available?" he shouted over the barrage of plasma tearing his ship asunder.

"One jump only. And we may end up in slipspace forever if we do it!" Daga answered. "We need just a moment to regain power."

"Thars hails you, Fleetmaster!" the communications officer shouted.

"Show him to me." Rojka looked up as his foe shimmered into being as a hologram in front of him. "Cousin Thars!"

The easy, informal greeting should have gotten a sneer from Thars, but his enemy was too gleeful. "You run! I am told your slipstream drive is being readied. I always knew you were a coward, Rojka. You are choosing to flee to Sanghelios. Back to where you are no longer considered a kaidon. Anyone of consequence you seek shelter from there will strip your ship from you in shame, brand you a failure, and give you menial work for the rest of your days."

Rojka shook his head. "Thars, you and I fight over our visions for this world. You have come for my throat because you think I am weak. I understand this, grievous error though it is. But Thars, you bear scars by my hand, for you have seen me fight. Even now, you waited until you had more vessels and more warriors pledged to your cause than I before you would even dare attack me. You may gloat now, but look deep inside yourself. You know what I am. You know what I am capable of."

Thars appeared to quickly sober. Confusion played across his face. "Then what is it that you are trying to do?"

"I hunt the Demon Three," Rojka said, and enjoyed Thars's stunned look. "I had them imprisoned in human stasis chambers until your ill-advised attack released them."

"I had heard rumors," Thars breathed. He twisted his head slightly. "And you let them live?"

"I did."

Thars remained silent, thoughtful for a moment. Rojka glanced at the engineering readouts as *Unwavering Discipline* struggled to prepare for its single, risk-filled slipspace jump.

"Rojka, did you wish to use the Demon Three for trade?"

"I did."

Thars waved a hand. "Unexpectedly clever of you. But you waited too long. So. I will allow you to die with honor if you tell me where they are."

"They will be like a thistle in a forest, cousin. Only I know where that thistle is."

"You lie."

"I have a tracker on their escape ship," Rojka said. "Kill me, and you lose it, and any hope of finding them. The last thing you want on Rakoi are three demons skittering about on its surface, no matter what happens to me."

"I have as much right to hunt them as you," Thars hissed. "They slew all that I knew as well."

"You have made enough of a mess. It is time for me to do the right thing." Rojka pointed at Daga. They didn't need to delay anymore: further conversation was unnecesary. "Slipspace, by my order!"

Thars disappeared as *Unwavering Discipline* punched through the void, quickly launching through slipspace before emerging hundreds of miles away, trailing debris from the hundreds of jagged holes throughout the vessel.

Rojka looked at the tracker's signal. It looked like the Spartans were heading for the human city, Suraka.

"Down," Rojka ordered. "Down toward the Spartans."

"Our hull is damaged beyond repair," Daga said. "We might not make it through the atmosphere. Our shields have fallen again, and we cannot reenter without them."

"Sir, Thars and his fleet are adjusting their orbit," an officer reported.

"They come for us," Daga said.

"To the surface, I said!" Rojka shouted. He found a certain calm in choosing his next command: "And inform the repair crews they have until we enter the upper atmosphere to get the shields back up, or we will all burn."

Hekabe sat on the remains of a concrete wall and looked at the growing pile of detritus the slave Unggoy were pushing up between the horrible-looking, burned-out human buildings on their perimeter. Some of the Unggoy utilized mechanized Goblins, peculiarly designed heavy-lift suits, which Hekabe allowed in limited numbers to expedite the process. They had bitten a large, circular chunk out of the entire city now, reduced the buildings in the circle to rubble, and created a great crater out of the debris.

Time was precious. He couldn't glass the entire city—he simply didn't have enough cruisers or opportunity to reduce everything around his underground target layer by layer. He needed to be precise. Fast. Accurate.

But they could start glassing this particular area. And in mere hours, unveil what he had come here for.

One of Hekabe's trusted captains, Terrillus, approached. "The Sangheili appear to have stopped fighting each other," he announced.

"Rojka has fallen already then?" Hekabe asked, surprised.

"No. His flagship is coming down out of orbit for the planet's surface. Thars chases him."

Hekabe stood up, alarmed. "Thars would not approach until he has killed his rival. This is unusual."

"Do you think he suspects something?"

"I would speak with him. Now!"

Terrillus loped off toward the low-hovering troop carrier that Hekabe had been using as a temporary command center, with the chieftain striding close behind. Orders were shouted, the carrier's Jiralhanae attendants ran around looking for a holotank, and moments later the three-dimensional image of Thars stood in front of them all.

"Thars. Why are you coming to the surface?" Hekabe asked, attempting to mask his unease. There was, after all, nothing in their compact that allowed Hekabe access to this world, and he had assumed the Sangheili would have battled it out above the planet for some time—giving him the window he needed to accomplish his purposes.

"I go where I please." Thars looked haughtily at Hekabe. "And that is none of your concern."

"What are you doing? Why has the battle ceased?" Hekabe seethed at the dismissive tone in Thars's voice but had to relent, as he too was in the wrong. *Enjoy your time, Sangheili,* Hekabe thought. *We will see if you speak to me in such a manner as I tear you apart.*

"I do not answer to you."

Hekabe growled. "I pledged ships to help your cause—"

"And yet you are invading the human city." Thars seemed to lean in closer, the hologram wavering. "This was not part of our agreement. I should ask what are *you* doing *there,* Hekabe? We agreed to give you weapons and ships, not a piece of our world. Shall we discuss this right now?"

Did Thars suspect? Did he *know*? "I—"

"*I* have business on this planet, Chieftain. *I* have holdings on this planet. That is why *I* agreed to our partnership. So now *I* am coming down, as is *my* right. I will not explain anything more to you. And I will deal with you in good time." Thars waved a hand and cut off the transmission.

Hekabe slammed a heavy fist down into the holotank, cracking its casing. "Tell the cruisers in orbit to begin the attack on the Sangheili! They either suspect something or are on their way to interfere."

"We were hoping for more damage between the Sangheili before we did this," Terrillus said.

"We knew the risk when we planned this operation," Hekabe said. "It is time. The Sangheili must not get anywhere near this city before we are ready. Destroy them. I do not care what it costs."

"I will give the order myself, Chieftain," said Terrillus.

"And call upon *Foebane* to begin the dig immediately," Hekabe added.

"There are hundreds of Unggoy still clearing rubble inside—" Terrillus started.

"They are Unggoy, what does it matter? Need I remind you of the urgency of our charge, Terrillus? We barely have enough to feed ourselves. Our clans are starving back on Warial," Hekabe snapped. "I do not care about the cost of life. We've waited too long already. Begin!"

CHAPTER 7

The Bumblebee tumbled end over end. Jai grabbed a harness and held tight as his whole world spun. He looked up past where Adriana had wedged herself and forward to the cockpit. "Mike!"

Jai felt like he was hanging in the air, the airlock turned into "down" and the cockpit "up," Carrow's surface flashing by the cockpit windows every few seconds. Then every second. Then everything blurred. Thrusters fired, thumping and tossing Jai around.

"Like flying a boot with a brick glued onto the side," Mike grunted.

A bulkhead screeched and cracked. Jai knew that the Bumblebee was breaking apart high above the planet's atmosphere, pieces shorn from its hull centimeter by centimeter. He glanced back at the injured civilian inside the harness, her legs jerking around in the chaos. With their armor lock, the Spartans might survive impact with the planet, but she'd be a bloody smear across whatever they hit.

Miraculously, the Bumblebee finally slowed its endless

spinning as Mike managed to wrestle control of the vehicle. Then, with a last wobble and thump of the thrusters, it flattened out.

"Apologies, everybody. That was a little rough," said Mike. "How's the civvie?"

Jai made his way over to her, grabbing harnesses as he went. There was blood pushing its way around the biofoam. "She's bleeding again."

A loud crunch and Jai lurched forward. "Sorry, airbrakes," Mike said. "Been trying to delay them as long as I could."

The clouds that had been far below seconds earlier now rose quickly toward them.

"The structural integrity of the lifeboat is failing. I can't make it to the city. I'm just looking for a place to land at this point."

"Understood."

"We're lucky we even got this far," Mike said, tapping touch panels near his knee.

"Not the first time we've jumped off a dying ship though," Jai said, squatting down on the floor.

"Not what I mean." Mike glanced back from the cockpit. "Lucky to have woken up. We were on a *Covenant* ship. What does that mean? We should be dead, you know. I don't understand why they didn't just kill us in the pod when they came across us."

Jai took a deep breath. Given what they'd been ordered to do, he was just as shocked to wake up on a Sangheili ship alive. "I don't know. I don't know what to make of it. I'm just trying to take this one moment at a time."

"We're going to need to talk about Glyke—" Mike started.

"Not now." Jai looked forward at Adriana, who clambered past him to sit in the very back of the lifeboat with the extra plasma rifles she'd liberated. She stared out the airlock window, somehow creating a separate world away from them both. She might as well have been in another star system.

"Adriana?"

"No," she said.

Jai winced. She'd been there in the fight. That was all that mattered. They'd deal with all this later. After they got help for the wounded woman.

Then they'd talk about Glyke.

But right now it was a distraction. And distractions got you killed.

The lifeboat popped loudly again and started to spin in a slow corkscrew.

"Damn it, we're coming apart," Mike said. "Hold on, I'm taking us down!"

Vice-Governor Lamar ran across the rooftop toward Ellis and the waiting Pelican. In the distance, past the skyline of downtown Suraka, the Jiralhanae cruiser hovered, blasting the ground beneath it with the tremendous energy of the ship's glassing beam. The air rippled all around what had once been the residential area of Suraka. It was turning slowly into a melted plain.

They'd debated about whether the cruiser would then come for the rest of the city. But whenever it approached the pile of rubble the Jiralhanae had turned into their fortified wall, it veered back toward the Uldt desert, evidently uninterested in the urban section of town.

Why? Why the edge of the desert? What are they after? Are they simply biding time before they strike the rest of Suraka? Are they looking for something else? The fact that she hadn't the slightest clue gnawed at the back of her mind like a thorn she couldn't pluck free. That was an unknown, though. She could only work with the known quantities she had in her possession and try to protect those who had survived. She'd just have to leave the Jiralhanae's motivations on the back burner.

"Governor! Governor!" Lamar shouted.

She stopped by the Pelican's ramp. "Lamar, what are you doing up here?"

"This is a *bad* idea," he said, taking her by the arm and moving in closer.

"No, Lamar, they need to see me," she said, gently pushing him off her. "The militia. People in the bunkers. I'm going to put my own eyes on the situation. Holed up in a control room, buried deep underground . . . I'm not going to be able to understand what's going on from there."

"The structure of command needs to be maintained during conflict," Lamar replied. "Head of state needs to be protected."

"You'll be head of state if I get killed," Ellis said.

Lamar bit his lip and shook his head. "The people elected you to lead. Not me. I apologize, Governor, for saying this, but . . . with all due respect, you can't run away from this and jeopardize Suraka's stability for the sake of your curiosity. The people need their governor safe if we're going to survive this mess. This is your duty."

He looked genuinely upset to have said it. And it felt like a slap to the face. Ellis started to turn away, but Lamar leaned in even closer, so Ellis had to face him head on.

"I spent some time working a hydropower installation at Lake Komeno on Mars," she said. "The lead engineer favored using readouts and drones to monitor everything. A pipe burst leading to the turbine. It didn't just cost him his job—it cost people,

people I knew, their lives. So understand this: I *always* walk the project. Okay?"

Whether Ellis had been inspecting new buildings in recently terraformed landscapes or getting down into the dark of the sewers to watch progress firsthand and talk to contractors to get their opinions, it was part of her DNA. Often enough, suited up in the same protective gear as everyone else, she went unrecognized. People gave her honest intel as a result, factors she could use from the top to improve things. The same would apply here.

"I don't like this," Lamar said.

"You don't have to. I can assure you, I'm not running away from anything. Go back down to the bunker." Ellis walked toward the Pelican. "When I get back, I want to see those plans you're working closely with the generals on."

Lamar folded his arms. "You told them you wanted to push the Jiralhanae back off the planet."

Ellis nodded. "Yes. I do."

"We have to look at things we can achieve, Governor. We won't survive a full press like that."

"Maybe not. But I want to see *all* the options. We can't cut anything out before we've even begun." She'd just accepted the fact that she wouldn't be able to make the perfect choice. But she was certainly going to try to make the ones that didn't leave her successors with more impossible decisions.

She had to win this war so they wouldn't have to fight one in the future. Whatever victory looked like now, it would *have* to lead to better paths down the road. Even if it meant great sacrifices up front.

"*Everything* has to be on the table, Lamar."

Ellis turned around and walked up the ramp and into the Pelican. The pilot looked back and gave her a thumbs-up. Ellis returned the gesture. *Let's get into the air*, she thought.

Another aide, Travis Pope, waved her over to one of the harnessed seats as the Pelican gunned into the sky. They swung around, the heartbreaking sight of the massive Jiralhanae cruiser annihilating the previously occupied section of the city tilting away from her sight. "You wouldn't believe the favors I had to pull to get you this!" he shouted to her over the noise of the craft.

"Thank you, Travis." Ellis took a datapad from him and looked over the schedule. "Did you get any of the refugee figures updated?"

"Yes, we're looking at twenty thousand who've moved to the farthest edge of the city—Sector 31—away from the Jiralhanae's concentration. Militia's helping them dig up areas to create temporary housing. They're using instacrete and sandbags and prefab materials from the early colonial days, trying to create some semblance of safety. The big problem out there is water. They've used some emergency hydrocables to draw from community wells out to the site, but they're basically out in the desert."

"What about food?" Ellis rubbed her eyes. She was fading.

"The vertical farms in Sector 24 weren't attacked, so we've got convoys to take anything we can harvest and get them to secure locations. Some of the grains we're diverting directly to the camps. We have a few days before we really have to nail the logistics on that, as people are bringing some basics with them. Finlay Ice Creams even took several vats of flavors out for the kids. Everyone else is demanding government credit. Redeemable after whatever this all is comes to an end."

After. That was optimistic. Ellis fumbled in her pockets and pulled out a stim patch. She peeled it open and rubbed it onto her forearm.

The governor's logistics staff had been scattered among a series of tunnels, fortified basements, and one offsite bunker on the outskirts of the city. They'd done a good job coordinating this response. Ellis felt a flash of pride that rode the slow build of the stimulants, returning her energy.

"Governor! Director Pope!" the pilot yelled back at them. "You'll want to see this."

They yanked their harnesses off and moved up the center of the Pelican. The pilot pointed up through the windows. "It just started—check it out. The Jiralhanae in orbit are now attacking the Sangheili."

Plasma fire lit up the sheetlike cirrostratus clouds far overhead in the upper atmosphere. It looked like an impossibly high thunderstorm that flashed lightning from cloud to cloud. They couldn't make out the vessels as anything more than specks, but the energy bursting out from them was clear enough. They were watching a vicious suborbital battle, Ellis realized.

"Another skirmish in this civil war we've been tracking?" Travis asked.

"There's nothing civil about the Jiralhanae," the pilot said. "They were aiding the Sangheili when this whole thing started."

Ellis nodded. "The alliance between those two groups in orbit may have only lasted as long as it could." She watched the dance of plasma fire and then tapped the pilot on the shoulder. "Take us back."

"Governor?" Travis looked down at his copy of the itinerary.

"They've turned on each other. They're going to be more focused on whatever they're fighting about than us. And two Brute cruisers versus the rest of the Sangheili fleet up there? That's going to be a mess. It brings odds down into our favor. We need to make sure we can take advantage of this."

This was a stroke of luck. Ellis wasn't going to waste it.

Travis didn't look as sure. He followed her back to his seat, grabbing hold of each passing harness as the Pelican looped around the financial district. "The Jiralhanae still have that cruiser and a lot of fighters on the ground down here. They didn't seem to need those two other cruisers to raise all the hell we're currently dealing with, ma'am."

"During the war, I heard of humans literally ripped apart by a Jiralhanae for looking it in the eye. *After* surrendering. Do you think these creatures are operating based on some rigid, logical strategy? They're loose cannons, animals. They're not like the Sangheili. They're probably making decisions based on emotion and instinct, which is why they're clawing at their benefactors' throats right now. This could be on the verge of falling apart."

"There's a lot of firepower still out there, Governor. I saw the preliminary reports on their strength. I'm not in the militia, but I can tell we're outmatched," Travis said.

"We'll need a definitive strike to turn things around." *Suraka has advantages*, Ellis thought. Surakans knew the layout of their own city better than the enemy. Their engineers and planners knew where the sewers and tunnels were. This was *our* city.

"Against the Jiralhanae's current air and ground occupation?" Travis looked dubious.

"Like I said, we're not fighting anything normal—these things commit atrocities without a second thought," Ellis said. "So we're not going to fight back right away. We're going to start rigging explosives. I want everything that can detonate packed around the occupied areas. We're going to move the militia there—all of it.

You'll need to start making plans to get the refugees to take over everything the militia is helping them do out there in the camps, Travis. Got it?"

Quickly taking notes, he nodded.

Ellis leaned in closer. "We might not be able to win in a straight battle. But we do need to convince the Jiralhanae that staying in our city won't be worth all the trouble we're going to cause them."

Rojka 'Kasaan looked at the constantly updated damage reports. *Unwavering Discipline* had lost large sections of its hull. Pillars and bulkheads had collapsed as the strain of reentry twisted the vessel; plasma fire had ripped through so many sections that Rojka wasn't even sure it could be called a *ship* as such anymore.

He was flying spare parts through the upper reaches of Rakoi's sky.

"Our shields are back!" Daga cried out.

The horrible shaking eased, and Rojka relaxed slightly. *Good.* He checked the location of the demons' lifeboat—dead ahead—and gave orders to continue the descent to intercept.

Two of Thars's frigates had now caught up to harass *Unwavering Discipline*. *Pure Resolve* and *Reprisal's Fire* rained plasma down on the raised shields, but they couldn't do much to the heavy cruiser's strength while simultaneously attempting to keep their own shielding up to prevent the heat of reentry from puncturing their much-thinner hulls.

It was just a temporary respite in the battle, Rojka knew, but it was welcome. The constant ship-to-ship warfare while falling out of space had been fierce. Now the remaining vessels had something else to focus on.

"Fleetmaster, the Jiralhanae cruisers," Daga announced.

"What?" Rojka glanced across all the naval stategy holoprojections and focused on scans of the fleet chasing him down out of orbit.

Two Jiralhanae cruisers were now recklessly slamming their way into the middle of Thars's ships, shields down, all weapons blazing.

"It would appear your cousin's much-vaunted allies have turned on him!" Daga crowed, moving forward to a top-down map of Rakoi's vast desert to better examine the ship movements.

"They are not even attempting to survive the journey down," Rojka said in near disbelief. *Pure Resolve*'s shields flickered, then suddenly died. Bit by bit, debris flaked off until something deep inside exploded and the ship simply blew apart.

Several of the bridge crew craned their heads from below the raised section of the command bridge, trying to see the bizarre turn of events for themselves.

"Did I not warn him?" Rojka said. "The Jiralhanae were never to be trusted. Now we all burn together over the skies of Rakoi."

He would have laughed, but *Unwavering Discipline*'s shields fluttered and failed a final time. The atmosphere clawed at their naked hull once more. *Perhaps we are next?*

"Generators!" Rojka shouted.

While the repair crews struggled to see if there was any possibility of reviving the shields, Rojka spat out orders. "Fire on anything trailing behind us! We only need to make it to the surface!"

What remained of *Unwavering Discipline* struggled and wobbled its way down through the clouds, trailing smoke and debris—a dark shadow of wrath bearing down on their prey below.

CHAPTER 8

The Bumblebee cleared the jagged rock teeth of a mountain, snowcaps whipping by just underneath, and then fell out of the sky.

"Brace yourselves." Mike possessed that overly calm way about him that pilots had just before catastrophe. This wasn't his first crash landing.

The forward thrusters fired and the Bumblebee sank further down. Jai felt his stomach lurch. Through the windows, he could see a distant desert rushing toward them. The lifeboat tilted forward. The scrub of foothills and valleys slipped to face them.

They struck and bounced off a rocky incline. The ventral thrusters continued roaring to keep them just above the slope of the hill as they sped downward. Jai glanced backward to see the mountaintops in the airlock's now-cracked windows, then twisted forward as a large pond reared up in front of them.

With an explosion of spray, the lifeboat struck the water and skipped back into the air, coasting just above the surface.

The thrusters kicked them off to the side, narrowly weaving around a column of rock that just grazed the Bumblebee. The craft spun slowly, turning sideways in the air as it passed the edge of the pond. The thrusters fired again and they were flying backward. Jai grabbed the nearest harness to keep steady.

Mike blasted the main rear thrusters at full. The craft slowed a little, and then the engines died out.

"Outta fuel," Mike said in mock cheer as they dropped yet again.

They struck the rocky ground in an explosion of torn-off brush and a wave of dirt. The airlock doors immediately warped and the window glass burst inward at the sudden collision, the back of the Bumblebee buckling.

They finally slowed to a grinding stop.

Mike immediately started calling for local assistance. "Mayday Mayday Mayday, this is Whiskey Tango Foxtrot One . . ." It was difficult to tell how far they had missed the mark and where the city was in relation to their current position.

Jai moved to the back of the lifeboat through smoke that was now billowing out of every crevice. He and Adriana kicked once at the mangled airlock doors, rending them from their pressure-locked hinges and sending them sliding across the arid ground.

"Mayday Mayday Mayday, this is Whiskey Tango Foxtrot One . . ."

Jai wrenched the harness off the civilian, who miraculously appeared unharmed, other than by her original injuries.

"We have a fire," Jai announced to Mike. "Clear out."

Adriana moved outside, plasma rifle swinging around to make sure there was no trouble waiting for them. Jai followed, carrying the woman in his arms.

Mike kicked through the cockpit windows and climbed out to avoid having to negotiate his way through the marred interior and out the back. The smoke now began to pour out of the bulkhead, signaling a chemical fire of some kind in the hull plating. "This fire will be a beacon for anyone who might come looking for us," he said. "We need to put it out."

The dance and flicker of orange light grew from breaches in the ivory armor, black smoke pluming out of the wrecked Bumblebee in an expanding column.

Jai laid the civilian carefully down on a slab of rock. "We hit water on the way down, didn't we?" he asked Mike.

"There's a large pond a hundred meters ahead. Let's push." Mike grabbed the side of the airlock and dug his armored boots into the ground. Jai put his shoulder to it. Adriana silently slipped in between them and did the same.

The Bumblebee scraped first slowly, then slid at a decent clip, eventually tumbling like a boulder with each coordinated shove. They'd disregard the safety of causing more volatile damage to the craft just to get it underwater as soon as possible.

It was the first time they'd done something this synchronized when not under fire since Glyke, Jai thought. He missed it, working together without talking or planning. Just knowing what the team needed and doing it.

They finally managed to shove the Bumblebee over the banks and into the large pond, letting it roll down a steep runoff and plunge onto the surface. It burbled and smoked a little before it slipped most of the way under the water, effectively putting out the fire.

A vast shadow fell over the mountainside they'd narrowly missed on the way in. Jai leaned back to see a Covenant cruiser thunder overhead. Smoke and flames streamed from rents throughout the hull and it wobbled as it desperately tried to control its descent.

"Damn," Mike said. Pieces of its hull broke free and showered toward the ground, slamming into nearby hills and valleys. Before they could even scatter for cover, it passed on, leaving a trail of black smoke the size of a skyscraper in its wake. It showed zero signs of stopping—or even being able to—but kept on going further toward a mountain range opposite where it finally disappeared beyond the horizon.

The faint sound of the impact rolled around the crags and peaks in the distance.

"Was that our ship?" Adriana asked, holstering her weapons.

"I think it was," Jai guessed.

"Look at that," Mike said, his eyes fixed in the other direction, from where the vessel had first appeared.

Beyond the mountains and the dark column of smoke left by the cruiser, dozens more ships fell slowly from the sky like burning angels seeking earth.

Unwavering Discipline struck ground, and it was almost as if the ship screamed as it died. The sheared hull elements shrieked in what sounded like anger and then began a mournful howl as more of the vessel's great belly pressed into the planet's surface and the ship's insides collapsed floor by floor. The command bridge was almost immediately plunged into darkness and Rojka 'Kasaan flew across the room, bouncing off the deck like a ragdoll until he smacked into a nearby pillar.

The roaring of his imploding ship continued for several minutes, even after the cruiser had come to a complete stop. Over the rending and warping, he could hear the occasional muted scream of a dying Sangheili, likely trapped as pieces of the ship fell down or buckled inward.

Silence finally fell over them like a gentle cloak.

Rojka lay still in the dark.

He still lived. *Unwavering Discipline* had lived up to its name and delivered him to the surface despite the hell it had endured.

He tried to sit up but couldn't. Something in the darkness and chaos had pinned him to the floor. Rojka pressed against it, spitting and swearing in his elders' tongue as he pushed. All he did was crush his chest even harder against the cool material.

Backup lighting and power somehow flickered on. He was trapped under one of the bridge's large, swooping holoprojector pillars. It was intractably pinned below the command dais, refusing to budge free.

He wasn't bleeding though. Something to be grateful for.

Feet thumped around the bridge's wreckage and stopped in front of Rojka.

Keza, one of his special operation commanders, stood tall over him.

"This is all your doing," Keza hissed. His energy sword sputtered as motes of swirling dust from the crash struck it. The surviving Sangheili glanced about, nervous. Fearing that one of the others would attack him, he also sought to strengthen his own courage. "Now I must end this madness."

Rojka looked around as best as he could. Other surviving Sangheili crew stood by silently, watching the scene unfold. It became clear that they would not stop Keza, even if Rojka ordered it. But they would not help the renegade Sangheili either. This was their way. Combat, even between a superior trapped in wreckage against a subordinate with an overwelming advantage, was not to be interfered with. Still, Rojka doubted that anyone here would follow Keza. They would likely soon kill him, as he was a weak commander, though clever at times.

Rojka had thought him loyal too. More bad judgment on his part.

The Sangheili were not patricidal savages like the Jiralhanae, but it was tragically clear that they had much more in common than Rojka would have liked to admit. In war, weak leadership needed, of course, to be rooted out for a clan to survive. Unfortunately for Keza, Rojka would not go so quietly into the night.

He still had other scores to settle.

"Do you think that Thars will reward you for killing me? He will kill you as well." Rojka forced himself to focus on moving his right arm. All he needed to do was free it. He pulled so hard he thought he could hear something in his shoulder pop.

"*You have led us to ruin!*" Keza screamed, and raised his sword high. "*You have done all that you could to destroy us!*"

Rojka managed to find enough purchase with his arm to finally reach his plasma pistol. As Keza swung down, Rojka twisted to pull his limb up and shot the commander in the foot.

Keza howled and dropped to his knees. But then he realized his mistake and quickly scrambled to recover, grabbing Rojka's wrist and forcing the pistol's barrel into the air just as the fleetmaster fired again. The shot veered wide, the plasma bolt splashing against the ceiling. Keza struggled to hold Rojka's arm down while also maneuvering into a killing position.

"You should have just killed me and gotten it over with," Rojka jeered, not letting go of the weapon as Keza tried to break his arm in two. Rojka fired again, just grazing the side of Keza's head.

"Fleetmaster!" Keza bellowed.

"I am no longer your fleetmaster." Rojka arched his back, panting, pulling his forearm toward himself. Keza's sword bit down into Rojka's side as the commander tried to finish what he had started. "I am simply your enemy now."

Both Sangheili roared in fury and pain, each trying to summon one last spasm of strength to finish the other off.

Rojka's arm moved a slight, nearly imperceptible twitch closer. He squeezed the trigger and shot Keza in the face. The commander's right mandibles burned away in an instant, leaving a gaping hole of melted flesh. As Keza jerked back in horror, eyes wide, Rojka finally yanked his arm free and jammed the muzzle into what remained of Keza's mouth, pulling the trigger again. Plasma burst out from the inside of Keza's helmet with a gush of sizzling purple blood.

The Sangheili's body toppled forward. Rojka grabbed it, brought it closer, and retrieved the dead traitor's energy sword still in his grip. He activated it, jammed it into the column pinning him, and started cutting, ignoring the molten splashes that seared his skin.

When he stood free, he kicked Keza's body aside and pointed around himself with the sword. His side burned where Keza had managed to injure him, but the sword had cauterized the wound shut. Rojka ignored it for now. "It is fair to attack your leader when you perceive him to be too weak or in grievous error. But I grow tired of those who wait for my back to be turned in order to strike! I am sickened of those who refuse to meet me in combat face-to-face!"

The other Sangheili, the ones who provided no aid during the skirmish with Keza, took a respectful step back.

The fleetmaster nodded. "I am Rojka 'Kasaan. *I* alone created our fleet out of the discarded and forgotten ships. *I* led us to this new world. We have lost all of that because some will not follow me. So . . . decide on your path now. Bow to my authority as kaidon here and follow me to avenge your fellow Sangheili against the Demon Three, or leave my sight. Make your choice."

Daga was the one who pulled himself up over the crumpled remains of the command dais and bowed to Rojka first.

Then, as one, the rest of the crew present all lowered their heads in submission.

"Good," Rojka said, deactivating the weapon. "Now let us see what we can salvage from our ship. We still have a hunt in front of us."

From inside the planning room, Ellis Gass glanced over the shoulders of General Grace and General Kapoor at the activity within the command bunker. The air here had changed. An anticipatory buzz now floated about, the hushed, funereal whispers shifting into nervous, determined chatter. The generals that had previously approached her with grim faces now had purpose in their stride.

They could all feel the sense of possibility here. That she was *right*. They would take advantage of this turn of affairs and exploit this weakness to make Suraka an utter quagmire for the Jiralhanae.

Their enemies would not take the city from her.

Several proposals floated on the screens around the planning room, as well as on paper. Old emergency schemes for dealing with UNSC occupation that had been kept hidden since the prewar days. Civilians throwing bombs, rigging buildings to blow, then escaping through sewers. Sneak attacks. Guerrilla warfare.

Engineers came in and out of the meeting rooms with more diagrams and blueprints of the area the Jiralhanae occupied.

"We've retrieved the thermobaric bombs from the high-security facility on the other side of the underground complex," one lieutenant reported, patching in from the field. "All twelve functioning excavation-grade explosives are now in place. They've been strategically distributed by scouting teams. At their current position, when they detonate they'll completely eliminate all enemy activity at the edge of the occupied area, but will not directly affect the majority of the city apart from anticipated collateral damage."

"We can get at most of the Jiralhanae on the surface with the bombs," General Grace said. "But there's still the matter of the cruiser above the city. They'll have a secondary force in there ready to deploy, perhaps more. And they can glass us from the air, obviously."

Travis Pope knocked gently on the window that looked into the planning room. Ellis shook her head. Now wasn't the time.

"There are some strategies on file that might be worth considering for the second wave," General Kapoor said, opening his briefcase.

Pope slipped in through the door and ghosted over to Ellis's elbow. "Governor, I think you need to come with me," he said in a low voice.

"What is it?" she asked, annoyed. The two generals had stopped talking and now stared at them.

"It's best if I speak to you somewhere private."

Something in his voice convinced her to follow him outside. "I'll be right back," she told Kapoor and Grace.

They looked annoyed at the interruption. They had people to lead, preparations to make. But they relented nonetheless. "Of course, Governor."

She stood and left the room with Travis.

"I'm really sorry for the intrusion," Travis whispered as he moved her through the command bunker toward her temporary office. "But we should discuss this away from everybody."

Lamar was already there, waiting inside. He stood up as she entered and Travis stayed back, closing the door behind her.

"Lamar, what's going on?"

"Governor, there's an after-action report," he said. "I've been holding on to it for confirmation."

"After-action report about what?"

"Okay . . ." Lamar blew out a breath. "It's from a survivor, someone from Jeff's squad. She's . . . she's the only one who made it."

"Oh God. What happened?" Ellis grabbed the edge of the desk to hold herself steady. "Tell me what happened, Lamar."

But she already knew.

"The Jiralhanae captured him during an engagement," he said with a solemn face. "Local command is listing Jeff as KIA. They don't have physical confirmation, but there's virtually zero probability that he survived based on the eyewitness account."

Ellis slowly nodded as her worst fears came true. The world faded until it was just her own breathing and Lamar's presence before her. "And they've taken no prisoners so far? You're sure about this?"

"Yes, we're sure. They've taken no prisoners."

"Why wasn't I told earlier?"

"This is not something I wanted you to hear from anyone else. I wanted some kind of confirmation before telling you. This is the best I could get." Lamar took a step closer. His hand closed gently on her shoulder. "I am so, so very sorry for your loss."

But it *wasn't* her loss, Ellis thought. It was Jeff's. Her son would never get to know anything else. A whole future had been extinguished. Her *son* had been extinguished. A light that had been so bright.

The smile. The sound of his laughter. She kept thinking about his wide eyes. She could still see the nine-year-old child covered in soot with a blanket wrapped around him as they evacuated to bomb shelters on the reserve when the Covenant first arrived on Mars. *You're going to be okay*, she had kept saying. *It's going to be okay.*

A lie.

"Please leave," she told Lamar. "I need a moment."

He exited without another word. After she closed the door hard, Ellis grabbed the guest chair and threw it against the wall. It didn't break. It needed to break. She picked it up again and swung it against her desk. Screens flew off the surface and shattered on the floor.

Not better, but certainly satisfying.

She launched the chair against the window, the view there on one of the underground loading bays. She saw a handful of passersby outside flinch as it struck. The safety glass starred and fragmented but hung together. Lamar just stood there in the corridor outside, his back to her, almost at parade rest. Travis remained there as well, looking down at the ground, hands folded in front of him, waiting.

Ellis closed her eyes and wiped the tears away with the back of her hand.

She was not the only mother who had lost a child in Suraka. She needed to be stronger than this, but that burst of rage and grief made her feel even weaker than she had before. Ellis took a deep breath and composed herself, warding off other thoughts of Jeff and summoning what little of her strength remained.

She opened the door and tapped her waiting second in command on the shoulder. "Lamar. Come with me. I need you with me in the planning session."

"Governor?"

"We have very little time," Ellis said, striding back toward the conference room, blinking her scratchy eyes.

Generals Grace and Kapoor stood up when she reentered. "Governor, we've been told," said Grace. "Our condolences."

"Recall our ships from Kiriken," Ellis said. "Issue it as an executive order directly from me to their naval commanders through our closed-band comm relay. We can't remain cowering here, letting them tear into us piece by piece. We need to strike while they're still focused on their skirmish with the Sangheili. We've got their ground forces covered by the bombs—let's take off their head," she said, pointing to the cruiser's beacon on the holographic map, "with whatever naval strength we've got left."

Grace and Kapoor looked at each other with uncertainty. "Governor," Kapoor said. "You've just received devastating news. This might not be the best time to—"

"We are under the occupation by an enemy military force that has the ability to kill every man, woman, and child in this city whenever they are disposed to. There is no best time," Ellis said wearily.

Kapoor hesitated, then said, "We agreed to hold the ships back for reserves."

"And now we need those reserves." Ellis calmly looked them all in the eye. "We will not be given a better window of opportunity. It's not the time to be cautious—it is the time to strike back. I'm not saying this because I just found out my son died. I'm saying this because we need to use everything we have to dislodge them from *our* world. Or everything we've sacrificed will have been in vain. Recall the ships. *Now.*"

Grace nodded. "Yes, Governor."

The Jiralhanae would pay in blood for blood, Ellis thought. It was time to stop worrying about elegant solutions and to speak the language of violence.

CHAPTER 9

Anexus scrambled up the remains of a collapsed building near one of the taller barricades that Hekabe was using to observe progress. For a moment the Jiralhanae warrior paused to look behind Hekabe and out over the glassed area a kilometer away, now beginning to dip slightly as the molten earth compressed downward.

"Report," Hekabe ordered.

Anexus nervously whipped around. "Three Sangheili frigates remain in orbit. But they are barely functional. They will not be able to attack us here. We have truly taken this world for ourselves, Chieftain."

Hekabe rubbed the top of his gravity hammer thoughtfully. He was not interested in this world. He was interested in what was inside it. "The price?"

"Their other vessels have all crashed into the mountains that hem the desert—they are far removed from this city. *Hammerstrike* and *Fighter's Blood* have fallen with them. Perhaps we should send the *Foebane* to the site to recover any survivors and weapons."

"No, we will need it for transport soon enough. *Foebane* is sufficient for what is left of our purposes here. These humans with their pitiful strength will not be able to harm a Jiralhanae heavy cruiser. Have any Sangheili survived?"

Hekabe caught a whiff of anxiety from Anexus that told him more than words could. "Some. But we have the planet. We have the *Foebane*, and our cruiser can destroy the enemy from the air whenever we choose," Anexus said, evidently overcompensating for any perceived weakness he'd shown earlier. "They will not be able to disturb us. Our clan is strong."

"Strong," Hekabe mused. "We *say* that. But when the humans and Sangheili joined forces, they hunted down what remained of our ships. They struck us down with impunity, even those who fled back to Doisac. They attacked without parley or mercy; they destroyed the very ships that protected our bloodline. Anexus, our clan's lineage may die with us. Do you still dare to say that we are *strong*?"

Anexus did not know how to respond. He clearly wished to be anywhere else but here right now.

Hekabe sighed. "What I mean is this: do you truly think any surviving Sangheili will just stay put where they landed? And those that ally with the humans—will they remain weakened now that they are on the humans' world?"

Anexus looked down at the ground near Hekabe's feet. "No, Chieftain."

"They will seek revenge." Hekabe paused, but Anexus did not react. "So we will need to strike first to protect ourselves, before they have a chance to gather their forces. Send whatever remains of the Unggoy and three hundred warriors out to meet them, now."

"The Unggoy are all dead. You ordered—"

Hekabe growled. "Then our warriors will have to suffice!"

Anexus backed down the hill. "Of course, Chieftain. What about the humans who remain in this city? We will be vulnerable with little protection."

Hekabe caressed his gravity hammer. "The humans are of no concern. We will have fifty Jiralhanae here. And we will have the *Foebane*. Or are you frightened?"

"Never," Anexus said, anger dripping from his voice at the suggestion.

"Then send out the packs. Nothing crosses the desert between the mountains and the human city. Do you understand? Nothing can be allowed to stop our progress here."

"How much deeper can we dig?" Anexus asked. "This planet . . . we will soon dig into the molten rock if we keep going. Maybe what you seek is not here."

"Oh, it *is* here," Hekabe said. "We are close, Anexus. Our time has almost come."

There were now only three Sangheili frigates left in orbit. Governor Ellis looked at the reports in her office.

Could they realistically engage them? Suraka's twelve surviving ships were armed but had no magnetic accelerator cannons. MACs had been the UNSC's weapon of choice during the war against the Covenant. Only a slug launched by a remarkably long coil of magnets and powered by a ship's engines could penetrate Covenant shields. But despite not having MACs, Suraka's ships did have retrofitted point defense guns welded onto the outer structures. That had to count for something if they now outnumbered the Sangheili ships.

A swarm of lightly armored merchant ships versus three

disabled Sangheili frigates that had just been in an intense fight with the Jiralhanae? It was a long shot. Sangheili ships were notoriously hard to hit. But they hadn't come to the surface when the others fell into the Uldt. All indications hinted that they were crippled. Ellis couldn't pass up the chance.

Lamar entered her office and closed the door behind him. "Governor." He was calling her by title mostly now, she noticed.

"We're not scheduled to meet for another fifteen minutes," Ellis said, irritation creeping into her voice.

"I didn't want to say this in front of General Grace." He stood in front of her desk in an odd way. Formal. "I've been reading over the last hour's intel."

Ellis stood up as well. She walked around the desk and tapped on the holo-display's file cache, bringing up the reports. "I've been poring over them too. It was right to recall our ships. We have an opening."

Lamar nodded but didn't relax his posture. "An opening, but to do what with? Until now, we've been under attack and fighting back where we could, figuring out what was happening. Now we have a moment to breathe, but we're still in fight mode. I know it's a bit late, and it's not on our contingency plans, but I strongly believe we should take a closer look at evacuating any civilians we can with the assets we have. Contingency plans never expected the loss of all our slipstream-enabled ships. I agree, we need to recall the ships. But I do not believe we should attack the Jiralhanae, or the Sangheili for that matter. Now is the time to use those ships to evacuate Surakans. We need to protect our civilians while we've got this window—while the Brutes and Elites are focused on each other."

So this was what had been eating him up for the last few hours. Ellis swiped the holo-display and brought a pane into view, showing a number of images pulled from close-band relays high above the planet's surface. "Did you see the satellite feed of the crash sites?"

Lamar glanced at it. "Not yet."

"The Sangheili survived. Both sides. But they are grounded. Many of them are heading deeper into the desert. They're moving toward Suraka."

"Which is why we need to evacuate."

Ellis slapped the holo-display's sensor, collapsing the images. "There are a *million* people in Suraka, Vice-Governor." If he was going to go on title, she could return the damn favor. "One. Million. How many people can we evacuate from the surface with twelve merchant ships? Seventy thousand? Standing side by side in cargo holds? And I don't think I have to ask you, but where do they go? The Sangheili targeted everything with slip-space capabilities. They did this for a reason. We do this and we condemn those citizens to being crammed into ships, to wait in orbit until the aliens shoot them out of the sky or until they run out of air, whichever comes first? Are we going to force them to evacuate, to become refugees *again*? They've already been through this."

"It's a chance for life," Lamar snapped. "Once they get into orbit and away, there's an opportunity they can wait for rescue."

"Who the hell is coming?" Ellis asked. "Our contacts in the New Colonial Alliance? They're engaged in battles of their own, and over the last three months, we've been tenuous allies at best. When we agreed to work with the UNSC and the Sangheili for peace here, the NCA stopped talking to us. If anything, we're probably on their list too."

"The UNSC had an envoy in that Sangheili fleet. They're sure as hell going to come looking for her."

"For one person? Yeah, eventually. They'll send one little ship to extract her. If she was even still alive."

"They've made an investment in getting us peace with the Sangheili, Governor. This conflict puts them at odds with the Arbiter and it places their entire alliance on shaky ground. They won't just let the dust settle—they've got stakes in this thing."

"But without communications, all they know is that things have gone dark. Earth has its own issues to deal with, Vice-Governor. This will be a political nightmare for them. They want peace with the Sangheili. They'll give us up in a heartbeat for a chance to keep the Arbiter's people by their side."

"Evacuation is not a good chance, but it's still a chance." Lamar stabbed his finger at her.

"And what about those left behind?"

"Evacuate as many as we can to the oases. Aza Oasis, Herndon Lake, Fallen Tree—there are places they can shelter."

"To be hunted down later."

"We take your path, then we risk everything. If we fail to stop either side, we effectively doom everyone, whether by the boots of the Jiralhanae or the swords of the Sangheili. Don't forget, there are still plenty of fighting Sangheili over in Rak who could cross the Uldt for our heads overnight. That's in addition to the ones already headed this way."

"You'd leave most of us stranded and defenseless with *your* plan," Ellis shot back. "It's foolish."

"It's at least something." Lamar's voice cooled. "It's better than sacrificing us all for a personal act of vengeance."

"Vengeance?" Ellis cocked her head. "Is that what you think this is?"

He couldn't meet her eyes but looked behind her at a point on the wall. "You just lost your son."

"Lamar." She kept her voice level and calm. But she hit the desk with the palm of her hand. "How the hell could you say something like that to me? I didn't lose my senses. I am grieving, but it has not overwhelmed my ability to look at the facts we face."

"It's too great a price to pay for the opportunity to gain air strike abilities," Lamar stated, but less strongly now.

"Could be." Ellis grabbed his shoulder. "Or it could be our chance to secure this world despite everything that stands against us. If we don't try this, we guarantee that we'll remain weak and at their mercy, especially if we just try to hide and wait this out. Coming here, it was a gamble. Deep down, we've all known this. We knew it wouldn't be easy."

"But we don't need to compound the risk. We've been at peace since we arrived here, Governor."

"We were fooled because those first years went so easily," Ellis said. "But now we have to decide whether Suraka lives or dies. Whether this world is ours, or whether we hand it over to these creatures and just give up. Whether this world becomes *Rakoi* for good, and the Carrow we've fought and died for fades into memory."

Lamar rubbed his forehead. "I've been at war for so long, Governor. UNSC, Covenant. I just want to stop seeing bodies in my dreams. I thought I could get away from it, here, help you build something different. And now I'm being asked to do it all over again."

She squeezed his shoulder. "Lamar . . . we'll do this together. I need you to stand with me. I need your wisdom, your advice. I can't fight you and these monsters alone. I just can't."

They both leaned against the desk. Lamar wiped the corner of an eye. "Okay."

"Also, please stop calling me 'Governor,' damn it. We're not going through hell and back just to have you refer to me by my title."

He laughed. "Sorry. Old grunt's habit."

"Old habits are easy to fall back on."

Lamar took a deep breath. "Briefing, then?"

"I'll follow in a minute—looks like Pope is all but jumping up and down by the window to get my attention."

Ellis watched Lamar walk out. She let out a deep sigh and rubbed her hands.

Travis took the opportunity and quickly slipped in. "Governor, there was a Mayday from a lifeboat. The officers who received it are debating whether or not to take it seriously or if it's a Sangheili ploy. The call came from the Karfu mountain range. It's an old UNSC channel."

"So there might have been a UNSC ship in that battle?" Ellis asked.

"Maybe they were keeping an eye on the proceedings. ONI might have been up to something. It's odd. The lifeboat's call sign is a bit strange too. One of the operators thought it might be a joke. The call sign is Whiskey Tango Foxtrot One."

"That has got to be human."

Travis nodded earnestly. "That's what I thought."

"Can we spare some patrols to head out into the desert and sniff around? Wait a second. Is this even on the briefing agenda?"

"No. But someone I know on the front lines was worried it wouldn't get up the command chain to the generals quickly enough due to the chaos. They back-channeled the intel to me."

"Keep this off any agendas for now," Ellis said. "I'll talk to General Kapoor afterward. And please keep it to yourself as well. At least until we know for sure if it's real and who made the call. Okay?"

She didn't want Lamar reversing course to go back to clinging to the hope that the UNSC would suddenly arrive to save them all. They couldn't afford that, no matter what this lifeboat meant for their situation.

The coming strike against the Jiralhanae still needed to go forward without any other complications. They needed to send these bastards the message that their world wasn't up for the taking.

Melody lay sideways on a flat, wide rock that radiated heat into her ribs. Despite the hard edges, she felt comfortable, almost sated, and didn't want to move at all. She stared at the snarled, stunted tree nearby for a long minute and enjoyed the faintest breeze across her skin.

But, she realized fuzzily, Sangheili ships didn't have stunted trees in them, did they?

She must have hit her head really hard. The last thing she remembered? Firing the plasma pistol over and over after she'd sat down in a storage bay on an ex-Covenant cruiser, blood dripping from her chin as she clutched her side.

Melody looked along her body, grabbing for the spot and wincing. The jagged piece of metal didn't stick out of her uniform anymore, but under the ripped cloth, biofoam leaked out of the wound.

Overhead, mountain peaks thrust into clear, saffron-tinted skies. *Where am I? Carrow?*

Melody struggled to stand, gasping and holding the torn skin just below her rib cage. A parched desert stretched away from her as she turned around, her back to the peaks. She was most of the way down the lower slopes of the mountains. Heat rippled in the air above the distant sand.

"Rojka! What have you done?" she called out. "Are we on Carrow?"

She staggered forward and dropped to her knees as the pain lanced through her stomach. The ground thudded as a half ton of gray armor slammed down next to her. Melody looked up to see herself in the reflective visor bent down over her. Her curly hair flew every which way, and she looked so weary. An older version of herself. A crazed version.

"Easy, easy," the massive Spartan said gently. "You can't be walking, ma'am. You'll start bleeding again. We're making you a stretcher right now. Come, lie down."

He delicately picked her off the hot sand and carried her back over to the rock. Melody grunted as he placed her down. "How bad is it?" She pressed her hand to the tear in the uniform.

"You have internal injuries. Our descent onto the planet was particularly rough." The Spartan removed her hand. "Please try not to move unless you have to."

Melody raised her hand. Dark blood dripped from her fingers. "We're on Carrow, right? Why are we down here?"

"Frankly, I was hoping you could tell *us* that, ma'am," the Spartan said. "We were revived on a Covenant ship, in the middle of a firefight between two groups of Elites, and dropping down here was our only option out of it."

Melody slumped onto the rock. Not good.

"I'm Melody Azikiwe. I'm an envoy for the Unified Earth Government. What's your name?"

"Jai Zero Zero Six."

"Gray Team, as I live and breathe," Melody said, half smiling.

Not that there would have been other Spartans in old Mjolnir armor frozen away in the holds of a Sangheili cruiser. For some reason, though, the confirmation buoyed her spirits. Slightly. "Are the rest of them with you?"

"I'll talk about who is and who isn't here after you explain some things to me."

Melody gave him an exhausted look. "I was the one who got you out of the cryo-chambers, and to be honest, we really don't have the time for all this. What happened to the Sangheili ship? How long have I been out?"

She may have sent her staff down to Carrow to hide and survive, but Melody now was on a completely different task thanks to ONI. Something that was more important than maintaining the Sangheili alliance, more important than extracting her staff, more important than even protecting the one million humans left on Carrow. She needed to get off-planet immediately and send a warning back to Earth. Passing out had really screwed things up. She was going to have to scramble to piece together a new plan.

"How'd you do it?" Jai asked bluntly, interrupting Melody's new train of thought.

"How did I do what?"

"How did you get onto a Covenant vessel and free us? We found you armed only with a plasma pistol."

Covenant vessel, Melody thought. *They don't know how much everything has changed around them.*

"Well, first of all," she told Jai, "it's been about six years since your team went under. A lot has changed. That wasn't a Covenant cruiser. It's *Sangheili* now. The fleetmaster, Rojka 'Kasaan, is the kaidon for the Sangheili city-state of Rak here on this planet. The Covenant, as you knew it, no longer exists. We won the war in a battle on Earth in late 'fifty-two. We allied with a sect of Sangheili rebels who turned against the Covenant. Allies like Rojka 'Kasaan.'"

"Late 'fifty-two?" The Spartan didn't move or say anything for a moment. The date seemed to hold a lot of importance. After processing that, his helmet tilted. "It doesn't look like *all* the fighting is done. We woke up in the middle of a battle."

"Yeah, well, that part's complicated. More important: where *exactly* are we right now?"

"We had a brief window of communications with a human city here on the planet right after we made landfall, but there was no response. We got as close as we could in the last three hours, but we only ended up here, in the mountains. By foot, we're still pretty far from the city."

"Okay. That human city is Suraka," Melody explained. "They began resettlement here on Carrow shortly after the war."

Melody relaxed slightly, now that she knew they weren't near Suraka.

Jai crouched down and looked up into the sky. "Wait a second. So there are Sangheili *and* human populations here on this planet, side by side?"

Melody nodded, then winced at the movement. "Carrow lies deep inside something the UNSC refers to as the Joint Occupation Zone. There are a number of JOZ worlds in this region that used to be part of the Outer Colonies. The UNSC, and our Sangheili allies . . . we're all trying to create some order out of the chaos. We had some setbacks of late—it's been challenging on a lot of fronts. Here on Carrow, human refugees came back to resettle Suraka. When they arrived they found Sangheili keeps *already* being built around a river on the other side of the Uldt desert. They'd been here for some time."

"The Sangheili are leaving their own worlds and just settling human colonies in the . . . JOZ?"

"No, not quite. The current Sangheili leadership wouldn't allow subordinates to just go off and do something like that, especially in a politically sensitive territory. But these Sangheili are special. They're the survivors of Glyke, one of their worlds that was devastated during the war," Melody explained. She noticed a slight shift in the Spartan's stance. "They actually *needed* somewhere to go, and they started their settlement shortly after the war's end."

Jai continued to look at her with that inscrutable helmet. She continued: "They had several months of a head start on the human refugees. They'd fallen through the cracks, so to speak. When the humans returned here and found the keeps, it was far too late. In some ways, I think the leadership in both the UEG and Sangheili circles were wondering if a jointly occupied world *would* actually work—if it was even possible. A true sign of interspecies cooperation. Maybe it was a social experiment, on their part. Whatever you want to call it. But human settlers out in the desert—people who separated themselves from Suraka—have apparently been clashing with Sangheili over various oases. Some fighting occurred, some people died. To the UNSC leadership monitoring this situation, it looked like full-on armed conflict here on Carrow was about to break out."

"So what happened then?"

"The UEG thought it best to formally broker a meeting between the kaidon of the Sangheili city-state and Suraka's governor, so here I am—the envoy entrusted with helping negotiate peace and harmony. Obviously it all kinda fell apart, didn't it?"

As she shifted her position, Melody spotted that the other two

Spartans, despite their incredibly heavy armor, had deftly snuck up on either side of her.

"But we saw Sangheili fighting each other, not humans," one of them said. The slight Slavic accent and voice, along with female Mjolnir body armor, confirmed for Melody that it was Adriana-111.

"At the time," Melody said. "But the opening attack was actually a Sangheili faction moving against Suraka. They disabled everything with slipspace drives and completely cut off any off-world communication so that Suraka couldn't call for help."

The other Spartan, who had to be Michael-120, stepped forward. "I'm confused. Who are the good guys now, ma'am?"

"Like I said, that part's a little more complicated," Melody said, concerned that this entire explanation was taking too long. Getting the Spartans up to speed was important, but time wasn't something she had a lot of. "I was embedded with Fleetmaster Rojka 'Kasaan, the kaidon of the city of Rak. My staff and I were to give him advice on how to communicate with the colonists, as they had ties to the Insurrection before the Covenant War. There were things the UNSC wanted out of the peace talks that made our presence something of a third party."

"You mean to tell me we're all back to fighting among ourselves again?" Jai said.

"There are splinter groups operating in the JOZ. Suraka is one of many. They are not considered hostile, though the UEG would like to figure out how to bring them back into the fold. Suraka wants to be independent but doesn't seem to have any intention of initiating any formal resistance."

"So they probably won't welcome *us* with open arms," Jai said. "We represent the UNSC."

"I'd say a Spartan presence would be met with a lukewarm reception at best, particularly since peace talks failed and the Sangheili destroyed all FTL-capable ships." Besides, Melody reminded herself, Suraka was not the direction they needed to be going. Heading into the city right now would be a big mistake.

"Who did the destroying though?" Mike asked. "We saw the Sangheili fighting each other. Guessing that someone in the kaidon's ranks didn't like the idea of making peace?"

"Yes, that's pretty much it. There was a big falling out between Rojka 'Kasaan and another called Thars 'Sarov. Thars really doesn't like humans. He initiated the attack, citing weakness on the part of the kaidon for aligning with the humans—though it was so well planned, I'm certain that there's a wider scheme at play for him."

"So we contact your friend Rojka and ask for a ride out of here," Jai said.

"Can't do that." Melody looked around at the three Spartans. They were so damn tall.

"Why?"

Melody let out a sigh. "Well . . . here's yet another part that's complicated. Apparently, Rojka wants you three dead, just as much as Thars does. There's something that happened, during your last mission? I couldn't get clearance to find out what. Rojka would always change the subject whenever asked. I know only that he found your lifeboat several weeks before I came on board. That's one of the reasons I was there. ONI sent me to get you all out. I was to try and secure your release on one hand while publicly negotiating peace for Carrow with the other."

Melody saw the Spartans look at each other, a slight tilt of the helmets. Then Jai said, "You need medical attention. We all need food and supplies. After that, we can figure out the next step to get back where we need to be. Any thoughts, Melody?"

Okay, so that's how it's going to be. "Still getting my bearings, but there's a research facility in the northern part of the Karfu range," Melody told him. "That must be this series of mountains."

"Haven't heard any beacons," Mike told Jai. "No one's responded to me."

Melody took a deep breath. "Yeah. They won't. It's an ONI facility. Gila Station. They're not going to break silence. But that's where we should go for help. My staff should be there. Resources too."

There she'd be able to use the ONI prowler that came in periodically to resupply the site and get the Spartans back to the proper authorities. And more importantly, she could call for help and get off-planet. It was imperative that she warn ONI about the potential compromise of their target on Carrow.

"Okay, Gray Team," said Jai. "I say we head to Gila Station and try to avoid everything out here that Melody says wants to kill us."

Mike had already ripped branches off a tree and lashed a makeshift sling between them with webbing. They placed Melody into it as she checked over a crude paper map she had kept on her person, not being able to carry anything too sophisticated aboard the Sangheili ship. It was covered in blood now, but she could make out enough to guide them.

Once he had rough coordinates from Melody, Jai grabbed one end of the branches and Mike the other. They casually lifted Melody in the air and started walking. Adriana followed behind them with a larger branch, twitching it behind her to erase their footprints.

"What's all that smoke from the other side of those mountains to our backs?" Melody asked.

"Sangheili ships, as far as we could tell," Mike said.

"Thars contracted Jiralhanae mercenaries for his coup against Rojka," Melody noted. "Some of those ships could belong to the Brutes."

"Then there were probably some Jiralhanae as well. Everything upstairs was beating the hell out of each other as we came on down. And Suraka has some cruiser hovering above it right now. When we patched in to the city's comms, I heard some chatter about Jiralhanae being on the ground there. Must be your mercenaries."

Jiralhanae on the ground in Suraka. That was even worse than Thars and his Sangheili. Melody wondered if she shouldn't have kept her other secrets from the Spartans.

The Spartans had chosen not to disclose why the Sangheili wanted them dead so badly. And Melody was keeping confidential information of her own. Strict orders. But under the circumstances, she wasn't sure how long she was going to be able to stay quiet.

CHAPTER 10

Jai ran across the desert, falling into a rhythm with Mike as Melody slept in the crude stretcher they carried between them. Adriana was still bringing up the rear, wiping their tracks and keeping an eye out for any surprises that might sneak up on them.

"Everyone is pissed off at us," Jai said via helmet-to-helmet communication. "We have a long run ahead with no water, no food, no supplies. Reminds me of training."

Mike waited several moments before responding. "I'm not sure if the biofoam will hold her together."

Okay, Jai thought. They were only going to talk about the task at hand. No pleasantries. "She held off Elites with only a pistol. She's a tough one."

"Or suicidal. You know she's lying to us, right?"

Yes, Jai had noticed that. "She has ONI ties. They keep things close."

ONI. Just saying that cast a dark cloud over both of them. They kept running along for another long spell of silence. Jai felt the team slipping away again. They would come together to fight.

To stay alive. But everything else he tried to say was met with cold indifference from the other two.

Jai had never had that much authority over Gray Team. The three of them, each orbiting around each other so tightly, had always moved together as one. They'd found each other in the hell of SPARTAN-II training. Since then they'd been inseparable. Gray Team against the galaxy.

But this last mission had become a real thing between them all right now, leaving Jai feeling like something had been ripped out from inside him, leaving a hole he couldn't fill.

"ONI has lied to us often enough," Mike said. "I'm not sure that what we're doing is wise."

"Saving a life?" Jai responded.

"Is that what we do?" Mike asked. "Save lives? I haven't done that in a while, Jai. I *take* lives. That and orders. And now we come back and find out that the war is over."

"But there's still some kind of war going on," Jai said.

"There always is, isn't there?" Mike pulled a little harder on the stretcher. Jai had to wobble to compensate and not spill Melody out into the sand. She groaned and stirred. "First it's the Insurrection, trying to keep humanity from falling apart. Then it was the Covenant, thirty years of hell. Now it's something else. There's always something else."

Melody flopped an arm out of the sling stretcher, waking up and trying to sit up to look around.

"You're okay," Jai told her. "You're okay."

"Doesn't feel like it," she said. Her dark brown face had paled even more since the beginning of the run. She was probably bleeding internally. "I'm tired."

"How did you get assigned to the Sangheili fleet here?" Jai asked.

Melody smiled up at him. "I speak the language. I've studied the culture. I did some work in Sangheili refugee camps out here in the JOZ."

Jai couldn't believe he was hearing the words. "Are you serious? A refugee camp?"

"You're going to hear a lot about what's called the Great Schism—that's what they call the big breakaway where the Sangheili rebelled against the Covenant when their Prophets decided to give the Jiralhanae military superiority. Their entire alliance disintegrated. The Sangheili paid a heavy price in the last days of the war and ultimately helped us win. So the UNSC sent volunteers to help Sangheili stranded across human-occupied space get relocated into JOZ locations."

"You mentioned the Covenant made it all the way to Earth," Mike said.

"Yes," Melody said. "Not long after they glassed Reach."

"And now we have Sangheili allies." Jai couldn't help the slightly confused tone in his voice, bitter and angry. It sounded crooked and disgraceful to him that after so much fighting, so many killed by Sangheili soldiers, they were now allies.

"The Sangheili who rebelled against the Prophets? They came to our aid. They fought against the Covenant with us . . . I mean, it was either that or extinction. Like I keep saying, it's complicated. Everything isn't perfect, but it's an important relationship now."

"But for some reason, the Sangheili *here* still want us dead," Jai said.

"They probably have very good reasons," Mike said softly.

Now it was Jai's turn to fall silent. He glanced behind them. Adriana had thrown away the branch and ceased hiding their footprints. But she still hung back, refusing to speak now that they were just eating up the kilometers.

Was she going to stay quiet all the way to Gila Station?

Jai couldn't force her to talk. Then again, maybe it was better they just never brought up what happened. It was almost six years ago, even though in some ways it felt like just yesterday.

The longer Jai thought about it, the more he wanted to bury it all in the past and pretend they had never experienced it in the first place.

But if they did that, could they ever fall back into being a cohesive team? Or would there always be this distance between them from now on? Was this the best it would ever be again—with this ever-widening rift of mistrust and doubt?

Maybe. And if the rift remained, it could well be the end of Gray Team.

But maybe we deserve it, Jai thought grimly.

Melody carefully watched the body language of the three Spartans while feigning disinterest. It could be hard to glean information about the super-soldiers, but by listening closely to their voices and looking at their interactions, even if masked by half a ton of powered assault armor, a trained envoy like Melody could see some hidden, underlying signs.

Something had clearly broken this team.

For one, Adriana refused to speak unless it was absolutely necessary. The rest of the time, she remained withdrawn from not just the team but really anything else at all. She was remote and detached. When she did interact with the other two, Melody could sense something angry and feral curled up inside her.

Mike, up in front, expressed his anger by questioning little things that Jai did. Bits of verbal sniping, followed by purposeful long silences and then changes of topic.

Jai was reined in behind an unspoken sorrowfulness, a black cloud eating up every last piece of invisible rage thrown his way as if he deserved it.

They'd been floating in deep space for years, undiscovered. Dead quiet.

Why were they there in the first place? Melody had some theories she'd worked on while aboard *Unwavering Discipline*. She was willing to bet that Gray Team had been behind enemy lines and engaging in some kind of unconventional warfare. The sort of desperate, last-minute things ONI cooked up when all of their other plans failed miserably. When their backs were against the wall in a war they were quickly losing.

The personnel she had interacted with from ONI wouldn't tell her anything about Gray Team's mission. All they had conveyed was that after six years MIA, they'd been found by Rojka 'Kasaan somewhere in Sangheili space just weeks before she was assigned to be envoy. ONI wanted them back, and unofficially Melody had been told to oblige any offer Rojka made to return them. ONI seemed desperate.

But no matter how many times she carefully made that clear, that anything Rojka wanted was on the table, the fleetmaster had refused to talk about them.

They are demons, was all Rojka would utter when they met privately about the Spartans, the very subject upsetting him enough that Melody would drop it. Her staff had looked terrified whenever Rojka acted like that. Even his own retinue, the handpicked few around Rojka whom he trusted with the knowledge that the Spartans were on board, seemed uneasy about the subject being brought up. *We will discuss their fate after the treaty, after we decide the fate of Rakoi—not before.*

Melody smiled. Her staff—Adam, Victoria, and Jens. It would be good to see familiar faces again. They'd bonded under some horrible circumstances. Refugee riots in Valles Marineris on Mars. People throwing bottles at her from behind a barricade of furniture, just outside an office building in the Tenderloin District. Shouting at the soldiers not to fire.

Usually, hard times pulled people in uniform together.

Not Gray Team though. Not on the last mission, whatever it was.

She looked over at the endless sand dunes that sprawled off to her right. The Spartans had been on the move for hours. They'd been thawed from cryosleep, shot at, dropped out of orbit, crash-landed in the middle of a desert, and now they were plowing on. Just how the hell did they do it?

One step at a time, apparently.

Or in Melody's case, one wheezy breath at a time. She coughed, wiping the backs of her fingers across her lips and looking at the blood on her fingernails.

That wasn't good.

She realized that she might have to tell them the truth sooner than expected. Give up that dark secret and hand over to the Spartans the burden of what she knew about this world. The real reason ONI sent her here.

They weren't cleared for it. But she had little choice, didn't she?

Melody Azikiwe knew she was dying.

The Jiralhanae cruiser *Foebane* hung over Suraka, its great weapons now silent.

Hekabe pointed at the bottom of the deep pit they'd excavated. "There!"

Anexus squinted.

Hekabe retrieved his gravity hammer as well as an object wrapped in old cloth and thorn beast leather from an armored receptacle he had brought with him from *Foebane*. He then carefully picked his way down the smooth, gentle slope at the side of the pit. The hole stretched several kilometers from one side to the other, with an increasingly steep decline toward the center, a hundred meters deep at the very least. In some places, the vitrified soil that remained still glowed red from the ship's plasma bombardment. The heat singed the unshaven fur around his legs, but he paid it no mind.

Anexus gingerly followed him. Hekabe had ordered the rest of his packs to stay back at the edge of the pit to protect his secret. "Yes, I see it!"

Smoke curled away from a fifteen-meter spire in the middle of the pit. As they approached, its details became more visible. The spire, which seemed to be a stark ivory color at first, finally caught the light and glinted, its oily blue and green surface shifting colors slightly as the sun played across it. Hekabe quickened his pace toward the spire, ignoring the heat of the barely cooled ground all around him. Anexus had paused to stamp at a small part of his leg that had caught fire.

"Exactly where the holy writs declared," Hekabe said, deeply satisfied. He grabbed Anexus by the arm and dragged him forward. "Now I can tell you what I seek."

"Chieftain?"

"When we displaced the Sangheili by the Prophets' side as Honor Guard, most of our kind assumed we had succeeded in everything. We were promised the richest planets, the greatest Forerunner reliquaries. Total authority over the Covenant military. We knew we would stand with the Prophets when the Great Journey began."

The ground cracked and popped as they walked across it. Anexus glanced nervously around. The crust under their feet threatened to break, dropping them down into the liquid rock that likely still roiled underneath. The oppressive heat made Anexus pant as he carefully followed. His weakness, even in the hour of their triumph, was dissatisfying to the chieftain.

"When the Prophets proved only to bring ruin on the Covenant by failing to secure the Ark and the Sacred Rings, still I did not lose hope. What remained of our people were scattered, fleeing from our new position of power to other hidden worlds. But I never rested, Anexus," Hekabe continued. "Most would assume our kind to be incurious and primitive. But I took advantage of the opportunities presented to me while we had power firmly in our claws."

Hekabe had used his newfound authority aboard one of the Covenant cruisers to wage the final battle against the human and Sangheili forces on the Ark, the Forerunners' great foundry-preserve that had created the ancient Halo ringworlds. The Sacred Rings were made to kill a mysterious parasite known as the Flood and usher their Makers into the divine beyond. But what remained of the Covenant was defeated by the Sangheili's treachery, and so killed any hope for the Great Journey. Hekabe thought it might also be the end of all that the Jiralhanae had achieved in their coup . . .

And then he found *this*, the leather-wrapped object he carried.

Stealing the object Hekabe had brought to this world meant risking his entire pack on a stealth attack in the middle of this tragic defeat. Hekabe had led his warriors on a mission deep into the underworld of the Ark, when High Charity, the Holy City of the Covenant, crashed into the foundry's surface, releasing the Flood across its surface. As the parasite infested the Ark, and Sangheili and Covenant ships fought above, Hekabe led his pack into the depths, finding this object—a holy relic—one of the most significant machines ever conceived of by the Forerunners. He had lost many good warriors that day. It was nearly six years later that he managed to decipher the relic's hidden meaning and find the world it pointed to—Rakoi.

Pledging the warriors he'd gathered to himself in those six years to the weaker Sangheili kaidon on this world and then betraying that arrogant rodent Thars had been the last step on Hekabe's long journey toward power.

Hekabe stopped at the foot of the spire. This structure, which he had risked everything to expose, was finally here in front of him. The spire was only the tip of what was buried deep, all the way to this planet's mantle. Its roots reached down toward the magma. Based on what he had encountered on other worlds, Hekabe believed that it could power itself forever off that molten rock.

"Do we blast our way in?" Anexus asked.

"Only if you wish to die. This is far enough."

He carefully put the relic on the ground, adhering to the ritual he had learned from the sacred writings.

The leathery covering sizzled and caught fire, quickly

dissolving to ash. A metal box was revealed, Forerunner hiero-glyphs imprinted on its sides. The symbols briefly flared with em-bers.

Hekabe opened the box by pressing grooves on its sides, ignor-ing the pain from the heat, and wrapped his large hands around a fist-sized, pearly metallic orb embedded into a blue-gray helmet-like device composed of strange ancient metal that seemed almost malleable. The moment he touched the object, blue arcs of energy traced their way through the metal, like the slow-moving lightning strikes he had seen many times sailing across the water-graves of Warial. The blue light lit Hekabe's face from underneath in a ghoulish glow.

"Remember this moment, Anexus," Hekabe said, as he care-fully lifted the alien device up into the air. The ruined ground be-neath them hummed, as though a mechanical sleeping giant rose from its slumber somewhere far below the crust of the cooling stone they stood on. Something indescribably vast, ancient, and powerful stirred. "This is the moment where Jiralhanae no longer struggle for their place. Where none of us will have to negotiate peace through weakness, but instead, we will demand respect by way of our strength."

The spire trembled. Seams appeared on its sides and began to open.

"Our homeworld has been shattered. We are reduced to steal-ing from other species just to survive. The Sangheili called us beasts of burden—mere thralls to be ordered—and they laughed." Hekabe shook his head sadly. "I say instead we will rise. We will take what is rightfully ours, what the Prophets could never pro-vide. And you, Anexus, you will one day tell others of this story, that you stood by me to see this glorious day."

The spire before them now split apart, opening like a giant

beak at first, then splitting yet again. Each sliver of spire lowered itself like a drawbridge, until what had once been seamless turned into four enormous triangular petals flowering before the sun. Each of the petals quickly fell open into the weakened rock, throwing up molten debris as their backs struck the surface.

Hekabe watched with interest as the nearest petal struck ground just a few strides away. Melted rock pelted down around his legs and feet, some of it sizzling on his armor. He moved forward with the device in his hand and stepped onto the petal. It was surprisingly cool under his foot, the heat unable to penetrate through the metal.

The petals had parted to reveal an open core—a sheer ledge that surrounded a hole which fell down into the darkest depths of the planet. Ornate ramps impossibly spiraled around the core, carved into the gray metal structures. They seemed to wend in and out of the raw bedrock. A red glow illuminated the empty abyss of the shaft. Entire handfuls of the tallest buildings in the city around them could be swallowed up in that dimness, Hekabe realized as his eyes adjusted to the scale.

"Come, Anexus," Hekabe ordered, "summon the war packs to join us. They too should bear witness to this event."

Anexus instead looked frightened, peering down the suddenly formed entrance to the structure. "What is it?"

"Power, Anexus. Power that the Prophets would have hid from us all. What lies beneath would have let us win the war against the humans and the Sangheili. It is what will make us strong again. Come with me, and I will show you what the gods attempted to keep secret, even from their own kind."

ojka 'Kasaan stood near a small body of water as one of his warriors crawled out of it onto its muddy bank. After the crash of the *Unwavering Discipline*, and after he had fought for his life while trapped on his own command bridge, he had overseen salvaging whatever the surviving crew could from the wreckage. They had dragged out weapons, equipment, and supplies onto the side of the mountain, and then quickly continued their hunt. "The humans' escape craft is down there, Fleetmaster. But there are no bodies."

Rojka looked at the disturbed water. Shimmering, rainbow-colored oil coated the surface. The tracker that Rojka had tagged the Demon Three's ship with had failed when they landed in this very spot. Presumably their arrival had been violent—he silently hoped there was injury involved, but not fatal: Rojka himself wanted the honor of providing that. Then the Demon Three must have shoved their escape craft into the water. "Was there a sign of fire in their craft?" Rojka asked.

The warrior looked surprised. "Yes, Fleetmaster." A number of Sangheili were scattered around the site, keeping their weapons aimed up the mountain in case of ambush. Others walked the grounds, looking for clues along the giant run of plowed earth the human pod had clearly made when it crashed.

"They pushed it into the water to extinguish a fire?" Daga asked. "But where did they go afterward?"

Scanning the location intently, Rojka walked the area in circles and stopped near a tree with several broken branches. He pushed at the branches, gauging their strength. "No one has found any demon armor?"

"No, Fleetmaster."

"The envoy is wounded and they carry her," Rojka announced. There were missing branches that had been broken free. He guessed they had been lashed together with some ties. It could feasibly carry a human, but not a Spartan. "That will slow them."

He looked at another broken branch from a leafy section of the tree.

Clever. They would use that to disguise their tracks.

"What is it?" Daga asked.

"Look for any disturbance leading away from the site. Not the prints of their feet. Any disturbed ground, something that could not have been caused by the wind. Everyone!"

As Rojka turned, he again caught the pillar of smoke up the mountain range. *Unwavering Discipline* burned still. Rojka growled in the back of his throat. Since he had learned to walk, he had looked up to the vessels heading into the inky black of space and wanted nothing more than to command one of them. He had all but worshipped the greatest and most renowned of Covenant shipmasters his entire life. And he had fought so hard toward the goal of being one himself. To stand with a control dais beneath his feet.

Life once had such purpose. Yet now his ship lay destroyed

on this planet's surface. Half of the surviving crew he had been forced to leave behind. They would attempt to fix whatever they could pull from the wreckage, then catch up to him. The other half, who now stood around Rojka, equipped with a handful of working vehicles, hunted the Spartans with no delay. And the crew who had perished, Sangheili who looked to him to pilot them among the stars, lay inside the ship. They had died fighting the intruders or as their own ship fell apart around them on impact. Their bodies too would become part of the pyre of his own dreams. All his hopes had been swallowed up by deceit and betrayal.

Thars 'Sarov. The envoy. The Demon Three.

Daga moved beside him, looking in the same direction. "We lost many."

"We tried to build something here on this world, Daga. Now it is all ashes. We cannot even defend Rak. Our lineages will be vulnerable to the Jiralhanae and the Spartans, maybe even the humans. We have failed."

Maybe the humans were right in the way they fought for life, not honor. Perhaps survival *was* tantamount, not the integrity of valor. Had he not been goaded into this battle with Thars, Rojka could have simply withdrawn to protect his keep at Rak. Or hidden away and waited until he was stronger.

He thought back to the cool river running through 'Kassan Keep. The cylindrical spires of his greenhouses and the columns of the courtyard in his half-built home. The trees, the farmlands just outside of it. Those who remained in Rak, who were right now likely laying supplies in the bunkers and wondering if they had a future.

So many things had changed. Would Rojka end his life

questioning everything? Was nothing he had been taught by his uncles on the sand of his keep back on Glyke set in stone? Certainly not, because Glyke itself had been destroyed. It almost felt like everything he had thought and believed on that world had been swept away along with it.

Daga had looked startled to hear his fleetmaster admit defeat, even tentatively. Maybe, Rojka thought, Daga too would try to kill him soon.

Was Rojka really a coward? Perhaps secretly, somewhere deep inside, his reason for coming to the surface was to survive Thars's attack in order to just live?

Rojka looked away from his ruined cruiser in the far distance. "We who live owe a debt to those who perished today. We must continue our fight."

"Those warriors have returned and wish to report to you." Daga pointed to three Sangheili standing farther down the slope, waiting. "They found the disturbed ground you ordered them to look for. It appears that the Demon Three headed out into the desert. They may have changed course once out in the sand though, as the wind has blown over their trail."

Rojka considered their path. "They will likely be headed to the human city."

So they could still hunt the Spartans and bring vengeance. He had that much at least. Rojka banished his dark thoughts with a blast of anger. "Send the Banshees we have up ahead to scout for them. But stay low. Thars might be still looking to see if any of us survived."

"Thars," Daga spat. Both Sangheili looked up in unison at the peaks of the mountains beyond *Discipline* and the plumes of distant smoke from the other crashed vessels.

They had been listening in on communications between Thars and his commanders. Some of his fleet had survived the Jiralhanae attack, but only at great cost and with severe damage done to their vessels. Without the ability to quickly repair their ships, and with limited resources themselves, Thars would be grounded as well—especially given that what little survived of his fleet, licking their wounds in a suborbital drift, remained completely out of communication range.

But Thars's patrols were headed for the remains of *Unwavering Discipline*. That much was clear. Soon the fighting would begin anew.

"Thars doomed us all with his poor strategy," Daga said. "To fight an evenly matched battle is to destroy both parties. It is something to do only if one is desperate and certain that the only enemy is the one you currently fight. We were not true enemies, Kaidon. Thars is a fool who should pay with his life."

"Eventually," Rojka said. But Thars was only a distraction. He looked back out at the desert. "First, we find and kill the demons. That is all that matters for the moment."

They had covered so many kilometers that when the three Spartans stopped, Melody was taken aback. She expected them to just keep running until they got to Gila Station. But they *were* human, she mused. They had to have limits at some point.

Mike dug a pit in the sand on the lee side of a dune and placed Melody's stretcher gently into it. The warmth from the sand seeped through her clothes. She wriggled gently against it, letting it form to her back. "Thank you," she said. "That's a lot more comfortable than the webbing."

"It won't be a long stop," Mike said. "We just need time to let some lactate clear out of muscle tissue. Then we can press on."

"Remember training, when Mendez's excuse was that he was just curious about how far we could go before collapsing?" Jai asked.

"I threw up three times," Mike said.

"You came up with the idea of carrying each other when someone needed rest so we didn't have to stop, just to mess with his head."

"Five hundred kilometers, three days. Mendez finally stopped it because he started to get worried," Mike said, with what might have been a slight chuckle.

Okay, they had limits, but not small limits, Melody thought.

She could easily tell each Spartan apart, but primarily by the damage to their Mjolnir armor: all their battle scars made each of them distinguishable. The bent cap over the visor, that was clearly Jai. Mike had two scarred divots over his left breastplate in a rough X. An energy sword had clearly come dangerously close to him—twice. Adriana had burn marks across the back of her greaves, as if something had blown up near her legs.

Those were the obvious bits of damage. Each Spartan had additional unique gouges and dents, as well as normal wear and tear. All of them told a story, some little piece of hell that Gray Team had somehow managed to survive.

"This isn't boot camp," Adriana spoke up. "We don't get to jog—we have to keep running and watch our backs."

The moment of levity broke. Melody watched Adriana wander over to a nearby sand dune. She faced north, her back to them.

"Thank you," Melody muttered as Mike made sure she was comfortable. Then he crested the dune to go and face the Karfu

Mountains in the west, where they'd come from. He disappeared from Melody's sight, though she heard his armored feet crunching across sand for another few seconds.

Jai silently settled down just over her head at the top of the dune.

"You *almost* had a moment of camaraderie there," Melody said to him.

"Almost," Jai agreed, his voice neutral.

"Is this going to affect your ability to fight if someone catches up to us?" Melody figured a challenge might draw the Spartan out.

"The only time we fall back to normal, Envoy, is when facing action. For a brief moment, after we woke from cryo, it felt that way again."

"Your team is broken," Melody said in a low voice. "It's obvious even to someone on the outside."

"Whatever you say, ma'am. We're still operational."

Melody shifted to try and get a better look at the Spartan. The movement sent a dizzying spike of pain through her stomach. "That's what you think. But what happens when things get really bad?"

"We woke up in the middle of a firefight on a Covenant warship. And now everything we thought we knew about what's going on out there is all wrong." Jai waved up at the sky. "Yesterday's enemies are now supposedly our allies, but for some reason they're still trying to kill us. We fight all the way down here, crash-land, and are now being chased into the desert by some very angry aliens. How much worse can it all get?"

Melody turned her head so that the Spartan couldn't see her expression. "Oh, believe me, it can," she said. "But I'm hoping it won't. I'm so sorry."

She sighed and ground her head against the sand.

"Sorry about what?" Adriana asked sharply.

"That I unfroze you and brought you into all of this mess. Now you have to deal with—"

"Shhh," Jai said.

"No," Melody continued quickly. She needed to know they could handle what came next if she gave them the truth—

"Something's coming." Jai stood up, sand cascading from his armor and blowing over her in a gritty burst of rain.

"Oh."

Adriana had now turned and raised her plasma rifle.

"Banshee," Jai said calmly. "Contact imminent. At least some things don't change."

The three Spartans waited in place for a brief moment. Melody strained her ears. Right on the edge of audibility, she could hear the whine of something swiftly approaching.

"Stay down," Jai told her.

Plasma fire shattered the peaceful scene as the Banshee suddenly appeared overhead and wheeled back around in a blur to shoot into the dunes. Molten sand sizzled and pooled. Jai leapt into the air, firing at the vehicle as it swung around for another run. Melody ignored his instructions and twisted around to watch him bounce from dune to dune, dodging the plasma fire and an intermittent explosive fuel rod that jettisoned from its undercarriage.

Adriana launched off into the air as well, the leap making her seem like an armored cricket. Her own rifle streamed plasma fire that seemed to perfectly curve up not to where the Banshee was but to where it was headed. She was leading her target, and at this range it was very impressive. The Banshee smacked into the line of fire and immediately wobbled. It attempted to swerve back to where it had come from, but Mike had already been waiting for that with a third barrage of plasma.

With a loud cracking sound that cut through the air, the vehicle's sealed carapace split open. A Sangheili fell out of the cockpit and down to the sand as the crippled Banshee continued its track and disappeared off into the distance, finally exploding between the dunes.

Adriana hit the ground next to the Sangheili. "Dead," she reported. Melody felt an odd twinge of sadness. She might very well have met that pilot while aboard Rojka's ship.

Jai looked toward the burning wreckage, smoke rising before the harshly orange setting sun. "Ninety-six kilometers to go," he said. "And now they know where we are. Time to get moving again."

Vice-Governor Lamar Edwards spread images out on a viewscreen in front of the generals as Ellis Gass entered the all-too-familiar confines of the planning room and its oversized conference table. She looked around. "What is this? Pope?"

Travis looked completely lost. "The meeting was last minute— I don't have an agenda."

"Vice-Governor?" Ellis asked, her lips pressing together, the words sharp and questioning.

Lamar pointed his index and middle fingers at the screens. "The Jiralhanae have been ruthless about any attempt by us to get eyes on what they're doing. They've used their cruiser to shoot down Pelicans. We've lost drones, recon teams, anything that gets near. Until now."

Grainy, motion-streaked pictures of the Brute-occupied terrain filled the screens.

"I thought there was going to be an update on our naval force," Ellis said. "I wanted a precise ETA on their arrival in orbit."

"An F-99 we had hidden at Aza was dispatched three hours ago and managed to transmit about a dozen images before they shot it down. We now have intelligence that needs consideration," Lamar said. "It places our decisions in a new light."

Ellis glided into a seat. Here was the old veteran who had once claimed to her over drinks that military intelligence was an oxymoron and laughed when he said it. "Lamar, at our last meeting we talked about the alternatives."

And now he was ambushing her.

"The Jiralhanae have not tried to expand out past clearly demarcated zones," Lamar continued. "We wondered if they were just holding the area. Now we know: they are excavating. We saw similar behavior from the Covenant during the war."

The three generals and Lamar turned to look at Ellis and Pope.

"So, Governor, it's not an invasion," Kapoor said. "I think we are just accidentally in their way."

"Right," Lamar said. He pointed at one of the images. "There was something buried under that part of the city."

"So then it's twice as important that we strike!" Ellis stopped herself from shouting by steadying herself before continuing. "Since when has an archeological dig by anything Covenant-related ever resulted in them uncovering something for the greater good? You've read some of the reports about the things the Covenant searched for during the war, so have I. This could spell disaster. The galaxy is apparently full of destructive Forerunner machines waiting to be dug up, and they usually wind up getting a lot of people killed. We need to hit them hard before they find whatever's down there."

Lamar swept most of the onscreen images aside and pointed to a single zoomed-in and enhanced photo of what appeared to be splayed out metal leaves on the ground. Ellis could see a vertical shaft and large spiraling ramps heading deep underground, like threads on a screw nut. "It's too late, Governor. They're already down there. The reason we were able to get close is that a large number of Jiralhanae are no longer present here—most have actually left the occupied area and gone into the Uldt."

"Lamar, what you're doing—"

"All I'm doing is presenting information and choices, Governor, Generals." Lamar pointed at the picture up on the screen again, his face nothing but earnest and concerned. "You mentioned the Covenant excavations in the past, Governor. Well, I've been on the ground when things like this have happened before. I've seen it with my own eyes, and I've seen the toll in the lives of people who've had to go through it. We need to think about saving people now, before it's too late."

"As of yesterday, Lamar, *everyone here* has also been on the ground for things like this," Ellis snapped. "That's why I want the damn ETA on the ships! So that I know we have something in orbit to attack the Jiralhanae before they *do* move to kill us all."

General Grace spoke up. "The fleet will hit orbit in four hours and twenty-five minutes."

Ellis looked at the generals. "Well, it appears my vice-governor is trying to pull something of a coup here," she said darkly.

Lamar looked horrified. "Governor!"

"Oh, call me *Ellis*," she growled at him. She turned back to her generals. "If what he says is correct, then we face an even graver danger than we did before. I understand I am the civilian authority. I understand I do not have absolute jurisdiction in a situation such as this, and I know I don't have your fighting experience. But we have each laid our plans out: fight or flight. Do you feel we can execute a direct strike to remove the Jiralhanae permanently? Or should we make plans to run? You need to tell me now. And once we hash this out, I don't want to have to figure it out all over again. Because if there's one thing I think everyone in this room can agree on, it's that we don't have the luxury of time."

"The price will be high," Kapoor said, leaning in. "Lives will be lost. But in the Brutes' weakened state, I believe we have a chance."

"You might not have fought before, Governor," General Grace said as she rubbed the side of her temple, giving Lamar a frustrated look. Judging by the angle of the images, Ellis had to assume the intel must have come from Grace's camp. Yet the general clearly hadn't been prepared to see the executive branch of Surakan government openly fighting in a meeting room. "But you were elected to run both civilian and military, even if this falls under an emergency protocol—it's ultimately up to the security council here. In my opinion, direct strike is the most viable solution."

Ah, Grace is furious with Lamar, Ellis realized. Apparently, Lamar should have met with the generals to gauge his support before attempting this end run around Ellis. But then, Lamar always said what he thought and *then* followed orders. He was a good soldier that way. Even now, he was sitting down and accepting that the room hadn't taken up his idea.

"That's a majority consent. Let's move forward with the operation: give the orders for them to move into position. We'll synchronize the attacks when air support arrives," Ellis said.

She'd thought they'd laid Lamar's desire to evacuate civilians to rest earlier. Instead he'd been quietly still working at it without letting her know he wasn't going to drop it. But she would have to deal with her unexpectedly rebellious vice-governor later.

Now was the time to act.

CHAPTER 12

By the moonlight, Jai-006 led the team up to a rock mesa. Here the desert had given way from dunes and scrub, to valleys and flat-topped stone carved into smooth shapes by intense winds and storms. Larger boulders dotted the slopes. It had been awkward getting Melody up around the boulder fields and sudden cliffs, but they'd finally managed by strapping the stretcher onto Jai's back.

"Do we need to know anything about defenses this place might have?" Jai asked Melody.

She took a moment to respond. "We're there already?"

"These are the coordinates you gave us. So how do we get in safely?"

"Low-power general transmission. It's proximity-based. I have to think about the passcode—give me a minute." She went silent. Jai put the stretcher down.

"Melody?" She seemed out of it, as if dozing. Jai tapped her on the shoulder, then clapped his armored gloves.

She snapped back awake, at first startled and then groggy. "I'm not sure if I'm going to make it, Jai," she muttered. "I need to tell you . . ."

"You were going to give us access codes," Jai prompted. "We'll come back to other things you need to tell us after that, okay?"

Melody nodded, pushing her dark, curly hair away from her face. "You want to broadcast, low-power, the following passcode." She rattled off an obviously memorized sequence of random numbers and letters. "Then tell them my name."

Jai followed the instructions.

"She's passed out again," Mike said.

"Not good."

They had spread out, each of them facing a different direction of the mesa's tabletop. Jai checked his plasma rifle. After the firefight with the Banshee, the remaining energy was low.

"No response?" Adriana asked.

"Nothing."

A rectangle of light stabbed upward into the night as a trapdoor near a cairn of rocks slid open. The top of the trapdoor was covered in dirt that danced random patterns from the vibrations of powerful motors inside, and a large boulder wobbled as the disguised slab of a door shifted aside. A skinny man with jet-black hair appeared from under the shadow of the entrance, and looked around.

Gray Team had their rifles trained on him in a split second, but the man didn't even blink; he just peered closer at them. "Spartan Twos!" he shouted. "On Carrow! I just had to come up and see it myself."

This wasn't the usual demeanor of the average ONI agent.

"I take that is Melody Azikiwe?" the man asked.

"Yes," Jai said.

"I was told to keep a lookout for her if things turned inside out. Obviously that happened, as we don't get visitors, as such, here.

She's not part of Naval Intelligence, but I know my supervisors gave her training and prep." The man cocked his head and stared at her slumping body on the stretcher. "We better get her downstairs. You're coming in too, right? Can one of you just carry her down for me?"

Jai looked around at the night sky instead of answering.

The agent saw the movement. "Yeah, there's a Banshee lurking about fifty kilometers away: it's the perimeter of a recon picket. The rest of the party is still further out. But it's secure down below."

"Okay." Jai and Mike picked up the stretcher.

"Excellent. I'm Commander Greg van Eekhout," the man said, sticking out a hand. The Spartans brushed past the gesture and he lowered his arm. "Yeah . . . good to meet you too."

He followed them into the well-lit cavity, roughly the size of a Warthog garage, and then down a flight of stairs built into the landscape as the heavy, shielded trapdoor thudded shut overhead. That wouldn't be easy to pry open without the proper codes, Jai noted.

"It's pretty flat up there, makes for a nice makeshift landing pad, though the pilots always complain about coming here anyway," van Eekhout explained. "The next supply run is actually in three days, so I'm afraid I've eaten most of the good stuff. We're down to the cans and freeze-dried stuff now. I may have some cheese that's doing well, possibly a bottle of vodka, but don't tell anyone—I had to bribe the resupply coordinator to get me it. God, I really miss beer."

Jai stopped at the bottom. There was now a good twenty meters of rock above him. He approved. "The envoy needs medical attention, immediately."

Van Eekhout shouldered past them and looked down at Melody. He leaned over and poked at the biofoam. "Follow me. I can fix her up."

"You have medical training?" Jai asked.

"No, no, not at all. You don't want me fiddling around inside you. But . . ." Van Eekhout led them around a corner and pressed his palm against a lock display.

The door opened and lights flickered on. Jai froze. The room looked like a Covenant torture chamber, packed with machines that extruded insect-like mechanical legs and a variety of devices that looked like energy weapons with cauterizing tools that flipped out from their ends like jackknives as they woke up.

"We do have an automated surgical suite. It's basically a Covenant design from a downed corvette that ONI gutted, installed here, and reprogrammed to . . . better handle humans."

"We've seen the originals in person before," Jai muttered. "On the Covenant ships."

A surgical table grew spontaneously out of the floor in the center of the room, machines folding together and apart in unison to create a perfectly flat surface. They lifted Melody onto it.

"And now," van Eekhout said, "we let the 'doctor' do its magic."

"I'm staying here," Jai said.

"No, you're not." Van Eekhout pointed around the room. "Surgical environment, Spartan—it won't operate with you here. It needs complete sterility."

"Have you seen the suite in action before?" Jai asked.

"Of course! Now come on, you need to wait outside." He waved his hands, forcing them back out of the room. Jai dutifully reversed his course to stand in the corridor. Van Eekhout smiled and tapped the lock. Part of the wall before them cleared to transparency, showing the surgical arms deftly removing cloth and probing Melody's wounds.

"Now." Van Eekhout put a hand up on Jai's armored shoulder. "It's not every day a Spartan arrives on your doorstep. I cannot waste this opportunity. Are you hungry? Can I get you a drink? Do you ever take those helmets off? Seriously, I'm really curious."

"We're fine, sir," Jai replied. "We're remaining battle ready for now."

"Good call," Mike whispered, helmet to helmet. "I don't trust this guy. Something's off."

"I'll distract him," Adriana said, responding via helmet.

She stepped in front of van Eekhout. "Let's see your drinks."

"Yes. That's what I'm talking about." Van Eekhout looked at Mike and Jai, then shrugged. "Okay, just me and the lady, then."

Jai turned back to the surgical suite entrance, looking back into the room. "I'll wait for the envoy." Adriana could metabolize any amount of alcohol given at a fairly rapid pace; the important part was getting the ONI agent away from them for a moment so they could assess the situation.

Mike watched Adriana walk around the corner of the corridor. "I'll go scout out the rest of this facility. See where the supplies are. Get a sense of its layout."

"Good idea."

"Are you worried about the envoy?" Mike asked.

"I'm worried about what she wanted to tell me up there," Jai said. "She's hiding something big."

Rojka 'Kasaan paused between boulders as one of his commanders hailed him.

"Thars has attacked the survivors that stayed behind at the *Unwavering Discipline*," he reported. "A few were able to escape the slaughter to report. He is coming for us next and has working gunships."

It would be hard for them to scout an entire desert. But with air support, eventually Thars would figure out where they were.

Rojka and the sixteen warriors that formed this strike force needed to move faster. The Spartans had stopped attempting to hide their tracks as they had pressed deeper into the desert and up through the mountains. But it had become clear that they weren't headed for the human city.

There was something else out here.

"We must be getting close," Rojka said. "The Demon Three will be within our reach soon enough. We will finally have our vengeance."

Melody woke up with a start. She kicked the warm blanket around her feet off and twisted about to examine the clean, white walls that surrounded her. She'd had a nightmare about being left inside the red-lit belly of some horrible Covenant machine that snipped and tore at her skin with terribly precise movements.

No more pain, she realized as she sat up. She was wearing a surgical gown, and judging by the hazy feeling of goodwill dripping from her pores, she was also heavily drugged.

Jai stood by her doorway, still in full armor, and leaning against the side. The cold white walls of the room reflected on his visor. "Envoy. How do you feel?"

"I don't . . . I don't know yet." Melody pushed the blanket away and stepped off the bed. The metal floor was cool under her feet. Where were her clothes? The surgical gown fluttered and she grabbed the back of it to keep it in place. "I need to talk to the agent assigned here. Right now."

She grabbed the blanket and wrapped it around her middle and over her shoulder like a toga. The tight feeling in her side shifted to a slight twinge. She may have felt good, but she wasn't fully healed yet.

"You should rest," Jai said.

Melody ignored him and walked out into the corridor. She didn't have the layout memorized, but she'd seen documents about Gila Station. It was a pretty standard hidden forward-operating center. Which meant the galley and briefing room would be in the center.

She walked inward with the curved corridor, spiraling toward the sounds of chatter. Jai followed closely behind.

Adriana was in the corner with her helmet off, thumbing an empty glass. She had striking Slavic features, despite her extremely pale skin and abnormally bright eyes, which had an unnerving effect. The male she assumed was Van Eekhout appeared to be in the process of asking Mike a steady stream of questions about the SPARTAN-II program. "Forgive me, Spartan," Melody said, her voice a bit fuzzy even to her own ears. "I need to talk to the agent."

"No problem, ma'am. Glad to see you're doing better."

"I'm presuming you're Commander van Eekhout, right?" she said, probing. She had never officially met him. She grabbed van Eekhout's arm.

"Shouldn't you be resting?" the agent asked.

"Where are Victoria, Jens, and Adam?"

"Who?" Van Eekhout slipped a shoulder under her arm and started to steer her back down the corridor.

"My staff," Melody mumbled.

"It's okay, I'll walk her back," van Eekhout said to Jai. "You've stayed with her most of the night. Why don't you spend some time here with your team? Relax."

Melody glanced back. "I don't think they can do that."

"We should all try anyway," van Eekhout said. "Life's too short. So, what about your staff?" The agent kept glancing back down the corridor toward the galley behind them.

"They came down in a shuttle during the battle. I gave them your coordinates."

"I'm sorry," van Eekhout said softly. "No one other than you and the Spartans have come here. Also, you know providing that kind of intel to a third-party violates protocol. You can't just be handing over these coordinates."

"They were my team. It was that or death."

"I'm really sorry to hear that. But you of all people know the stakes and why we have these rules in the first place."

"We knew the risk, but I didn't think—" Melody said. But even in the heavy cloud of painkillers, she felt an ocean of grief strike her. Her knees wobbled. "I-I don't think I can walk anymore."

She drooped against the wall, trying to grab it to hold herself up. The tears that she'd kept bottled up because she'd been too busy trying to fix the situation, do her best, living minute to minute, finally caught up. She sank to the floor.

Victoria, Jens, and Adam were probably dead. *Thousands* were probably dead in Suraka. Somehow, as she'd watched the attacks from orbit, it hadn't hit home how each pinprick of light, each explosion on the ground, meant lives lost. Individuals.

"Hold on a second," van Eekhout said. "This will be uncomfortable."

He slapped a patch on her forearm. Melody jerked back away from him, struggling to her feet. "What's that?"

"Stimulant." Van Eekhout placed a hand over it, stopping her from trying to rip it off. He didn't look jovial anymore at all; his eyes narrowed, and he spoke with calm certainty. "Just hold on a second. I need you clear-headed, Azikiwe."

A blast of energy poured through her. Melody's eyes widened. "Oh . . . this can't be good for me after surgery."

"No," van Eekhout agreed. The welcoming personality had completely disappeared. Van Eekhout's jaw clenched; the mask had come off. *This* was truly ONI now, through and through. "We don't have time, Azikiwe. I've tried to pry a few answers out of the Spartans and I've been keeping track of the general battle in orbit. Are you aware of the Jiralhanae incursion into Suraka?"

"I know one of their cruisers is hovering over the city. Did they start already?"

"Yes." Van Eekhout turned around and stood by the wall, his face grim. "They knew exactly where to dig. And a Surakan intelligence drone captured some images showing that the Jiralhanae have already entered the structure."

Melody stared. "*Already?* How is that possible?"

"I don't know. We thought it would take them months. ONI has readiness contingencies. None of them are forty-eight-hour plans. The first ship to reach us will be here in a day and a half, but it'll probably get eaten alive by anything sitting in orbit. We're in a lose-lose situation. I've already sent up the emergency beacon, for what good it does."

"They should have had a fleet right here, waiting on the other side of Kiriken," Melody said. "That could get help down to the planet faster."

"Politically awkward," van Eekhout said. "The Sangheili would have probably detected it and been upset by a larger UNSC fleet practically sitting on top of a colony they're trying to make peace with—and that doesn't even account for Suraka, which wouldn't have approved either. The New Colonial Alliance could use the opportunity to stoke more unreset in the JOZ and beyond. And you know as well as I do, the UEG wouldn't want extra ships taken away just for babysitting. They've been doing their best to not draw attention to this world. That was before everything went to hell."

"We could appeal to any nearby Sangheili loyal to the Arbiter."

"And then reveal that we knew about this possibility, but didn't tell them? Why not set back relations with them, sure."

"Screw politics. We're beyond that. We're deep into 'everyone's going to die' territory," Melody said.

"But we didn't *know* that ahead of time. There are a lot of secrets scattered across many worlds. We can't stick a fleet on each one. It's expensive enough to construct ONI facilities near the ones we actually discover to monitor the situation. Let's stop processing what *could* have hypothetically been done and focus on what we *can* do immediately to mitigate this situation. Gray Team has been reactivated. That means we have on-the-ground capabilities. We need to put them to use. Adriana tried to get me drunk, see if any intel came pouring out of me. Mike has already broken into several systems to verify everything I've told them and see what can be shaken loose. They're sharp, Azikiwe, and very much on their game."

Melody cautiously said, "I don't . . ."

"ONI didn't ask you to retrieve the Spartans out of goodwill," van Eekhout snapped. "They're the closest thing we have to a backup plan for if and when things go bad in Suraka, which is right now. We have emergency authorization and we need resources on the ground. Desperately. We need Gray Team. This is what they're trained to do—take orders and execute them against threats to humanity."

Melody remained silent.

"Look," said van Eekhout, "this is the first time we've met, but I can imagine the training they put you through. When things went sideways, you had to know that if you got the Spartans out of that mess up in orbit, it might come to this. And you knew they'd be effective weapons."

"Things aren't exactly fitting ONI's predictive models, Commander. I'm not sure they're ready to take orders like that right now," Melody said.

"It doesn't matter," van Eekhout said. "They're probably already listening to us right now."

"That's correct," Jai said, stepping carefully around the curve of the corridor.

Van Eekhout smiled coldly. "Well done. I almost didn't hear a footstep."

Adriana thudded around from the other side of the corridor, not bothering to sneak up.

Melody did her best not to flinch as the half-ton of armor halted just in front of her. The towering female Spartan, her helmet back on, raised a finger that could kill them in a heartbeat and pointed it at van Eekhout. "So, ONI already has plans for us. To use us as weapons? But you thought it would be a good idea to keep us in the dark?"

Van Eekhout straightened. "There is more happening on this planet than you know. *Much* more. The UNSC needs your help. Humanity needs it."

"Nice speech," Adriana said, dismissively. "I know that's what

ONI created us for. We don't need a stirring, 'once more unto the breach' speech. You don't know what we've done and seen out there. And you certainly don't know Gray Team. We're not just going to jump because you bark at us."

The floor shook slightly as Mike stepped into view. "We've always been a little . . . different," he said. "Even from other Spartans."

And that was true; Melody knew that from the briefings. Adriana had gone undercover in civilian populations when they were at Twenty-Three Librae. They'd temporarily "reappropriated" ships from ONI in the name of accomplishing their objective. Even in training as children, they'd been hard to control.

These three were considered wild cards.

And yet they always got the job done, even if they didn't play by the rules. In humanity's most desperate hours, they'd been depended on to fight against the Covenant on countless worlds. And now Melody had to depend on them once more. There was no other choice.

Adriana half-turned to look at Melody. "Tell me, Envoy, are you part of the Office of Naval Intelligence—something you might have failed to mention earlier?"

Melody saw no point in lying to them. She had been just hoping to get them off-planet and warn ONI that Jiralhanae were digging up the city. But she hadn't expected things to move along so quickly. She needed their help. "I work for the UEG. But yes, I'm also serving as a liaison for ONI. I don't have formal rank in their org. I'm not even on the books. For this mission, I was trained by them for one thing. To break out Gray Team if things got out of hand. That's why you're awake right now, that's why you're alive and not slag in *Unwavering*

Discipline's debris field. I'm still one hundred percent Diplomatic Corps. But I'm with van Eekhout here—this world needs your help."

The three Spartans looked at each other, their thoughts impossible to read behind reflective visors.

"Okay, then," Jai finally said. "How bad is it? I mean, what exactly are we facing here?"

He sounded tired, behind that mirrored visor. Tired but grimly resigned.

Melody hesitated. "I'm not going to lie to you. It's bad. Very, very bad. And it's going to get far worse now that the Jiralhanae have broken through the ground and found what they're looking for."

Hekabe now led three heavily armed war packs down into the bowels of the ancient construct. The Forerunners had excavated deep, creating under the planet's crust a tower of empty space the size of a small city. As they descended, Hekabe could see through struts along the exterior wall. The chasm hidden below was large enough that where it reached the molten lava, it could house three swooping Forerunner towers that would dwarf any of the human buildings above them. Delicate bridges, which looked vaguely like an insect's legs, reached out to sink into the walls of the chasm to hold the towers above the red-hot glow below them.

Why the entry point wasn't a lift or portal of some kind, Hekabe was uncertain. The ways of the Forerunners were often inscrutable. The air around the central shaft rippled with heat as the packs followed Hekabe down the curving ramps carved into the walls. The red glow battled the blue tracing light of the Forerunner architecture as they slowly all spiraled deeper and deeper in longer and longer arcs.

The structure wasn't limited to just the shaft and the towers hovering above the pit of molten lava. As he walked farther down, Hekabe saw corridors leading away from the shaft, like spokes on a wheel, on every level.

While he could not guess what machinery and purpose the places in those spokes held, it was clear this had been a site of great power for the Forerunners. "Surely this is a hell," Anexus growled as he looked over the side of the ramp.

Hekabe did not respond. This was not hell. It was destiny.

Above them, the pale circle of the sky grew smaller as they circled down toward the magma.

They finally reached the last curving ramp and approached the bridges leading to the great towers in the heart of the void. *A city within the city*, Hekabe mused to himself. *A fortress within a fortress.*

"Are you sure of this, Chieftain?" Anexus asked. "Up ahead, do we truly know what waits? The Forerunners have kept this a secret—perhaps it should remain so. Even the Prophets would not have dared such a thing!"

Hekabe laughed at the captain and raised Oath of Fury. "Anexus, look at this weapon. It is unwieldy. It does not reach far. But the impact is so strong that with it I can stand against any threat in hand-to-hand combat. Yet it was not always my own. I had to first *take* it," he said, grasping it tightly. "I have learned that the only thing worse than fear is the failure to act—to take what should be mine by right."

Anexus stared at the weapon with lust. "It is said you took your hammer from one of the Banished."

Many Jiralhanae were flocking to the Banished, seeing their growing strength and pledging to follow Atriox, their infamous leader. They were a powerful sect that had begun well before the Covenant's demise. But Hekabe was no such follower. He still believed in the ancient ways. "One of Atriox's best warriors—the chieftain called Odanostos—died struggling to hold on to this very handle. I rent it from his grasp and smote his face with it in front of his own soldiers. Now they all know who wields the Oath of Fury."

If Anexus's eyes could get any larger, Hekabe thought, *he would look like one of the Prophets themselves.*

Hekabe waved them on through the cavernous tunnel. They jogged across the final bridge until Hekabe stopped them in front of the towers. These massive structures reached high into air, vanishing into the darkness that masked the ceiling. The collection of angled spires were connected at their bases by a single, imposing wall, with ramparts and walkways slung across the upper levels. It was clearly a citadel of some kind. A defensive fortification.

Directly in front of them, an enormous entrance led deeper into the citadel—wide as the bridges they had ventured across, even large enough to navigate a Lich gunship through with ease. But it was closed, completely sealed off by a seemingly immovable wall.

Hekabe kneeled before the great arches of the entrance and took off his battle helmet, placing it on the ground beside him. Then he once more opened the engraved container. The strange blue-gray machine inside—an ancient helmet itself of some kind, embedded with the orb he had first used to gain access to this place—surged with arcs of electricity that coursed along its organic shape. Hekabe forced himself to hold his hands steady in front of the curious eyes of the war packs watching him.

"Understand this, Anexus," Hekabe said. "We do not need to fear anything because I already know what waits for us inside this place." He slowly set the Forerunner device onto his head. Initially the device seemed too large, doubtless because it was made to be worn by gods.

The metal shifted with new purpose. Nanotechnology inside met the warmth of organic touch, and parts of the device wriggled like a living thing, then jammed threads down in through the chieftain's skull. Hekabe wanted to gasp, but he bit the impulse back as blood dribbled down his forehead. Hekabe wiped the stinging fluid from his eyes with the back of a hand. He had known of the object's power beforehand, that it contained the technology of the gods inside, mysteries that were incomprehensible to him. Hekabe had read an account of what would come next. The device he'd rested on his head would be reconfiguring itself on a molecular scale as it studied his living matter, his brain tissue, and adapted itself to him.

He knew he didn't have much time before the pain of the tendrils reaching down to interface with his own neural tissue would burn through him. He steeled himself for the excrutiating sensory trauma.

"An entire generation has passed since the Covenant first set fire to our world," Hekabe reminded them all. "And they laid waste to us until we accepted them as masters, accepted their ways, and welcomed their oppression. We survived on the scraps they threw us. We ate the Sangheili's pervasive scorn, we lived underneath their boots for decades. Now, after all our sacrifices, our kin starve and we stand at the edge of thralldom. But we have tasted power before . . ."

The device, this ancient Forerunner machine, kept reaching deep into his brain. Explosions of light dazzled Hekabe, his ears roared from the surging rush of blood. A vast and powerful storm swept forward to grab his mind.

It's just a machine, he reassured himself. *Ancient and powerful. But technology and power to be wielded, like anything else.*

"*Do you remember?*" Hekabe shouted, trying to hear himself over the din inside his own mind. The howling wind of ancient software was trying to rip at his thoughts. "Do you remember that brief moment when everything had been made right after we thrust the Sangheili out, when we stood near the apex of it all? It is time to stop fading away! It is time that we grasp for that same power once more so that we are never weak again! We will feed our children once more. We will gorge ourselves on fresh meat. We will cease begging for scraps. *It is time for the Jiralhanae to rise!*"

Hekabe knew that his voice had risen to a scream, but he could not even hear his own words. He realized then that he had not so much taken possession of the machine, as the machine had taken possession of him.

A blinding light that only he could see finished tormenting him in one last, frightening burst so that Hekabe could watch in silence against the inner storm as the great wall that barred entry to the citadel suddenly slid below the ground, finally revealing its inner contents to him. Racks and racks of stasis fields, the blue lights each like the lit tip of a candle from the distance.

Hundreds of thousands of points of light glowed. Inside each field, a shadow held firm by the stasis field's embrace.

Deep in Gila Station, surrounded by an edgy Gray Team who seemed to be ready for combat to break out at any moment, Melody half turned back toward Commander van Eekhout as he held up a hand.

"You'll want to think very carefully about what you are *actually* cleared to talk about," he said.

"I understand," Melody said. "I'll own this." It'd be her career thrown on the fire, and maybe her life—it was ONI, after all. They could just hunker down here and wait. Do nothing. She'd retrieved the Spartans. She'd done her best to stop this war. Now she was going to follow through with the rest of the plan. Even if it meant deploying a broken Gray Team.

The last thing she was going to do was to keep critical intel from them.

She would just lay her cards on the table.

"In fact," van Eekhout said softly, "my orders were to convey the intel directly to them on the off chance that this opportunity were to materialize. I have rank and command privileges in this facility. No one does anything here without my clearance. They go when I say they go, and they stay when I say they stay."

Adriana said, "Go ahead and pull rank. But you can't force us to stay here. I wouldn't guarantee your safety if you try."

"You might be surprised," van Eekhout said, an assured coolness in his voice.

"I've already poked around at your defenses," Mike said. "She's not wrong."

Melody stepped into the middle of the group. "Let's not get into threats. We're all on the same side: Gray Team can't be kept in the dark, van Eekhout. We're the ones on the ground. We need to make the decisions here."

"Sure," Adriana remarked. "We said that when ONI gave

us orders deep in Sangheili territory, after we went dark behind enemy lines."

"You sure you want to talk about that right now?" Jai asked.

"Well, we all seem to be on the cusp of putting everything out in the open," Adriana snapped. "This is as good a place as any to talk about it. We've been avoiding it long enough."

"We made a choice, together," Jai said.

"Was it the right choice?" Adriana asked. "You've heard the things the envoy's been saying. The war ended in December of 'fifty-two. It was done, over with. So what did we do back there on Glyke, when we followed our original orders? You know damn well why those Sangheili want us dead."

Jai shifted to face Adriana and Mike. Melody remained utterly silent.

"That far into enemy territory," Jai said, his voice wearied by this burden, "with what we were asked to do . . . we all had to agree. We'd lost communications, so we fell back to protocol—all we had were the orders. We didn't know the war was over."

"We did what we did. It's done and we can't change it," Mike said. "It was what we had to do. It's what we've always done. Now is as good a time as any to explain it to these two. They'll need to know, since those Elites will still be out there tracking us. They won't give up. The envoy's and agent's lives are just as much in the line of fire."

Jai turned to Melody. "It was called Operation: SUNSPEAR. You won't find any records of it—it was activated just after Reach fell. I don't know if you remember how desperate ONI was in 'fifty-two, how desperate it still feels, at least to me, even though you've told us the war has been over for six years. That humanity actually won . . ." He shook his head and stopped.

"The Covenant was right on our doorstep," Melody prompted

him, leading him. "We all thought our species would be extinct. And there were certainly some desperate measures by ONI. So what was SUNSPEAR?"

"Retaliation," Jai said solemnly. "Specifically against the Sangheili naval commanders who led the fleets that destroyed our worlds. There were those within ONI who . . . wanted the Elites to know they were not invulnerable on their homeworlds either. We needed to extract a price from them for what they had done."

He'd gone quiet again.

"I get it. It's not an unknown strategy in total war," Melody said. "You're talking about a long strike: we couldn't invade back, but we could demonstrate that we could reach them."

"Early on during the war, we targeted prominent commanders and religious leaders," Jai said. "We made sure their backup strategic minds were under the constant threat of assassination. Then, as things got worse and more human colonies fell, we were asked to *do* more."

Van Eekhout looked rather concerned right now about where this conversation was headed; whether he knew or not what kind of confession was about to come from Jai couldn't be immediately determined. "Spartan, you don't have authorization to—"

"No," Adriana continued. "We do. What happened next was that an emergency order came through. Condition Endgame, it was called. It meant the Covenant had appeared in the Sol system, that the Cole Protocol had finally failed to protect us after all these years. We couldn't reach Sanghelios itself—it was too well protected. But ONI made a breakthrough with intel in 2552. They learned the locations of a number of enemy strongholds, so we were immediately deployed to the Sangheili world of Glyke.

"We brought a NOVA bomb with us."

Now Melody took a step back. *Glyke*, she realized. *For Rojka 'Kasaan, it was all about Glyke.*

She had to suppress any emotion, any judgment, as she continued to listen. All her Diplomatic Corps training was kicking in. Glyke had been utterly destroyed in the wake of the war, only days after the UEG established a tentative peace treaty with the Arbiter. Billions of Sangheili, civilian and military, gone in a blink of an eye. Some had blamed the Jiralhanae, others had more elaborate theories of clan disputes on the planet itself—but now it appeared to have been ONI.

And Gray Team was responsible for carrying it out.

"We voted," Jai said. "We took the intel we had and we made a decision. We followed protocol. With Earth backed into a corner, we were confident humanity was about to be destroyed. So. What would you do if you knew everything you'd spent your life fighting for was about to be erased?"

This was it. This was the darkness that had settled over Gray Team and dogged them since Melody had met them, threatening to rip them apart.

Again, Melody would have to draw on her Diplomatic Corps training. She needed to help them come back from the edge of whatever precipice they now found themselves on.

Melody bit her lip. "You had to follow orders. You retaliated for Earth. You hoped the slaughter would stop our extinction."

"And now you know why your Sangheili friend was willing to risk everything and come hunt for us," Jai said.

"Those same Sangheili glassed entire human worlds!" Melody said. "Killed billions themselves! It was *war*, Jai. And we were *all* in a war for survival. Humanity was on the brink of *extinction*."

"Our deep-space comms equipment was damaged," Mike said. "We never got the orders to cease or withdraw. We didn't know the war was over, never mind that there was peace. So we followed through with SUNSPEAR and lit the nuke."

"We got out before the destruction," Adriana said. "We watched from orbit in our escape shuttle. An entire planet ripped apart. Every living thing on it killed in a moment. Zero probability for survival, no matter what kind of lifeform. By the end, it was just empty debris where a planet once had been. And that's when I actually started wondering—where does this armor stop and flesh begin?"

A rather introspective statement from a Spartan-II, Melody thought. They were struggling to process what had happened out there.

"The prowler we had originally deployed from was damaged during the blast. All we had left was a lifeboat. After a few days waiting for pickup, we went into cryosleep," Jai said.

Those long hours, sitting in the dark. Wondering if they'd done the right thing. Waiting for rescue. Wondering if there was anything left that even could rescue them. Wondering if everything they knew was lost.

"You're concerned about your functional viability as a team," Melody said softly. "I take it that it wasn't a confident unanimous decision when you finally decided to activate the NOVA. Now you're being thrown into another war and you're not sure which end is up. I understand your reluctance."

Melody was willing to bet her pension that if they took those helmets off right now, Gray Team would be looking right through her. The "thousand-yard stare" they'd called it in the first machine-gun wars on Earth. When soldiers fought from trenches and shivered in the mud while artillery rained down on them.

Van Eekhout shook his head. "This is a scenario modifier. What was supposed to happen in the unlikely event that you managed to retrieve these Spartans was that they were to be immediately redeployed to secure—"

"What lies beneath Suraka," Melody supplied.

"Yes." Van Eekhout nodded, mouth quirking slightly. He seemed to view that as too much information. "If what they're saying is true, then we need to get clearance from my superiors to redeploy them. Otherwise we risk intensifying the situation on Carrow exponentially—and even having it spill over into our ongoing peace negotiations with the Sangheili. I didn't know they were directly responsible for Glyke, but this is certainly a new factor and it requires new mission parameters. The Sangheili here on Carrow are mostly Glyke refugees. We throw the Spartans into the mix—who they would likely consider war criminals—and we're adding fuel to a raging fire. We need to keep them here for now and wait for new orders. Gray Team can't be redeployed without my superiors' clearance, or we could be risking everything the UEG and Carrow were trying to accomplish here."

"Maybe," Melody said. "But we're in a desperate situation now ourselves. With the Jiralhanae's strike and the rogue Sangheili making a play for the planet, there are over a million human lives in Suraka that need any help we can give them. And that's not even considering the overall Suraka situation. If ONI's models are correct, and the Jiralhanae have gotten to what's under the city, our greatest risk isn't human-Sangheili peace relations. It's whether we'll all survive what they get their hands on."

"I'm going to reiterate that this is classified information. We need to have Command reassess the situation given these new factors before we provide any more information. Gray Team does not have the clearance—" van Eekhout started to say.

"With Suraka's slipspace relay down, there's nothing to piggyback off of, and that means days. We don't have days,"

Melody said. "And it's classified information that everyone is shortly going to find out about the hard way if the Jiralhanae get access to what's down there. Anyone trapped on this planet deserves to know what's coming, including these Spartans."

Melody turned to Jai, serious, and leaned forward. "Have you ever heard of the Sharquoi?"

CHAPTER 13

By the light of the lava flow around them, Hekabe stepped forward to the nearest stasis field in the first row of seemingly hundreds. The Forerunner machine had sunk more pieces of itself down into his skull, leaving only small shards still glinting from random spots on his head. Inside, more connections were being formed, reaching deeper into Hekabe's consciousness. The immense presence that came with the neural link and the mysterious nano-machinery that now burrowed into Hekabe's skull began to press in on him.

So many of them are lurking inside those stasis fields, Hekabe thought. *All of them waiting to be unleashed.*

Hekabe stepped closer, just an arm's length away from the shifting energy patterns formed by—incredibly—the sustained breach of slipspace being perpetuated right in front of him. The bristles on his shaved arms twitched.

The figure behind the curtain of energy stood twice as tall as Hekabe on thick, trunk-like legs. The chieftain caught a glimpse of a gray, leathery skin over heavily bunched, corded muscle. Hekabe looked up at its fists, bigger than his head, shifting in and out of view under the wash of blue light. *My hand looks like a young whelp's next to these*, he marveled.

And from just above the hands, two massive bone spikes jutted out, larger than Hekabe's thighs. This creature could impale a Jiralhanae on them and simply pick it up to look at it with idle curiosity, like a mere toy. The rest of the creature was shrouded in the swirl of energies.

Hekabe knew what would come next: the chieftain swallowed as he merely willed the field to release its contents. The neural interface inside his mind twitched, the ancient machine now embedded deep inside his brain responding as it decoded Hekabe's command.

The slipspace energy snapped like a foam bubble hitting seashore, with both time and space releasing its prisoner so that Hekabe could now gaze upon it unencumbered.

What looked like a single, cyclopean eye dominating the creature's forehead was actually a lump of light-gray bony tissue, Hekabe now saw. It thrummed as it pinged the room around it with sound. Below the heavy head, the squat, powerful shoulders shifted as the arms stretched underneath a strange armored collar of Forerunner design. Hekabe stared at the beast's jagged razorlike teeth that jutted awkwardly out over its jaw as its neck craned forward, taking in the room through sonic mechanism.

This was a creature designed for destruction, strength, and power. To see in the dark or in the light. To lay waste to any threat despite the environment it was faced with.

Hekabe tightly gripped Oath of Fury with both hands. It was to reassure himself. An instinctive response. Though what could his weapon do against something like this?

Anexus would not follow his chief any farther. He had stopped a few paces behind Hekabe, gaping at the stored beasts in their stasis fields. The rest of the nervous packs all remained at the threshold of the citadel's gate, staring up in fear and awe.

"What is it?" Anexus asked, terror seeping from him and fouling the air. "Chieftain . . . ?"

"*Sharquoi,*" Hekabe whispered. He stepped forward and left Anexus behind. His eyes blurred with sweat and blood as he walked up within the creature's reach.

ONI Commander Greg van Eekhout looked like he'd swallowed something very distasteful. "Azikiwe, I'm going to ask one last time: are you sure you want to do this?"

"Yes," Melody said firmly. Her mouth was dry. There was an electricity in the air. Was van Eekhout going to try and somehow lock down Gila Station to keep them all here? The Spartans would rip the place apart if he tried something stupid; she was sure of that. "And you're going to help me because you know just how high the stakes are. We don't have days for ONI to assess the situation. We need to move now."

Van Eekhout nodded, resigned. "All right. Come with me."

"Thank you," Melody said.

He didn't reply but led her and the Spartans to a ready room and turned on a holographic projector. "During the early days of JOZ integration, the UNSC debriefed a lot of Sangheili seeking political asylum or just trying to find a place to call home in the middle of their own civil war. One of our higher-target interviews was with a shipmaster who spent a great deal of time on the

Covenant's holy city of High Charity. His statements validated a long-standing suspicion based on rumors: within High Charity, there was a reserve weapon the Prophets had planned for the final attack on humanity. Something so powerful that the releasing of it would spell the absolute end of whatever world they had targeted. And even though they didn't have many of them—according to his records, at least—once they located a target high in population and of sufficient morale value, like Earth, they would unleash it."

Van Eekhout waved at the projector. A series of hand-drawn images appeared. Melody stepped forward. "This is a religious mural replicated by hand from the shipmaster. At the top are three San'Shyuum Prophets. You can see the headgear and physical appearance, even in the crude art. Here are the other species that had been part of the Covenant, and one Sharquoi. Here's another hand drawing of a Sharquoi from a Sangheili zealot who claims to have seen one. The Prophets secreted these things from the high-ranking Elites in the military and government, guessing that they hoped to keep the mythos of these creatures intact."

Jai looked at the sketch of the creature. Oversized limbs, a tiny head, what looked like an eye on the upper forehead, randomly jagged teeth that stuck down over its jaw. "Is that a single eye?"

"Unconfirmed. We've never seen one in person. Some evidence we've drawn suggest it's about five meters in height—basically a giant. Lots of muscle. We think that some of the armor designs for the Mgalekgolo—the Hunters—within the Covenant may have imitated the older Sharquoi size and function. The Covenant used them as a template, so to speak. But if any of this evidence is true, the Sharquoi themselves are far, far more dangerous than Hunters."

"We've fought Hunters," Jai said. The Mgalekgolo were massive and strong, yet still fast in close spaces. Despite being colonies of bizarre Lekgolo worms inside nearly impenetrable armor, they fought as if they were one body. Not easy to kill. "But I've never heard of *these* things."

"What makes the Sharquoi such a problem, other than their size?" asked Adriana.

"See the head?" van Eekhout pointed with a finger. "It's not just a size and perspective thing, it's really that proportionately small. According to our intel, the Sharquoi aren't all that bright on their own. They get intelligence by being connected. We're not sure how. Or about range. Certainly the Forerunners' technology would be advanced enough to solve most of the things we see as problems."

"So they pool their cognitive resources?" Jai asked.

"No. It's not a collective group mind," van Eekhout said, shaking his head. "Our understanding, based on some obscure inscriptions we recovered from artifacts on Onyx, is that the Sharquoi are controlled by a single individual when deployed. Like an ant queen and a colony. Every Sharquoi somehow becomes an extension of that individual's will."

"That kind of control sounds like fantasy, make-believe," Mike chimed in.

"It would certainly make the perfect soldier," Adriana said skeptically. "Compliant and ready to take orders. Oh, I can imagine ONI must be *very* interested in finding these things."

"Agents died to find out more about this threat," Melody said, catching that acid in Adriana's voice. She turned to van Eekhout. "Show them the helmet footage from Operation POLECAT."

He turned around. "Yeah, why not. We're already in too far." The holograms disappeared to show a flat screen projecting a camera feed from an ODST's helmet. "We *have* seen them in person before. Once. There's a lot of pertinent footage, but all you need to see is this."

A blue stasis field faded away at the center of the ODST's heads-up display. A glance left showed a column of ODSTs with weapons ready. Easily a hundred soldiers moving slowly forward toward the location where the stasis field had been. A Sharquoi standing on the dais in front of them shifted. It towered over them like a small building. Jai couldn't help thinking of a cyclops, or troll, from ancient human mythology—a massive pillar of lethality.

"Operation POLECAT used Sangheili contacts and one trusted Sangheili crew on an ex-Covenant destroyer to hunt down a remote world where the Prophets had allegedly kept their Sharquoi hive," Melody said. "A handful of Sharquoi were found there. One was accidentally released while ONI personnel were trying to access the site's terminal data."

The Sharquoi's head twisted. The eyelike bump on its head thrummed, probing and searching the air around it. It seemed to notice the weapons aimed at it and bellowed. There may have been words in some strange alien tongue, but they were washed away by the immediate chattering of bullets as the ODSTs opened fire.

The creature roared and leapt into the air, shattering any assumptions that it was slow and lumbering. The ODST's camera feed struggled to follow it as it landed in the middle of the column of shock troopers. Melody paused the footage just as the Sharquoi lifted up an ODST by his leg and smashed him between two fists, armor disintegrating under the impact.

"One Sharquoi alone killed fifty ODSTs during this operation. Later, the hive was nuked from orbit and then glassed by the Sangheili ship for good measure," Melody said. "They're not something anyone at ONI wanted to get out."

"How come we've never heard of these things before?" Adriana asked.

"How much do you know about the Forerunners?"

"Only what we saw in briefings before SUNSPEAR," Jai said. "About the Master Chief and the Halo installation out in deep space."

"We believe that the Sharquoi were engineered by the Forerunners who built the Halo Array," van Eekhout answered. "And after the Sharquoi were first discovered by the Covenant, they were immediately hidden. No one really knew about them. They were created for protection against the Flood—a parasite that threatened all thinking life in the galaxy—as the Forerunners retreated into the galaxy's periphery. But evidently, only a few ever were discovered by the enemy, fewer still used. During the war, some Sangheili and San'Shyuum that knew about their existence begged their High Prophets in secret to release them against the humans, but they never did. That's why we've never formally encountered them."

"So why didn't the Prophets release them in battle?" Jai asked.

Van Eekhout smiled. "The assumption is that they had the ability to *release* the Sharquoi, but they lacked the means to *control* them. The control device the Forerunners used was hidden away on one of their installations. The Covenant never had possession of it. If they had ever released them, it would have been only for raw power. A show of destruction and strength. The threat of Sharquoi was somewhat manageable before today . . . before the Jiralhanae chieftain Hekabe showed up."

"Hekabe?" Mike asked. "Who's this?"

Melody spoke up. "Hekabe is a rogue Jiralhanae who leads several packs, and we believe he's the one who landed here on Carrow. Some embedded moles we've had among the ex-Covenant think that Hekabe may have acquired the control device in question during one of the final battles of the war—he's apparently boasted of such. But it's taken him six years to sort out where to go to unlock its power. He must have finally figured out about the hive here."

"And this hive here—so no one knew about it?" Jai asked wearily.

Van Eekhout took that question. "There's a Forerunner structure deep underground on the outskirts of Suraka. Judging by ONI seismic scans before the reoccupation of Suraka, it matches the design of the only other known hive but . . . we believe that this structure has the potential to store hundreds of thousands of Sharquoi. A scale unlike anything we've ever seen. We don't think the San'Shyuum knew it even existed. They tended to . . . *misinterpret* a lot about Forerunner artifacts."

"An understatement," Melody muttered.

"Hekabe must have obtained new knowledge of the hive's location, and that led him here," van Eekhout said.

"And you just let people come back to Suraka? And Sangheili?" Adriana said. "Settle here? And all the time, knowing this was down there?"

"We couldn't stop the planet's refugees from resettling without a major political upheaval from those who felt like the UNSC had abandoned them during the war," said van Eekhout. "It would have been a logistical and PR nightmare with some of the emerging separatist movements like the New Colonial Alliance. Think

Insurrection-scale problems. We also couldn't afford any of this leaking out. We figured the city would act as a buffer to discovery. But just in case, I've been here for the past few years. Monitoring." Van Eekhout looked slightly martyred. "There were . . . contingency plans."

"So," Melody said, looking right at Jai. "There's a very angry Jiralhanae chieftain in Suraka who has just figured out how to break into a Forerunner facility buried below the planet. He plans to take control of the Sharquoi inside. There's a strong chance this poses a threat not just to Carrow but to anywhere Hekabe can carry the Sharquoi in his vessels. You're now fully up to speed, Spartan. I had been trying to get back to warn the UNSC or ONI, but without a long-range communications relay, I'm afraid we're on our own. Are you willing to help us?"

Ellis woke up as her head slipped forward and struck her desk. Utterly exhausted, she swore, rubbed her forehead, and looked down at the datapane she'd been scanning. Lists of Surakan militia who waited on the rooftops with shoulder-launched guided missiles. Pelicans and several Sparrowhawks prepped to be rolled out of hardened bunkers, procured through backdoor channels years earlier—probably through the New Colonial Alliance, Ellis wasn't certain. Maps of militia positions around the occupied area also needed rechecking one last time.

But they were all coiled and ready.

The pane suddenly blinked several times, signaling an incoming call. Ellis tapped it and General Grace appeared. "Our ships are about to enter orbit. The Jiralhanae frigates that remain are pulling back from them rather than moving to engage. We have the high ground."

"Thank you, General. Keep me posted," Ellis said, and cut the connection. Her vision blurred, doubles of everything she was looking at swimming around in front of her.

How long had she been up? Three days? The human body wasn't meant for this. She pulled out another stimulant patch and ripped it open. She rubbed it against her forearm and waited until the blurring faded away. The pressure behind her right eye took a step back.

She got up to leave and Lamar quickly appeared in the hall to stop her at the door. "Ellis," he said, "with the Jiralhanae frigates drawn back, this is our last chance."

"Lamar . . ." Ellis rubbed her scratchy eyes. "I understand you want to do what you think is best. I won't hold this against you afterward. Or ever, really. But I need you with me, by my side, to help us do this. I need your expertise. If you can't give it to me, let me know now. We can't afford to fight each other. Not with this threat on our doorstep."

Her vice-governor took a step back. "I had to ask one last time. I have a conscience, Ellis."

She gave his shoulder a squeeze. "I know. And I really appreciate where you're coming from. Thank you, Lamar, for all your counsel."

Of course, when this was all over, she was going to ask for his resignation. Ellis wouldn't be vindictive; she was better than that. But it was the end for him. Never mind the smile of reassurance she gave him now—that was to make sure he followed through until the enemy had been pushed back.

The operations room's walls dripped screens patched into surveillance all over the city. They now had a decent line of sight on the rim of the massive crater the Jiralhanae had glassed to get down into the Forerunner structure. Other screens showed feeds from orbit: Surakan ships transmitted a bevy of new data as they waited to head planetside.

Two generals sat in the room, a variety of other militia officers, and three aides. Everyone crammed in close, with those lesser in rank crouching in the corners out of the way while murmuring orders or requests into earpieces.

"We are go for Operation BUZZHAWK," General Kapoor said.

"Good," said Ellis. "Let's send these Jiralhanae back to where they came from."

On her orders, the Surakan ships began to descend from orbit and break for the surface.

CHAPTER 14

Rojka's assault team still consisted of the sixteen trusted warriors he'd handpicked after fighting the traitorous Keza to the death while trapped in the wreckage of his own command bridge. Most of his crew was dead, either from the crash or by Thars's wrath. Those who survived had only a handful of working vehicles—two Ghosts, a Spectre, and a single Phantom—salvaged from the debris of the *Unwavering Discipline* and operated by a few of his most skilled Sangheili. This other group had separated from the main pack and methodically picked their way to the outskirts of the Uldt desert in order to divert and delay their pursuers, while Rojka's own force raced ahead. This lean, fast-moving fighting force had found the remains of the Spartan shuttle quickly. From there they continued to follow their enemies across the desert.

Yet it hadn't been enough. Because now Thars had finally caught up to Rojka before the Spartans could be dealt with.

Rojka's best were not enough to take on the one-hundred-strong enemy Sangheili arrayed on the dune tops around them, and any communication with the few vehicles they had would only give up their location. If they stood any chance for survival, he would have to wait on recalling them. Thars's own Phantom gunship had thundered overhead in the early morning darkness as they approached the mesa where Rojka had tracked the Demon Three. Thars's troops dropped to the ground and quickly formed a broad semicircle around Rojka's smaller force, all shadows scattered around the dunes. Rojka held a dune top of his own, for what little good it did.

At least he wasn't positioned down below and between the dunes, forced to look up at Thars and his conspirators.

"Can we escape?" Daga asked.

"No. We will not be cowards." Rojka looked back in the direction Thars had not blocked off. There would be something out there, waiting. Ships with bigger guns. Thars would crow for eternity if he killed Rojka in the process of retreat, the shameful end his enemy dreamed of.

Thars trudged up to the top of the nearest dune across from them.

"Greetings, cousin!" Thars shouted from a safe distance. Several of his heavily armored commanders moved quickly to stand at his side. "I see you have paused. Do the Demon Three worry you?"

Rojka looked toward the wall of rock ahead of them. "We are studying the enemy's keep," he said. "It is a human-made base, hidden from sight, and it will have defenses. We need to know how many are inside. Or if we can lay a trap for them when they leave." For many, it would have been difficult to discern the humans' structure embedded in the mountainside, but Rojka had seen enough of Rakoi, and of this vast desert in particular, not to be fooled. He knew what was real and natural and what wasn't.

Thars made a sound of amusement and disdain. "You no longer have any ships. You have few to command an attack. Rojka, right now, I see only the dead standing before me."

"I have enough to take my revenge. Revenge for all," Rojka said.

"Possibly," Thars said. "But if Sangheili attack a human facility, it is a strike against the humans' government. You are willing to die fighting for vengeance. We who live after your glorious deed will be the ones who suffer the consequences of this, however. What will the humans do to us on this world afterward?"

This, Rojka thought, was uncharacteristically forward thinking by Thars.

Then again, maybe not. Thars always made sure to take care of his own hide. *"You don't wish to see the Demon Three dragged to justice?"* Rojka shouted, letting rage seep into his voice. "After the family we lost to them. Our nephews dead. Our traditions erased. The history of our peoples brought to nothing with the destruction of our home? Glyke was your world too, cousin!"

"Oh, I want this," Thars said, his voice silky and thoughtful despite the distance. "But I puzzle over the more effective way to kill them without upsetting the humans who will arrive soon."

"You have thoughts on this," Rojka said.

"I offer you a bargain," Thars said. "We will let you attack. But you will spare any humans inside other than the Demon Three. Once you have accomplished your task, we will rush in and rescue the remaining humans from you."

So that was why Thars surrounded and stopped him instead

of striking directly. Rojka made a show of nodding thoughtfully. "And then you will kill me and my warriors."

Thars spread his arms. "An unfortunate consequence of the fighting," he said. "I will tell the humans that you were sympathizers with one of the Covenant sects that is causing them problems. These days, that would be easy to believe. But all Sangheili will know you died in glory, cousin. And my previous offer stands: I will allow your bloodline to live on."

Given the circumstance, it *was* a generous offer, Rojka knew. And even though Thars was a traitorous wretch, with so many eyes on him for such a public proclamation, Rojka doubted Thars would slaughter his bloodline when back at the city of Rak. Thars would likely attempt to claim to have killed the Demon Three alongside Rojka and steal a share in the glory, of course.

So before him was a choice. Run out into the desert, away from Thars, and die at the hands of a hundred former brothers, or attack the human base and perish when Thars swooped in afterward.

Rojka looked at his sixteen trusted warriors. They were poised, preparing for the battle to erupt at any moment, but also waiting for him to make the first move. Daga caught his eye and nodded. *Any which way*, his eyes glittered.

Their lives were gripped in his hands, Rojka knew. But more importantly, their legacies all were being decided right in this moment. What would be sung about them for generations hung on whatever he chose to do next.

"Very well. I will attack and spare the other humans," Rojka said with grudging respect. "It is a worthy plan." It would certainly give anyone under him their honor. And it would allow him to finally exact revenge on the Demon Three. Perhaps he could also silence the envoy, who brought this all on him to begin with. And it might even protect whatever remained of their lineage left in Rak.

Might, he thought heavily. A small word from which to hang the fate of lives.

Rojka waved his fighters to move with him, toward the large numbers of Sangheili in front of them who now opened up a path to let them through. As they passed, Rojka turned on his armor's stealth camouflage.

"Let us find a way into this human keep and then kill the Demon Three," Rojka said to Daga as they left Thars behind them and walked toward the mesa. "And end this once and for all."

In the ready room, Jai crouched on the floor with his back against the wall. Melody sat at the side of the table on a chair a few feet away.

"You are persuasive," Jai told her. "But I can't convince this team to do anything right now. Not after what we've been through. We were forced to make a big decision out there, on our own. That call is still breaking us."

"I gave you the information so you'd hear what was at stake. Your team listened. That's all I can ask." Melody leaned forward. "What are *you* going to do, Jai Zero Zero Six?"

She was using his number on purpose. *A call to duty*, Jai thought. She was good, the envoy. And she wasn't wrong. The long, silent inner turmoil that he'd carried across the desert had eased slightly when she'd made the request that they assist. "I'm going to try to help you. This is what I was built for, wasn't it? This is the information we have, what you gave us. That's a hell of a fog of war. Doesn't seem like there's much of a question."

"I truly believe this is the right fight, Jai," Melody said. "I wouldn't have put everything on the table if I didn't think you guys should know it all."

"I know." He cocked his head. But believing something strongly didn't make a person right. Insane asylums were filled with people who felt the same way. Conviction was a poor substitute for tactical thinking. "But the intel you just shared is the reason why I'm going to do this."

"What about the rest of Gray Team?" she asked.

"What happened on . . ." Jai paused as he struggled with the way he'd phrased those words. "What we *did* to Glyke. I don't know how we'll ever come to terms with that. How *I* will. Yes, maybe it *has* broken us. But right now, because of the stakes, because of what's at risk, we'll fight. That we know how to do."

An explosion shook the rock walls. Alarms blared. The comfortable brightness snapped off, replaced with emergency red lighting. Van Eekhout leaned around the doorframe with a BR55 battle rifle in hand. "Something violently breached the south entrance. Sensors show mass but no visuals. Computers are running through visual analysis, but they're already inside."

The Sangheili had arrived. Jai stood up. "Active camouflage," he said.

"Probably," van Eekhout agreed. "And once you get close enough, even to a shielded bunker like this, their sensors would be able to show them enough to get in."

Adriana skidded to the door behind van Eekhout. "We need to get to your armory," she said.

Mike thudded in to join them. "Sangheili?"

"Yes," Jai said, and looked back to van Eekhout. "The armory?"

"There's no time," van Eekhout said. He tossed the BR55 at Jai. "Take my rifle. You can do more with this than I can. You need to get out of here, now!"

"No," Jai said. "We're Spartans. We fight."

Van Eekhout stepped inside the ready room and squared off against Jai. "Really? Then get to Suraka. Because fighting here doesn't help anyone—it just wastes time and resources. But we sure as hell need your help fighting Hekabe before he releases the Sharquoi on everyone and everything we're all trying to protect."

Jai glanced at Mike, then Adriana, who shrugged. "The ONI boy has a point," she said.

Van Eekhout pointed down the corridor. "Here's what you need to do. Follow this corridor. Take the second tunnel on your left. It dead-ends on a shielded hatch. Tap the code four-five-eight-six-one-eight to open it. There's a ladder down the cliff face and a Warthog hidden at the bottom. Drive east thirty kilometers until you hit an old streambed. Then drive along that south until you get to Suraka. Other than that, good luck."

"Melody?" Adriana asked.

"She can't make it down the ladder in time like you can," van Eekhout said.

Melody rapped Mike's armor. "Get out," she said. "They won't touch me. Van Eekhout and I are worth more alive than dead. You're the ones they have a vendetta against. Go—they're in here already!"

Gray Team took off down the corridor. Jai glanced back—leaving someone behind just felt wrong, he thought.

Melody watched the three Spartans turn the corridor. Once they were gone, she said to van Eekhout: "We need to fall back to the armory and bolt ourselves in."

"There is no armory. We had a single battle rifle, and I just gave it to them." Van Eekhout ushered her into the ready room and closed the door behind her. He tapped a password into the screen by the entrance.

"That's not good," Melody said. "Those Sangheili are coming for us, and they're all pretty angry. It won't take long for them to find their way here and break into this room."

Van Eekhout walked to the back of the room and sat down. He put his feet up on the table. He wasn't wearing any shoes: he must have rolled out of his bed and come running. "They're always angry," he said. "At this point, which one do you think is coming through that door?"

Explosions rocked the installation. A bit of dust trickled down from the ceiling.

"I took the Spartans away from Rojka. He might kill me for that," Melody said. "If it's Thars, he might kill me too for choosing to help Rojka all this time. They might kill you as well."

The blade of an energy sword burst through the door. Embedded electronics spat sparks and hot cinders. It wouldn't take long now.

"So, death at either door?" van Eekhout said, almost cheerfully. The dead-serious ONI agent had faded away to be replaced once more by the friendly van Eekhout. She wondered which was the facade and which was real.

"Maybe." Melody stepped back from the door.

"I knew I was screwed the moment I got assigned to this back-water planet."

The door blew inward and sliced through the conference table in the middle of the ready room. Thars stepped through, energy rifle aimed at Melody's head. "Envoy," he growled. "You do not even try to fight us. A dishonorable capture. I expected no less."

ekabe, eyes closed, stood in front of the massive Sharquoi. He swayed slightly to the left, feeling the presence in his mind still seeping further and further in. The fearsome creature, just a few meters away, also slowly shifted its body to the left in perfect synchrony with Hekabe.

He could feel the Sharquoi, its potential. It was a speck of will deep inside the universe toward which he extended his own mind. Though the Hekabe of just hours ago would not have understood these words properly, because the words were only abstractions that didn't quite capture the true *feeling* of control.

That Hekabe was gone. Vaporized the moment the Forerunner technology had bitten down through his forehead.

Yet there was a seed of the will and desire of the old Hekabe that still lived here. Like a flame in the distance.

He had learned so much in these last few hours. An unknown element deep in the substrate of this machine's reach had embraced Hekabe and educated him. A presence of something that had taken on this mantle long before Hekabe. An ancient whisper of experience, or memory, guiding him. Something that had touched the Sharquoi long ago, and had left some residue.

Here is how to dwell in this new consciousness, it told him, if he strained to listen.

Those ancient snatches of memory gave Hekabe the glimpse of vicious surgical devices cutting deep into Sharquoi skulls to crack them open. Intelligent Forerunner machines delicately reaching down past viscera to stamp implants securely into brain tissue. Implants of incomprehensible power that could effectively control the Sharquoi.

It was a challenging process. A desperate gamble and complete forsaking of ethical standards long held by the Forerunners. They were attempting to create soldiers out of a half-witted but physically imposing species, beings who had, for some inscrutable reason, proved completely resilient to the Flood plague. They were the perfect weapon, but they needed guidance, they needed to be controlled. And through a deft balance of stimuli to specific cerebral tissue and a burst of engineered hormones, the one who wore this strange device had near-absolute governance over the creatures' physical functionality.

And now, here, it meant Hekabe could control the powerful thing before him.

The Sharquoi raised its fists into the air.

Hekabe could see it with his own eyes.

But he saw himself from the Sharquoi's eyes as well. The neural twitches translated from the Sharquoi through its implants and then back to Hekabe. Looking down from above, the Sharquoi saw him as a small thing: tiny and weak. And Hekabe also saw himself standing in front of the Sharquoi from the perspective of three more of them that now stood off to the side. They had been awakened and had emerged from their stasis fields. Had *he* done that?

Yes, some part of him had. It was a part muddled with the memories of his own mind that was now fusing with the power buried throughout his skull.

The three Sharquoi stepped forward to flank Hekabe.

From all the Sharquoi, he could now look back over his shoulder, where Oath of Fury still rested, and he could see the Jiralhanae packs fearfully staring at him and the mysterious creatures.

The ground shook as something far overhead exploded. Even the Sharquoi could feel that. Dust drifted through the air in lazy patterns.

Anexus, clearly grabbing hold of his courage, approached them. "*The humans are striking back at us!*" he shouted. To Hekabe's own body, it sounded like a distant murmur from behind a closed door. But the Sharquoi could hear it, so through them, Hekabe could as well. Ground-based weapons thudded away at their excavation site.

"Let them strike," Hekabe said. Anexus scrabbled back, eyes wide. The words had come, deep and terrifying, from the Sharquoi nearest to him instead of Hekabe, who still had his back to Anexus. The words were slurred, coming from an alien mouth, but recognizable and filled with vitality.

"We will be lost," Anexus said. The stench of fear roiled off him. "The *Foebane* is taking damage from human ships."

"*We are not lost!*" Hekabe now shouted with anger, through all of the Sharquoi. The packs collectively took several more steps back, edging closer to the bridge they had come across. One of the Sharquoi moved to release its brethren, which staggered out from their containment fields, freed from eternal suspension. "Tell *Foebane* to stand its ground at all costs. No one enters the citadel while we are down here. No one."

He would need more Sharquoi to put a stop to the human counterattack. He would need more Sharquoi for all that he had planned.

Hekabe growled in frustration. He would have preferred to have had additional time to learn how to properly control these new charges. But this was time he didn't have.

Accept everything, an instinct counseled him. *Stop fighting, stop trying to bend their minds; your ways will not hold here. Direct them. Guide them. Unleash them. Be them.*

Hekabe roared and punched the ground with massive, clawed fists. He saw this through other eyes. It was no longer Hekabe the Jiralhanae, but Hekabe the Sharquoi.

The Sharquoi's arms struck with the same force as a gravity hammer, rippling the air with energy and concussive force.

A curious Jiralhanae warrior that had approached too close now flew back, tumbling into the air away from the point of impact and over the edge of the bridge.

As the luckless Jiralhanae screamed, dissolving in the lava, Hekabe opened his own eyes.

"Release more of them!" he shouted at the wind in his mind, as the human bombs above his head thudded and exploded against the top of the Forerunner structure.

Whether he could control the Sharquoi or not, it was time to unleash as many as he could. It was the only way to stop his enemies now.

Outside the ONI facility, Jai fell a hundred meters to the ground and hit solid rock. Pulverized pieces of debris flew away from the point of impact. The gel inside his Mjolnir armored hardened to protect him. The Spartan rolled and tumbled with the fall, bouncing off a boulder and sliding down scree until he came to a bruising, dizzying stop.

"Check in," he groaned.

"The Warthog is up against the rock under the ladder," Mike said.

"Here," Adriana grunted. Jai stood up and spotted the Warthog. It had jet-black paint like others he'd seen ONI deploy, but it was immediately clear that, over the past six years, it had seen a number of design changes to its chassis. Adriana already limped toward it. Mike had bounced a bit farther on down and was scrambling over the rocks, heading for Jai.

"I don't like leaving the envoy," Adriana said, clambering into the Warthog's rear bed and setting up on the Vulcan anti-aircraft gun.

Surprised, Jai said, "You think we should head back up?"

"It feels like we abandoned her," Adriana said, echoing Jai's thoughts. "And we don't really know how those Sangheili will react."

"But they know more about that situation than we do," Mike said. "These things the Jiralhanae are looking for are clearly a greater threat. Sometimes—"

Jai fired the Warthog up, interrupting him. Mike immediately attempted to access the vehicle's command console to assess its capabilities. But Jai didn't pull the Warthog out from under the shade of the rock recess; he turned in his seat to face the two other Spartans.

"Listen. We've already been through hell. What happened on Glyke . . . I take the blame for that. I'm responsible for pushing the team in that direction and not waiting for more intel. That's my fault. We're in a similar spot right now, without clear direction. So I need to make sure we're all on the same page. I need to make sure this is a decision we make as a team."

"We're going to Suraka," Adriana said after a moment. "Even if I don't agree with leaving the envoy behind, even if we're in the dark about what we should do next. If the Jiralhanae are attacking humans in the city? That's an easy fight to jump into."

"Yeah," Mike said. "We're still Gray Team. It's us against everything else, same as it ever was. Even when it's all gone to shit. We head toward the fight, not away from it, and we'll figure it out when we get there. That's what we do."

Jai didn't say anything. Just nodded and accelerated the Warthog out onto the dunes, headed east at full speed.

Melody Azikiwe stood defiantly as Thars stalked around the ready room. "And you swear you have not seen Rojka 'Kasaan?"

The Sangheili seemed puzzled.

Again, she shook her head. In the corner of the room, Commander Greg van Eekhout hung from between two Sangheili soldiers' arms, having been bruised and battered by Thars for the past five minutes. "I have not seen Rojka since orbit, Shipmaster," Melody said quietly in flawless Sangheili.

Thars kicked the ruins of the conference table. "Again! He runs from me again!"

Thars had apparently arrived expecting to find a very different situation. This didn't make sense. Last time she was with Rojka, he was preparing to fight Thars to the death. For some reason, Thars had now expected the kaidon to be here, according to some mutual plan. *What the hell is going on?*

"You still refuse to tell me where the Demon Three have gone." Thars stopped pacing. He looked thoughtfully over at van Eekhout. He pulled out his energy sword. It flared to life.

Melody stepped forward. "Shipmaster! What are you doing?"

One his commanders backhanded her in response. Melody sprawled to the floor, hitting the pieces of table. She scrambled back up and wiped blood from her upper lip with a sleeve.

"Humans will find horrible things done to you two, atrocities that they will believe *Rojka* committed in this station, and I will apologize to them profusely that I was not able to reach you in time to stop it," Thars said. He arced the energy sword through the air, slicing first into van Eekhout's head, then shoving the blade slowly down to cut his body in two. The Sangheili on either side stepped back in disgust as each half of the remains of the ONI agent fell by their respective feet.

Melody stifled a scream.

Thars turned back to her. "My cousin Rojka feels there can be a peace between our kind, Envoy. But after all that has happened, do you also believe it? Do you think you can let go of seeing an ally killed like this before you? Will that hatred with which you now stare at me be something you could dam up?"

"I'm willing to do so." Melody tried not to look at the ruined body of Commander van Eekhout. She swallowed bile and stared directly back up at Thars's pale, unblinking eyes. "We have to be. Or all we'll do is destroy each other. There will be more war. More hell."

Thars scoffed at her. "What do you know of war's hell, Envoy? Sitting in your comfortable negotiation rooms and dining with ambassadors as you travel around in comfort. You are soft, and you talk all the time."

"I am *Kenyan*," Melody snapped at him. "I was there when the Covenant attacked the East African Protectorate. I have lost more than you suspect, Shipmaster. And yet here I am, fighting for peace. Fighting for the survival of our species. I'll fight for it until I die. But never lecture me about loss when all my family and friends lie dead under glass by the actions of your kind."

"These are just words to me. You do know what horrors the Demon Three unleashed, well after our peoples had established peace?" Thar raised his voice. "*Do you know about Glyke?*"

"Yes. I know what they did." Melody defiantly refused to close her eyes. And if he killed her right now, she would stare him down until the last moment.

"And yet since your kind is without justice you still will not give them over to me," Thars said. "I assume they run for the human city, Suraka. Which route do they take?"

Melody swallowed and looked at the remains of van Eekhout, the sight of his mangled body and the smell of cauterized flesh threatening to overwhelm her. "I will not tell you that."

She tensed, waiting for the killing strike.

Thars cocked his head. "You know I will find them. We found you here."

"If you find them, your fight will be with them," Melody said. She was doing her best to remain steady. *Just keep him talking*, she thought. She was only trying to buy time at this point. The longer Thars stood here, the better chance the Spartans had.

"Do you see?" Thars announced to the other Sangheili in

the ready room. "All humans are the same. This one protects the Demon Three. What difference does it make whether they killed Sangheili innocents after we had laid down our weapons, or if it was her that did the killing? She helps them *now*. Perhaps she even worked with those who plotted the genocide of Glyke back then. You see how all humans are complicit?"

"And have you not stood in the command bridge of a ship that murdered innocent civilians by the millions, at the order of the Prophets?" Melody asked. "Are you truly any different than the Demon Three?"

"Guard your tongue, human." Thars raised his energy sword and turned to her, his voice calm. "I will now ask my questions a final time. You will answer, or suffer an end the same as your friend's."

Melody took a deep breath as she tore herself away from staring at van Eekhout's body and back directly to Thars. She needed to keep the Sangheili engaged, but she wasn't sure how much longer she could do that. *Take a big gamble, then*, she thought. *Tell him everything you're not supposed to.*

"Do you know what the Jiralhanae you allied with are *really* here for? Why they really agreed to come to this planet? You have spent all of your time asking how you might take control of Rak from Rojka . . . but since you brought Hekabe here, this has been the wrong question," she said.

Thars did not respond. Melody continued.

"I need you to think about threats to your people, your keeps, here on Rakoi right now. You need to know what the Jiralhanae are planning to do. They will destroy everything you are fighting for. They are going to release something horrible onto not just this world but Sanghelios, Earth, everywhere."

Thars pushed the very tip of his energy sword into her shoulder. Melody screamed as skin and muscle sizzled.

Thars stepped forward. "I do not care about the Jiralhanae. Where. Are. The Demon. Three."

Melody tried to grab his forearm, but was struck from the side. She gasped as the wind was knocked out of her and she rolled into the wall. Something invisible had grabbed her. She could see the edges of whatever held her down shifting as it moved, the other side of the room gliding over it: it was active camouflage.

"Traitor!" Thars bellowed.

Melody's head snapped as she was picked up and the invisible figure sprinted for the door. Plasma fire splashed hot against the frame.

They veered down the corridor and more invisible forms started firing back as Thars's own Sangheili spilled out of the room to give chase. Thars's fighters ducked back inside as ignited plasma grenades flew through the air to stick to the floor in front of them.

Explosions rocked the corridor and a powerful blast of heat roiled down between the walls toward the invisible fighters. The active camouflage flickered and failed as a large form appeared crouching, protecting Melody from the explosion.

Melody gasped, staring at a familiar Sangheili face. "Rojka?"

Rojka's fighters appeared around her, their active camouflage deactivating and their armor shields flaring. Rojka yanked her down the same tunnel the Spartans had used to escape the facility. Melody could see the desert through a hole the Sangheili had blown in the now-glowing rock.

He continued running for it, holding Melody all the while, his fighters falling in behind them. They were laying down covering fire back at Thars.

"Rojka, go, I can't survive that jump!" Melody shouted. They obviously weren't going to be using the ladder down.

"Trust me, Envoy," he told her.

Then his strong, saurian legs tensed. They had to be hundreds of feet above the desert.

"No, wait!"

Rojka leapt out into the hot void.

They hit something a second later with a metallic bang. Melody opened her eyes and saw that Rojka held on to the bay door of a Phantom dropship with one hand, and her waist with another. He pulled her into the vessel's open bay while it drew away from the mesa's rock wall.

Rojka's fighters were jumping out of the hole for the ground below, some of them finding purchase on the same dropship. Others fell toward the ground, hitting it in an explosion of dust and leaping into a run. More of his own soldiers awaited in a small assortment of ground vehicles a hundred meters from the mesa's base.

"Why the rescue?" Melody asked, shouting as air whipped at them in the bay.

"You know where the Demon Three are going," Rojka said, letting go of Melody. "We came to retrieve that information from you. Then I witnessed Thars renege on his word to protect you. And there is also the interesting query you raised about the Jiralhanae."

"You're still hunting Gray Team?" Melody shouted back, hyperaware that all Rojka would have to do was shove her out of the bay and she would plummet to the desert floor to a certain death. "Will you be trying to torture that out of me?"

"We now have little time. I suspect I already know where the Demon Three will be: Suraka. What I require now is more information about the Jiralhanae. Were you being honest, human? You were claiming to warn Thars of them. You said all Sangheili here on Rakoi are in danger. I have a duty to protect them. They are mine. These few vehicles are the last of what remains of *Discipline*, all that I have left to protect my people. Tell me more, Envoy. Why was there such a human facility hidden here in the desert? What is really happening?"

Melody looked back at the mesa through the open bay. Pain tore through her shoulder at the movement, making her gasp. The seared skin under her ripped and bloodied Diplomat Corps uniform was cauterized, but not ready for her to move. Rojka's leap had torn some of the charred skin apart, and now Melody could feel blood trickling down under her arm.

The mesa's entire rocky top jumped up slightly into the air, disturbing dust and sand. Then explosions ripped through the space above and the rock face, and it imploded down into a giant cavity—the entire facility swallowed up with a belch of fire. Rojka looked back, somewhat startled. "What was that?"

"I think that was Commander van Eekhout's last gift." She'd always dismissed rumors about ONI installations that would self-destruct if they couldn't confirm that the station's authorized keeper was alive. She'd wondered if she'd been playing for time inside a ticking bomb.

"Indeed. *That* will slow Thars down," Rojka said, approvingly. They watched the fireball over the desert slowly dissipate.

"You think he survived?" Melody asked.

"Doubtless." Rojka leaned out the open bay as smoke curled upward from what remained of the mesa. "Thars would not have wasted any time exploring the facility for clues. He is too impatient, he would have left the structure to get to his vehicles. He will be pursuing us shortly. I'll be sending a Banshee and a few of my fighters off in another direction to confuse him."

With a grunt of pain, Melody moved to stand beside Rojka and figure out the next decision she had to make. Rojka had been an ally. But ultimately, he was Sangheili. If ONI had requested the utmost secrecy from her, prohibiting her from telling the Spartans about the Sharquoi without authorization, what would happen if she told Rojka?

Nothing good.

Here, in the middle of battle, she needed to make a choice that might have far greater implications down the line. Could Rojka be trusted? How long had she really known the Sangheili kaidon and fleetmaster? Was it too late to even matter?

Rojka realized she'd moved. He snaked his head down to be level with hers.

"You told Thars he asked the wrong question," Rojka said. "What question should *I* be asking?"

Melody looked from the burning facility to Rojka's large, unblinking eyes.

"The question you should be asking is . . . what are the Sharquoi?"

CHAPTER 16

The attack on the Jiralhanae cruiser hovering over the edge of the city began from the ground. The Surakan militia had kept a dozen Kodiak mobile artillery tanks in a reserve underground. The large, heavily armored vehicles were easy to navigate through the streets, and quick to reposition themselves where needed. When ready to fire, they moored themselves to the ground by stabilizers to launch powerful anti-armor rounds at targets. The Kodiaks now opened up, hitting the cruiser's well-defended belly all at once.

But this was just a diversion. Jiralhanae patrolling gunships—a collection of Phantoms and the cruel machines the Brutes referred to in their native tongue as "grave-makers"—chattered loudly as they pressed toward the Kodiaks, opening up a mixed barrage of directed energy and searing hot metal projectiles.

As the positions of the Jiralhanae shifted, six Pelicans swung in from the Uldt desert, flying low and kicking up sand as they rose up toward the cruiser. While the Brute gunships engaged the mobile artillery and the anti-air squads protecting them, and firefights ripped the streets apart, the handful of Surakan aircraft began the first wave of attacks. They banked hard as they climbed along the enemy ship's hull, gaining altitude to jettison the highest nonnuclear payload Suraka had in its reserves directly onto the cruiser. The vessel's shields shimmered under the bombardment but continued to hold.

Wising up to this diversion, a number of Jiralhanae Phantoms disengaged from the street fighting in order to deal with the Surakan aircraft. They climbed swiftly into the sky, attempting to cut the Pelicans off.

The Pelicans at first dodged ferocious waves of enemy firepower from the cruiser's point defense system, which halted abruptly as the Jiralhanae's own gunships veered too close. The Pelicans took advantage of that to break free and launch back down toward the surface. The Phantoms would have likely pursued but were frozen by what they now saw in Carrow's sky.

From the east, three glowing fireballs fell from the sky, leaving long trails of smoke. From the west, eight Surakan merchant ships emerged from the cover of clouds and began pummeling the Jiralhanae cruiser with their own point defense weaponry. The concentrated firepower lit up the side of the cruiser.

"This is the tricky bit," General Kapoor said, observing the entire battle from the wall of screens in the underground operations center. General Grace sat nearby, arms folded, eyes fixed on the scene, and Ellis stood just behind her.

The Surakan ships were also a diversion—the three balls of light that plummeted toward Suraka from the east were the real attack. Several half-mined asteroids had been jockeyed into stable orbits between Carrow and its moon, and then brought dangerously close to the suborbital plane before being shoved out of orbit by the four remaining Surakan ships. They used an advanced coralling technique with hull-mounted magnetic grapplers and terraform vices, a procedure that had—up until just the last hour—only been untested theory. Now it was the real thing.

It was a huge gamble. If the Jiralhanae cruiser fled, the Surakans would be effectively bombing themselves. But if the encroaching ships could keep the Jiralhanae pinned in place just long enough, they would never be able to counter the three giant space rocks.

The front line of Surakan ships continued to lay into the cruiser. It responded, a devastating cloud of blinding white fire that quickly ripped four of the vessels apart. The survivors continued unabated, targeting the shields, and the Jiralhanae cruiser bore the brunt of a concentrated attack from the ships above and artillery below.

More focused on the threat the Surakan ships posed, the enemy ship didn't acknowledge the burning asteroids cutting through the atmosphere toward it until it was too late. The closest Surakan vessels pulled off to the side just at the last second as three chunks of metallic space rock struck the Jiralhanae cruiser in quick succession. The first one failed to penetrate, but megatons of kinetic energy had suddenly been released. Its shields flickered, already stressed by the incessant barrage dealt to it by the Surakan ships.

The second rock exploded against the cruiser and a brilliantly white fireball blossomed on the hull.

General Kapoor pumped a fist in the air. "There it goes!"

The third rock struck.

The Jiralhanae cruiser appeared to fold in midair, gushing blue and white flames and canting over as it dipped out over the far edge of the crater, a giant wounded beast trying to escape the harassing Surakan ships, which now descended and began nipping at it.

The Jiralhanae cruiser finally pitched to the ground just outside

Suraka and crumpled between the city and the rocky hills that led out into the Uldt. The rumbling sound followed for those underground a few long seconds after.

"Governor." General Grace turned in her chair to face Ellis. "I'm proud to say, we have taken back Suraka."

Aides and military personnel clapped and cheered, and even the tired generals took a moment to smile. Ellis stared at the screen, looking at different feeds of the Jiralhanae ship burning at the edge of its crater: the horrible monster had already dug its own grave. The cruiser had been hovering above the city for so long that it seemed odd to see the sky now clear.

Grace started giving commands. Dropships to be landed on the city's outskirts to release extra troops. Militia to be moved down toward the massive hole in the earth and flush out whatever remained. "I don't want a single Jiralhanae walking around the city. We start mopping them up, now."

Travis Pope put a hand on Ellis's arm. "This is a triumph, Governor."

She'd done it. She'd fought them back. Kept the city alive and steered her people through hell. Ellis numbly looked around the room. She should be celebrating, but her nerves felt too raw. The idea of not being focused on one emergency after another felt dangerous. She wasn't sure she knew how to switch off.

Sleep. She would have to go to sleep. But she didn't want to. She didn't want to dream. Didn't want to have to grieve her son's death. Didn't want to have to feel.

"Pope, ready a Pelican. I was interrupted the last time I tried to go out and put eyes on the situation. Now I want to see firsthand what we're going to need to do for reconstruction."

He nodded and left to make arrangements.

Lamar detached himself from the corner of the room. He

looked exhausted and more than a little sad. She wondered if he regretted his actions. Would there be an apology from him after he'd tried so hard to stop her?

It didn't really matter.

"Governor." He looked down at the raw patch of skin on her forearm. "You haven't slept in days. You need to get some rest. Trust me, I've been here before. It's going to hit you. You can't put it off forever."

"Rest is close at hand," she told him coolly.

He heard the rebuke in her tone, which she wasn't bothering to soften now. He nodded. "I understand. Is there anything else I can do for you?"

He had to suspect now that she would be asking for his resignation. Eventually. But he still stood in front of her, awaiting her orders. "I want teams sent down within the hour into that structure they dug up. We need to take whatever the Jiralhanae were willing to fight so hard for and get it ourselves before the UNSC arrives. Whatever it is, I'm willing to bet it will make all of this hell worth it. Drones go in first. Let's be very careful. Whatever they've got left down there is going to be cornered, and they'll fight like it."

"I'll arrange it now."

Of course, Ellis knew that he would. Even with everything that had happened between them, he would do what was necessary.

"I hope you'll let me make a secondary suggestion?" Lamar asked.

She gave a small sigh. Okay, here was his slack. "What?"

"We still have the perimeter mined. Let's leave it in place until we know what we're dealing with down there."

"I'll do more than that," Ellis said. "Grace says we still have a couple of rocks in geostationary orbit left with four of our ships.

We'll get them prepped to aim for the area if we discover that we need to. We may have our disagreements, Lamar, but I am an engineer. I always have backups."

Lamar looked relieved. "Thank you."

Hekabe could barely tell who or what he was anymore. The howling wind in his head that was the computational matrix of all the Sharquoi neural networks connected through a quantum entanglement array and then plugged into his own mind had scraped away anything and everything that he'd once been. It had then spread throughout something greater, and it was growing faster than he could control.

All this new neural tissue. It both empowered and energized him. But at the same time, it stretched him out so thinly across the Sharquoi.

How many of the creatures had he released?

A thousand?

No. Three thousand.

Hekabe had to stop and think, pull himself together, concentrate on finding the answer that might be slowly floating to him. How could he control so many Sharquoi at once?

He saw himself collapse to his knees, blood streaming from his nose.

You're still fighting, the echo under the wind said. *Let go.*

Hekabe finally did so.

The wind struck him harder now, searing through every neuron. Hekabe wept from the pain of it but did not fight anymore. He let the fury of it all wash right through him.

And then he stood. He wiped the blood from his nose and

looked at the terrified packs strung out midway on the bridge. They gaped at the multitude of Sharquoi placidly lined up and waiting to cross. Some of the Jiralhanae glanced overhead, nervous about the commotion above. It had died away only seconds ago with a violent thunder.

Those who remained with Hekabe would be well rewarded for their loyalty. Though clearly some of them had unwittingly been caught with their packs, Hekabe could see they still stood here because they regarded their leader with some measure of respect.

"Our enemies gather overhead," Hekabe said, using his own voice. So small, so weak. "We have sacrificed much to be to where we stand right now. But I promise you, it will be the beginning of a new age for our people—for the Jiralhanae. An age where we are finally restored to our proper might!"

The packs cheered, but it was halfhearted. They were uncertain of the Sharquoi or of the humans who had rocked the surface of the planet above.

Hekabe stepped forward toward his packs, beginning to cross the bridge. The massive Sharquoi lumbered forward around him as they responded to Hekabe's will.

He raised his voice with a shout of triumph. The masses of Sharquoi responded with their own deafening roar and began marching past the packs over the bridge, their movement drowning out the sound of burbling lava. The nervous Jiralhanae stared as the army of giants rumbled past them, headed up the spiraling ramps carved into the sides of the shaft that led to the surface.

Jai hit the Warthog's accelerator and swerved past a boulder in the dry riverbed. A blast of plasma struck the rock, shards of white fire raining and rattling into the vehicle. There'd been some human ships deorbiting in the distance, explosions in the clouds over Suraka. He hoped they were getting there in time, but it didn't look good from here.

"Adriana!" Jai yanked the wheel, zigging and zagging them around and up the side of the banks, the wheels kicking up dust before ducking the Warthog back down into the riverbed.

"Just a second."

A Banshee flipped around in the air and resumed its strafing run.

"Whichever Sangheili they're working for sure knows where we are now," Jai muttered.

"We're ten minutes out from Suraka," Mike told him. Something boomed up ahead, the shock waves felt in the Warthog. In the distance, a blanket of dirt and dust washed across the desert like an enormous wave.

"Earthquake?" Jai asked, as the plasma fire raked across the ground in front of them and he cut the wheel to avoid it.

"Nah. Something rang the bell," Mike replied.

Adriana ignored them and walked a stream of bullets along just in front of the Banshee, letting the pilot slam into them. The Banshee took a dozen in its side before it wobbled and dipped toward the ground, striking an outcropping with a spectacular explosion.

"We're out of ammo," Adriana said, pushing back from the Vulcan and retrieving her plasma rifle from the magnetic latch on her thigh.

Almost there, Jai thought, just as the streambed abruptly ended. The Warthog roared as they jumped out onto hard dirt and scrub. The distant skyline of the city rippled on the horizon, an oasis of greenery and steel rising up from the stark barren wasteland surrounding it.

"Somebody took out that cruiser," Mike said, impressed.

The remains of the Jiralhanae vessel burned off on the horizon. It had plowed into the desert on the other side of a small range of rocky hills that had blocked them from seeing its demise earlier.

"What do you think took it out?" Mike asked, as two more Banshees vectored in from their side, flying low against the ground. These new craft were different—they were a hybrid of familiar Covenant alloys and strange Brute iron, covered with extra cannons, and boasting a menacing rose of spikes welded to their fronts.

Out in the open, there was nowhere for Jai to hide. On the first run, the Banshees strafed a line of fire down the dirt and into the side of the Warthog. The vehicle bounced up onto its side, riding up on two wheels for a second as Jai fought to control it. Metal hissed, blackened from the strikes.

"These aren't Elites," Adriana said. "Must be Brutes."

The Warthog started shimmying badly as they slammed back down onto four wheels.

"I thought they were still in the city," Jai said.

"There's been a lot of activity over there—maybe they got pushed out?" Mike said. "Or maybe they're sentries, just making sure no one gets into the city."

Another strafing run. Jai veered hard to the left and accelerated straight at the Banshees, trying to shake them off. He pulled up the battle rifle the ONI agent had given him, preparing to give it to Mike, and jammed a boot against the wheel. To his back, he could hear Adriana's plasma rifle open up.

The Banshees kept closing in, pressing their attack. And then the one on their right started to smoke near its canard, losing altitude. "Focus on the left one," Jai said.

From out of nowhere, a rocket flew languidly along and struck the left Banshee before Adriana could redirect her fire. Pieces of it spiraled apart and then fell out of the air just as they passed underneath. Jai let the Warthog slow to a stop as the other smoking Banshee slammed down into the ground and detonated.

Mike looked back to where the rocket fire had originated. "Humans. Look. They're coming in weapons up," he observed.

A squad wearing green and brown camouflage and slightly modified marksman rifles ran full tilt toward the Spartans from a rocky outcropping they had apparently been stationed at. "Lower your weapons!" the woman in the lead shouted. "Now!"

"Let's stand down and be friendly," Jai said.

"It's going to slow things down," Adriana said, hopping down from the Warthog's rear bed.

Jai raised his hands and started walking forward. "I know. But these are local fighters, not UNSC. I want our first encounter to be on solid terms if we're going to be working side by side with them."

"Nice and slow!" the squad leader yelled. Jai didn't recognize the uniforms or the insignia, not even among the colonial ones he had known from six years ago. The Suraka military had certainly broken with the UNSC in look—scrappy, functional, with only a hint of structure. A rip-away name patch on the squad leader's left chest said "Carson."

The squad leader's eyes widened. "Holy shit, you're Spartans," she said.

"We're here to help," Jai said. "We'd like to speak with whoever is in charge."

The squad leader smiled. "You're too late to help." She jutted her chin back in the direction of the city. "We've already taken care of it. Shot them right out of the sky. We're in the process of cleaning up any Brutes in the outskirts. But it'll be an added bonus to have Spartans as well, so we'll take you in."

They're too sure of themselves, Jai thought. This was not the reaction of an army that had faced something like what the envoy and ONI agent had described back at Gila Station. It was clear that they had no clue about the danger that still lay beneath their city.

CHAPTER 17

Rojka 'Kasaan had gathered Melody—he now gave the human envoy the respect of using her name—and his closest remaining personnel in the bay of the Phantom dropship, which had become somewhat cramped with the newcomers. The three fighters who'd stayed behind at the facility reported that, as Daga predicted, Thars had left the human facility before it exploded. They'd been unable to lure him in the wrong direction, so Rojka ordered them to head back for Rak. Thars was tracking Rojka, and now he needed to make decisions about where to go, and what to do, next.

Daga sat across from Melody and his remaining fighters, warily watching the human. The fleetmaster's most trusted commander had never liked the envoy, now apparently even less so. She pushed a hand to her shoulder to slow the bleeding there, Rojka noticed. Enigmatically, she did not appear the least bit embarrassed about the dishonor of spilling her own blood on the Phantom's deck.

He decided to ignore it.

"You tell me that these creatures from Sangheili legend truly exist," Rojka said. "I traveled to High Charity many times before its demise, yet I never saw nor heard anything of this before. I find it hard to believe."

"It would not be the first time the San'Shyuum lied or kept secrets from your people," Melody said.

"That is true." Rojka scratched his mandibles and sighed.

Sharquoi. Rojka wasn't sure what to believe. Giant creatures that could rend one asunder with their bare hands, deployed and controlled in the thousands through some kind of neural network that the Jiralhanae had evidently discovered. The human claimed other Sangheili knew of these creatures, but there were never enough to be a significant concern . . . until now.

Could she be lying to me?

Yet the Jiralhanae had risked everything to get to the human city. The humans already had a hidden facility here on the planet. The pieces of the story fit well together.

"Even if everything you have just told me is true, I have only a handful of warriors at my command. I have no ships. I have nothing to offer. I have lost so much. You want me to sacrifice the one thing I have left: vengeance against the Demon Three."

"I have lost even more," Melody said firmly. Something in her voice caught Rojka's attention. He realized he knew so little about the envoy. The human had worked tirelessly to understand so much about him, but Rojka had never bothered to reciprocate. "I lost *everything* when the Covenant attacked Earth. I joined the refugees fleeing New Mombasa. I left and tried to rebuild everything in a refugee camp on Oban. There were too many of us displaced by the war, so we lived in plastic-lined shacks, huddled around makeshift fires at night, far displaced from civilization. My government was still reeling from thirty years of nonstop war—so many people without homes—and they didn't know what to do with us.

"There was so much suffering, so much death. Every night, I listened to one of my neighbor's children cough, until one day she stopped. I was so glad when I saw her at the mass burial fields later that day because I knew she wasn't in pain anymore. There wasn't enough medicine. Not enough food. You have lost so much, Rojka . . . that means you must know how I feel."

Rojka looked away from her. "I never participated in the attack on Earth. I was rebuilding ships, maintaining the fleets." And, he realized, she was trying to manipulate him. Words were her own weapons, he could see.

And she was a good warrior. A good envoy.

"I don't blame *you*, specifically," she replied. "But for years, every night, I would wake up in a cold sweat, listening for the sound of Covenant ships torching the ground and waiting for plasma fire to sweep me away. When *my* own demons appear in my nightmares, they look like Sangheili firing into crowds of civilians while we tried to run for safety. *My* demons look just like you, Rojka."

Rojka snarled under his breath, the words striking him as solidly as the jab of a spear. "Then why do you make such an effort for peace between our kind, if you think of my kind like this?"

"I'm here to build something new, something different, Rojka," she said. "I want a future. I want to look ahead, not behind. And I know you want to build something too. You came here to build a city; you risked much to come here and build something new as well."

"Like you, I had little choice. I was a refugee as well," Rojka said. He turned her attacks back on her. "When I learned that my family, that much of my bloodline, had been destroyed on Glyke, I took command of the fleet I was tasked to repair. I led what survivors I could here even as both your kind and mine ignored the treachery at Glyke."

He felt dishonor at first simply complying with the Arbiter's request to bury his rage and forget the life he had on Glyke for the sake of peace between their species. But then Rojka had seen a chance to found a new lineage on a new world—and, with him as Rak's kaidon, he might be able to finally make this dream a reality.

The envoy thought about that. "Then we are all in the same position, on this world. We are all survivors of war trying to start something new. And the Jiralhanae threaten both Suraka and Rak. If the Jiralhanae are able to use the Sharquoi to whatever ends they seek, we will lose everything. Everything on Rakoi. All the fighting between us will have been meaningless."

It was Rojka's turn to ponder. "It's not just this planet we might lose. No, the chieftain, Hekabe, will surely raise his sights higher than this dust world if he has the strength of the Forerunners behind him. He could attack both of our homeworlds if he is able to get his prize off the planet."

"That's my thinking as well. So we have to stop this from happening, however we can. No matter what demons either of us must face."

Rojka handed Melody a plasma pistol, amused at how large it looked in her hands. The last time she'd had one like that, she'd been shooting at him from behind the door. He suppressed his sudden anger at that past betrayal, then found some small measure of gallows humor in the strangeness of the battlefield. "Very well, Envoy. Let us fight this new threat together."

But I will watch you carefully, he thought. He had once believed that he could anticipate what she would do next, only to find her releasing the Demon Three and turning against him. This was a temporary alliance of convenience. Nothing more.

The envoy could use all the grand words and clever arguments at her disposal, but Rojka understood where she would ultimately put her true allegiance now more than ever.

He was, after all, one of the demons that haunted her nightmares.

Ellis pressed on toward the massive crater, picking her way across the rubble with a small team of milita surrounding her. They had their rifles slung, but still remained alert and wary. Ellis clambered up until she crested chunks of cement lining the outskirts and looked down into the district-sized basin the Jiralhanae had burned out of Carrow's surface. Several militia squads had already taken position at what was apparently the Forerunner structure's entrance, hundreds of meters away, at the far bottom. Warthogs and heavier machinery drove cautiously down the slope. Some of the Surakan ships had dropped all the way down to the surface, hovering near the crater's edge with their large hangar doors open in order to provide those working the area with easy access to supplies.

Behind her, in a medical tent, she could see the bodies lined up in silent rows, like mummies. She'd stopped by the rows on her way up, dozens of them. *This was the price*, she had told herself. This was why victory wasn't some cartoonish celebration and cheering. Each human life meant a loss of potential. Whatever they could have been, created, or invented, was forever lost. The lives they would have influenced would remain forever untouched.

Their families would feel the sudden emptiness that she now experienced.

Ellis swallowed. Jeff had died out here at the hands of the Jiralhanae. That thought had come and gone over the long hours, each time returning with more grief. She wasn't here among the rows of dead, thanks to people on the ground at the excavation who had fought, like her son. Jeff had given his life, and now she wanted to see the reason why.

There was a Jiralhanae body lying under debris nearby. Ellis stared at it. There were lots of the aliens still slumped and scattered all over the city. The Surakans hadn't bodybagged any of them. So what to do? Bury them? Or heap them into piles and just burn them?

Were their packs going to mourn their dead as well, on some distant world, like Ellis mourned her own son? Had some of these Jiralhanae been full of potential as well, just like Jeff?

This thinking wouldn't do anything useful, she decided, so she abandoned it.

Her hands shook now. She could barely hold them still as she applied another stimulant patch. How many more of these things could she endure? Could too many kill you? She needed to take stock on how many patches she'd used and at what intervals. It was strange; usually she'd be so precise about balancing something like this. But that care had been lost in the madness.

But as the new patch sharpened her senses again, she reminded herself that others had paid a far greater price. What were some shakes compared to that?

Pope scrambled up next to her. "Governor, General Grace wants to talk to you."

The general and her staff were down at the bottom of the

rubble. Ellis followed Pope over the lip of the basin and back down to the street, where things began to look more normal.

"Is the structure cleared yet?" Ellis asked.

The general's staff parted to let her through to Grace. "We're almost ready to begin. But I thought you'd like to know that a patrol heading out to secure the cruiser crash site picked up three Spartans heading into the city. They claim they want to help."

"Spartans?" Ellis frowned. "Have the UNSC arrived? Did something change?"

"There are no ships in orbit. That we know about, at least." General Grace cocked her head.

"Tell the squad to bring the Spartans in for questioning. Once they're detained, we can inform them that the UNSC has no jurisdiction here. We have the situation under control and we don't need their help against the Jiralhanae. But I do want them questioned. I want to know what they're doing here and where the hell they came from."

General Grace bit her lip. "Governor, you want me to *detain* Spartans?"

"Yes."

"That could be . . . difficult if they decide they don't want to cooperate."

Ellis looked around. "If they decide that, then we'll know whether they're really here to help or cause trouble. Make it happen."

General Grace nodded. Ellis kept walking along the street with Pope following a few paces behind. "Travis?"

"Yes, Governor?"

"We're going to have to start figuring out where people are going to sleep since so many homes were destroyed. People who had holed up until this was done will be coming out of the cracks. We'll need to deploy resources to help them, escort them to Sector 31 if there's space. We can't have people living in the streets."

As they started figuring out the details, she smiled at Pope. "It's nice to be thinking about zoning and planning committees again. Building things."

Travis glanced over at the rubble. "Well, it'll take a while before we're back to normal."

"But we're headed in the right direction," she said. "We're moving forward again."

And for the moment, even through her pain at losing her son, something actually felt good.

Jai watched, incredulous, as the Surakan squad came into the bunker room with weapons up and tight to their shoulders.

That's saying a lot, he thought.

"I'm afraid we're going to have to ask you to fully disarm," the squad leader said. "Sorry, orders. Then I've also been asked to read you a formal statement regarding the UNSC and Surakan jurisdiction."

"You have got to be kidding me," Adriana said slowly. Jai saw her hand twitch toward the rifle the ONI agent had given them.

Jai looked at the wide eyes and sweat on the squad leader's upper lip. "We're here to help," he said. "You can stand down."

"Sir, we're to disarm you and you're to remain here," she repeated.

"There's a greater threat we need to warn your superiors about," Jai said. "Ma'am, if you'd just—"

"I'm not authorized to talk to you about any activities outside my field of authority. You'll have to take that up with my superiors when they arrive. I've been ordered to hold you here till then. *Please* disarm. Now."

This squad leader knew that the Spartans could run right through them if they wanted to, and that there wasn't too much the unarmored Surakans could do about it.

"Let's just see where this goes for now," Jai said to Adriana and Mike via helmet-to-helmet communications.

Adriana reluctantly set the battle rifle down on a nearby table. The squad leader visibly relaxed. It was the symbol of the gesture: they both knew that the Spartans were still just as dangerous.

Jai raised his hands to shoulder level, placating the squad. "Okay, as a show of good faith, we're disarming, even though it's about to get really messy. You may want to put a rush request on your supervisors' getting here, so that it's not too late."

"Spartans, as representatives of the UNSC, I'm ordered to inform you that your presence here is illegal and unrequested. I'm to ask you how you arrived, what your mission is, and other pertinent queries about your presence here. Your answers will be recorded and put on file."

"So you're about to be attacked by something that could wipe humanity off this planet permanently, but yes, we will stand here disarmed," Adriana grumbled.

"We can still help," Jai said. "They want to ask questions, while we need to pass on what we know to the highest authority possible."

The squad leader rubbed her forehead, clearly stressed. "Look, there's what I've been ordered to do and what you *need* to do. I'm not an idiot. I'm going to try to find some overlap here. If you have intel that's important, I'll want someone to debrief you even if everyone upstairs would rather that you just sat still here. I'm going to try to hunt down someone who can get the gears moving."

"How long are we talking about?"

"Give me twenty minutes," she said. "I promise, I'm not going to leave you blowing in the wind. We Surakans may have struck out on our own here, but we fought side by side against the Covenant. I've seen Spartans in action firsthand. Personally, if you're worried about something, *I'm* worried about it. Give me some time to get things moving though, okay?"

"Thank you." Jai nodded. He checked the name patch again. "Carson, what's your rank? What do I call you?"

"Sergeant Rae Carson, sir." She moved forward and shook his hand.

As the squad left and locked the door, two of them posting up outside, Adriana laughed. "Different military, same shit. Paperwork and hierarchies to get things done."

"You saw the city. It's a large ship to steer," Jai said. "They're moving as quickly as they can without causing themselves trouble."

"But will it be quick enough?" Mike asked. "You know we can still leave at any moment, right?"

Jai walked over to a slit in the bunker and looked at the city's skyline.

"We have to hope this'll be quick," he told them. "Give them a chance. I want to play aboveboard, after all that's gone down. The last thing we need is to start another war between Earth and the colonies just because we picked the wrong planet to land on after a six-year nap. We're going to need their support anyway, when it comes to it. And I have a feeling they'll be forcing weapons into our hands before long. This hasn't even gotten started yet."

CHAPTER 18

D *id the ground just tremble?* Ellis stopped looking over her notes from where she sat at a desk in a makeshift control center, hastily set up in the bombed-out first floor of a bank. Was that her imagination? Maybe it *was* time she got some rest.

But there it was again. A loud thump resounded from the crater.

"What was that?" she shouted.

Outside the bank, militia ran for the edge of the crater only a few dozen meters away, as shouted orders punctuated the air. It looked like a hive of camouflage ants had been kicked as Surakan soldiers boiled out of tents. So far, only drones had actually been sent into the hole at the center of the crater, but they were lost. They had ceased transmission shortly after descending the shaft. The Surakans had been prepping a recon team per Ellis's orders just moments earlier.

Whump. The noise and vibration came again. From her seat, Ellis could see the heavy-caliber guns placed on struts up along the rim of the crater all firing at once. The deadly chatter of weapons fire didn't stop, filling the air with a constant *braaap*.

Ellis moved out from the bank, into the street. The sound of the guns were drowned by several Pelicans that appeared overhead, firing missiles down into the crater. The street shivered again. A piece of building facade cracked and fell off rebar, slumping down to the ground in a cloud of gray dust.

Travis Pope ran up to her. "We need to get out of here!" he shouted.

"What's going on?" Ellis asked.

"They're pouring out of the crater." Travis grabbed her arm. "We need to get to safety. Now!"

Ellis shrugged his grip off, ignoring his urgency, and crossed the street to the rubble pile.

"Governor!"

She quickly crawled up toward the nearest emplacement. Three militia surrounded a fourth with another heavy machine gun on a tripod, shooting down into the crater. Hot casings showered the emplacement. One of them noticed her approaching. "Hey! No civilians. Get back to a bunker!"

Keeping low, Ellis continued to scramble her way into place just behind a large chunk of debris that shielded the gun. As she got there, the gunner finished the belt. They changed the ammunition as one of them shifted over to her.

"Get. Back. Down," he yelled at her. "You too!"

Travis had crawled up on his hands and knees, following Ellis. "That's the governor!" he shouted. "Sergeant, that's the *governor* you're talking to."

The sergeant swore and pulled his helmet off. He jammed it down on Ellis's head. "What are you doing here, Governor?"

"I have to see what's going on." The machine gun blasted away, the rest of the firing team ignoring the shouting as they continued shooting downslope. "What are the Jiralhanae doing?"

"Those ain't Jiralhanae!" the gunner spat, pausing as they fed yet another belt into the gun.

Ellis crawled up to the edge of the rock and peered over.

Hundreds of gray monsters were swarming out from the excavated structure's entrance at the center of the crater. They looked like cyclopean nightmares, enormous bipeds with muscles bunched and corded—something from ancient mythology that had suddenly become very real. Their elephant-thick legs thudded as they moved, giants above the humans, destroying everything within arm's range, but they operated in an eerie synchrony. Like bees escaping a hive, clusters of them flew toward threats and crashed into them. Militia Warthogs roared around the crater, trying to engage the sudden menace, their machine guns kicking as they fired away.

"They're too big!" Ellis said, her voice drowned out by the sound of the firefight that had erupted. She'd never seen these creatures before. One of them plowed into a Warthog, punching the vehicle with its clawed wrists and flipping it end over end.

The monster half turned upslope, revealing what looked like a single eye fixed and staring in her direction. But it wasn't an eye—it was fleshy, a part of the creature's bony forehead.

A surface-to-surface missile struck the monster, fired from another nearby Warthog. The explosion shook the ground, and the familiar *thump* reached Ellis. The fireball faded away and the massive creature still stood there on the blackened ground, unmoved. The beast struggled forward, skin burning. It didn't seem to feel any pain as it reached for the Warthog skidding past and yanked a soldier from the vehicle.

Ellis gasped as it ripped the man apart. Blood sprayed through the air as limbs smacked to the ground.

Another missile struck, and this time the beast toppled forward.

But more creatures were streaming out of the ground to replace it. Hundreds now. They overwhelmed the few Warthogs left in the crater like a gray wave of raw power and violence, pummeling and crushing them almost as though the many forms were a single creature.

"They're breaking through!" the sergeant shouted, and pointed.

The creatures had now jumped over the far ridge, destroying gun emplacements as they pounded and flowed their way through.

"They're going for the ships!" Ellis yelled. In the distance, the creatures were striking militia deployed around one of the larger Surakan vessels. One of them vaulted over the defenders and bolted inside the ship's main hangar bay. Ellis didn't even want to imagine what it would do to anyone inside the cramped quarters there.

"Fall back to rally point bravo!" The sergeant grabbed Ellis by the wrist and pulled her down the rubble. Just a hundred meters north along the rim, a wall of gray surged its way up and over the slope, barreling through a shower of gunfire and slamming into the gunner.

Ellis stumbled and hopped down the debris onto the road.

"What the hell are those things, Governor?" the sergeant asked.

"I don't know." Several Warthogs screeched to a halt on the road nearby and more militia jumped out. They ran up the rubble to the crest, weapons ready. Then artillery started booming from down the streets—heavy machine guns and munitions launched from within the city. Small, fiery mushroom clouds bloomed over the crater.

"Governor, we have to get to safety," Travis said.

"No," Ellis said, dazed. "*No! W-we won.*"

"Governor!"

Three of the creatures smashed over the ridge, plowing through the militia there.

It wasn't supposed to be like this, she thought numbly, staring at the blood. Screaming came from everywhere. Bullets pinged off the rubble pile as Travis yanked her across the street. Personnel streamed out of the command center and ran down the road away from the sound of weapon fire, but then stopped as more of the hulking creatures thudded down out of the crater and pursued them into the street.

"Governor," the sergeant said. "We've been cut off from our rally points." A squad now surrounded her like bodyguards. There was nowhere to go. Travis had picked up a rifle from somewhere, dropping everything else in the process. Important papers. Rebuilding plans. Blueprints. *Our future.*

She took the helmet the sergeant had jammed onto her head earlier and gave it to him.

"No, Governor," he protested, but she silently pushed him back and stared at the horrors around her.

These massive, towering creatures clambering through the streets, openly and with incredible speed, actively seeking out their Surakan prey. A cluster of them moved in sync to attack a Kodiak artillery tank at the nearest intersection. Despite militia firing at them nearly point-blank, the monsters moved unimpeded—almost completely oblivious to the attack—and slammed their fists into the tank's cannon until it bent and the vehicle exploded.

What the hell had the Jiralhanae found down there? Ellis squinted as she watched the destruction move down either side of the street, the gray monsters annihilating anything in their way. Fear choked the back of her throat, but she forced it down. Suraka needed her. The fight wasn't finished yet. She might be about to die, but her mind still kicked into overdrive. *Everything is connected*, she thought to herself. *Examine what you know.*

The creatures were too coordinated to be individuals, so there had to be something driving their activity, as if they were part of a greater mind. *They must be related to the Forerunners. And they must be under the control of something.*

Or someone . . .

Up on the lip of the crater, Ellis noticed the first living Jiralhanae she'd seen since the start of the attack. Large and proud, he wore the armor she'd previously seen designated for their chieftains. Shards of strange metal gleamed from his skull as he climbed up onto the debris and looked out over the chaos, intently focused on the creatures.

She understood, almost instantly, that this was why the Jiralhanae had come here. This was what they had been after the entire time. This one was somehow orchestrating all of the chaos. She pointed to the squad. "Shoot that Brute. *Now!*"

But there was no one who could even try. The chieftain was too far away, and the surviving militia in the streets had to focus on the massive gray creatures. One of the beasts, fists dripping with fresh blood, finished its carnage with a stomp of its trunk-like leg and turned toward the small group of militia around Ellis at the base of the building.

It charged, and the entire squad opened fire as it came at them.

Ordnance smacked into thick flesh and muscle. Purple blood dripped from ragged holes, yet the creature continued inexorably forward.

The squad rushed it in an effort to protect the governor. It batted them aside as if they were a bare nuisance. Bodies hit the nearby buildings with a red smack and didn't move again.

Travis ran forward and fired his rifle directly at the thing's head. In response, it speared him, the movement a snakelike, rapid snap, with the two jagged spikes on its right wrist. Travis writhed and blood gushed out of his mouth as the creature lifted him into the air as if to examine his body.

Ellis screamed in a mix of rage and fear. She'd known she was going to die as the whirlwind of carnage took over everything around her, but now it hit her like a wall of anger.

I stopped all this! This isn't supposed to be happening!

A rocket streaked through the street and hit the creature's chest. The blast threw Ellis back, and she slammed her head against the asphalt.

Dizzied, she sat up as the creature's enormous charred body hit the ground.

A smoking helmet bounced at Ellis and stopped at her feet. She picked it up and stared at it.

A Pelican flared out hard, spinning in the air just above the road and striking brick facade with its rear fins. The entrance ramp lowered into the road and her vice-governor stood on the edge of it. He wore an armored vest and had a rocket launcher over one shoulder. "Governor!"

Ellis stared at him.

"Get in!"

She launched like a sprinter off the line. The moment her feet hit the ramp, the pilot opened the throttles. The Pelican clawed into the air as Lamar fired another rocket, knocking an approaching creature back down to the road.

As they spiraled up into the air and over the crater, Ellis could see hundreds more gray forms spilling over the crater's edge, flooding the streets, and expanding out into the city. From this height, they looked like a murky and vicious disease invading a body.

"What's that?" Lamar asked, pointing to the charred helmet in her hands.

Ellis looked down, not realizing she still had it in her hands. The edges burned at her palms. She dropped the helmet, startled.

"Pope," she said. "That was Pope."

And a sergeant she didn't know the name of. And his team. And all those other soldiers who had died in the last ten minutes for Suraka.

As well as everyone else that was about to die now.

✺

Grit and sand smacked the Phantom as the Sangheili pilot dropped out of high speed to swing low to the ground, clipping its flight and landing abruptly. Melody winced in pain, the shaking jarring her injured shoulder. She kept a hand up to it. None of the Sangheili had offered her so much as a bandage; they'd just tried not to look at the blood that had seeped through her fingers, likely out of shame for her.

Rojka stood behind the pilot. Something had their attention.

"The humans managed to destroy the Jiralhanae cruiser over the city," Rojka said, sounding mildly surprised.

Melody, still pressing a palm against her shoulder, stood up and walked past Sangheili fighters to the armored cockpit. She looked at a curved display that perfectly recapitulated the lay of the land, presumably through hull-mounted sensors.

The remains of the Jiralhanae cruiser were buried in the desert to their left. And Suraka, finally, was directly ahead. The metal and glass skyline shimmered like a mirage in the heat that lay between the distant city and the Phantom. Rojka had made this team travel far out into the desert instead of making a straight beeline for Suraka, part of a set of maneuvers—including splitting his warriors into three groups—to keep Thars from tracking them. One group took to the sky in the Phantom, the other two remained on foot, dividing the ground craft between them. Rojka had since lost contact with three warriors who had reported Thars's survival at Gila Station, though he wondered if they were still traveling to Rale or had possibly taken a route closer to Suraka.

Delays in evading trackers aside, things were about to come to a head. The skyline was in their sights now. They were only a minute or two out, and now they had to be cautious about human attacks.

"You know, they may not need our help after all," Melody mused, spirits lifting slightly at the sight of the burning Jiralhanae vessel.

The Sangheili pilot snorted dismissively and pointed toward the far side of the city. A Surakan ship wobbled above the skyline, smoke trailing from one of its engines. It appeared to be struggling to rise above the city.

"There is trouble yet," he said.

As they watched, the ship's hull burst gouts of flame and then exploded.

Amid the falling debris was a tiny, gray form, which struck a building in a shower of glass.

Sharquoi, Melody knew.

"They do need our help. The attack you warned us of has already begun," Rojka said somberly. He turned around to his Sangheili. "Prepare to disembark. We move on the ground from here."

The pilot dropped the Phantom low to the ground, spinning it about. Daga pointed a fist and the rear ramp dropped open, unloading the Sangheili in two columns.

Rojka glanced back at Melody. "There are two camouflaged human scouts up ahead who have set a trap for us. I suggest you walk forward alone, Envoy, and gain us safe passage without interruption from any . . . *miscommunication*."

Melody followed the Sangheili out the back of the Phantom and onto the hot, dry sand. "We may be too late," she told Rojka, as she looked at the vast crater to her distant right and saw plumes of smoke rising from it.

"In that case, perhaps we will still receive that honorable death we were both cheated of."

Sergeant Carson and her squad had hustled Gray Team across Suraka's sandy boundaries to a new bunker on the city's fringe. More armed militia waited for them by the sandbagged entrance to escort Jai and his team inside.

Jai looked around the control and operations room deep inside the centimeters of concrete and at the dozen or so nervous-looking civilians silhouetted by the glow of displays.

"This is taking far too long. We're running out of time," Adriana noted with distaste.

Jai looked at the pale faces and muttered conferences happening all around them. "They're taking us very, very seriously now. Something's changed."

A tall woman covered in gray dust and soot waited in the bunker room. She pointed at the Spartans. Another man with civilian clothes and an armored vest stood just behind her. Everyone in the room stepped out of their way as she crossed the room.

They both reek of "in charge," Jai thought.

"Tell me everything you know," the woman snapped in Gray Team's direction.

"I'm sorry, ma'am, who am I talking to?" Jai asked, unwilling to give her control of the conversation at the start.

"I'm Governor Ellis Gass. This is my vice-governor, Lamar Edwards. The citizens of Suraka are trapped here, unable to get off this planet, while we face some new threat that I believe you know something about. So tell us what you know."

Jai saw the vice-governor's face twitch as she said that: something was off. But he was forced to pay attention to the governor, who had now moved right up to his visor.

"What the hell did the Jiralhanae release?" Governor Gass demanded. "And don't give me any ONI 'official secrets' bullshit. You're here for a reason. What is it? We don't have time for red tape. We're far past that point. This is *my city* we're talking about! Our people are dying! *My* people are dying!"

The pain in the governor's last words was obvious. Everyone in the control room stared at the confrontation, work forgotten. The strain of battle weighed heavy on Ellis, Jai thought. He understood the pain in the governor's eyes.

"We came to help," Jai told her softly.

Governor Gass shook her head. "To *help*? Is that it? Spartans can do a lot of things, maybe even take on *one* of those monsters out there. But that's not what we need right now. We need *intel*, we need to know how to stop them. So you need to tell us *everything* you know. Then we'll all form a plan together."

"They're called the Sharquoi—" Jai started to say.

The vice-governor had stepped back in the meantime to listen to something being whispered to him. Now he interrupted: "Madam Governor," he said formally. "There are Sangheili at the city's edge asking to lend assistance, along with the Unified Earth Government envoy, Melody Azikiwe."

The governor frowned. "Oh, the one who was supposed to broker that new era of peace between us and the Sangheili?" Bitterness laced her words.

She raised a finger as the vice-governor looked about to say something. Jai took the halted moment to jump in. "You'll want the envoy," he said. "She knows more about the Sharquoi than anyone else."

Governor Gass turned. "She *knew* about this?" The venom in her voice all but dripped.

If there'd been time for sympathy, Jai would have offered it. Instead he said, "It's complicated. And we can argue about it later. We don't have time to fix what happened in the past. Like you said, people are dying. We need to face what is *about* to happen."

"He's right, ma'am," the vice-governor said to her. "We need all the information we can get. Now is not the time for us to assess the failures they made in the past."

The governor took a deep breath. She seemed to take the vice-governor seriously, though it did not appear easy for her. Something had passed between them with just a look.

"Fine. Okay then," Governor Gass said, her voice dripping with sarcasm. "Let's all find out what secrets the Office of Naval Intelligence has been hiding from us here on our own world. Sure, bring the envoy and her friends right on in! In the meantime, Spartan, tell me what *you* know and how you can help us."

"Ma'am, I am not an expert: we just learned about them a few hours ago ourselves," Jai told her. "But my team has a plan we've been working on since we were briefed about the threat."

Governor Gass leaned forward, her eyes glittering with glassy fatigue in the emergency lighting. "Go on," she said.

"It's simple," Adriana said. "Get us close enough so that I can take out the Jiralhanae leader. Those creatures on their own aren't much more than feral animals. They're augmented by their numbers and cohesion."

"But they're being controlled through a Forerunner device that the Jiralhanae chieftain possesses," Mike added.

"Kill the Brute, you kill the threat," Adriana said softly but firmly.

The governor thought about it for a moment. "Well, you'll certainly get no argument from me about the directness of this. And I've seen the chieftain. With my own eyes."

She swallowed. Jai noticed a small tremor in her hands.

"Give me some time to set it up with my generals," Governor Ellis finally said. "I think we can get you close."

"Your vice-governor mentioned there were Sangheili with the envoy?" Jai asked.

"Yes. Is that going to be a problem?"

Jai opened his mouth to respond, then realized the words weren't coming. Finally he said, "If the envoy says they can help, I believe we can trust her."

The governor turned to face Adriana. "Spartan?"

"Ma'am?"

"Don't miss."

"I won't."

Hekabe stood in the late afternoon sun of the desert world, enjoying the heat on his face.

He also moved through the cool shadows of a stairwell, hunting a terrified human warrior.

He perched on the edge of one of the pitiful human buildings, looking out over the crater and back at himself—the Jiralhanae chieftain standing on a boulder. From the distance, he could barely make out the metallic contours of the Forerunner device sticking out from his skull in random, jarring directions, shining in the sun.

Hekabe was everywhere.

He forced his way awkwardly into the bellies of a handful of human ships, the Sharquoi he controlled leading Jiralhanae from his war packs as they boarded the alien vessels. The humans had surprised him with these ships. He had thought them defeated in orbit, but they had actually just run away—behavior typical of their kind.

The Jiralhanae followed behind the vicious giants as they destroyed the human defenders on each craft, allowing them to storm their way onto the command bridges and take control. So now he had mobility.

Hekabe laughed at the irony, and the laugh came from thousands of alien throats.

Anexus walked up toward him. "My Chieftain." He stank of utter obedience and total subservience. *It smells sweet on the air*, Hekabe thought.

"Come."

Hekabe started walking. Multiple Sharquoi fell into step beside him, like protective walls towering on all sides. He felt invincible.

"It is an honor guard the likes of which even the Prophets never had the courage to summon," Anexus proclaimed, glancing around nervously.

Hekabe ignored Anexus. Something odd had occurred to distract him. A Sharquoi with a broken leg, head half dashed in from a human explosion, roared in pain as it pulled itself down the road away from the crater. There was sullen determination in its movements as it tried to crawl the span of a city block toward Hekabe's original form.

"That one is not a part of me," Hekabe told Anexus. "Interesting. I cannot see into its mind. The implants in its skull must have been damaged."

A long smear of purple blood trailed the road behind the wounded Sharquoi.

Hekabe made a circle around the persistent damaged remnant with the five Sharquoi that he now kept around him as his personal guard. The dying creature looked around, what remained of its forehead thrumming as it attempted to echolocate and build a picture of its surroundings. *This is a Sharquoi, as they were before the Forerunners.* It bleated something that Hekabe vaguely understood. *It just wants to run. To be free of pain. To be free.*

That would not do.

Hekabe tightened the fist of the Sharquoi around the fallen one and unleashed them with his thought. They moved deliberately toward their injured brother and started to kick it as it held its clawed fists up, begging for mercy. Anexus watched as they stomped the creature until the head tore free and rolled across the ground.

The decapitated body of the Sharquoi stopped quivering.

Hekabe focused his attention on five ships as they took off. They wobbled for a moment as they rose, likely controlled by Jiralhanae barely able to adapt to human controls. After a moment, they corrected their ascent and flew out north over the desert. They would trace search patterns across the wasteland until they found the Sangheili ships that had managed to survive the fight in orbit. Then they would disgorge Sharquoi and kill them all.

Anexus watched them depart. "We should send word to our fellow Jiralhanae clans. We could even call the Banished to us. Atriox would send us cruisers to transport these Sharquoi back to our homeworld. We will be safe forever. Just as we planned. The Jiralhanae will no longer suffer when all see our new weapon."

"No." Hekabe looked out from Sharquoi senses spread throughout the city, seeing humans moving to aim missiles down at the crater from the top of a building. He burst out at them, shouldering through the stairwell that he barely fit in, smashing walls apart to break free, and they screamed and scattered before his Sharquoi frame. He impaled them on his claws and threw each of them down to the street, bellowing from the rooftop in victory. "We will truly make certain we are safe from our enemies forever, but we will do it on our own. We do not need the other Jiralhanae, and we do not need the Banished. All that we need is already here."

The wind in his mind had hinted at its power before, but it became more and more clear to Hekabe as the Jiralhanae-controlled human ships—filled with Sharquoi in their hangar bays—moved farther away from the city. The Forerunner device that had embedded itself into his skull had more reach than he had even imagined. It could operate on far more than just a world. It could reach light-years across into other distant places. The only constraint was the strength of his own mind.

"Chieftain, we will need a carrier large enough to transport the Sharquoi," Anexus insisted.

"We will not cower and beg for assistance!" Hekabe shouted at him. "We will not hole up on our own worlds and wait to take abuse! Instead, we shall seize what we have here and go to our enemies. We will strike them down on their own worlds. We will reduce *them* to nothing but ghosts and shadows!"

"And how will we go to them?" Anexus asked, frustration rolling off him. "We have only a handful of weak human ships."

Hekabe pointed west. "There are Sangheili on the ground repairing their cruisers even as we speak, thinking that they will take us by surprise. They are sorely mistaken. The Sangheili cruisers will be ours soon enough. Our strength will prevail!"

"But what if they're not repaired in time? What if—"

Anexus screamed as two of the Sharquoi nearby unceremoniously grabbed each of his arms and pulled. The limbs tore free like petals from a flower, his flesh ripping and joints popping free as the Sharquoi casually flung the torn appendages aside. Anexus dropped to his knees in front of Hekabe.

"Mercy!" he frothed, blood pouring from his destroyed shoulders.

"There is no more mercy," Hekabe said as the Sharquoi standing directly behind Anexus picked him up. "If the Sangheili vessels fail me, then there will be human ships that arrive here soon. I will take what is due to me, one way or another."

The Sharquoi simply crumpled Anexus in its giant fists, like balling up a piece of trash. Hekabe could feel ribs shatter and poke at his palms.

Everything here would be his. *Everything.* And once he sat on the ruins of all this planet had to offer, other worlds would feel his wrath.

Safety and respect were no longer his goal. Dominion was what he now sought. There would be a true Jiralhanae empire to rival even the Covenant. An empire ruled by him. And Hekabe solemnly promised himself it would be unlike anything the stars had ever seen.

CHAPTER 19

A Pelican flanked by two smaller Sparrowhawk gunships cut through the air just above Suraka's skyline, banking hard as they approached the fighting. Surakan militia had fallen back almost eight blocks from the crater. The gray tide of Sharquoi was implacable, plowing into the city's defenders and leaving only a trail of carnage behind.

"It's a damn massacre," Sergeant Carson said, looking out over the pilot's shoulder.

Jai agreed. But in order for them to have a chance at stopping this, they needed the Sharquoi and their Jiralhanae leader—the chieftain by the name of Hekabe—preoccupied. So rather than retreat, the militia kept on fighting.

"Where to?" Jai asked Adriana as the Pelican looped around again, avoiding stray fire that came from the battle raging above the desert.

"We won't be able to stay up in the middle of this for much longer!" the pilot shouted.

Suraka had thrown almost every flying vehicle they could get into the air in order to harass and distract the vessels that the Sharquoi had taken. Melody believed that Hekabe's strategy, now that his cruiser had been destroyed, would be to secure vessels in order to carry the Sharquoi off-world.

Transmissions from the bridges of these ships confirmed that Jiralhanae now had control and were moving the stolen vessels deeper into the desert, for reasons yet to be made clear.

Surakan aircraft had assaulted them en masse: Pelican gunships, Sparrowhawks, and even some effectively armed Nightingales had initiated the strike. But the aircraft over the crater, completely outmatched in firepower, were being shot down by the Surakans' own point defense weapons on the Brute-controlled ships. The distraction wasn't going to last too long.

The Surakans were paying a high price to get this team into position.

Jai glanced out of the Pelican's rear bay to the left to see a Phantom keeping pace with them and in perfect formation, lazily swooping and twisting to match the human pilot's evasive maneuvers, providing protection for this effort.

How strange it feels to be flying into combat with an old enemy beside us, Jai thought.

Rojka 'Kasaan had not said a word when he'd joined them in the staging area with the envoy by his side. Although everyone present seemed at ease with a Sangheili holding conversation in the same room as them, Jai found it rather challenging. It must have been tough for the rest of Gray Team too. Most of the people here had grown accustomed to human–Sangheili relations since the war had ended six years ago, despite all that was happening on Carrow. But for Gray Team, the war had ended only hours earlier. It was difficult to keep instincts trained for years in check, instincts that told him to kill and protect at the sight of the enemy.

Rojka, for his part, did not seem to mind, though he was virtually impossible to read, especially in a neutral posture—something

Jai had rarely ever seen from an Elite. The Sangheili had just stood mostly silent as the envoy explained they were here to help take out Hekabe.

But there was still the matter of Glyke. Which pretty much guaranteed that no matter what he looked like, this Sangheili was *anything* but neutral.

"The technology used to control the Sharquoi is tied to a single individual—we all know that much," Melody had told the Surakan generals, boosting their plan. "So we target the chieftain, Hekabe. That's the best chance we have to slow or stop this mess."

The Sangheili with Rojka had been visibly uncomfortable. Jai and the rest of Gray Team remained on the other side of the governor and envoy, giving the Sangheili their space. They'd pooled their arsenals to start this last-ditch attack, a unified strategy that had to work if there was any chance to stop Hekabe. The Spartans would take a Pelican, and the Sangheili would take a Phantom.

War, Jai thought, *makes for strange, shifting allegiances.*

"There," Adriana now said, pointing to the top of a building. "Our line of sight is good there."

"That's right on the line," the pilot warned. "We don't know how long we can hold them back before they overrun us."

"If what Azikiwe says is true, all I need is one good shot and this is over," Adriana said. She made her way to the side compartment of the Pelican's rear bay and retrieved the SRS99-S5 AM sniper rifle provided the Surakans. "And I'm far, far better than just a good shot."

"That's right over the edge of that rifle's range," Sergeant Carson observed.

"One good shot," Adriana repeated slowly. "Let's go. We're wasting time that no one has to spend."

"Set us down," Jai said to the pilot, grabbing an M392 designated marksman rifle from the wall mount and fixing it magnetically to his back.

The Pelican swooped around and dropped down onto the roof. Mike, Jai, and Adriana leapt out, followed by Sergeant Carson and her squad.

"If we're overrun," Jai shouted inside the bird, "don't try to come back for us! We'll make our own way out!"

"Yes, sir!" the pilot called back.

The Pelican roared into the air. As it spiraled away, a large bolt of plasma fire from the crater struck its tail, immediately killing one of its engines. It spun around in an uncontrolled dive and crashed between buildings several blocks away.

Carson's squad stared at the dying Pelican, but Jai needed them to focus. "Get into the stairwells!" he ordered. "Make sure nothing gets up to the roof!"

The squad scuttled into motion, Carson leading the way. "We'll mine the stairs," she shouted back at them, ducking through the door. "It'll slow them down even if they do get past the line."

The three Spartans stood together for a moment of silence, then turned to look at the Phantom circling the building around them like a buzzard.

"You know, if the Sangheili lied to the envoy," Adriana said, nodding toward the gunship, "then they're probably going to ambush us now. This roof is just as good a place as any for them to try to take their revenge."

An enraged kaidon, bitter at the destruction of his homeworld because of their actions. If he chose to attack, there was little Gray Team could do to stop them.

But the Phantom stopped wheeling about and landed on a

neighboring building, deploying Rojka and eight of his fellow Sangheili.

"They're not joining us on this building," Mike said.

"Did you think they would literally stand shoulder to shoulder with us?" Adriana asked.

"No. I guess this makes sense," Jai said.

"They agreed to carry comms so that the envoy can reach them for us," Mike said. "That's pretty damn close to shoulder to shoulder."

"I can't imagine that they'd be inclined to do much more than stand by if one of those creatures caught up to us," Jai said. "But maybe I'm wrong about them."

As Adriana quickly set up her rifle, Rojka walked to the edge of the opposite building and looked across the gulf at the Spartans. Jai cautiously faced him as well.

Then Rojka solemnly turned, his Sangheili falling in with him, and disappeared down the building's stairwell.

"What was that all about?" Jai asked.

"We who are about to die salute you," Adriana said, extending the sniper rifle's tripod. "Those of us who are also doing something really risky salute you right back."

Adriana set up the rifle on the edge, where she could lie prone and take in all of the vast crater. She began scanning for their target.

"Mike, spot?" Jai was already heading down the stairwell.

"I'll spot," Mike said, checking the sights on a modified Surakan MA37 assault rifle. "But where are you going?"

"Helping our Surakan friends out," Jai said.

He hopped down from stairwell to stairwell to make time, slamming into the metal floors and denting them when he landed. He found an area with a broken window looking out on the intersection. The crossroad was packed with sandbags, and missile pods fired down the street toward the Sharquoi. The massive creatures never stopped pressing forward despite the constant fire. All firepower could do was contain them: one Sharquoi would die and another would appear around the corner, climbing over the bodies of its own kind for an opportunity to attack the Surakans.

Jai smashed the rest of the windowpane out and set the bipod of the DMR on the edge. It didn't have the range of Adriana's sniper rifle, but with the custom high-explosive ammo the Surakans used, it would do well enough at this range.

He looked down through the scope. He made a tiny adjustment to find one Sharquoi lumbering up the street, shrugging off gunfire. Jai moved his aim up to the creature's strange head atop its broad, muscled shoulders. He focused on the large lump on its forehead. He wasn't sure if it helped it see or connected it to the chieftain. Either way, it looked vital.

Jai held his breath.

He slightly increased the pressure on his index figure until the rifle fired. The tissue on the giant's head vaporized and Jai started breathing again. The Sharquoi stumbled and landed on its hands and knees. It crawled forward at the sandbags as it blood gushed from its head onto the road.

Jai reloaded, listening to Mike calling out to Surakan militia for a sighting of the Jiralhanae chieftain over the channel. The Surakans had now withdrawn their aircraft, but militia hiding in buildings behind the lines or with sight lines on the crater constantly reported in, tracking enemy movements in the city and in the crater.

"The Jiralhanae we're after—he's the one without a helmet? He has shards of something sticking out of his skull, looks Forerunner?" Adriana said. "Yes?"

Melody's voice crackled in their ears, patched in from the operations center. "Yes, that's our guy. The technology—it's a neural reader of some sort. Very invasive, and ONI theories say it might even have melded with his entire brain cavity by now."

Jai reloaded. Got a bead on the crawling Sharquoi, bleeding out. Five of them had battled through the last barrage of missiles, RPGs, and a near-constant hail of gunfire just to get within reach of the Surakan barricade down by the first floor of their building. One was down, four remained. Jai fired and watched the shot hit the next Sharquoi in the side of its head. An RPG struck it a second later, sending it to the ground in a heap.

It finally stopped moving.

"The Jiralhanae chieftain is wandering into my sight line," Adriana said. "Send visual through the closed-comm. Can I get a confirmation on the target?"

"Confirmed," Melody said.

Three surviving Sharquoi moved at an alarming pace and crashed into the Surakans as the crossroads below erupted in the chaos of close-quarters fighting. Jai hefted the DMR and tried to find a shot but couldn't at this angle. The Sharquoi rampaged through until nothing recognizable of the human defenders remained.

One of the Sharquoi now stopped, its head slowly turning until it seemed to look up at the window toward Jai with that strange socket in its head.

Melody half jumped as the vice-governor tapped her on the shoulder. She'd been leaning in to answer Adriana-111's question. Screens showed grainy feeds from militia shoulder cameras scattered all over the city, but she was focused only on the feed the Spartan had patched through from her heads-up display.

The vice-governor looked concerned. "What happens after the kill?" he asked.

Melody glanced back at the video. She'd told Adriana she was clear to take out the chieftain, but she could see that Hekabe was roaming past rubble along the crater's edge, moving in and out of her sight line. Adriana seemed to be waiting for a perfect moment. Melody could feel every heartbeat inside her own chest.

"I don't know, Vice-Governor," she admitted. "The Sharquoi will no longer be under Hekabe's control, but they will likely still pose some kind of threat. We have little information as it is, and ONI said nothing about how they would function outside of the control mechanism the Forerunners implanted."

"Please call me Lamar," he said. "So this undirected chaos . . . theoretically we could fall back and engage as needed, right?"

"These are all just best guesses, Vice—" she stopped and corrected herself, "Lamar. It's all theory. Whatever it is, it will be significantly more manageable than what you're currently facing."

Governor Gass tapped a screen showing a distant feed of Hekabe as a tiny dot walking around the far side of the crater's rim, likely from a patrolling drone. "When he drops, we need to get to that thing from his head before someone else does."

"There is a fast-response shock team standing by with orders," said Lamar. "They'll jump-jet out of a Nightingale to the spot. It should get them there faster than anything else we have. I also have squads on the ground to provide cover and rush there, if necessary."

Melody gave them both a dubious look. "The Spartans aren't going to take that thing."

Governor Gass gave her a similarly impatient look. "We can't make any assumptions. You told us Gray Team has been behind enemy lines in cryo for the last six years. How am I supposed to believe they won't? We have Sangheili here hailing from the same group that started this mess to begin with. I don't truly know what they're doing here either, or what their motivations are."

Or yours, her eyes accused Melody. The governor looked frayed, intense, and full of anger. The war had taken a toll on her. Melody needed to be very careful here.

"I am telling you everything I know," Melody said reassuringly. "I am trying to help. So is Gray Team."

"And yet," the governor said, "we are only just now learning about these things. You've kept many secrets from us. Those are my people dying out there, Envoy. It could have been prevented. The blood here is on the UNSC. All we wanted was our own peace."

"Hello," Adriana murmured over the speaker. "We have a good shot, I'm taking it."

Everyone stopped talking and watched the screens.

Rojka's active camouflage faded away. His fighters hung off the sides of the alley, their fingertips dug into window ledges, looking down at him from high above as he approached one of the Sharquoi standing near the entrance. They had worked their way down through the human building to a level with access to the outside. Clambering down the exterior walls, Rojka reached the ground first and signaled for his soldiers to remain where they clung while he approached the street outside the alley.

Rojka was here to study this new threat. To learn how to fight it. If he died here, they would at least leave with information about how to attack one of these creatures.

This Sharquoi threw sandbags at the retreating humans in the street. Vehicles and debris were strewn around it; preoccupied with the humans before it, it had its back to the Sangheili. Another Sharquoi several meters away destroyed the missile pod the humans had operated, slamming it to the ground until small pieces fell from its clawed fists. Every impact had shaken the street like a gravity hammer, causing pieces of metal to ricochet off the sides of buildings.

The Sharquoi nearest to Rojka finally turned and noticed him. The lump of flesh in the bony forehead vibrated intensely. Some sort of echolocation, Rojka realized. *Not* an eye, but it served the same purpose.

"*Roffka!*" the creature roared below its jagged teeth, surprising the Sangheili.

"Hekabe," Rojka said. He had never met the Jiralhanae chieftain before, but the chieftan apparently knew of him thanks to Thars.

"You will all die," the Sharquoi said in a guttural voice, speaking Hekabe's words. "I will hunt you all down. Then I will go to your keep and destroy all that you built here, until your bloodline is gone forever."

Rojka activated his energy sword, the blue light of the contained plasma reflecting off the walls. He realized then that dying in a human alley was not the glorious death he had thought to attain. But he would meet this new challenge with everything at his disposal nonetheless.

The Sharquoi thudded forward, shoulders brushing the sides of the buildings. The creature was over five meters at full height, so Rojka had an advantage keeping in between these tightly spaced human structures: he could move with ease, but this creature would be limited by its size.

Rojka tensed as the beast closed to within meters. He would need all his speed to dodge those wicked claws. But if he could get up near that thick neck . . .

The distinct sound of a single high-powered human sniper rifle's shot cracked from the rooftop above.

Another thudding step.

This was it.

The Sharquoi stumbled, however, and shook its head in confusion.

Instead of running forward, Rojka took the creature's new motion in stride and stepped back so he could continue observing. *Had the demons actually done it?* The Sharquoi's head leaned back, as if trying to comprehend the sky above it. It grumbled under its breath and then pushed against the walls, turning back toward the street.

"Fleetmaster: the Spartan has taken the shot," the envoy confirmed, her voice crackling loudly from the small communications device she'd clipped to Rojka's harness.

The Sharquoi startled slightly and turned its head back down into the alley at the sound of the words. The thrum of echolocation filled the area, bouncing down the narrow human corridor. It made another rumbling in its throat, seemingly confused. The air vibrated again as Rojka shifted his position, and the body language of the creature changed. The muscles in its great thighs bunched and the Sharquoi bellowed.

Behind it, beyond its great legs, Rojka saw the other Sharquoi milling around on the road. They were wandering about with an aimless curiosity.

Bullets struck them without warning. They swung their attention back toward the human militia down the street from them and charged.

"The creatures are attacking again!" Daga shouted from his vantage above.

"Assist the human warriors!" Rojka ordered.

The Sharquoi in front of Rojka bellowed again, edging closer to the Sangheili. This was the moment of truth. Although a thinking being, these creatures no longer seemed connected to Hekabe.

Will it attack? Is it aggressive by nature?

Rojka deactivated his sword, and backed away as if trying to calm a wild animal.

"See, I am no threat," he said softly.

The Sharquoi thudded into motion, lunging toward him with impressive speed. It stabbed at him with one set of claws, but Rojka rolled out of the way. The Sharquoi was still quick, but it lacked the strategic intellect: it acted now only on instinct and anger.

Rojka activated his sword just as the impact of the Sharquoi slammed into him like a massive ocean wave and they both burst through the alley wall in a cloud of debris.

CHAPTER 20

Hekabe fell back and his head bounced off a hard slab of concrete. It felt like he had been slammed in the face by a gravity hammer. Then he became immediately aware of being disconnected from the device in his head. He was dwelling only in his own limited mind once more. He felt naked. Small. Insignificant.

Sniper. It had to be a sniper. He had heard the shot through other senses. He had seen the trail the bullet left in the air leading back to a building near—his thoughts scattered and came back together—the Sangheili fleetmaster, Rojka.

He had *spoken* to Rojka.

He had seen himself fall backward, blood splattering around him. *His* blood.

Now he lay still.

But he wasn't dead yet. He was still thinking. And he was in pain.

He *should* be dead, by all rights.

He writhed on his back, hardly able to stand the burning in his left eye. He could feel the warmth of the blood seeping down the back of his skull. Then he felt something else . . .

A cold sliver of metal slipped around his forehead once again, this time on its own, and dug under his skin, scraping tendrils against the bone of his skull. The shot had injured him grievously, but this ancient machine somehow survived.

The pieces of the mysterious object that he carried so far to this world, that had burrowed inside him, now wriggled and crawled even further down through his scalp. It penetrated even deeper than before.

Hekabe could sense the Forerunner device actively seek out the damage and seal it off, doing its best to repair the chunks of his missing flesh and stop the bleeding. The same technology that could weld itself to his neural tissue to control the Sharquoi could apparently also hold it together when damaged.

He must have lost brain matter with that impact—excruciating pain welled up where his left eye once was—but the rest of the Sharquoi network now moved to compensate. Hekabe felt that pieces of his own mind had spread out through the implants in the Sharquoi's minds, and that the part of himself that he had deposited with each Sharquoi now returned back to him, igniting the ancient connection again. Hekabe could feel his own essence pouring back out into the network of Sharquoi.

He had control of it all once more.

Hekabe looked down at himself. Four Sharquoi surrounded him, their bodies creating an effective shield of hardened gray flesh, blocking any potential threats. Hekabe peered at himself through their eyes to see the horrible gaping hole in his left eye and the shattered bone around it. It all now glittered with Forerunner metal, holding his empty eye socket in place. It had shoved small fragments of itself throughout the bullet damage and fused Hekabe's skull back together.

Hekabe grabbed the arm of the nearest Sharquoi and, leaning

on Oath of Fury, he pulled himself to his feet. The pain began to drift away from him.

Three Jiralhanae had run up the side of the crater to see if their chieftain was still alive. Now they backed away from him, eyes wide with shock.

"*Do you see?*" Hekabe shouted. "Do you now see the power I wield? *I cannot be killed!*"

Hekabe closed his good eye to focus. Through his extended presence, he could feel the distant tickle of that other information deep inside the network. The wind. Some kind of ghost in the great biological spiderweb, with Hekabe at its center. Maybe this was how it always functioned—the Forerunner machine engulfing one's mind into it and then distributing it all around so that he could survive.

Could it be that something else lived in here with him?

No, the distant voice inside told him. *You alone wear the vertex.*

The vertex? Was that what they had once called this machine? Hekabe wondered if the voice was some kind of thinking machine that assisted any who wore the device.

It wasn't like that, though. There were strata. The echoes of another mind that once controlled all this had somehow remained behind in the vast deep that connected him with the Sharquoi. These things in this place could now become a part of him. But he was still the central power. The controller.

He was not immortal. He was just that much harder to kill. And if he died, parts of him would still live on in this deep place.

Hekabe, shielded by Sharquoi, turned and walked down the side of the crater.

There was still so much more power to understand here,

Hekabe realized. But it was time to ensconce himself in a safe area and barricade the doors. He would have the Sharquoi he released continue the work he had given them.

It was also time, Hekabe thought, to release the Sharquoi that still remained in stasis below.

He had been unsure of how many he could control with his will at any given time. But now he saw that he had underestimated the humans. They were indeed clever, but this injury would be the extent of their victory. He would lay hold of the Sangheili ships on the far side of the desert and redouble his efforts against the wretched human city, tearing it to the ground one stone at a time. He would flood the planet with Sharquoi and rid it of human and Sangheili meddlers forever.

He would make them all suffer.

Rojka pulled his energy sword out of the Sharquoi's neck and struggled out from underneath its bulk. Debris shifted and a section of wall slumped down to the floor, crumbling across the dead giant's frame. He coughed as the gray dust swirled around him. A cracked rib made him wince. Every bruised muscle screamed as he limped forward in the lobby of the Surakan building—the same one upon which the Spartans had landed.

"Rojka?" It was Melody's voice, warbling slightly. The human communications device was cracked open but somehow still working. "We show movement from your location. Respond."

"Yes, Envoy, I am here." Rojka leaned against the railing, taking a moment to control his pain. The Sharquoi had overwhelmed him, exploding them into the bottom of the human building. Although intended to be a killing blow, the Sharquoi's attack allowed

Rojka the opportunity to force the hilt of his sword into its neck. As the building had fallen onto them, a twist of his arm severed the creature's head from its body.

Rojka had woken with a start and struggled to claw free of the debris many long moments later.

"A message from Sergeant Carson—she flew in with the Spartans. You should fall back to the roof," Melody said in a hurried Sangheili. "Carson has mined the stairs and her team is about to detonate them. There are more Sharquoi coming. You've got about forty seconds before they get to you."

What about his Sangheili warriors? Rojka limped through the ruined wall back into the alleyway. He had last seen them leaping for the street to fight alongside the humans.

Rojka stared at the street where his fighters lay lifeless, scattered in awkward, unmoving poses throughout the area next to their human counterparts, their bodies destroyed together, smashed by the force of Sharquoi fists.

"Daga!" Rojka shouted. He stumbled out of the shadow of the alleyway.

"I'm sorry. They fought bravely," Melody said.

"Daga!" Rojka could see three Sharquoi dead. The humans and his warriors must have fought fiercely. Blood dripped from walls, plasma and bullet scars marking every open space.

"You need to move quickly," Melody said. "More Sharquoi are coming. You've got thirty seconds."

Rojka could see where four humans and Daga had made a final stand. He had to get one step closer to see the details. He would be responsible for witnessing and conveying to his clan Daga's final act of heroism in battle.

Rojka felt shaking under his feet.

"I heard you say that the Spartans shot Hekabe," Rojka said. He had seen the Sharquoi that attacked him in the alley appear to lose contact after Hekabe had spoken through it: one moment it had recognized him, the next it moved like a wild beast, completely on its own. "You humans thought this would end the conflict. What is happening now?"

"We're not really sure. Get upstairs, Rojka. There's a Pelican coming in. You only have twenty seconds before they trigger the mines."

Rojka left the street for the lobby of the building. He scanned the lower floor and found the stairwell—seemingly large enough for a Sharquoi to breach—in the far corner. He ran through the demolished interior, past the giant creature he had killed, and clambered up the stairs as quickly as he could manage. It hurt, and he had to use the railing to pull himself along. But his anger carried him past his pain. Daga had been by his side since they had hatched. They had fought in the sands of their keeps by their uncles. They had refurbished the greatest ships of the Covenant together. They had fought together. And they had stood together against Thars.

Gone.

A team of four small humans looked down from one of the intervening floors and waved him on, gesturing at him to keep going further up the stairs. Rojka groaned but pressed on, taking the remainder in one last bound, passing the humans as he neared the rooftop.

Rojka paused for a moment and leaned his head against the wall, overcome by anger and pain from his pulverized body when a series of booms sent shock waves through the air and the whole stairwell shook. The explosives blew dust and fire up the well, knocking Rojka to his side.

He leaned over the edge and looked down from the floor he had reached. The large system of stairs below him had disappeared in a haze of roiling smoke, the exterior wall collapsing to reveal the alley outside.

"Humans?" he called out in a broken version of their language.

One of them stepped out from behind a pillar and looked up at him from across the destroyed gap. They had survived a few floors below. This was part of a strategy. She shouted, pointing up.

Rojka stared at them. They had trapped themselves on the lower floor and were now going to try and hold off the Sharquoi while *he* left for safety.

No. Rojka limped around to join them. *We will all make this stand*, he thought. He would die just like his own Sangheili.

A Sharquoi slammed through the pillar at the bottom of the structure, the main support system for what remained of their side of the building. The human spun around and opened fire without even blinking. Two rocket-propelled explosives slammed into the creature from the side as the rest of the human squad moved quickly to attack it, but two more of the creatures burst in through the walls below, ripping out the column and sending the remainder of that side of the building to the ground.

The humans fell into a blossom of dust and debris several floors below. Even if they survived the fall, they would all die in seconds. The Sharquoi would not spare them.

More of the stairs crumbled and fell down to the floor below.

Rojka backed up to the wall and felt a hard tug on his arm. He turned and froze, finding himself face-to-face with a Spartan.

One of the Gray Team.

"I heard the explosions," the Spartan said through a translation device. The Demon spoke Sangheili—a benefit of the comms technology the humans no doubt used for their behind-the-lines activities during the war. "We leave. Now."

Rojka grabbed the Spartan's elbow and let him pull him along as they ran up the stairs. A Sharquoi below them bellowed at their escape.

The Spartan leaned over and looked down. "They can climb walls," he reported. "Let's move faster."

"Did you not kill the Jiralhanae?" Rojka asked.

They spiraled up another floor's worth of stairs. "We thought we got him. It was a good shot," the Spartan said.

"So what happened?" Rojka asked.

"It didn't kill him. The chieftain stood back up and now the Sharquoi move with him in control again."

They broke out of the stairwell and onto the open roof. One of their angular dropships waited for them, their independently maneuvering lift engines blowing dust off the deck and onto Rojka's legs as it pivoted into position.

"How is that possible?!" Rojka shouted.

"I don't know. We'll have to figure out how to kill him better next time."

Two more Spartans from the Gray Team fell in on either side of Rojka. They all piled into the Pelican as a Sharquoi burst out of and *through* the stairwell behind them, debris flying everywhere. One of the Spartans swung behind a large machine gun mounted on the rear bay of the Pelican and opened fire as the transport took off.

The Sharquoi ignored the flak and jumped at them, launching through the air at incredible speed.

Rojka snapped his energy sword on and waited for the impact.

A human sniper rifle cracked twice, just above his right shoulder. Rojka's hearing cut out and his head rang. But the Sharquoi's head got the worst of it. It snapped back and exploded in a burst of viscera. Its gnarled hands narrowly missed the edge of the ramp and it plummeted down, lifeless, to the street below.

Rojka deactivated the energy sword and leaned back against the inside of the Pelican, grabbing a handhold. "I would now think we have made Hekabe much more wrathful than he was before this effort," he said to the Spartans. The Demon Three.

The one who had saved his life turned to look at Rojka, and then nodded. "Agreed," he said.

Lamar intercepted Ellis just outside her office and deftly steered her back inside. She tried to spin away, clearly annoyed. But Lamar just as deftly blocked the attempt. "A moment, Governor," he said, while closing the door behind him.

"Lamar—"

"We spent a significant amount of time lacing the crater with explosives. We need to use them. We need to fire the trap."

Ellis shook her head. She'd already thought about this and looked at the situation, as well as a number of possibilities, including using the four merchant ships that remained in orbit and even jettisoning more space debris—none of them plausible given the circumstance. "The militia have fallen nine blocks back from the mines your people laid. They won't be able to cross that to try and retake it: there are too many of those things out loose in the streets."

"This isn't about retaking it. We need to slow down the flow of the Sharquoi still coming out of the structure. We need to buy ourselves time to get away, or at least fall further back. We still have those ships; they can take people."

A spike of anger surged through her. "We are *not* falling back, Lamar."

"Suraka is lost, Ellis."

"No!" Ellis swept everything off her desk with shaking hands. "*No!*"

Lamar took a step back. "Ellis . . . it's true."

She closed her eyes, unwilling to look at him. "My son . . . my *son* died here to protect this city. So many others did too in just a few short days, Lamar. What was all that for? Our plans. *My* plans. *My* leadership. *Their* blood. The planning done by the generals. *What was it for? Tell me that, goddamn it!*"

Lamar leaned forward, hands on the now-empty desk. "When I was in officer training, the instructor told us about one of the ancient battles back on Earth, a battle that the Athenians had with the Persians."

"Now is *not* the time for anecdotes, Lamar."

"Those who don't know history are forever doomed to repeat it," Lamar said. "So, the Persians attacked the city of Athens. It stood for everything the Athenians were, contained all their great buildings and their culture. No doubt many patriotic leaders swore to resist the Persians at any cost, to the last dying warrior. But instead the Athenians built boats and took to the sea en masse, abandoning their city to be burned and looted by the Persians. After the frustrated Persians left, the Athenians . . . just sailed back in."

Ellis opened her eyes. "You're suggesting we do the same? Just walk away?"

Lamar nodded. "The Athenians had an epiphany. They knew that they just couldn't match the Persian might on land. They also knew that a city isn't just a place, Ellis. Nor is it just a collection of buildings. Or even land. The true heart is its people. Protect a city's people, and you protect the essence of it. Governor, we need to protect our citizens. Not a patch of dirt or what's built on it. Those are just things that time will see erased. We need to see the big picture here."

"Lamar . . ."

"We have lost Suraka before and come back. This isn't new territory for these folks. And we will come back again. But only if we save our people first."

"Did the Athenians have to deal with neurally linked alien monsters?" Ellis asked.

"No." Lamar smiled sadly. "In fact, the Persians may have had a civilization more recognizable to us today than the Athenians'. But the strategic principles still stand, Governor. This isn't our war, Ellis. This is a UNSC problem; it's just in our backyard. We should just let them deal with it and come back when things return to normal."

Ellis sighed and gave him a haunted look. "Jeff died here, Lamar."

"I know, Ellis."

She gave a small frown, then said, "Okay. Okay, do it. We abandon the city."

"You need to give the order, not me," Lamar said. He guided her by the elbow toward the door. "Come on."

Ellis blinked as they crossed through the ops room to where General Kapoor and General Grace waited expectantly.

Ellis gripped the edge of a panel and gathered strength from deep inside. "Blow the mines," she said. "Evacuate the city."

Kapoor had the orders already pulled up. He presented them to the governor for a thumbprint.

That triggered a sudden burst of activity inside the bunker.

New video feeds flashed up, aides scurried around, officers began murmuring commands. Drones flying at a high altitude focused in on the perimeter of the crater, where the vice-governor's thermobaric bombs had been hidden.

Melody Azikiwe moved through the throng toward Ellis. "Governor, what's happening?"

Ellis pointed to the cluster of central viewscreens. "You just watch, Envoy. Any moment now."

Melody turned. The feeds of the crater flickered and then the ground along the rim abruptly sank and crumpled in on itself. A split second later, a geyser of dirt fountained into the air. The explosions continued around the rim, like high-grade mining demolitions. They looked small and inconsequential from the screens, but having been there firsthand, Ellis knew the area of effect was significant.

Dust rushed toward the nearest cameras and knocked them out, leaving nothing but static on the viewscreens.

An aide in the corner clapped once, twice, and then stopped.

Lamar turned away from the screens. "This isn't a win, people," he said loudly. "This is just a distraction to buy us some time. Now we need to evacuate every civilian we can. Send them to the oases. Herndon Lake, Aza Oasis, Fallen Tree—there's water and shelter in those places. Any valley in the mountains with a stream, any waypoint out in the Uldt with a supply of water. We need to get them out of here and to safety."

"What about the four ships still in orbit?" Kapoor asked. "Should we use those to engage the Sharquoi, or to evacuate more people?"

"I vote to keep them up and in orbit," Lamar said, turning to Ellis. "If we call them down, we risk turning them over to the enemy or, at the very least, attracting them to our evacuation efforts. Right now, we can take people through the underground passages to the trading outposts and move out from there on foot. That's the safest."

"I concur; if we need the ships they'll be on hand. The vice-governor is going to be directing this effort," Ellis said. "Take your orders from him."

"This won't stop Hekabe," Melody said separately.

"I know." Ellis pivoted to face her. "Apparently we needed nukes for that. Something the UNSC obviously doesn't trust us with. We could have rigged the ships, but they were hijacked, and the others would be too risky to bring in at this point. We're going to evacuate and let the UNSC come here to clean up their own mess."

"What about our 'power source'?" Grace asked, phrasing it carefully.

"Power source?" Melody pressed.

Ellis sighed. *What did secrets matter at this point?* "We have just one repurposed Havok bomb running emergency power to this bunker."

"You have an illegal nuclear weapon?" Melody asked, visibly shocked.

"Yes. Are we going to argue about secret keeping?" Ellis snapped back, annoyed. "I'll check the score and see where ONI places. But before you get any ideas, it's ours and I've already made plans for it. So, no. ONI cannot have more of our materiel."

Melody smiled awkwardly. "I'm only asking questions so I understand our situation," she said, raising her hands. "I want to talk about the bigger picture. Like containment. We need to make sure there's no way the Sharquoi can get off the planet."

Ellis experienced chills as she realized the envoy was effectively writing Suraka off. What was one city in the panoply of worlds under the Unified Earth Government's thumb, after all? "You're worried about Earth, right now? Is that it? When a million of us are wondering if there's going to be a tomorrow?"

Melody remained calm yet stern. "Yes, actually. If you are evacuating out of the city to havens, then your problems are almost over. Everyone else's are just getting started. Hekabe's not going to stop with Suraka or Rak or anything else on Carrow. He's going to leave this place and I want to stop him. Now, I was told none of those ships the Sharquoi took with the Jiralhanae are capable of slipspace travel. Is that true?"

"Your hinge-head friends destroyed all my ships with drives when the fighting broke out. Remember, when we began making plans for your peace summit and everything went to hell?" Ellis's voice was cold. "So if you're worried about slipspace, go talk to the Sangheili and leave us alone."

Melody said carefully, "Maybe I can get Rojka to try to open communications with Thars, if he is still alive. Or Thars's people if he isn't. It's possible his people know about the Sharquoi at this point. Maybe they'd even be willing to work with us. I want to find solutions, Governor."

Ellis grimaced. Enough with the UNSC's "solutions." Hadn't they already cost enough lives? She looked over at the new team working their way into the bunker, specialists that she'd called for to help her work on new ideas for saving the city with one last effort. "Rhodes, over here," she called.

Ellis's lead nuclear engineer, Brandon Rhodes, saw her and acknowledged with a wave. "Governor. I have the whole team assembled and ready."

"Excellent, let's get started, shall we?" she said to Rhodes.

"Governor, we need to discuss—"

Ellis turned away from Melody. "No, Envoy, we do not. I

have pulled together a group of our city's best scientists and engineers. I'm going to see if I can stop the slaughter of my people. You can do whatever you want. But just do not interrupt me or ask for me again."

Jai looked over the shoulder of the Pelican's pilot as the vessel swept quickly around the crater's rim. Piles of rubble had slid down, filling in some of the center after the scores of thermobaric explosives that the Surakans had rigged all around the excavation pit had gone off at once. The blast was incredibly powerful, stemming the constant tide of Sharquoi for a moment.

"Damn," the pilot said, briefly awed.

Forms struggled slowly out of the debris. Many of the Sharquoi had been stunned for the moment by the explosion but were getting back on their feet. Many didn't move, however, and remained scattered around the edges of the crater and tossed in between buildings.

The ones that lived all began to walk unsteadily back *toward* the crater's center and the entryway down into the Forerunner structure, the very place to where Hekabe had fled.

More and more of them trickled out from streets or crawled out from under rubble. Some of them began dragging machinery with them for purposes unknown.

They turned their backs to the Surakan militia, which had previously been their sole focus, to begin digging through a fresh pile of rubble at the center of the pit.

"Did that blast destroy the Forerunner facility below ground?" Rojka asked from the back of the Pelican.

Jai could see the glint of the spire still intact. Forerunner. That probably meant that it was buried but no doubt just fine. Forerunner materials had absurd resiliency. "No, it'd take a nuke to cause damage to that thing. Those bombs did help. They bought us time," he responded, as the translation software converted his words into Sangheili.

"Then let us use that time well," Rojka replied.

CHAPTER 21

The envoy was waiting for Rojka when the lift came to a stop with a heavy jerk as they returned to the underground control center deep under Suraka. Rojka walked between the Spartans and toward her. How strange that he could move so easily in the Demon Three's midst without wanting to kill them right then and there.

"Kaidon," Melody said, rushing toward him, while the Spartans peeled off for the armory.

Rojka felt a wave of weariness sweep over him at the reference. He was kaidon of a people that were still very much alive back in Rak. He had been counting on his death for the past few days, but it hadn't come—not yet. He still had to be kaidon, and think like a kaidon. Everything was at risk. Everything he had tried to create here. He wondered about his bloodline—clan and kin. Would they survive? He even wondered if his carefully tended gardens around the cool waters of the Astlehich River would burn. Whether the columns of the keep would be pushed over and buried.

She called him kaidon, as if he truly ruled anything.

What *should* she call him, though? There was no fleet left for him to master either. Who was he?

Rojka.

That was all.

Alone. And yet surrounded by these hated aliens.

"Envoy," Rojka said evenly, "we find ourselves with the same problems yet again."

"We need to mitigate the consequences of our failure to contain the Jiralhanae," Melody said. "If Hekabe sends the Sharquoi to other worlds, this all spreads. Then he gets access to more powerful weapons and ships, and it gets worse. I've been using the Surakans' orbital relay to track the stolen Surakan ships from here. At most they're only a few hours away from reaching Thars's ships, and I need your help to stop them."

"My help?" Rojka was astounded. "What help could I possibly give now?"

"Thars is still alive."

Rojka grunted, recalling the report he received earlier. "He is worse than an insect you cannot squash. But what does this have to do with me? Thars is no doubt waiting for me to leave this city in order to ambush me and then strip me of what little honor I have left."

"I reached out to Thars," she told him. "The Surakan drones show he has ships laying low, far beyond the mountains. Activity around them suggests some of them are either fully repaired or in the final stages. They'll likely be ready within the next hour. You are our best link to Thars and his ships. You and I both know he has to get them off-planet or destroy them. If the Sharquoi get there first, they'll have the means to leave this world."

Rojka hadn't seriously thought about Thars since he entered

the city. The conflict with his cousin felt like a previous life, after all that had happened since his escape from the human facility in the desert.

Melody continued. "Using the long-range comms channel, I was able to find his frequency and broadcast a request to talk. He was unwilling at first, but I managed to convince him to listen to me."

Rojka looked down at the envoy. If anyone else had told him this, he would have refused to believe them. Yet he somehow had no doubt that she had forced Thars into a conversation.

"I told him about the Sharquoi," Melody said. "I told him everything he needed to know. I told him to take any slipspace-capable ships and get them off the planet before it's too late, or simply destroy any ships he couldn't fly off with."

As good a negotiator as she was, Rojka knew how Thars must have taken *that* suggestion. "And how did he respond?"

"He did not take my suggestions gracefully," Melody said.

"No," Rojka agreed. "He would not be willing to do any of that. You waste your time trying. If you want to make sure that Hekabe cannot use Thars's ships, you need to convince the humans to take whatever ships or aircraft they have left and strike his vessels now, before it's too late. Where are your Surakan allies?"

"Governor Gass will give us nothing. In fact, it's a miracle I was allowed to tap into their comms and relay system. She's locked herself in a room with a team, working on something. The vice-governor, on the other hand, is reserving all resources for evacuation. I have nothing left but you, Rojka. I need your people, your weapons. Your will."

"I am nothing but what you see before you," Rojka said. "The warriors and the vehicles that we brought here were consumed in the diversion."

Melody paused. "Are you certain there's nothing left?"

"At best, I could warn those in Rak about what has happened. But Thars and I have mobilized everything under each of our own commands. There is nothing left to spare."

Melody took that in. "There aren't even any of your Sangheili still out in the desert? Any of those who attempted to throw Thars off our trail? What about from your downed ship?"

Rojka opened his mandibles as if to respond, then stopped. Finally, he said, "Thars has killed them all, except for three of my warriors and a single Banshee, who remained behind to confuse Thars when we secured your rescue. I ordered them to return to Rak some time ago as Thars did not pursue them. I do not know if they are still alive."

Melody looked disappointed. "Even if they survived, three more Sangheili is not enough to help us. Damn."

But she had Rojka's interest. His mind was now churning. "Tell me again—how much time before Hekabe's stolen ships reach Thars?"

"Two hours, maybe three." Melody said, chopping the air with a hand. "Two hours for us to change the direction of everything."

She then led him down the corridor.

"I find it . . . difficult to do what you do," he said slowly to Melody.

"What would that be?" she asked, puzzled.

"You talk," Rojka said.

"We all talk."

"But you talk things into being," Rojka said. "They do not exist at first. Then, after you speak, they become real. It is almost a magical thing. You talked, and the possibility of peace conferences came into existence. You talked, and Thars saw his chance to best me. You talked, and despite all my convictions otherwise, we joined forces with that which I hate most of all: the Demon Three."

"I only help us uncover possible solutions," Melody said. "That's my job—it's what I do. I know these things are hard. But all of those things were possibilities before I voiced them."

"But *you* were the one who voiced them." Rojka cocked his head. "I have known you now long enough to know you want something specific from me."

Melody took a deep breath. The human way of gathering strength. "I need you to speak directly to Thars. I need you to be convincing. I need you to do what I do: talk new possibilities into being."

Rojka considered this. "You want me to convince Thars to voluntarily destroy all his ships?" Even *she* had not been able to speak such a thing into being.

"Or come up with a better idea and make it happen. Worlds are at stake, Rojka 'Kasaan. Like it or not, we need Thars. He doesn't know it yet, but he'll need us right back in a few hours."

Rojka nodded. Three fighters, out in the desert. And she had forgotten the other weapons she had access to, that the Governor did not—three of them, in heavy armor. "Very well. Let us attempt this negotiation with Thars. But remember, Envoy, I tricked him and then betrayed him openly before humans. I do not believe I will get very far."

"We have to try," Melody said. "Or many will die."

"I think perhaps I can convince him that the Sharquoi threat is real. I doubt he is completely ignorant of all that has happened here. If Thars listens, he and his people will have some measure of warning. Maybe they can hold the Sharquoi back and cut off access to his own ships."

She looked surprised that he agreed, but she nodded. "I'll contact him again then."

A few minutes later, in a small ready room that Rojka had to lower his head to enter, Thars appeared on one of the human viewscreens. He burst into a mocking croak, the closest Sangheili expression to human laughter, at the sight of his cousin, his sworn enemy.

"You have run to hide among the weak ones," Thars said with scoffing glee. "Is it truly that difficult to face me?"

Rojka pointed wearily at the screen. Thars would not listen to reason. It was almost certain that Thars had lied to Melody that he would even consider negotiation. But Rojka saw a way to either die honorably himself or truly give the humans a chance to destroy Thars's ships once and for all. It was a slim way, but it was still a way.

"You had the upper hand earlier, cousin," Rojka said. "So let us meet and face each other on the sand, just the two of us. Then we will see who truly is the strongest warrior."

Melody whipped around to stare at him, anger on her face. "This isn't negotiation," she hissed at him. To her it seemed to be sabotage, no doubt.

But even Thars wouldn't risk his neck in single combat. No, Rojka had to lure the coward out. There was only one thing that would work.

"I will hand over to you the Demon Three," Rojka said. "If you will meet me in the desert at a location of your choosing."

Thars gave it thought, then said, "Done. You give me the Demon Three. And the envoy too, so that I can negotiate with the humans when they arrive in greater strength. Then we can face each other, cousin, and I will slit your throat."

"You tell the humans here where we shall meet. I will bring them to you." Rojka then turned and abruptly left the room.

Melody skidded around the door out after him a moment later, having received the coordinates of Thars's rendezvous spot. "What the hell was that all about?"

"I have created a way to get Thars closer in short time," Rojka said. "If I can capture him, perhaps we can force him to destroy the existing slipspace drives. And if he kills me, then I know that I will die with some honor left in a very dishonorable situation."

All in all, Rojka felt pleased to have found some small good out of the madness they all found themselves in. The envoy did not look convinced.

"Going out there to die—that's not a good solution," Melody said. "You know there's no chance in hell Thars will show up alone."

Rojka nodded. "I know he will not. But we are out of good solutions, Envoy. This one gets Thars within reach. No great stories will be told about us. What we choose now is how we die. How do you wish to die, Envoy?"

"You were in the middle of choosing exactly how to do so back on the *Unwavering Discipline*. That changed, didn't it? We can change this as well."

"I have lured Thars out. Now we can face him. If you are correct, then perhaps we will be able to change our fate, somehow. If he just listens to reason."

"How will you convince the Spartans to go with you?"

Rojka looked down at her, incredulous. "I will not. I do not intend to bring them, nor you. I intend to go and fight Thars and die, alone. But before I do that, if he believes me about the Sharquoi, I might give the human city the time it needs to evacuate its people. And by extension, the keeps of Rak might survive as well. Thars is devious, but he also values his life more than anything. If I can show him that Hekabe puts his life at risk, he will run."

"This is not a good plan," Melody said.

"I never said it was."

But it would be a Sangheili fight.

Rojka looked at her. "I require transportation of some kind. I can operate most human vehicles. This is all I ask. Consider it my last request."

The evacuation numbered in the high hundreds of thousands. Some chose to stay and hide underground, far away from the scouring eyes of the Sharquoi in a single passageway that led to a series of trading outposts in the wasteland beyond. Others stayed to fight.

Vehicles of all kinds were requisitioned to pull sleds, refitted with sand-capable tires. Some surviving Pelicans even shifted from military duty to flying parents and children out to the oases and mountains first, with supplies to last. Caravan lines of tens of thousands of people snaked out of the outer eastern districts of Suraka. People on foot, carrying whatever they could, striking out northeast into the Uldt desert.

Ellis looked up as Lamar took a break from managing food drops and reassigning militia resources, crossing over to the ready room that her team had taken over for its wall-to-wall viewscreens:

"I was just informed the envoy has set a meeting with Thars," he reported. "We could try to open negotiations about getting some of our citizens off-world with his ships."

Ellis paused a simulation of scanner data. "Lamar, are you serious right now? Thars started this fight to begin with, he's killed our people already—and you're looking to just give him more? What Surakan would even consider going along with this? Please, stop disturbing us." She walked him to the door and pushed him over the threshold. "Do whatever you need to do, Lamar. I will not stand in your way. Just let me handle the Brutes."

She shut the door on him.

He stared at her through the glass pane for a moment. And in response, she turned her back on him. For a moment, everyone in the room stopped what they were doing and stared at the two.

"Back to work, people!" she growled. "We don't have time."

The room quickly returned to a buzz of people poring over information that had been retrieved. This made sense to Ellis—the technicians, the engineers, the analysts. It may be a crisis, but they weren't jockeying over diplomacy or soothing ruffled feathers. The complete opposite of the last few days. No one needed managing. Yes, engineering and science still had interpersonal rivalries and relationships. But here, in this pure moment, that all fell away as they focused on a common goal.

For almost an hour they'd been using advanced analysis systems and metric quantifiers to rip through every piece of information they had. How was Hekabe controlling the Sharquoi? They knew it was via the implants within the ancient machine sticking out of his head. But how did that Forerunner technology work? No signals had been discovered. Line of sight? The Sharquoi did just fine inside buildings and still followed Hekabe's control. Maybe it was loosely connected to quantum entanglement, though that was outside of human ability to interfere with: even if it was true, there was little they could do. But that led to a more probable solution: maybe the communication happened in slipspace?

Based on the information, this seemed to be the most promising possibility.

Now they had to find a way to disrupt it.

And the answer would be somewhere in the data here.

Brandon Rhodes, who'd taken the lead on a whole section of electromagnetic spectrum analysis for Suraka, clapped the table loudly enough to startle everyone into looking over at him. He pointed at one of the viewscreens. The feed showed two panes: one was of Hekabe in combat, controlling Sharquoi, and the other was a waveform readout.

"There's consistent, measurable electromagnetic activity that we can detect from the device on the Jiralhanae's head," Rhodes reported, standing up to point at waveforms displayed on another viewscreen.

"Is it for communication?" Ellis asked.

"No. This is probably the device picking up Hekabe's brainwaves, not controlling the Sharquoi. But it *is* a sign that the device is vulnerable."

Ellis raised an eyebrow. Dare she hope? "How?"

Rhodes grinned. "If an electromagnetic pulse hit it, it could disrupt it."

"We have the one Havok nuke powering the bunker," Ellis said. "What if we rebuild it, and we set it off over the pit?"

Rhodes shook his head. "That's the problem. The Forerunner facility is completely shielded. An EMP would not penetrate. And since Hekabe retreated, we've been unable to locate him. We don't know how big it is down there, we don't know where it leads to or what he might have as an exit contingency. If we'd known about this before, when he was outside, we might have been able to disrupt the object. We can't do that now that he's down there and shielded."

Ellis shut her eyes. "So if the UNSC had told us about this before, if they hadn't hidden critical information from us,, we might have been able to stop this earlier?"

Rhodes looked a bit nervous. "I couldn't say, Governor."

Ellis let the datapad drop to the desk. Her fatigue was so intense now that she felt nauseous. At this point she had gotten only a few hours of sleep during the brief reprieve, and even that was uneasy. She rubbed the most recent stim patch; her skin was numb underneath it.

She looked up guiltily, realizing that everyone was staring at her. "Hekabe will come out at some point," she said.

"And if he doesn't?" one of her technicians asked nervously.

Ellis realized it was time to leave the realm of data and structure and pull herself back into the messy real world. Something she had become very familiar with. "We go in after him," she announced. "We can build something that will neutralize his control and buy us time to take that facility out from the inside. We need some kind of electromagnetic pulse cannon, like the ones we saw used on Mars. Something that will fry that device in his head. Then we need to get that Havok inside the facility."

Some of the engineers looked around the room, rolling the idea around in their heads and nodding slowly. Others still hadn't bought it; they leaned back and folded their arms. She needed Rhodes. If he thought it was possible, they could pull it off.

"We only have one Havok," said Rhodes. "That's it. And we'll need a hell of a power source if we want to build anything strong enough to shut that device down. That means the Havok if you want something mobile—whether for the cannon or as a bomb. There might be a way we could do both. If we patched the Havok's power conduits into something like a rail gun or gauss cannon—maybe one of the M68s—we might be able to use it to power a short-range, concentrated EMP blast. The Havok could potentially still be capable of a local detonation if it's used right."

"Why not just bring the Havok down and detonate it near the Brute's position?" someone asked from the corner. "There's no way he could survive the blast."

"Technically, true," Rhodes answered, "but if this thing is tethered to some strange slipspace confluence, I'm not so sure we have that guarantee. Hekabe managed to survive a direct hit to the head with a fourteen-point-five millimeter round."

"And again, we don't really have any intel on this underground facility," Ellis reminded them all, pulling Rhodes further into her line of thinking. She could feel the room's mood shifting around her. "For all we know, a hundred Havoks detonated down there might not even touch him. I've seen stranger things from the Forerunners."

Rhodes nodded, agreeing with her once again in front of the others. "The EMP at least neutralizes the immediate threat: the neural machine controlling the creatures."

"There's something else," Ellis said in a distant voice. "The Forerunner device itself. It doesn't belong to the Brutes, it doesn't belong to the UNSC, it doesn't belong to the Elites: it belongs to *us*."

Rhodes turned to her, an eyebrow raised.

Ellis continued. "Using the EMP does one very important thing a Havok detontation can't: it keeps this object in Surakan possession and out of the hands of our enemies. What if other

Forerunner sites exist on this world with more of these things? We can't be forced to experience this hell all over again. I won't allow that. Not again."

The others in the ready room looked at her with mild curiosity. Some were clearly intrigued by her line of arguing, perhaps even inspired by it, but others clearly frightened.

"Get the nuke," she ordered. "Hook it up to a gauss cannon and get something functional in the hour. We have to make sure we hit him hard—and we can't let anyone else get their hands on that device once we do. We'll only have one chance to make this happen."

Melody Azikiwe dodged the Surakan militia headed to their Warthogs; the military was at the edge of a makeshift compound overseeing the evacuation process on the far side of the city. One of the officers driving by stopped.

"You're the UEG envoy, right?"

"Yes?"

"We're clearing out of this area, so I'm to tell you that now's your chance to hop on for a ride to safety. There are Sharquoi infiltrating the tunnels and buildings further down the block. We're taking whatever supplies we have with us right now and moving to escort the evacuation before the creatures pick up the trail and discover where we're headed."

"I'm staying. I have work here still," Melody told him.

"Understood."

The driver peeled out, leading a small convoy of Warthogs and even an Elephant. Melody was surprised at the volume and pedigree of materiel this small peripheral colony had at its disposal, apparently all early gifts from the NCA for mutual support. She also wouldn't be surprised if the xenophobic Sapien Sunrise group was sending them equipment, given Suraka's struggle to coexist with Sangheili. Yet the weapons and vehicles had remained largely unused for years—until now.

Over in the corner of the loading bay outside the bunker, Melody saw one of the Spartans step behind a bale of dry goods that had been pushed off a truck so that militia could hastily load boxes of ammunition. She frowned and walked around. She hadn't seen the Spartans since just before her conversation with Rojka. "Jai?"

In the shadowed side, she saw the doubled-back knees of a Sangheili shift. Rojka turned to her. "Envoy."

"What are you two doing?" Melody asked. While Rojka seemed to have at least temporarily swallowed hatred to work with those he called the Demon Three, finding them all talking in the shadows made Melody nervous. Rojka had wanted to kill the Spartans. He had *reasons* to kill them.

And here they were *talking?*

They had every right to do it. And yet it troubled her.

They were up to something.

Adriana swung off the top of the bale, startling Melody as the Spartan hit the ground with a heavy thud. She guided Melody away. "Private conversation, Envoy," she said.

"About what?"

"About Rojka's proposal for our surrender to Thars," Adriana said. "But don't go too far; we may need you soon enough."

"Wait a second. He said earlier that he would do it alone and not involve you," Melody said. Adriana, ignoring her, had already turned back to Jai and Rojka.

The Spartans surrendering to Thars? Melody didn't believe that even for a moment. And the humor in Adriana's voice told Melody that the Spartans would not just walk meekly across the Uldt desert to their fate. Obviously something else was at play here, something different than what Rojka had told her in the command complex.

What were they truly planning? Melody strode off, thinking furiously.

What did she really know about Gray Team? They liked to operate rogue and had a very long leash, yet ONI kept working with them despite any problems that caused—Glyke being the understatement of the century. Dangerous times called for dangerous methods.

But what motivated Gray Team anymore? If they were worried about being viewed as war criminals for their actions on Glyke, they could make any number of bad decisions.

She wasn't sure that being around Rojka, one of the only remaining survivors of Glyke, who had himself seen so much blood on his hands in the last days, was healthy.

What *were* they planning, really?

"Vice-Governor!" she called out, spotting Lamar in an operations canopy, getting things together for his own departure. "Can I have a moment of your time?"

He looked at her. "A little busy right now. The entire bunker's being evacuated. I told someone to take you out of here already. I'm trying to set up a fallback command center at one of the outposts before evacuees' arrival so that we can manage their flow toward the oases."

"I understand. I've kept you updated: you know Thars is willing to talk to us and I'm trying to get him to prevent the Sharquoi from getting off-planet. But I might need to ask you for resources to help contain the Spartans if . . . they cause any trouble with that."

The vice-governor started laughing. "You want me to try and contain three Spartans? Are you insane? They're *your* responsibility, Envoy! And I don't have the time or the resources needed to detain them."

Melody suppressed her anger. "I'm trying to find solutions, Vice-Governor. I'm trying to stop Hekabe from getting off-world and causing more harm to other people."

But Lamar was, of course, focused only on getting civilians evacuated from the city. And she couldn't blame him. That was the immediate need, and the UEG had done very little to commend itself to Suraka, especially with regard to the secret Forerunner facility and the Sharquoi threat it held.

"Maybe the Inner Colonies will just have to deal with that problem on their own," the vice-governor said. "I know you're just trying to do your job. I know you're not at fault. Your superiors left you deep in the mud here. And I am not as angry as Governor Gass is. But, Ms. Azikiwe, the bombs we detonated have bought us a brief window with the bulk of the attacking force. So I've got to get these civilians to safety. Apologies, ma'am."

He turned away.

Melody leaned against a pylon of the operations canopy. She'd fought hard for so long on this mission. Every minute, trying to make things happen. She'd known it was all falling apart but had kept opening doors in an attempt to make some kind of difference. Now it all felt like she had accomplished nothing. Everything she grasped at slipped away like sand between her fingers.

They had just over an hour before the Surakan merchant ships, piloted by Jiralhanae and filled with Sharquoi, assaulted Thars forces and took his ships for themselves. Even if Rojka managed to beat the ships' arrival and make contact with Thars, it was very likely that he would be killed by his cousin. The Spartans, if they were now suddenly going along, might let themselves get captured alive. Maybe they saw this as a way to get off the planet quickly now that the Sharquoi threat had became clear. Continue the fight from there.

That was logical, she thought.

It might feel like cowardice to fly away from Suraka as it burned. But it wouldn't be the first planet the Spartans had been forced to leave while it was under attack.

She was tired, and it was getting harder to see things for what they were. But she knew one thing for certain: Hekabe would kill anything alive here in the city, and wherever else he might track down new prey.

An armored glove tapped her on the shoulder.

Melody turned to see the hulking figure of Adriana-111.

"We've come up with something of a plan," Adriana said. "And unfortunately, you're a part of it."

"Am I going to like this?" Melody asked.

"Well, you certainly don't want to be sticking around here. We at least need to get you out before those things show up here and start causing problems."

Melody looked up at the faceplate. "You need to tell me what you're up to first."

"The fleetmaster promised Thars that he would deliver three Spartans and an envoy," Adriana said. "From what we've seen of Thars, and knowing that Rojka tricked him the last time, he'll likely want to visually verify we're all there before we can get close enough."

"You know Thars won't actually come alone, right?"

The Spartan nodded. "We are ready for that contingency. But we need you there for our best chance at luring Thars out."

Melody bit her lip. "How will we even get out to the meet point?"

"Mike's off ahead of us requisitioning a Pelican."

"The vice-governor said they didn't have any spare resources for us."

"Mike can be very persuasive. Can we count on you?"

There's little point arguing with a determined Spartan, Melody thought, and nodded.

CHAPTER 22

Ellis walked through a dark, cavernous bay toward a pool of light. The militia had left nothing behind in the underground command complex but shadows and emergency lighting that glowed from the gray concrete pillars.

Her team had set up a hasty workspace under the glare of several battery-powered lights in the most remote part of the complex. Benches, tables, testing equipment, a few mobile viewscreens, and in the center of it all a very old, bulky Havok nuclear bomb sat on a mobile trolley, partially stripped apart. The pod-like capsule exterior lay in parts on the floor, different sections labeled with markers or pieces of plastic taped to their sides.

The warhead itself was ensconced in a cradle of heavy wires and fiber-optic cable. This one was larger than those the UNSC had employed in recent years. It would need to be dismantled and reconfigured carefully for this EMP weapon to work.

Readouts flickered from screens, showing radiation levels and power outputs.

There had been programs that turned nuclear weapons into fuel for civil use for hundreds of years. People had even been doing it since shortly after the invention of nuclear weapons.

Here the engineers scattered around the Outer Colonies had reverse-engineered an entire system that they could plug a bomb into to get the power they needed. Rapid, effective, convenient, and built in such a way that if someone needed the nuke's core, the cradle ejected it after just fifteen minutes of automated reassembly.

Some rumors suggested that the cradle procedure had been cribbed from UNSC documents. It had been a way for them to create reactors out of bombs but keep the weapons available on short notice. An asset that had come in handy during the Insurrection.

Ellis wasn't sure if that was true, but it certainly sounded like something they'd do.

She carefully peeled another stim patch from her forearm and threw it on the floor. Almost five days running nonstop. That was the limit, wasn't it? Somewhere toward the end of that period, one started hallucinating. Or just collapsed. The brain couldn't take the time to process and cleanse itself, so it would begin to blur the line between reality and the unreal.

Lamar emerged from a side corridor, startling her as he stepped into the pool of light.

"I've shut down all operation centers within the city limits and destroyed all applicable drives," he said. "Everything is on the move to Command and Control Four-East, by the third outpost marker."

They'd moved militia command and control out past the farms and well into the desert, to an old quarry that had been used by the colony's first traders.

"I'm not leaving. We need to finish this," she told him. "Continue to evacuate from the east tunnel and I'll follow when I can."

"I can't walk out of here and leave you behind," Lamar said.

"One of us needs to be at the top of the command structure during the evacuation process. It should be you right now. I need to be here to see this through."

Lamar looked over at the bomb. "We should be using that to slow the Sharquoi down, instead of taking it apart to chase this Brute down a hole."

Ellis bit her lower lip. "You're probably right, but I'm not ready to give up on this yet. As long as that Brute is alive, the people of Suraka are at risk. Evacuating was the right thing to do, but a final effort needs to be made. I need to make sure of it. Go, Lamar. You're in charge now. I've already passed the documentation along to military leadership: they're looking to you from now on."

"Ellis . . ." Lamar wasn't sure what to say next. "It shouldn't be like this."

"But it is. How much time do I have?"

"Probably a half hour before the Sharquoi can break through the complex's defense." They'd originally thought it would be hours, or she wouldn't have started stripping a damned nuke apart in the underground bay. But the Sharquoi were getting better at penetrating human defenses. No, *Hekabe* was getting better at controlling them. "Militia are posted up in the forward tunnels and the bay. They're part of the reason you've got your thirty minutes."

They'd be dying up there to slow the Sharquoi down. "And if you pull them away?"

"Fifteen minutes. Maybe."

"Cutting it too close," Ellis said, emotionless.

"They stay. No sense in risking so much to guarantee a loss. They'll give them hell before those things get to you. Mines, rocket launchers, mounted machine guns—a death sentence, but they'll sure as hell go down fighting. What if the Sharquoi breach before you finish here?"

"Then we'll use the bomb for its original purpose," Ellis said. "It's ready to be detonated in a matter of seconds. It'd take the complex, probably most of the city above."

Lamar paused. "It was close, Ellis," he said. "It could easily have gone the other way. You could have gotten that win back there in the crater. And I would have rightly been in the wrong. That's the way it is, sometimes."

He held out a hand. Ellis shook it firmly. "Good-bye, Lamar. Good luck."

"You too, Governor."

Lamar had been faithful to the people of Suraka, even during their disputes. Ellis respected that. She knew where she had been wrong. She knew she could have handled things differently. But all that was over, water under the bridge. He was in charge now, and she had one thing left to do.

In the distance, gunfire popped inside one of the tunnels.

No time. Ellis turned her back on Lamar as he left. "Rhodes. The focusing elements from the M68, how are they coming along?"

Rhodes raised his head from another mess of circuitry toward the far edge of the large table where a wild Frankenstein of a machine was being created between the Havok's core and an oversized, dismounted gauss cannon. It was intimidating to see it up this close, lying on its side. "We're there, Governor."

She wanted the maximum amount of energy coming out in a focused beam, one that they could bring into the Forerunner facility and control. They weren't using the nuke for its destructive power: they needed it to power the gauss cannon's disruptive EMP energy right at Hekabe, to sever his connection with the Sharquoi and neutralize any tech buried in the chieftain's skull.

Since they were using a repurposed M68 gauss cannon—
normally mounted to Warthogs or other mobile vehicles—they
had some options on what exactly they could attach the gun to.

And if the electromagnetic pulse didn't work, well, there was
always the nuclear option.

Quite literally, in this case, she thought.

For Ellis, that sort of final act and sacrifice would be her penance for being wrong. Penance for all those lives lost at her hands.
Penance for those who had been forced to leave all they had called
home.

And the final revenge against the bastard that took her son's life.

Melody walked out of the Pelican into the hot desert. The Spartans
fanned out in front of her, and Rojka grunted as he stepped forward from under the shade of the Pelican's wings. They were fifty
klicks from Suraka, at the coordinates where Thars had agreed to
meet them. It was an empty and bare swath of land, well removed
from Thars's own ships.

Melody shielded her eyes against the sun. Above, a Spirit dropship made a slow circle around them.

"He's thinking about it," Mike said.

The Sangheili ship finished a second pass, then began to sink
toward the sand.

"It's landing," Melody said.

The Spirit dropship came to a stop just above the sand, heat
rippling up around it. Twenty Sangheili climbed out of its arms
and spread out in a long semicircle in front of it, with Thars at the
center.

Melody raised her hand to her shoulder. The burned flesh

where Thars had shoved the edge of his energy sword into her skin still scraped against her dirty uniform.

Her hands shook as she pushed her hair back and tied it with a handkerchief. She was scared to stand here. To walk knowingly into what had to be some horrible trap. *How do the Spartans do this so calmly?*

"It's okay," Jai reassured her, glancing back at the Pelican parked to their backs. "We'll protect you."

"This is so far from okay I'm not even sure how to describe it. You still won't tell me your plan."

"We're all going to go say hello to Rojka's cousin," Jai said. "And we're going to watch for an opportunity."

Melody didn't believe that. "You must have something *else* planned, right?"

"Plan is an ambitious word," Adriana said, approaching from behind her with Mike. "Just be ready for anything."

"You should really tell me what you're going to do."

Melody so wanted to be able to see past those faceplates. They didn't truly trust her, and that made her nervous. She had continued to wonder about their own goals on the flight out. Were they planning to trade her: was she actually the prisoner? No, that couldn't be it. Thars wanted Rojka, and he wanted the Spartans even more. He likely couldn't care less about a random UEG envoy. As they had said, she was just here to sweeten the pot.

But why keep her completely in the dark?

They had to be concerned that she would hint that something was about to happen. Maybe they needed her in the dark in order to sell a legitimate conversation and hide whatever they had really planned? She was going to have to believe that.

They were all teetering on the edge of unknowns and doubts and suspicions. She would have to be the one to trust them.

Melody felt like she would throw up if they didn't need to keep walking forward. But she needed to monitor the situation second by second. She was looking for an opportunity to pivot anything that happened in a different direction. Better that than wait for what felt like an inexorable bloodletting of some kind lurking ahead.

There's still time, she told herself.

Rojka threw the hilt of his plasma sword to the ground as a show of peace and walked out in front of the group.

"Here we go." Jai dropped his rifle in suit. Mike followed along.

Adriana carefully set her sniper rifle down on the sand. Next to it, a pistol. Then another pistol. She added the submachine gun slung over her back. A dagger from an ankle. Then she stood back up. The Spartans moved forward.

The further they got from the Pelican, the more Melody's mouth dried up—not what an envoy needed just before a conversation with the enemy. She glanced from side to side, watching as Thars's Sangheili cohort moved to surround them.

"I rescued you, only to lead you to your deaths," Melody whispered as she caught up to Jai, voice shaking.

"Don't take all the credit. We were running toward death long before you ever showed up," Jai replied. "And you can't lead us anywhere we don't willingly follow."

Twenty plasma rifles and carbines were aimed in Melody's direction. If Thars gave the order, all this would end very quickly.

Adriana slipped to Melody's side as Jai walked confidently forward.

"Take a deep breath," Adriana said. "This is the real edge of the knife."

Thars stepped out from the protection of his Sangheili. "On your knees! Move no further!"

His energy sword flared to life at his side. Melody and Gray Team came to a halt behind Rojka, who faced his adversary.

"Thars." Rojka slowly sank down into the sand with the look and posture of resignation. Melody did the same. And the Spartans followed as well.

Thars walked around Rojka, and from Spartan to Spartan, eyes narrowed with suspicion as he examined the armor. His sword, a white blaze of plasma, still remained casually at his side. He stopped in front of Melody.

Melody stared back up at Thars. "Kill me and you will be at war with the full might of the UNSC."

"I do not see the UNSC here." Thars looked around with a kind of theatrical exaggeration. "Do you?"

"You know they're coming."

"Oh Envoy, everyone who could tell the UNSC anything about this meeting will be long dead when they arrive."

"Thars. There are bigger issues at stake. The Sharquoi are headed—"

He struck her face with the back of his massive hand, the blow knocking her down onto the sand. "You will live a little longer, Envoy. At least long enough to see the Demon Three dead before you. At *my* hands. Their blood will soak the sand, an unfitting cost for the atrocities at Glyke, but it will have to do. My people will call me the Killer of Demons. Rojka too will see my sword the moment before he dies. Payment for his bloodline's preservation in Rak. And then—"

The familiar sound of another energy sword activating interrupted Thars's speech.

The sword's blue light burst out from the chest of one of the Sangheili in the semicircle. The warrior looked down, stunned, and then he was lifted into the air by something invisible as he squirmed against the weapon and screamed.

Another scream cut through the shocked silence of Thars's Sangheili. A Sangheili on the other end of the semicircle fell to the ground, killed by a blur of motion wielding an energy sword.

Melody instinctively crouched closer to the sand.

"Here we go," Adriana said to her, calmly. "That was the plan."

Jai ran full speed at the nearest Sangheili the moment Rojka's three camouflaged warriors attacked. The surprised fighter fired at him twice. That was all. The plasma fire crackled across Jai's armor and his shielding hissed. Then he slammed into the Elite. They rolled in an explosion of dirt and sand down the ridge behind him. The Sangheili fought hard, scrabbling to get his rifle up for an opportunity to hit Jai point-blank.

But the rifle flew away when Jai cracked it with his elbow, using the rush of gravity and his own inertia to his advantage.

The Sangheili was resourceful though. His energy sword fired up in his other hand as they slowed to a stop. He launched up and forward with it, shoving it into Jai's chest armor, dragging the blade up toward Jai's neck. Jai pulled himself closer to grab the hilt of the energy sword. They both strained to overpower each other and control the direction of the blue energy spitting in the air between them.

Then Jai slowed his breathing. He looked past the flickers of readouts blinking warnings on the inside of his helmet and time slowed down. He concentrated on his enemy's own strength as he shoved the sword upward between them as hard as he could.

The Sangheili gurgled and spat as Jai slowly pushed the sword up through his jaw and deep into his skull.

Two more Sangheili tackled Jai when he stood back up and pulled the crackling sword free. Jai threw the first over his head and sliced the arm off the next one. The Sangheili screamed and rolled in the sand as Jai stabbed him in the chest and picked up his rifle.

He barely had time to lift the rifle and blindly shoot another attacker nearly a meter away. The last two Sangheili should have shot him from a distance, Jai thought, but their preoccupation with honor was their undoing. He might not get that advantage with the rest of them.

All around him Sangheili screamed, fought, and died. Adriana and Mike attacked in concert, blitzing the enemy and using the Sangheili's own weapons against them. Rank-and-file Elites were incredibly strong natural warriors and their combat harnesses made them resilient, but against Spartans it was never a fair fight. Especially when the trio of Spartans was augmented by three camouflaged Sangheili—Rojka's invisible wild card, the only survivors that remained from his cruiser. To the Elite's surprise, his three warriors had not returned to Rak, but instead traveled toward the besieged Suraka, intending to fight alongside their kaidon to the bitter end.

They'd kept that part of the plan secret from the envoy, to prevent her from inadvertently betraying something in her body language to Thars.

"The dropship!" Jai shouted.

Some of Thars's Sangheili were folding far quicker than the Spartans had expected. They covered each other as they fell back to the giant tuning fork of a Spirit dropship, whose long bays began to re-open from one end to the other.

Jai ran for the dropship as well.

Two Sangheili faded out of active camouflage and hurried alongside him. Rojka's surviving fighters.

Rojka himself was now in a fierce duel with Thars, their energy swords slamming together with an unfettered, raw hatred Jai had rarely seen.

"Where is the third one?" Jai shouted midsprint. Some ten Sangheili had piled back into the two bays of the dropship. Three on ten, and the Spirit itself—not the best odds. The dropship's ventral cannon ignited as it rose from the ground and plasma fire swung in Jai's direction. He dove with the two Sangheili behind the safety of a rock. The craggy outcropping shook from the impact of heavy plasma.

The heavy droning sound of the ship's engines kicked up several octaves.

"They're taking off! We need that Spirit!" Jai pulled back from glancing around the edge of the rock and shoved his back against the rock in frustration.

A Banshee whipped past them, flying just a few meters above the ground. Jai rolled away from the rock to see Rojka's third fighter bank the vehicle slightly to draw the dropship's fire and then rise up through the barrage of plasma fire.

The Banshee fired back, scorching the closing bay of the Spirit with a trail of white flame and throwing two Sangheili clear. Their limp bodies struck the sand in two quick thuds. The dropship's ventral weapon caught up and danced across the Banshee's right canard, blowing it free. Rojka's third soldier lost control and the fighter careened toward the ground but not before it collided into the back of the Spirit. The resulting explosion rocked the entire dropship. Secondary detonations ripped through the inside.

Thars's loyalists were now leaping from the vessel for the desert floor as the dropship listed, slid, and then finally crashed. Impaled in the sand, the ship's insides glowed blinding white and then exploded, sending debris and sand in every direction.

Jai stood at the ready and scanned the area for survivors. There were none—all of them had been consumed by the blast. Adriana and Mike had killed those who hadn't been able to retreat. Rojka and Thars, who now stood alone on the sand, warily circled each other with energy swords out.

Jai watched the debris burn, cursing under his breath. They'd needed this dropship, intact.

Melody Azikiwe staggered to her feet from where she'd taken cover on the ground, her face now grimed with dirt. "What the hell just happened?" she asked as she walked past him.

"We failed," Jai said, looking her up and down.

Adriana kneeled in the sand over a dead Sangheili, retrieving a plasma grenade from its side. Mike walked toward Jai, armor featuring a new burn mark on his right thigh.

"We needed that Spirit to get to Thars's ships," Jai said.

"Don't kill him!" Melody shouted to Rojka in Sangheili.

Jai turned. Rojka, his harness battered and covered in Sangheili blood, had smacked Thars's energy sword away. Rojka's entire posture crackled with fury. Weaponless, Thars sunk to his knees in front of him and looked down into the sand.

"Do not give me orders, human!" Rojka roared, raising his energy sword high in the air to slice through Thars's neck.

Rojka roared, his rage boiling over. *Thars.* The one who had riven the Sangheili here on Rakoi. He had destroyed everything Rojka had worked so hard to build.

Then the words of the envoy finally sank in.

He slowly lowered his energy sword.

"Contact them," Rojka said, breathing heavily. "Tell them to destroy any slipspace devices still working."

They had fought a brief but savage duel as the attack unfolded around them, paying little attention to anything but each other. It had been a contest of sheer strength and cold bloodlust, until Thars made a fatal error and lost his energy sword with one fateful blow from Rojka. Now Thars, fully spent, waited on his knees.

He had lost his war: this was the end for him. But Rojka needed something else. Not blood satisfaction but something more important. As strange as it felt to think in this way, thanks to the envoy.

"You still think a Jiralhanae *worm* will attack my fleet?" Thars asked through his bloodied mandibles.

"Do you think I risk my life, do you think I delay my vengeance, for no reason?" Rojka moved the sword closer. "I have seen the Sharquoi with my own eyes. Yes, they are *real*, not some myth as the elders of old spoke of. I have fought one myself. I have even heard Hekabe's voice from a Sharquoi itself. He controls them. *He* is our true enemy, cousin."

Thars snorted blood. "I do not care if the Forerunners themselves walk this world again. I will not tell my fleet to destroy their engines, nor will I give you control of anything I have wrested away. I expected a trap. My commanders warned me that you could not be trusted. But I thought I had enough fire power and fighters to survive it. I was wrong. But this is how I will die with my honor nonetheless: You will not have my ships."

Rojka grabbed Thars by the head and twisted him around to

face Suraka in the distance. The clouds of smoke above the city flickered with explosions. In the quiet they could all hear the distant gunfire and artillery. "Look, cousin. The human city falls. It is being eaten from underneath by a wretched hive of monsters which Hekabe controls. Rak will soon be overrun as well. So will other worlds, if Hekabe gains the use of your fleet."

"No," Thars said. "My fleet will burn the human ships out of the sky. We are not ignorant, Rojka. We have been watching. Preparing. After my people destroy the human ships that currently approach, they will come for me. And then they will come for you. If you wish to see your bloodline survive, you need to consider—"

Rojka shoved the tip of the sword into Thars's shoulder and watched him scream as flesh sizzled. "You have no honor."

Melody moved between them. "Shipmaster, you risk our homeworlds," she hissed down at Thars in Sangheili. "All of them."

"I am already on my homeworld right now," Thars said with venom in his tone. Rojka pushed her aside with his free hand.

"Rojka," Melody begged him, "we can't let this happen. They've got minutes before the Jiralhanae arrive with the Sharquoi."

Thars leaned back, satisfaction dripping from him. "The only thing you can do now is let me open communications with my fleet. Let me show you how great our power is as we destroy this thing that makes you cower. Then they will attack here in great numbers once they're done with this annoying alien threat. But at least you will die knowing that your world is safe."

"I will kill you before your people arrive," Rojka promised.

"We need to warn them what they're up against," Melody said to Rojka. "We need to let Thars open communications."

Rojka snarled. This would just hand Thars what he wanted. A second chance at them all. But then the image of Sangheilos burning dripped in the back of his mind. No, he could not risk such a thing.

Thars graciously spread his arms, then winced. The cauterized wound along his shoulder oozed Sangheili blood. "Give me the information to fight these new creatures, and I will be generous in the manner of your death."

Rojka shoved Thars toward the Spartans. "Open communications. Help his commanders, if they'll listen. And if they survive to come for us, we will deal with them then."

Thars staggered forward, glee seemingly on his face, as the Spartans trained their weapons on him. He pointed toward a holo-grip lying in the sand, a handheld comm projector used by the Covenant before the end of the war.

"Here," he wheedled, slowly picking the device up and brushing it off. "I can make contact from here. I will bring my ships to bear on the threat, and then they will come here for me."

"Understand," Rojka called out to him. "These Sharquoi are no normal threat. You must listen to the envoy's words."

"Of course, of course." Thars half scuttled to the side of a large rock, leaning against it while clutching his shoulder.

Melody leaned over, talking to Thars in measured but rapid tones as she brought him up to speed. Occasionally Thars glanced back at Suraka, or nervously toward Rojka.

It would not be so difficult to stride over and stab that satisfied look out of his face, Rojka thought.

Thars finally activated the hologrip with a snap. The hologram of one of Thars's commanders appeared over him, hovering in the desert air. "Shipmaster, you are alive! The enemy approaches. Our defenses are ready. We are just minutes away from finishing repairs on our drives."

Thars looked pleased with himself. "Begin targeting the

human ships, Commander. I will have adjustments to battle strategy based on information just given to me. But we must not delay engagement. Shoot them out of the sky."

The image of the captain flickered out, replaced with a feed from some stationary camera, possibly on the mountain peaks around Thars's camp. Rojka took in the scene: four Surakan ships flying over the mountains toward the Sangheili fleet, which was now just a handful of cruisers and corvettes. They were damaged but well armed.

In a few moments, Thars's boasting would prove either true or empty.

Everything hung on this.

Ellis heard something large and angry pounding at the blast doors leading into the bay. The last of the tunnels had been blown up to slow the Sharquoi down. The militia gunfire had faded away in spurts and screams.

Every thud made her team jump.

"Almost there," she murmured. They had the original Warthog the gauss cannon had been pulled from ready to go. The hybrid weapon lay on its side in the bed and was being assembled frantically by what was left of her team. They hadn't had time to mount it on anything.

The doors creaked and bent inward.

"There are no more militia out there," someone said, voice breaking.

Ellis's hands shook as she applied a last piece of solder from where she crouched on the rear bed. Smoke curled up past her nose. She looked over and saw the door bend further. Thick, gray fingers reached underneath the lip and the Sharquoi on the other side bellowed as it struggled to force the door up.

The heavy blast door moved a half meter upward with a screech.

"We have to go," the driver said. The Warthog lurched forward. Ellis yanked the soldering iron back just before she would have shorted out a circuit.

"No, not yet!" she shouted.

"They're coming in!" the driver shouted back.

Rhodes ran over to another bench, pushing tools aside. "Do you think the gauss cannon will be enough? It can only knock out the Forerunner machinery for a minute or so."

"Yes. If we can get to the Jiralhanae leader, it will be worth it. We need to finish wiring this up," Ellis said.

Rhodes picked up a rifle from the table and fumbled around with it until it clicked. The bay door jerked upward again as the Sharquoi continued pulling at it.

"Go!" Rhodes shouted. He aimed the rifle down at the door's lip and fired a burst. Bullets smacked the door, hitting a meter above the Sharquoi's fingers. Rhodes aimed lower. Fired again. Bits of gray flesh splattered the floor as the shots tore chunks out.

The Warthog shuddered and started rolling through the bay. Ellis perched on the bed with what could only approximately be called a pulse cannon and held on as tight as she could. "Rhodes!"

She swore at the driver to stop, unwilling to leave one of her team behind, though she knew he was right to leave. They had run out of time. Two more engineers ran toward the door to join Rhodes. They carried knives and crowbars.

This was insanity.

Rhodes dropped to a knee and kept his rifle aimed right at the door. "Keep going," he shouted in a shaky voice.

The door buckled and flew forward. It struck one of the engineers, killing him instantly before it bounced on. Three Sharquoi rushed into the bay. Rhodes stood in place and kept firing, right up until the moment one of the creatures took hold of him and swept him against a pillar in a spray of blood and concrete.

The driver slammed on the accelerator as Ellis desperately tried to get straps over the cannon and tie it into place. No time to wipe her tears away or even look back at the thudding and crashing as the Sharquoi continued Hekabe's relentless attempt to kill them all.

CHAPTER 23

Melody crossed her fingers. If Thars's fleet managed to stop the Sharquoi attack and turned this war against Hekabe around, she, Rojka, and the Spartans would likely be dead when the UNSC arrived. His Sangheili fleet, which only needed to hold off the attack for a short while before being able to fly once more, would come for him and kill with impunity.

But they would have saved many, many lives.

So every deep, hot, sandy breath out here felt so damn electric. It was another moment of life. But it might just be one of their last.

"We begin," the Sangheili commander's voice said. *He sounds smug*, Melody thought. *So smug.*

She watched the holographic image of tiny human ships hanging in the air over the blazing sandy desert as the device projected it in the center of the group. Rojka had slowly moved back to stand near the injured Thars, who leaned against a rock while holding out the hologrip in his hand. The Spartans kept their weapons ready and likely one eye on Thars, even though he did not look very mobile anymore.

"First wave," the Sangheili commander's disembodied voice informed them. Plasma leapt into the sky, rising inexorably toward the human fleet, striking and piercing ships at a distance. "We are successful, Shipmaster! These humans are piloting barges—they are not made for war. We are swatting them out of the sky like flies!"

Melody watched the carnage. For a brief moment, hope fluttered up from under her rib cage. The Sangheili sounded so confident of their win as the human ships rose upward, exposing their bellies as they climbed higher.

"Our drives are online!" the commander shouted. "We will rise to meet them—Wait. What? This is odd."

"What's going on?" Melody asked, though part of her already knew it wouldn't be anything good.

"There are . . ." the commander began. "They—"

Thars struggled to his feet, suddenly concerned and ignoring the flash of Rojka's energy sword as it pointed warningly toward his head. "Tell me what is happening. Tell me everything!"

The hologram shook. A new camera view materialized before them all, likely from one of Thars's own ships. The human ships aimed to get *above* their enemies, not trying to get close to them. They passed through the plasma fire, not even bothering to attempt evading the horrendous and steady barrage. Torn apart, vomiting debris, they now plunged toward the camera, evidently on suicide runs.

"They cannot destroy all our ships that way," Thars protested. "This makes no sense."

As the Surakan ships fell through the fire, bursting apart from the Sangheili's anti-aircraft fire, large gray bodies launched from the human ships' hangar bays and plunged through the sky with uncanny speed down toward the Sangheili ships. Thars's ships tried to take aim, but this was far more than the plasma could destroy.

"There are hundreds of them!" the commander hissed.

"Sharquoi! They are truly the Sharquoi!" another Sangheili officer said in the background, voice awed.

Another shift took place as various cameras suddenly went offline: a view from the side of a cruiser. Sharquoi struck the ground. Many of them didn't move after impact, but enough survivors did. Lumbering to their feet, shaking their heads, they waded into battle with any Sangheili that approached them.

Some Sharquoi managed to breach the Sangheili's hangar bays, led by a handful of Jiralhanae with jump-jets. Other Sharquoi landed atop the Sangheili ships, their wicked claws tearing at the sides of the hulls.

"They are trying to rip their way in!" the Sangheili commander reported, shocked. "This cannot be real!"

"*Destroy your slipspace drives!*" Thars screamed at the hologram. "*Destroy your ships! Turn your weapons on each other before it is too late!*"

"You gave us orders not to—!" the commander shouted.

"No, I was wrong!" Thars replied.

"Shipmaster!" The hologram shifted to the commander again so that he could see Thars face-to-face while on his bridge. Other Sangheili worked frantically in the background.

"*Do it!*"

The all-too-familiar form of a Sharquoi broke through a wall at the rear of the bridge and smashed into the commander. The Sangheili's body flew away, limp, and the camera went offline.

Thars dropped the projector in horror. Then he scrambled through the dust as it rolled away, shouting for anyone to listen.

Melody felt sick . . . and then came a faint moment of relief. She would live for a while longer, as Thars had lost. But at what cost? Her worst fears had been realized. "Hekabe and the Sharquoi are now able to get off-world."

Rojka began to speak. "Thars, you are a small-minded hatch-ling of little strategic ability."

Thars did not appear to even hear him, huddled over the sand in utter defeat.

Rojka took a step forward and continued. "You were arrogant. You thought you could be kaidon, but you did not properly secure this world. You acted before you had true strength over me, doom-ing your fleet and mine. You never had strength over Hekabe. You risked not just Rakoi, cousin, but all other worlds, even Sanghelios itself, by your actions."

"It was not I who released those things! I did not do this!" Thars shouted.

"You brought Hekabe here to do your fighting for you, and therefore it is you who bears the shame for it. You have failed, Thars. You have failed in every possible manner, and in all things."

Thars half twisted around in horror, struggling to get away as Rojka took another step forward and swung the energy sword into his cousin's neck. The strike, long and clean, was so fast that Mel-ody saw it only as a blur.

Melody held her hands over her mouth in shock. "I can't be-lieve you did that."

Rojka snapped his energy sword off. "Believe it."

She let out the gasp she'd been holding inside. "It doesn't mat-ter, does it? We failed as well."

"It is true. But today I saw my enemies perish before me. So I will carry that memory with me until it is my time to go, how-ever long or short that time may be." Rojka sounded pleased. "Though I had hoped Thars would give me a greater challenge than this."

Jai stepped forward. "You'll get that from the Sharquoi and

Hekabe." He pointed back toward Suraka, where smoke spilled above the distant horizon and lazily gathered in the sky. "They still need Hekabe to control them, if they want to leave Carrow. We know where he is. We need a new plan."

Ellis sat next to the pulse cannon latched onto the rear bay's floor as the Pelican swung out over the Uldt desert sands. Only half her team had managed to escape; they were all strapped into the Pelican's jumpseats now. The militia who'd picked them up were quietly staring out of the open bay door of the Pelican. Everyone appeared to be exhausted, not to mention covered in grime and blood.

Then there were those people from her team left back in the tunnels as she and her group made their way to the evacuation point where the Pelican waited.

So much death in the running retreat.

Long lines of civilian evacuees passed under them and entered the underground corridors, which led through the adjacent mountain range to the wastelands beyond. This passage would provide them the cover they needed to escape the Sharquoi. Lamar had no doubt plans to rig them with proximity mines, which could take the entire mountain down on anything that got close. Ellis gave the migration one last look as the Pelican leveled off and put the skyline behind it. Citizens fleeing on foot, carrying whatever they could into the Uldt heat.

There were pockets of militia running hunter-killer patterns against the Sharquoi, trying to draw them away from the evacuation. This would be a noble effort, but Ellis doubted any would survive. They were basically playing the role of diversion while the hundreds of thousands of humans who could fled into the belly of the earth. Eventually, their luck would run out.

"They'll need to move quickly once they reach the other side. They won't survive long out in that environment," someone muttered over the comms.

How long could *she* survive out there, though? Ellis lived and worked in a major urban center. That was *her* life. She knew nothing about the desert, other than how nice it was to camp in or hike through. If they made it to the oases, they should be fine. But if they got caught out in the wasteland, during a sand storm— *husbands, wives, children* . . . Ellis shook off the thought. That was Lamar's problem now.

"They're out in the open once they get past the eastern mountain. If he manages to locate them, Hekabe will herd them however he wishes and kill them all," Ellis said, in even more of a whisper. "So our plan needs to work."

She was going to have to swallow her pride and find more allies in the fight ahead. She couldn't do this alone.

It was now up to Ellis to get this makeshift weapon into the alien structure and end this once and for all. And for that, she needed Spartans. It would be risky. She had to take it though. There was no way the handful of militia on this bird could last a second down there.

"Found them!" the pilot shouted. "They didn't disable the Pelican's beacon, which made this a helluva lot easier." Lamar had been furious to find out the Spartans had 'requisitioned' a Pelican for themselves. He hadn't even wanted to give Ellis one. Every Pelican counted for the evacuation.

Their own Pelican flared out and landed. Ellis unbuckled

herself and clambered out to the edge of the ramp. "Envoy! Spartans! Sangheili. We need to talk."

They'd watched the approach warily. Now the alien kaidon, UNSC operative, and Spartans trooped up the ramp of Ellis's Pelican. There were fresh burn marks and chips on the Spartans' armor, but they were otherwise all still alive and functioning. Sangheili bodies littered the desert, and what looked like a Covenant dropship burned in the sand.

They've been busy, she thought.

"Did you gain control of the fleet, Rojka 'Kasaan?" Ellis asked. Melody began to translate but the Sangheili seemed to anticipate what she asked. He shook his head, causing Ellis's heart to sink.

Melody stepped forward. She was the worse for wear, Ellis thought. Covered in dust and sand, and looking as tired as everyone else seemed to feel. "Thars is dead, and the fleet has been lost. The only comms chatter we're getting from Thars's camp—what's left of it, at least—suggests that the Sharquoi and Jiralhanae crew who survived are preparing the Sangheili vessels to attack Rak next. They're deseperate to find more ships and get off this world."

Ellis took a deep breath, plans realigning in her mind. She might not have access to support from the air, but if Hekabe's stolen fleet was heading for Rak, they had an opportunity—and more specifically, they had time.

"*I* want to stop Hekabe." She singled out the Spartan leader and directed her words at him. "Our militia is dying in the streets of Suraka, trying to hold back the Sharquoi so that civilians can get to safety. Everything we've got left is devoted to the evacuation. My vice-governor and my advisors will not let me take resources away from that. There isn't much I can commit to an attack, so I need your help."

The Spartans loomed large in the dark cabin of the Pelican.

Ellis couldn't tell if they were considering her offer or not until their leader cocked his helmeted head. "What do you have in mind, Governor?"

She pointed at the cannon. "We built an electromagnetic pulse cannon out an M68 and a repurposed Havok core. Based on all the data we culled off Hekabe during the siege, our chief engineers believe this machine will be powerful enough to disable the Forerunner device the Brute uses to control the Sharquoi. It's designed to fire a highly concentrated EM burst, which we believe will sever the Jiralhanae's connection and make him vulnerable."

"How sure are you that it works?" Melody asked, stepping forward and looking dubiously at the tangles of cables and power leads. Ellis knew it looked like an unholy mess of random, and probably dangerous, parts at this point. The half-disassembled Havok was welded onto the leg above the mount, and the gauss cannon was slung out on a large metallic frame.

"Sure enough that I'm going in with it," Ellis said. "We designed it to be bolted onto a Warthog, or something that could move quickly if necessary. I need a team to support us during the attack. I need to get close enough to Hekabe to use it, and I need your help to do that."

The female Spartan squatted down, leaning in close to the Havok. "This is a suicide run," she said, sounding completely unconvinced. "We would be marching into the heart of Hekabe's fortified position to attack him directly. With all of those creatures in there with him."

"I know that. And I'll need to be with the machine, in case anything happens to it. That's why I came to you," Ellis said, with one final effort to convince them. "Spartans who've been living behind enemy lines for years in secret seem like the kind of operatives I need to get this thing close enough to Hekabe. I've lost good people to build this weapon. Are you a soldier willing to use it?"

Jai looked over from the jury-rigged electromagnetic pulse cannon to Mike. "How's the engineering side of this?" It looked like the mother of all rail guns to him, only with more cables and some unconventional mount. And it still had a viewscreen. Not many handheld weapons came with readouts.

"I think there's a small chance it might just blow us all up when we fire it," Mike said. "So if we do this, we need to make it count. We should make sure we're standing right next to Hekabe."

"Adriana?"

"I want a second good shot," she said.

Jai studied the governor one last time. She was trembling slightly. Not out of fear—just too many stimulants. He wondered when she'd last slept. Could they trust something built by someone shaking like a detoxing drug addict? Probably not, but they didn't have a lot of other options at hand.

"Hekabe has burrowed deep down into the Forerunner structure at the center of the crater," Jai said. "Last seismic readouts I saw indicated that it's a long straight shaft three hundred or so meters and then it flattens out into a larger chasm. Beyond that, we've got nothing. Right now, the crater is crawling with Sharquoi. We can't fight through everything down there—but we have the skies free. So we do an insertion drop. Fast, drop down the shaft, and pull chutes or jump-jets just before impact. Then we move through the installation, no stopping or gawking."

"Can we fly a Pelican with a Warthog down there?" Ellis asked. "The opening has been uncovered by Sharquoi already."

"No. Need the air drop, so that we're hard to hit. I'm not even sure a Warthog would work well," Jai said. "Do you have anything small and nimble that we can mount this weapon of yours to?"

"Jackrabbit would work," Mike said. "You have any of those?"

Ellis thought about that. "We did at one time. Lamar will be using them for the evacuation. I can try, but don't get your hopes up. Like I said, we don't have a wealth of assets anymore—not ones I have access to. Everything has been leveraged to get people out of Suraka safely."

"If we can get one, this could work," Mike said. "A low-altitude drop into the shaft, we go on foot, and I'll guide the bike in and drive it once we're inside. They're highly versatile. We can park and shoot it. It'll get to just about anywhere we need."

It was a long shot, Jai thought. They all knew it.

"One small question," Jai said. "How do we find Hekabe when we get inside? A Forerunner structure can be pretty vast, and the recon feeds we've seen go blank after they hit the bottom."

"We have sensor data that gave us information about Hekabe's electromagnetic activity. It's a signature we can track once we're inside. That's what this is for." She put her hand on the pulse cannon's display. "It's built into the EMP weapon. But we're running out of time. We need to go now before Hekabe's larger force returns from the desert and takes over the airspace around the crater; otherwise we'll never get in."

"I'll go as well," said Melody.

Adriana shook her head. "You're not trained—"

"I'm the one who freed you and almost died in the process. And I'm familiar with the site and what we're up against—more than anyone else here. You'll want me there."

Rojka stepped forward and conferred with Melody. After listening, he spoke briefly in Sangheili to them all.

Jai smiled as he heard the translation in his earpiece, and he gave the Sangheili a curt nod.

Melody said to Ellis, "Rojka says he pledges himself to your battle against Hekabe and his Sharquoi. He adds that we will destroy him or die gloriously in our attempt."

Jai looked around. A ragtag band of fighters and one cobbled together EMP cannon running off a repurposed nuclear bomb.

"Okay, that makes six of us," he said. "Let's do this."

CHAPTER 24

E llis fumbled with the straps of the pararchute as the Pelican flew low over Suraka's roads. She would be flying tandem with Jai. "This thing opens automatically, right, if something happens to you?" she asked him.

"No, it does not," Jai replied. He patted the ring on the strap against her shoulder. "If anything happens to me, pull this as hard as you can once you enter the structure. Flex your legs right before you land on something."

"How do I steer?" she asked.

"It's too late to show you now," Jai said. "You shouldn't worry about it. If something happens to me, with you this close, you'll probably be dead anyway."

Ellis flinched as the pilot flew them underneath a bridge. "That's not as reassuring as you might think."

Jai looked back at the bridge through the open ramp of the Pelican, and the swaying Jackrabbit magnetically anchored to the dropship's tail. Mike already sat inside, staring back at them.

Jai ignored Ellis's statement and continued. "We're gonna be just high enough that the Sharquoi can't reach us, and low enough to get in before they can formulate a response."

Plasma fire whipped down the steel and glass canyons of Suraka's skyscrapers toward their transport. The attack came from Jiralhanae gun platforms that had been combing the streets, high above the Sharquoi infestation. Ellis held on to the Spartan as some of the plasma grazed them. The dropship shuddered, the pilot struggling for a second to get altitude and regain control as the Jackrabbit swayed wildly.

The vehicle faced backward, the larger rear single wheel hanging just above the Pelican's ramp. The yellow, single-pilot chassis of the Jackrabbit shook, the two wheels on booms at the front bouncing slightly as another splash of plasma fire shook the Pelican. Usually a heavy gun sat over the rear wheel, but they'd replaced that with the significantly bulkier pulse cannon that Ellis and her team had cobbled together.

Ellis had convinced Lamar to let go of one single ground vehicle for this operation. That was all they had: one Jackrabbit, and a crate of small arms and explosives. They had successfully rigged the vehicle with the pulse cannon and a chute, ready to be deployed once they reached the shaft. The installation process had gone smoothly. The Spartans seemed to be comfortable with the habit of regularly soldering guns onto things.

The other concession Lamar had granted paced them in their wake: a second Pelican with an alternate squad of eight Surakan milita. Led by a Corporal Wyse, Lamar had pulled them from running diversions in the streets to assist with the drop.

Jet wash kicked up debris on the street below as they raced on. Ellis wrapped her hands around the straps and tightened her grip. She looked forward through the pilot's cabin again and saw the crater rapidly approaching. The female Spartan and the envoy would be jumping tandem, and the Elite would go on his own. They were all making final prepartions.

Then we face Hekabe and his monsters.

The Jiralhanae chieftain had taken everything away from Ellis. She wanted to rip everything away from him in return. She wanted him to *see* her rip it all away. For him to know, deep down, this same horror and helplessness she felt.

Ellis closed her eyes, her rage dancing in the flickers of light behind her lids. She was exhausted, but there were reserves of strength somewhere below, torrents of energy that now came to the fore.

Their Pelican burst free of the cluster of buildings and screamed over the rim of the crater. Sharquoi littered around the basin floor turned to face them as they passed overhead.

"Almost there. Get ready," Jai said to her. Her harness connected directly to him. Thanks to the Spartan's size, Ellis felt like some kind of pack strapped to his back. Ellis gripped her straps tightly as Jai climbed out of the Pelican's bay and onto the Jackrabbit's frame, nothing but air whipping past below her legs, the ground a blur far below. Her heart hiccuped and she gritted her teeth.

Jai, on the other hand, didn't seem at all bothered by the height or the fact that the dropship was still racing forward as he casually maneuvered into position on the Jackrabbit.

Adriana, with Azikiwe strapped to her back, moved out of the Pelican's rear bay onto the other side of the Jackrabbit. The kaidon, Rojka, followed a moment later, climbing onto the bike's rear wheel and hanging on to a series of grips underneath the pulse cannon.

Then the Pelican nosed straight up into the air. Ellis was slammed into the Jackrabbit's cage by the sudden climb. Below them, the crater fell away as the Pelican gained altitude. They were now right over the petal-like iridescent green opening to the aliens' underground structure—which, at this point, looked like a small dark cavity.

From this height, it looked far too small to drop into.

"Five." Jai reached up behind his helmet and tapped her shoulder, and held up five armored fingers.

"Four."

Ellis closed her eyes and held her breath on three.

". . . two, one, go!" Jai said out loud. There was a short metallic clank and then they fell.

Ellis swallowed a scream as the wind struck her face and the Jackrabbit tumbled, dizzying her as she opened her eyes and saw crater, buildings, Jai, and the Pelican whip end over end around her. She closed her eyes again. She opened them again just in time to see the Pelican struck by plasma fire, its tail blown free by the blast.

The second Pelican had pulled the same maneuver, climbing up into the sky before releasing its passengers out of its back. Bodies tumbled out with arms and legs stretched out to control their descent. Corporal Wyse's militia joined them in the air, arms outstretched as they fell. Plasma bolts soared upward but couldn't get a bead on the small targets—just as the Spartans had planned.

Jai and Adriana pushed free from the Jackrabbit, flying up behind it. Rojka followed suit. Mike and the bike plummeted toward the splayed Forerunner petals and the shaft at the center. Above, both the Spartans twisted in the air, controlling their descent.

The petals around the opening of the structure started slowly raising themselves off the ground to close back up into a tower. Even more plasma fire rose into the air around them. This time Ellis could see the source: Jiralhanae gunner positions stationed across the crater. The energy snapped and hissed around them.

Ellis screamed as one of the bolts zipped by, searing the air by her arm as she threw it up to protect her face. She pulled her arm away and looked back down.

The shaft grew larger, even despite the closing petals. A series of stairs and structures wound around its walls into the dark reaches below. Even as they rushed toward it at terminal velocity, it still looked too small to aim for.

Ellis had studied the scans of the structure and saw how much space was down there radiating out from around the central shaft. It was a vast series of underground caverns, and Forerunner structures coiled throughout.

The petals were trying to snap shut before they dropped through the shaft. If they did, they would all be dashed against them and it would be over in an instant. Hekabe sensed their approach and was trying to react, no doubt.

Then the hole grew wider, massive even, and the closing petals rushed past in a sudden blur as they dropped through the center of the structure. Floors of blue-gray metal flew past her until Ellis violently jerked to a stop. She smacked her head against the Spartan's armored back and spat blood.

"You okay?" Jai asked.

He and Adriana had deployed their own parachutes, as did the Sangheili. And then the Jackrabbit followed suit, punching upward with a quick jerk as its canopy spread. The Spartans pulled at their cords, controlling their descent as they spiraled quickly inside the dark shaft in the middle of the structure.

"No. I'm not okay. But I'm alive," Ellis said.

The Jackrabbit hung slightly forward, favoring the twin booms connected to wheels. Mike swung around again, using his own weight to aim for one of what appeared to be descending ramps situated around the edges of the open bore, running down the middle of the structure. The Jackrabbit bounced horribly as it landed but appeared to survive the descent.

Right before their own impact, Jai cut Ellis free. She dropped to the ground at the base of the shaft. Adriana dropped Azikiwe to the ground and landed. Armor screeched against the floor as Adriana and Jai slid and came to a stop, severing the chutes and letting them blow into the shaft's interior wall.

"No Sharquoi—it's a quiet spot," Jai said. "They weren't expecting this stunt. But be ready, they'll be coming."

Ellis reached for the pistol she had taken from the armory, unlatching its strap as she steeled herself for what lay ahead.

The Surakan militia came in hard next, one of them collapsing on impact. As squad leader and medic, Corporal Wyse ran over and crouched by the soldier lying on the ground. She wadded the parachute under his head and ripped open a pants leg. The limb underneath had been completely shattered.

"Corporal?" Ellis asked. "We can't carry anyone, this isn't that kind of mission."

Wyse hit the man with a dose of painkillers and looked up. "I know. I'm stabilizing him. We need to find somewhere to try and hide him as best we can. Everyone deserves a chance to live."

They dragged the injured soldier to a shadowed corner at the side of the shaft, then readied their weapons and followed Wyse behind the first group.

Ellis walked along the back of the Jackrabbit, checking the pulse cannon over, looking for any damage from the landing. So far, so good. She breathed relief.

"Sharquoi," Rojka called out from ahead, the word recognizable to all of them. He stood upslope, looking out across a large chasm with an ambient red light filtering upward. His body language was clear: impatience. He was ready to fight and Ellis couldn't really blame him. She wanted this to be over more than anyone else.

Mike spun the Jackrabbit around toward Rojka. Jai grabbed on to the vehicle's frame, locked into positon next to Mike.

"Ready?" Mike asked.

Adriana pulled herself onto the other side of the vehicle, holding on as the Jackrabbit edged forward. She had a sniper rifle magnetically anchored to her back, and a battle rifle in one hand at the ready. "One good shot is all we need," she said softly.

The metal ramp under them trembled with the sound of even larger feet thundering their way.

"Hop on back," Jai said, offering Ellis a hand. She climbed up behind him, holding on to his armor with her hands and her foot lodged into a groove on the bike. The vehicle moved methodically into the cavern, and Ellis peered out across a vast bridge slung over a lava pit.

Then a Sharquoi came around the bend.

Jai looked down the chasm as Mike gunned the Jackrabbit around a corner and onto a bridge. The chatter of a rifle echoed back down from where they'd come, followed by three explosions. Jai glanced back. The injured soldier they had left behind hadn't been able to remain hidden, or had chosen not to. That was the sound of his last stand.

The rest of the squad sprung around with only a few pained glances behind them, weapons trained forward as they all proceeded across the large bridge.

"The Sharquoi arrive!" Rojka shouted, Jai's earpiece translating.

"Hekabe has found us," said Mike over the comm. "Remember:

watch out for synchronized behavior. They fight as one, not individuals."

Two Sharquoi bounded directly across the bridge at them. Adriana leapt from the Jackrabbit and pulled out her sniper rifle. Two direct shots, and the lead Sharquoi slowed. It stumbled and fell to its hands and knees. Blood and brain matter leaked onto the bridge floor. Still it fought to drag itself toward them.

Rojka lunged for the other Sharquoi's limbs. The energy blade flashed in the gloomy light as Rojka sliced the creature's arms free of its body. It roared as it struggled to get its footing and fight Rojka. The Sangheili instead kicked the creature in the back, forcing it over the edge of the bridge and down toward the lava below.

The half-dead Sharquoi on the ground crawled painfully on its hands and knees. Rojka now walked over to it. He leaned down to glare at it.

"We are coming for you, Hekabe!" he roared. "We are coming!"

He drove his sword into the creature's skull.

"Not as heavily defended down here," Adriana said. "Most of the Sharquoi are outside and above us. I don't think Hekabe expected that we would jump right into the hole like this."

"Who would?" Jai asked, stepping from the side of the Jackrabbit. Ellis and Azikiwe followed, as they warily walked across the bridge and toward a series of large towers that came into view.

Rojka slipped back to a position on their left. "Hekabe knows only violence and trickery. Not general strategy. We shall use this to our advantage. We will attack the human way."

Jai wasn't sure if that was intended as a compliment or as an insult.

Mike braked to a stop as they reached the center of the bridge that spanned the dull blaze of liquid rock below. The glint of fire reflected off distant walls.

Jai looked back to Ellis. "Governor? Where next?"

She climbed up onto the back of the Jackrabbit and looked at a screen strapped to its frame. "Deeper. If something happens to me, know you need to just keep going deeper."

"If we go too much farther, we'll end up pretty warm!" Mike shouted. "In case you didn't notice all the lava."

"I see the lava," Jai said as they continued crossing the bridge. "I also see the Sharquoi waiting for us."

Fifty gray forms waited for them at the end of the bridge, where an island of earth held a Forerunner structure comprised of a large wall, towers, and an opened gateway. And far more Sharquoi than that now thundered down the shaft's spiraling ramps, corkscrewing along the walls rising above them all. The creatures poured in from the surface in a landslide of Hekabe's will that would bury them soon enough, Jai thought.

Rojka paused as the Spartans stopped in the middle of a bridge.

Standing on the shallow apex of the bridge Rojka could see the enemy Sharquoi waiting for them at the end. This Forerunner fortification must have been where the governor's scans located Hekabe.

Jai stepped aside to ask the human governor something. She looked across the bridge toward the structure and shook her head.

"Why have we paused?" Rojka asked the Spartans.

"The closer we get to the device, and to Hekabe, the more impact the cannon will have," Jai said, walking back. "The governor says we are not close enough yet."

"Then it is my time," Rojka announced. He had known this would come. "Spartans, we must surround and trap Hekabe."

"What?" Melody looked at him, then back at the wall of Sharquoi at the end of the bridge. "We're the ones surrounded, Rojka."

"If you live," Rojka shouted at her as he moved down the bridge toward the waiting Sharquoi, "speak of my bravery! I want my bloodline to add it to their battle poem!"

"What are you going to do?" Melody asked.

"I will be the spear of our assault," Rojka told her. He pulled his energy sword, but didn't activate it yet. "Wait until you see me scatter them in confusion. Then you will know it is time to press your own attack!"

Rojka ran ahead in a dead sprint. He knew the Sharquoi could tell he was coming. Echolocation would track his movement. He launched down the bridge, leaving the others behind. It felt good to run and stretch his legs far out. Ready to kill. To hunt.

These creatures were not to be feared. Rojka would pass them like a whirlwind.

Would Hekabe be able to trap him eventually? Possibly. But not before Rojka got close enough. Not before Rojka tied up Hekabe's attention on his own suicidal attack.

As Rojka approached the end of the bridge, the Sharquoi retreated toward a dais at the very front of the Forerunner structure's entrance. There were towers behind the large wall. It was a strange keep, certainly a fortress of some kind, Rojka thought. And through the entry and beyond the wall, he saw his Jiralhanae enemy, gravity hammer at his side.

Hekabe waited inside the structure, surrounding himself with Sharquoi like a wall. Still visible pieces of the Forerunner machine coiled inside his head reflected the cavern's light.

Sharquoi jumped from one and two levels above Rojka down to the base of the bridge, abandoning some kind of perch at the top of the towers. Apparently Hekabe took this sudden, sole threat against him rather seriously.

"Hekabe!" Rojka screamed, snapping on his energy sword. "Hekabe, I am here!"

It was madness, of course. Ten Sharquoi moved directly in front of him with incredible speed. Alone, Rojka stood no chance.

But Rojka fought to be remembered, for his honor, and to give this strange team of allies he stood with a chance to kill Hekabe and save countless worlds.

The Sharquoi charged, and the Sangheili met them in kind.

As he struck the first beast, sword flaring brightly, Rojka heard the humans' vehicle roar and gunfire chatter as the team rushed down the bridge after him.

Dropping low to the ground, Rojka slashed his sword through yielding Sharquoi flesh that sizzled as he cut the trunk-like legs off at the knees. The creature's large claws snapped through the air over his head.

Two of the Spartans joined the attack, their armored boots stomping the stone floor as they landed nearby. Rocket-propelled grenades from two militia soldiers exploded around him, and the death cries of Sharquoi filled his ears. Maybe Hekabe was taken off guard by the direct attack, maybe the Jiralhanae was being defensive, doing his best to keep a wall between him and the Spartans who had already nearly dealt him a mortal blow. Either way, the creatures seemed to scramble to deal with the swarm of enemies around them.

A Spartan engaged one of the Sharquoi off to Rojka's side. The demon dodged the creature's blow near the ledge, throwing it off-kilter. It swung around and threw the Sharquoi over the side and into the lava below, no ammunition wasted as they ran toward the dais.

Far behind them, at the other end of the bridge, the remaining human soldiers struggled to slow the Sharquoi rushing down from the rear. They had brought the heaviest of their infantry weapons to deal with these monsters. But the humans fell one by one, inexorably. All they really could do was buy the Spartans time. Time to get the vehicle and its cannon further down along the bridge, without the Sharquoi destroying it.

The floor around Rojka shook. Sharquoi streamed out of the towers and the walls that enclosed them. Dozens more emerged from the magestic alcoves that shimmered with blue energy. This must have been where the Forerunners had kept them all these thousands of years.

Rojka fought like a demon himself, jumping, diving, weaving for his life. For all their lives. He was drawing the Sharquoi into a close-quarters battle where they were forced to fight against their numbers, often damaging each other with their great size and powerful blows. Here, in the thick of their mob, their great strength was turned against them.

Four Sharquoi lay dead by Rojka's hand as he pierced the protective wall of creatures, and now Hekabe himself stood just a few bounds away, just through the Forerunner wall. Hekabe turned his attention from Rojka to the humans and then back again.

Without warning, a Sharquoi slammed into Rojka before he could get inside, throwing his body across the ground toward the lava pit. Rojka's sight blurred and the world darkened as he momentarily blacked out from the intensity of the strike. Instinctively, he jammed the blade of his sword into the cavern's floor as he tumbled toward the edge. His weapon snapped free from his hand, but Rojka caught the ledge just as he slid over, nearly falling to his death. He glanced over his shoulder at the lava below him, then pulled his way back up and rolled to the right.

As his vision returned, he paused for a moment to assess the battle.

His gambit had worked. Hekabe had pulled the Sharquoi to himself in a protective reflex. That had given the Spartans and human militia time to get down here. The Sharquoi's concentrated numbers actually played to the Spartans' advantage, making the smaller and nimbler targets difficult to kill.

But as Rojka watched, a Sharquoi fell from the air and struck the front of the small human vehicle as it moved toward the base of the bridge. Sparks and flames erupted from its front end as the one called Mike leapt free, rolled to the side, and shot the creature at point-blank range. The beast reeled backward and fell over the side of the bridge.

The governor ran up to the pulse cannon from her safe position behind the vehicle, where she and the envoy had remained during the battle. Jai and Adriana darted back to join her, providing cover fire as Sharquoi pressed toward their position.

Rojka looked back toward Hekabe, still within the Forerunner walls. Dozens of new Sharquoi flowed around him, coming from the base of another cylindrical tower at the very heart of the Forerunner structure. They poured out of the front gate.

Overhead, more of the creatures began to leap from ramps and bridges connecting the towers high above them. They would fall for hundreds of meters, then strike the bridge as living bombs. Each impact jostled everything on the bridge as the creatures landed with deafening thuds. Rojka wondered how long the bridge could hold under such duress.

The governor and the Spartans reached the burning vehicle at the same time. The small human machine had held their best hope to stop Hekabe. Now it looked irreparably damaged.

Rojka roared in frustration and returned his focus to the Jiralhanae and the muscled wall of gray surrounding him.

"It is time to die with honor!" Rojka shouted.

He leapt at the Sharquoi, his eyes fixed only on Hekabe behind them.

CHAPTER 25

Ellis skidded to a stop next to the wreckage of the Jackrabbit. She climbed onto its back to examine the weapon.

"Keep pushing it forward!" she screamed at the Spartans. Sharquoi bodies struck nearby, gore exploding across the bridge, each strike shaking the entire structure to its moorings. The further they got toward the Forerunner towers and Hekabe, the harder it would be for the falling Sharquoi to hit them.

Jai grabbed the two wrecked front booms of the Jackrabbit and lifted the vehicle up. He started pushing it as Ellis shoved damaged pieces of equipment aside and tried to figure out if the cannon could still work.

Adriana and Mike provided cover, unleashing a torrent of fire at encroaching Sharquoi.

"The cannon?" Adriana asked, walking backward with them.

"I don't know, I don't know," Ellis muttered, her mouth dry. The Sharquoi had hit the front of the Jackrabbit; the back had snapped up into the air and remained there, the frame bent. Mike had kept the Sharquoi from doing any more damage, but it may have been too late.

She watched the readout run through a quick self-assessment

as she also hurriedly checking the wiring. "It has power. It's functional!"

"It will take too long to push it closer," Jai said, turning back to her.

He stepped forward and grabbed the mount. He ripped it slowly free from what was left of the vehicle. She could hear his power armor groan under the stress, then the shriek of metal as the weapon tore free from the back of the Jackrabbit. The Spartan hoisted it above his shoulder to awkwardly carry the massive cannon, its framing hanging by his chest and waist. This was a death trap, if the enemy got close enough.

"Let's go, Governor," he said, voice strained as he thudded forward. Adriana and Mike fell in before him to provide cover and Azikiwe trailed behind with a battle rifle raised.

The Sharquoi had congregated around the Forerunner structure that held Hekabe, evidently attempting to protect the chieftain from Rojka, who they could no longer see in the forest of gray bodies.

Ellis glanced behind to see her fellow Surakans had fallen back to the top of the bridge, which was now covered in viscera from the falling Sharquoi. The militia was attempting to stop Sharquoi from getting across the bridge. Corporal Wyse was bent over one of the few remaining squad members. Her hands dripped with blood as she tried to stop him from bleeding out. But the soldier pulled free to load a rocket-propelled grenade and fired it into the stampeding mass of Sharquoi coming toward them across the bridge.

One of the alien beasts reached the squad. It mercilessly grabbed for Wyse, claws ripping through her stomach and yanking her away from the wounded soldier. He managed to reload again and fired at it, but a second Sharquoi crossed the distance to join the slaughter. It kicked his head in, the gore splattering against the gray hide of its thick feet.

Ellis swallowed bile, wondering how many of the Sharquoi from the surface Hekabe had recalled to his position. Looking up, she saw more coming down the shaft's side and making their way to the bridge by the second. She patted her side for the pistol she'd been given, but couldn't pull it free. She realized she couldn't fumble around with the weapon if she also needed to help with the pulse cannon.

She hurried to keep up with Jai. When she looked back behind her, all she could see were Sharquoi on the top of the bridge.

With her and the envoy at the rear, the Spartans pushed on, battling Sharquoi that broke forward from the huddle around Hekabe. Behind that, deeper into the Forerunner citadel, more chaos erupted as other Sharquoi massed to try and stop Rojka from getting close to Hekabe. Seeing even more of the creatures spilling out of the towers behind them left Ellis feeling dazed.

There are so many.

The entire cavern shook with the thunder of feet, open combat, and Sharquoi falling onto the span from above, many of them killing their own kind in mindless sacrifices.

Rojka, now surrounded by Sharquoi himself, saw the Spartans approach and howled defiance in words that Ellis could not understand.

"Rojka is right," Jai said, dropping to a knee with the cannon. "This is as close as we get to Hekabe. Governor Ellis, fire it!"

Time felt like it slowed to a halt and everything went silent, like a dream, as Ellis scrambled up to Jai's side and the jury-rigged cannon's controls. He had sighted the gauss cannon aimed straight through the entrance at Hekabe, who was screened by a shifting, muscular wall of Sharquoi that he only occasionally appeared through.

A mist of purple blood burst over them as another Sharquoi struck the ground nearby, knocking four other creatures off the ledge and into the lava below. Out of the corner of her eye, Ellis saw yet another one just miss entirely and fall past the edge. A column of yellow and red magma rose from the surface with the impact, spilling across the bridge.

"Governor!" Melody shouted from behind her, panic clear in her voice. Ellis returned her focus to the readout. She could sense that the Sharquoi were close. Deadly close.

She powered up the cannon and quickly set its parameters.

One of the Spartans—she thought it was Mike—narrowly survived a massive blow from two Sharquoi. He was tossed across the ground toward the ledge, his pursuers close behind. Nearest to Hekabe, Rojka disappeared under a sea of corded gray muscle.

Ellis waited a split second for the shifting bulk of Sharquoi to reveal Hekabe, then quickly turned the switch and stabbed the firing button with a thumb.

The cannon whined. The blue Forerunner lighting in the structure ahead of them flickered, the EMP taking its toll. The blast was mostly silent and sightless, invisible to the naked eye.

A few last thuds and roars punctuated the cavern before an eerie silence dropped down over them. The Forerunner structure went dark with only the lava below to light the cavern interior.

Ellis could see enough to know that the cannon had worked. Hekabe stood stunned on the dais, his hammer dropped from his hand, as the Sharquoi suddenly lolled around him. One Sharquoi to her right staggered over to the side of the bridge and simply disappeared over the edge.

"Strike confirmed," Jai said. "Adriana, Mike! Report!"

"We're going to get him again, just to be sure." Ellis quickly reset the keys on the cannon, and fired again. Alarms flashed and buzzed on the weapon's display. Wisps of smoke rose in the air from burned-out circuits unable to handle the sheer amount of power dumped through them.

She checked the screen of the power unit. "The cannon's shot. The Havok powering it is still functional though. If it comes to that."

The Sharquoi still wandered around, ambling as though blind or asleep. Ellis imagined that they were not sure what was happening, having been suddenly yanked free of their neural connection. Whatever it was, they likely had a limited window.

"Governor?" the envoy called out. "Did it work?"

Ellis didn't answer but ran toward Hekabe, cautiously weaving between the lumbering Sharquoi before they could come to their senses. She passed under the massive Forerunner entrance and through the gate. Behind her, Jai heaved the pulse cannon to the ground and the other Spartans came up from behind, lights on their helmets activated.

She was close, so close now. The Jiralhanae crouched on the ground, vomit and blood pooling in front of him. It seemed as though his injuries were taking their toll without the Forerunner device functioning to hold him together.

This was her chance. Suraka would never be attacked again.

Forcing aside fear, Ellis swung her legs over onto the alien's back and dug her fingers into the metallic pieces of the Forerunner device that stuck out of his skull. She began to pull. Pieces of the device slowly separated from his head with a sickly ripping sound. They flowed back to and joined each other in her hands as Ellis pulled them free of the Jiralhanae's skull. Tendrils covered in blood and tissue slid out of Hekabe as Ellis yanked even harder.

"Governor!" Melody shouted.

Dozens of confused Sharquoi scuffled, bellowing and howling behind Ellis. Untold numbers of them filled the great chambers and passageways of the darkened Forerunner structure. They would be shaking free of the last of their confusion. But who knew what they would do when fully unhindered. They were like wild animals.

Ellis used her legs to push against Hekabe's back to pull the last tendril free. The Jiralhanae cried out in pain as the final section of Forerunner machinery broke away. Ellis fell to the ground holding the device, which looked mangled and strange in her hands as it seemed to struggle to flow back into some memory of an original shape.

"No!" Hekabe gurgled, clutching at his head as blood gushed down over his face. He slumped over and began to crawl, blindly searching for something.

"The Sharquoi are approaching us!" Adriana shouted.

"Don't shoot them—they're confused!" Jai announced. "Stay clear. Even better, stay still if you can!"

But stillness could only last so long. Gunfire lit up the dark near the far ledge, and Ellis caught a glimpse of a Sharquoi chasing down the third Spartan, Mike. He narrowly dodged its blow, but others had now been signaled. They approached threateningly from the side.

The Sharquoi might not be coordinated by Hekabe anymore, but there were hundreds of these things still up above in her city. How many more of her people would die, hunted by the Sharquoi now free of Hekabe's control? What if Sharquoi found citizens being evacuated? Or the oases?

"It's time for all this to stop," Ellis said. She held up the gore-covered device. It shifted around in her hands, coming to life and slithering down her forearm as the Forerunner structure behind her returned to a blue glow. The EMP was wearing off. "My people will be safe once more."

Ellis held the alien machine over her head and then let go. The Forerunner technology burrowed down through her temple and eagerly wormed its tendrils through her skin and into her skull. She screamed as blood—Hekabe's and her own—dripped down her face as the artifact bore its way down into her brain.

Rojka scrabbled out from underneath a heap of dead Sharquoi in time to see the Forerunner machine burrow down onto the human governor's head. As she began screaming, the now dying Hekabe jerked at the sound and fumbled about on the ground. His movements were confused, no doubt due to massive brain damage, as he appeared to look for something.

With a groan, Hekabe managed to stand up with the aid of his gravity hammer, swaying back and forth for a moment. Then he stumbled toward the human. Rojka wasn't quite sure how the Brute could even survive after what had happened to him, yet Hekabe did, against all odds.

Rojka looked around for his sword, but turning caused him to ache despite himself. A broken left arm and several cracked ribs were bad enough, but something inside him hurt enough to leave him breathless. Hekabe was not the only one dying, Rojka realized with painful insight. The Sharquoi had dealt Rojka too many punishing hits.

The mostly blind Hekabe heard Rojka's cry and lashed out

from his stupor to strike with his gravity hammer. The blow to the chest shattered Rojka's harness. He flew back, landing hard against the base of the nearest tower.

Spitting blood, Rojka stood again, shaking himself back to consciousness amid the sound of Sharquoi thudding about and someone screaming angrily. Now the human governor had stepped forward, just outside Hekabe's reach.

Her eyes blazed with a hatred that, Rojka suddenly realized, was aimed not just at Hekabe but at himself.

He thought about the immense losses her people had taken in this pointless war that Thars started. Thought about Melody Azikiwe's words: *My nightmares look just like you . . .*

"Governor?" Rojka rasped. "What are your intentions with that machine?" It would be easy for her to take revenge, wouldn't it? To give in to fury and anger. To try and wipe this world clean of any threats to her city. Including Rojka, and all his kind. *"Governor?"*

A large, clawed Sharquoi hand forced him down to his knees and pinned him to the ground. Rojka saw the Demon Three surrounded by Sharquoi as well. A single creature held on to each Spartans, forcing them into a defenseless position. He wondered how many Sharquoi had died to capture them while he'd lain against the base of the tower, shaking himself back to consciousness.

"Would you like to try and kill me?" Ellis intoned, still standing beyond Hekabe's reach and ignoring Rojka.

The Jiralhanae, still free but unable to see out of his ruined face, spun around in the direction of Ellis's voice, following the sound. Then he raised the massive hammer and blindly lunged forward.

Humans! Hekabe thought, though his mind reeled and struggled to deal with all that had just taken place. He knew he wasn't whole. He knew he was a blade's edge away from death. He knew it was something to do with his head and his eye. He was missing so many things: memories, thoughts, even feeling in his body. Physically he was completely insensate. But he was familiar with the emotion he felt upon hearing these creatures.

Rage.

He was consumed with it. They had wronged him. And now they threatened *everything*, all that he had labored years for.

He desired only one thing: to utterly annihilate this human right where she stood. Hekabe could feel Oath of Fury high in the air over him, faithful and ready to do his bidding. His back muscles strained to hold it and then bring it swinging down toward her head.

Within a split second, he would have safety. Everything would be made whole again.

The gravity hammer struck something and stopped halfway down. Struggling to see through the blood and flesh that covered his one good eye, Hekabe looked up to find a giant gray fist above him, holding the hammer's head like a small trinket. A Sharquoi had stopped the weapon in place just centimeters over the human's head. She had not even bothered to move out of its way.

Hekabe let go of the hammer and reached for the human's neck, but the Sharquoi grabbed his wrist with its other hand. Another Sharquoi swiftly moved in and took hold of his other arm. Hekabe's chest stretched and strained against the impossible tension threatening to rip him apart.

He bellowed, spitting blood and defiance at the human in front of him, the one who dared to ursurp his power over these creatures.

Then two massive claws ripped through his chest, punching holes through his body that could never be repaired.

He looked down at them in confusion. Blood dripped from their tips onto the ground. *His* blood.

Hekabe tried to scream his anger again, but all that came out was a burbling froth of red.

The claws moved, taking him with them. They pulled him away from the human and lifted him into the air. Hekabe writhed, trying to pull himself free and continue his attack. It was all that was left in his brain, the last piece of a mental command that his body worked to fulfill.

Get the vertex once more, and all of this could be mended.

But the Sharquoi that speared Hekabe on its claws threw the Jiralhanae out and away from the citadel, over the ledge and down into the pit below.

Everything, Hekabe thought, *had been within my grasp.*

Now everything fell away from him as the world grew brighter and infinitely hotter.

CHAPTER 26

The person who used to be Ellis Gass watched Hekabe fall through the eyes of a dozen Sharquoi. The small form struck the lava far below and something like a surge of satisfaction rolled through her.

She could feel herself expanding out further through this new space. It was deep and rich, and it flooded her with new energy.

This victory had been a close thing. Even as Hekabe attempted to kill her, she'd been struggling to figure out how to control the swirling pieces of the storm that whipped past her. But the storm had spoken.

Calm yourself. Relax, don't fight, it whispered.

And Ellis, who hadn't slept in well more than five days, who was beginning to see the edges of her vision melt and blur, fell toward the reassuring embrace of near omniscience with relief. She'd been so tired, so ineffably tired.

Now, as Hekabe's threat faded completely away, Ellis began to percolate her attention through the Sharquoi and back to the spot that her body swayed upon.

She knew she might collapse soon. It should have happened already, but her body was riddled with chemicals abusing her

— 355 —

adrenal functions and resetting her neurochemistry. Fleeing out into this larger consciousness was like waking up after running on the edge for so long.

Ellis noticed Melody Azikiwe slowly pick up a battle rifle. "Don't do that, Envoy," she said through the Sharquoi that surrounded Azikiwe. "Or I will be forced to neutralize you."

The envoy is ONI, Ellis thought. She should have had a Sharquoi do that from the start.

She was only just now learning how to wield this power, still.

Azikiwe dropped the rifle to the ground by her feet and raised her hands. The other dangers—the Spartans—were held in their place by many Sharquoi. The creatures also now gripped the Sangheili kaidon, tightening their fists as he struggled in place.

The threats to her had been negated. She could relax now.

Relax.

Rojka 'Kasaan stared at her. "You planned this," the Sangheili said. For some reason, she could understand his alien language now, through the senses of the Sharquoi.

"No." Ellis looked at Rojka through sonar, his body a set of shifting audio reflections. The moment she had seen Hekabe on his hands and knees with the Sharquoi milling about in confusion, she had known exactly what had to happen. Although she had previously wanted to secure it for Suraka and stop the menace, it was only at the end that she could bring herself to do what truly needed to be done: take the machine for herself.

There was no other choice.

"It was the only way to make us safe," Ellis told them.

"Then why are you holding us?" Jai called out.

Ellis shifted her attention to the captives just outside the Forerunner walls. With a single thought, the Sharquoi dragged the Spartans back toward the base of the bridge, and she used another

Sharquoi to nudge the envoy along. Another Sharquoi hoisted up Rojka, who still bucked under its iron grip, and followed the others. Ellis joined them, using her own shaky human legs, and stopped by the ruined pulse cannon. She used her own tired, human eyes to look at the Havok nuke was buried in the depths of the wires.

"I don't trust you," Ellis said. "The Sangheili warred against Suraka. The Spartans are tools of ONI, created to attack people who want to govern themselves without interference from Earth's government. You are all threats . . . but I now have the power to protect this world."

Rojka glared at her. "You sound like Hekabe," he hissed.

"*I AM NOT HEKABE!*" Ellis screamed from hundreds of mouths, the sound echoing all throughout the cavern.

Rojka pulled against the Sharquoi, still trying to break free. "And what does this new world look like? Will my people still live here?"

Hundreds of Sharquoi appeared at the far side of the bridge. They marched in lines back toward the Forerunner towers.

The moment the machine had burrowed into her skull, Ellis had begun calling all of the Sharquoi back to her. All throughout Suraka, the creatures were doing everything within their power to return to the Forerunner structure. Many of them dragged Jiralhanae that they had captured, despite the fact that a mulititude of the defeated Brutes had been trying desperately to hide, cowering away in the dark.

As the Sharquoi returned, they threw screaming Jiralhanae down into the lava below.

"The Jiralhanae, at least, are not welcome here," Ellis said softly. "Understand that this is *my* world. I will not let anyone harm it any longer."

Jai's joint popped loudly in his ears as his right shoulder nearly separated. Only the Mjolnir armor prevented it from being completely ripped out of its socket by the Sharquoi who held him. Alarms and his heads-up display told him the armor had been pushed far beyond tolerance levels. Any more pressure from the Sharquoi and he would literally be torn limb from limb.

The searing pain would have left any normal creature unable to even think. But Jai dug deep, breathing slowly. "The UNSC will not allow this to stand. You'll bring far more destruction upon yourself than you've seen so far."

"Ah, Earth. Always threatening us as well. You kept this a secret from us, and we paid for that instead of you." Ellis reached down through the cannon's wires, accessing the Havok core's readout pane. She tapped the display. "There's a voice in here with me. It's telling me I shouldn't be doing this. But I know what has to be done. I have to make a hard choice. I'm pulling all the Sharquoi back in here right now—all of them. I'm going to end this."

Jai was beginning to suspect that they had an entirely new problem on their hands.

"Governor? What hard choice?" he shouted. "What are you doing with the nuke?"

A gray wall of Sharquoi moved forward, forcing Melody further back onto the bridge. The Sharquoi holding the Spartans tossed them next to her with less care. They tumbled to a stop, with Rojka joining them a moment later.

"There won't be much time," the governor said through the mouths of all the Sharquoi around them. "I have already reopened the facility to let the remaining Sharquoi back in. The Havok's timer is set for ten minutes."

Jai, flexing his abused shoulder, glanced over at Rojka, who looked like he was in much worse shape.

"But there are wisps of other things here with me," the Sharquoi around them all said together. "Memories of others. They're . . . very strong. They do not want me to do this, but it must happen. Or everyone will keep trying to gain this power for themselves. The voices here, they'll try to stop me before long, so you should leave now. I might have to trigger this manually before the countdown. This is the only way to stop others from using this machine. It's the only way to protect Carrow. So run for your lives, right now. This world will be safe. It will be free."

"Ellis!" Melody called out. "We can't leave you!"

"I said *RUN!*" the Sharquoi all boomed at once.

Gray Team fled. Mike hefted Melody and Rojka limped behind, his legs too damaged to keep up. They passed hordes of Sharquoi who moved across the bridge slowly and without direction.

"The nuke will take out part of the city! There's no way we can get clear!" Melody shouted as they reached the bottom of the main shaft and began the race to the top.

"I'm calling a Pelican," Mike said. "Comms are spotty, we're so deep down here. We'll need to get higher to be sure they're hearing us."

"Can we trust her? The governor?" Jai asked Melody.

"She was overusing stimulants. She was in a bad place to begin with. But I think she loves this city, so that's why she's doing this."

The Sharquoi lining the sides of the ramps began to roar. They looked as though they were awaking from a slumber. The running Spartans climbed closer to the top with Rojka trailing behind. But it was a long way to the top via the spiraling ramps around the shaft's walls.

"I'm feeling naked without a weapon here," Adriana said, wary of the Sharquoi's new behavior.

It now seemed like Ellis was struggling to control the Sharquoi. Some of them lunged at the Spartans. Clearly a great internal battle was raging inside the governor's mind.

"I don't think we're going to make it," Melody said, looking up toward the sky at the top of the shaft. If Ellis made good on her promise, the nuke would go off in only a few minutes, and they still had a long way to go to the surface.

CHAPTER 27

Ellis wobbled and nearly fell. As her consciousness faded, the Sharquoi stepped back from her. She was losing her footing, both physically and mentally.

No! She needed to hold.

Where are the Spartans? She cast around inside the whirlwind and found them only halfway up the winding ramps leading to the crater.

She wasn't going to hold it together long enough. And as her mind dissolved, the winds that dwelled inside fought to survive. Yes, she could still control the Sharquoi. But the machine's nature had been stained with traces of consciousness before hers, and these traces were fighting to live.

Even a shadow of Hekabe swam somewhere around here in the deep.

Ellis skipped from mind to mind in the network of Sharquoi that hadn't made it back to the underground structure—until she found what she needed.

She stood outside now. The militia had seen the Sharquoi turn around, give up the fight, and start moving back to the installation.

The Sharquoi had formed lines and scrambled across the Uldt, through the city streets, out of buildings—all to get to where Ellis had summoned them.

One of the Sharquoi turned back to the cautious militia shadowing them. They raised their weapons ready to fire.

"This is Governor Ellis Gass. The Jiralhanae are no longer in control." The words came out muddled—she had to hope they could be understood. "I need you to do something very important."

As a part of her spoke to the militia, another part of her saw the last of Hekabe's pilots aboard the command bridges of Sangheili ships—the same vessels that had attacked her people only days ago.

The Jiralhanae intended to use these warships to assault the Sangheili keeps. They'd already made several passes, destroying buildings from above with plasma fire. If she did nothing, within moments they would continue to rain fire down on the Sangheili. They would never recover. Humanity would reign over Suraka, supreme and unchallenged. Ellis could take vengeance for the attack on her own city. Eye for an eye. Blood for blood.

Make them pay, a voice whispered to her. *Ensure Suraka's safety.*

Ellis balled her hands into fists and dug deep. Past her desire for revenge and through the pain. Sharquoi charged past the Jiralhanae and began battering against the ships' controls and displays until something critical was damaged. The Jiralhanae on each ship attempted to fight back, but it was too late. The ships plummeted toward the Uldt's desert floor. Nothing would survive impact. Connections to the Sharquoi fell away, one by one, as each alien vessel crashed into the ground.

Ellis was trying to clean the entire mess—a war that spread out across Carrow.

And all the while, she was slipping away herself, like dust in the wind.

Jai stopped in the middle of the ramp and looked up at the shaft. They had several hundred meters to go. "We have four minutes," he said. "We can't make it to the top by then. Mike?"

"Still no comm, maybe if we went a little higher . . ." He didn't sound confident, Melody thought.

Melody's heart raced. These were going to be her last few minutes alive, then.

Noise thundered down the central shaft. *This is it!* she thought.

One of the Sharquoi leapt down from the mouth of the hole high above, dropping down to their level.

"Go!" it shouted.

"We can't make it!" Melody said. "Ellis, there has to be another way."

The Sharquoi looked up into the sky and then, without further explanation, launched down into the darkness below.

A single Pelican dropped carefully down through opening, the roar of its engines echoing all throughout the core shaft. The large rugged shape obscured any sunlight from above.

Melody moved closer to the edge and waved her hands, Gray Team and Rojka quickly joining her.

With a blast of hot air, the Pelican dropped level with them and spun about, wobbling as it backed the bay's ramp as close to them as the pilot could manage.

Jai grabbed Melody by the waist and made the long leap first. Adriana and Mike came next. Rojka, though severely injured, refused assistance. He hobbled into a run and launched into the back of the Pelican, then clattered across the floor toward the front of the aircraft. He lay where he slid to a stop, unable to move any further. Jai crouched by him. "He's badly injured, more than he'll let on. He's unresponsive. He needs medical help."

"The governor sent us," the pilot interrupted. "Should I drop lower to get her as well?"

"No," Melody said. "Get us out of here. As soon as possible."

The ramp closed and the Pelican awkwardly rose, climbing up with increasing speed. Jai stood up and stepped over Rojka's slumped form. "There's a Havok down there about to blow. Aim for the sky and punch it."

"Got it, sir," the pilot said.

As the Pelican's engines raised in pitch, everyone grabbed hold of something.

Darkness slowly ate the edges of Ellis's vision. Sharquoi advanced along the bridge, breaking free of her control and looming over her. She looked up through the shaft from another Sharquoi's eyes a final time and saw the Pelican climbing overhead, the air underneath it rippling hot from the howling engine exhaust.

Peering down the tunnel to the pinpoint in the center of her fading vision, Ellis stumbled over to the Havok.

Two minutes left.

But those three Sharquoi coming for her weren't going to wait. The winds inside this thing, this—the name popped into her mind: *vertex*—weren't going to let her destroy it. They would protect it no matter the cost.

Ellis flipped the controls over to manual. Turned the keys, pushed her palm out over the remote ignition she'd welded onto the frame.

Blindness finally took her. The vertex fighting back.

How far away were the Sharquoi? How much longer could she delay this?

She'd given the others every last second she could. It was time to secure Suraka's future.

Ellis took a breath and thought about Jeff. His voice and his smile.

She wondered if she would ever see him again.

Then she pressed the button.

The Pelican burst out of the Forerunner structure nose high and engines screaming. Gray Team clutched the bay's jumpseats, and Rojka slammed into the back of the vehicle with Melody piling on top of him.

Jai looked ahead through the pilot's viewport. Only sky filled the view.

As the aircraft righted itself, dipping forward to vector away from the crater, it banked hard, revealing the entire pit below through a starboard window. The ground shuddered and trembled. With a single jolt, the earth fell down into darkness. It looked as though something was sucking the entire crater down in on itself, as if the planet were taking a deep breath of dirt.

Then the earth lifted up, rock, dirt, and debris blown outward by an enormous fireball that liquefied and burned through everything, vaporizing the entire pit in a matter of seconds. The shock wave from the explosion raced below the Pelican and struck Suraka.

The dropship shivered as a wall of dirt struck its belly. The force of the blast had risen higher than the pilot estimated. Alarms wailed and the aircraft began to spin as the engines guttered out.

"Crash positions!" the pilot shouted.

Ahead of them, the shock wave struck the outskirts of Suraka. At the edge of the destruction, buildings swayed and collapsed. All the windows in the buildings that still stood disappeared in a spray of glass. Debris rained toward the ground.

After everything it had suffered, the city would endure still more destruction.

The Pelican spun around dizzyingly as the pilot fought to control the dead weight of the craft as it careened toward tall, impossible-to-navigate buildings. Flaring hard, the pilot brought the dropship down low and attempted to stabilize it before impact.

They struck the street and slid for half a block. The Pelican finally came to rest at the bottom of a bank, the floors gaping open to reveal the inner workings behind what had once been silvered windows.

"Gray Team?" Jai called.

"Mike here."

"Adriana here." She sat up and rested her elbows on her knees.

"Rojka?"

The Sangheili could only groan in reply.

"Melody?" Jai asked.

"Yeah, I'm alive," she said.

The pilot dropped the ramp and Jai stepped out. A black cloud rose above the buildings. All that remained of the excavated crater now was an immense canyon cut deep into the planet's crust. It roiled with a thick blanket of dust—all that was left of what had once been one of the Forerunners' darkest secrets.

CHAPTER 28

R ojka watched the desert tilt and whirl from the back of a Pelican as they approached Rak with the rear bay ramp opened. The spires and great domes of the Sangheili keeps appeared in view as the aircraft banked once more for its descent.

Home, Rojka thought.

He never thought he'd see Rak again. Especially at the very end. The sight now felt like a dream, as if a mirage had appeared in the desert.

The Pelican's engines whined as it touched down on a sparse field just outside the city. Rak itself sprawled out along the valley, rock outcroppings jutting up into the air between the keeps. The river Astlehich burbled down through the center of the entire city, surrounded by carefully maintained gardens that wound alongside it. A bright green paradise hidden in the middle of a vast wasteland.

Rojka thought back to contemplative walks he'd taken along the many decorative paths and bridges that crossed the Astlehich. He silently hoped he would be able to do so once more.

"Do we need to worry about that?" the pilot asked Rojka, the dropship's comm system translating into the Sangeili's own language.

Thirty Sangheili in full combat harnesses spread out around the edge of the field, weapons in their hands.

"I do not know," Rojka admitted. He looked down at his own harness, battered beyond repair, and his empty hands. He was still exhausted, nursing broken ribs and strained muscles in his legs. It had been two full days since the event at Suraka. The humans had put his arm in some sort of sling, but he refused to use it for this return home. If these Sangheili were coming for him now, there would be little he could do to fight them. "Thank you for the transportation, pilot. You should leave as soon as I step clear."

"That's the plan, yes, sir."

Rojka wearily got to his feet, limped down the ramp, and stepped out onto the field.

As promised, the moment he was clear, the Pelican lifted off and arced away over the rock outcroppings. Rojka looked at the blurred forms of the approaching Sangheili through the dust. Had they pledged loyalty to Thars? Did they want to take control of the keep for themselves?

Even with painkillers, set bones, and human medical care, Rojka fought to stand strong in the middle of the field.

"Kaidon Rojka!" the Sangheili in the lead shouted.

Rojka squinted. To die here would be good, Rojka decided. His death would not go unnoticed.

He then recognized who addressed him. "Kaidon Akato 'Dakaj."

Akato's warriors surrounded Rojka at a careful distance, their weapons in hand.

"So, you have returned. What are your intentions in these keeps of Rak?" Akato asked.

"My intentions . . ." Rojka had spent the entire flight across the desert mulling that over. He looked past Akato. "I wanted to see the city again. My city."

"Your city?"

"A poor choice of words," Rojka admitted. "I claim no ownership or leadership. But I put everything I had into building this place. I risked it all to come to this world. But during this war, I came to realize that I might never see Rak or my own keep again. I wanted to see both at least one last time."

Akato's hands moved away from his sides. "We have lost our fleet, Fleetmaster. We suffered at the hands of the Jiralhanae. The Sharquoi almost entered the city. You do not have many friends here, Kaidon."

Kaidon. Rojka felt a sliver of hope uncoil in his chest at hearing the word. "Many of the Sangheili in Rak chose Thars. Thars is now dead. I have taken my vengeance. He wasted our fleet in pursuit of his own plans. He invited the Jiralhanae to this world, and he rightly bore the punishment for this. I do not seek the support of Sangheili who have turned their backs to me. But I am not interested in vengeance any longer."

"Even against the Demon Three. I am told they still live."

"I fought with them," Rojka said. His shoulders hunched, then rose again as an invisible weight slid from them. "We spilled enemy blood together. We stood side by side to save this planet. I will not take their blood. Enough have died for the cause of war. I see no vengeance satisfied here. The war is over . . . and now I just wish to see my home."

Rojka stood before Akato, waiting to see what might happen next. Akato had been a lesser kaidon, relatively new to Rakoi. Rojka did not know him well. A profound change in the leadership of the keeps had certainly occurred here in Rojka's absence.

Akato must have taken an opportunity to rise to power, because none of the kaidons who had lent Thars their fighters were here to meet Rojka.

That meant they were all dead.

That also meant that Akato was now trying to decide if Rojka was an immediate threat to his new leadership.

"The Jiralhanae began their attack," Akato said softly. "And without either your fleet or Thars's, we were vulnerable. You fought to your end to try and stop this. But it should never have happened in the first place."

Rojka inclined his head but said nothing.

"Even though the attack ceased with their deaths, which we now know was thanks to the intervention of the human governor, we are still vulnerable. My most trusted advisors agree with me that without our fleet, this is the truth, Rojka. There is nothing above us. Not a single ship. What are we without a fleet, kaidon?"

"I do not know," Rojka admitted.

"So we must face a new future, as a result. One that acknowledges that all creatures living on this planet are vulnerable. You have clearly established an alliance with the humans. We need a speaker to them."

"And you believe I can be this?" Rojka asked. In some ways, to some Sangheili, this would be a lesser role. It was clear that Akato was asserting his authority.

"Do you not think so?" It would be a difficult position. But Rojka could still lead through influence, if not brute strength. Just like a human. He could influence both species that lived here, he realized. He could, like Melody Azikiwe, speak things into being.

"I agree that we do need the humans now," Rojka said. "We are both rebuilding. We would be stronger together. The humans' Earth government will have their own fleet in orbit soon, and their attention. Sanghelios will no doubt be looking far more critically at us as well. I want Rak to survive. That is all I wish. I pledge that I will pose no threat to your leadership, Akato. I will speak to the humans for you."

It felt so alien to say such things. He was turning his back on many years of yearning and aspiration for leadership through combat and other means.

Both the Sangheili and the humans had lost so much to war. But there was the rebuilding to oversee if either of them were to survive here. There was a peace to be secured with the humans. A future to work toward.

A future that, Rojka had learned after all he had been through, he wanted to see made.

"I will be your envoy," Rojka said.

Akato nodded to the group of Sangheili. They opened the circle up and fell in behind as Akato swept an arm out toward the keeps lining the valley. Rak. "Welcome home then, Rojka. We have much to discuss. The future of this city, and of this world."

"Thank you, Kaidon." Rojka fell into step beside him, walking back toward his home, and a very new and different future.

Yet one he now welcomed.

The heavily armored, gun-like shape of the UNSC frigate *Welcome to the Snipehunt* popped out of slipspace just above Carrow.

When Jai saw it approach from the cockpit of the Pelican, he turned to Adriana and Mike. "Are we ready for this?" he asked privately over the team's helmets.

Melody, up in the cockpit, glanced back and gave them a thumbs-up.

Jai nodded to her.

"Time to face the music," Adriana said. "The war is over. The Covenant is gone. Maybe we'll be discharged. To be honest, I never thought about what the end of our fight would look like."

"Do you really think ONI has changed?" Mike asked. "Or that the fight is over? They used us before the Covenant showed up. You know they'll keep doing it afterward too."

There was a long silence in the Pelican as the dropship moved to meet the frigate's open hangar bay.

Mike looked over at them. "We're Spartans," he said. "I don't know anything else. I have nothing else."

"So we stay together and see what's coming?" Jai asked.

"There are still threats out here," Mike said. "We saw what happened to the Surakans. The Brutes and the Elites. I don't think fighting is over."

"What about Glyke? There's a possibilty they'll try us as war criminals to save face for what happened to that world," Jai said. "You know that, right? You're prepared for that?"

"I'm ready for anything."

Welcome to the Snipehunt swallowed the Pelican, which settled into the hangar bay. It had been six years since Jai had been inside a UNSC ship. *Six years.*

Jai paused as the ramp opened enough for him to see what was waiting for them.

"What is this?" he asked out loud.

Dozens of crewmembers lined the hangar bay in full dress uniforms, positioned perfectly by their rank. One of them called out a command to salute, and they responded in unison.

Melody stepped into the middle of Gray Team. "They're here to see you," she explained. "Not many Spartans of your generation survived the war."

"This is strange," Jai said.

"They're here to honor you. Take it in, Spartan. Look around. Know that your enemies have died and that you lived," Melody said.

Those words, Jai thought, *are very Sangheili*. She'd spent a lot of time with the aliens; he wondered how much had rubbed off.

"Earth survived," Melody said. "And now Carrow survives. We're still alive to build a future, because of the sacrifices you all have made. Do you still believe in futures, Jai?"

Jai looked at the crowds waiting expectantly. "I didn't think there was one when we were floating around Glyke, before we went under. Didn't think there was one when you unfroze us."

"And now?" Melody raised an eyebrow.

"A lot changed down on Carrow," Jai said.

"Well then," Melody said, "try believing in one."

She walked past him and stepped down off the ramp. Jai followed her, with Adriana and Mike flanking him. The landing bay filled with deafening applause that reverberated off the walls.

"Jai's right. This *is* strange," Adriana muttered.

"You've come back heroes," Melody told her.

"We're not heroes," Adriana said to her. "We just followed orders as best we could in a horrible situation."

"They see heroes. Now come." Melody led them through the assembled crew and to the officers waiting to receive them.

The officers saluted the Spartans as Melody introduced them.

"I'm so sorry, we have to cut this short," Melody said to them. "I'm told we have a meeting in one of the briefing rooms?"

"Of course," a visibly disappointed lieutenant said. "Chief Petty Officer Dunkirk here will lead your way."

CPO Dunkirk looked less starstruck than the lieutenant. He silently led them through the ship's corridors. Jai found the familiar angled doorways and long hallways reassuring. He'd come home, in some way. CPO Dunkirk stopped outside a briefing room near the bridge.

"Thank you," Melody told him in a tone that clearly relieved him of any further need to hang around. She looked at the battered Spartans. "Ready?"

In answer, Jai opened the door and stepped in.

An ONI officer waited there. He looked briefly annoyed when he saw Melody. The look disappeared under a familiar mask of calm. "I'm Commander Yarick. I'm here to help Gray Team reintegrate. Most of the commanding officers Gray Team dealt with are no longer operational. I'll be taking over where they left off."

"Before we talk about reintegration—" Melody started to say.

"Ms. Azikiwe," Yarick interrupted. "You've already detailed your concerns. Our current admiral has experience with the SPARTAN-II program and its pressures. She is quite familiar with the situation and what is needed moving forward. We have the best people at our disposal to work with Gray Team. The first step for them will be some basic functionality analyses and some shore leave back on Earth."

That seemed to mollify Melody slightly, but she didn't back down. "This team has given a lot out there. You understand that, right?"

Yarick's lips thinned. "Ms. Azikiwe, you work for the Diplomatic Corps. While your services to the Office of Naval Intelligence are highly regarded and valued, they are also no longer required. Now, I need you to leave the room while I continue to debrief Gray Team. I understand you need to be making arrangements with Governor Lamar Edwards for a continuing mission here on Carrow?"

Jai watched Melody realize she had been dismissed just as matter-of-factly as she had dismissed Officer Dunkirk.

But Melody wasn't about to back down, so Jai decided to defuse the situation before it escalated. "It's okay, Envoy. We'll be all right. There's still a lot that needs to be worked out with Suraka. Thank you for looking out for us. We'll talk to you, after this is all sorted out."

Reluctantly, Melody turned around and left the room.

"Sir. What about what happened on Glyke?" Jai asked after she left. The question had been waiting over their heads like a dark cloud.

Yarick folded his arms. "You have a choice in front of you, Spartans."

"Go on."

"Some are recommending decommissioning Gray Team. A general discharge or hardship discharge. A reintegration team would be assigned to you, but there would be some . . . conditions attached to it." Yarick looked at them, curious as to their reaction.

Jai looked over at Adriana and Mike. "I didn't think ONI let Spartans become civilians," he said.

"I didn't say that we did," Yarick responded. "There are other ways we can employ your skills that don't involve public exposure. Only a handful of people know about what happened on Glyke. Some of them are Sangheili allies that we'd like to keep in our graces. This would be a public-facing decommission only. The bottom line about Glyke is that although it was tragic, it was not novel. Planetary genocide was effectively done to humanity repeatedly over the course of the war. The Sangheili know this and we know it—which is why we're putting the decision in your hands."

Jai nodded slowly, the world around him pulling back into a

focus he hadn't realized he'd lost. "We're Spartans, sir. We can't be anything but Spartans. We're not stepping away. That's not Gray Team."

He had spoken on their behalf. He tensed, expecting an objection. But neither Adriana nor Mike said anything. They gave him quick nods, their visors tipping forward ever so slightly.

Gray Team is back, Jai thought.

"The war we were fighting appears to be over," Jai continued. "We've obviously got some catching up to do. But even we can see that whatever is left of the Covenant is still causing trouble. The UNSC can barely control whole worlds like Carrow this far out from Earth. You're not done with us, sir. I think we all know that. So, what's the other choice?"

Commander Yarick smiled. "You're right—ONI would prefer to keep Gray Team intact and active. The Forerunners left a lot of secrets littered around the galaxy; many of them have been popping up on human colonies. Artifacts and technology are scattered throughout the Joint Occupied Zone, which obviously makes our peace extremely tenuous. Humanity is vulnerable, Spartans—especially way out here. We need a specialized strike force that we can send out into the dark, where the UNSC doesn't have formal coverage, that can keep us safe."

"And you think we are that team."

"Part of it." Yarick held out his hands. "See, if you agree to come back on in this capacity, we can offer you a formal pardon that the Arbiter—the Sangheili leader Thel 'Vadam—has put together along with others under him. Then you would join a team."

"We *are* a team," Mike said. "We don't work with others, sir."

"Right," Adriana said. "We go out. Alone. That's how we've always done this."

Yarick smiled. "I'm actually talking about an interspecies

team, trained to work together to face whatever out there that is threatening us."

"We've never worked with others," Adriana said, tapping the table. "Not even other Spartans."

But that isn't true, Jai thought. They'd worked with Rojka. They'd fought alongside Melody. "We'll need some time to think about that," Jai said.

"If you want back in, this is how it goes."

"Can you believe this?" Adriana said privately via Jai's helmet. Then, disgusted, "ONI."

"If we do this, I want a UNSC prowler at our disposal," Mike said to Yarick.

"What?" Yarick asked, twisting to face Mike directly. "That's—"

"I'm not doing this unless we have a stealth corvette, something fast and with slipspace capability," Mike said. "We're not hitching rides anymore. Or taking six-year naps. We get our own ship. *A prowler.*"

Yarick looked around at the Spartans. "If you're amenable to what I'm proposing, I'll see what I can do," he said.

"I have requests as well," Adriana said. "If the Sangheili are our allies now, I have a whole other list of weaponry I want to stock up on. It's an extensive list."

Jai smiled. It would take a long time for that weight they'd been carrying to fully slide away. But they'd turned a corner. They were broken, they were bruised . . . but they were still Gray Team.

Melody walked through the hallways of *Welcome to the Snipehunt*. Soon they'd be under way. Back to Earth. Back to suits and cocktail mixers with diplomats. Paperwork and the hum of offices.

She'd go back having saved a world though. There was a future to be built on Carrow. Soon there would be ships with even more diplomats on their way out here as the UEG created official channels. Formally, they would claim that a portion of Carrow that contained Suraka was an Outer Colony. A piece of this world would fall under the jurisdiction of the UEG. They would bankroll repairs and handle any fallout as a result of the Sangheili and Jiralhanae attack.

Sangheilos would likely do the same for Rak, which meant that somewhere out in the Uldt desert, between Suraka and Rak, would be an actual land border between the UEG and the Sangheili.

In practice, Melody knew the UEG didn't have the ability to force Suraka back in right now. So at least for the next few years, a form of realpolitik would have to be exercised here. Likely the same for the Sangheili. Carrow would be treated like it was independent although on paper everything would change. Melody would be an unofficial ambassador. Not just between Suraka and the UEG, but between the UEG and the Sangheili.

Now where would that put her on the climb up the organizational chart? That sort of fieldwork would go far in her working her way up the ranks. It would unlock assignments she hadn't even dreamed of.

In the past, she would have been quite elated by that.

But instead she was here walking the corridors of the *Snipehunt*. When was the last time she'd slept? Or thought about her staff. She would have to write the letters to their families.

How am I supposed to feel after a battle?

In the last couple of days, whenever she lay down and tried to close her eyes, sleep fled from her, like she was trying to hold on to water.

They'd given her sleeping patches. She knew she'd be poked and prodded a whole lot more when she arrived back on Earth. It had taken years of therapy for her to come to terms with growing up as a civilian in a war. How many years would it take for her to come to terms with what had just happened?

Did that mean that, just like back then, she wouldn't stop feeling dazed? That she'd never feel relief? That she had another long journey ahead of her?

The thought frightened her. She'd been keeping busy the past few days since coming back up out of the Forerunner structure. Trying to keep all that buried.

Melody stopped in front of a cabin door. She knocked gently on it, ignoring the comms system. "Hello," she said when it opened.

Adriana-111 stood on the threshold, wearing shorts and a halter top. No helmet. No armor. Her pale face stood out in the dark. Too much time under the armor. Too much time under an alien sun. Adriana ran a hand through buzz-cut hair.

"Can't sleep?" Adriana asked.

"No."

"The patches work."

"They yank me down into the dark. I don't like the feeling."

"Come on in." Adriana stepped back from the door. "Even in the dark, those things in your mind, they never really let go of you. The drugs just make them invisible."

Melody came inside and the door closed behind her. "No one else on this ship would understand what we've been through." She needed to stop running these things through her head. They'd been focused just on surviving for so long. Now the world was opening back up for her.

"Some of them have been in war," Adriana said.

"But nothing like the one *we* just saw."

"It's always the same," Adriana said.

Melody sat on a chair in the corner of the small cabin. "Do you know what Gray Team's going to choose?" she asked. She'd been told they'd be offered some sort of out, or more work with ONI.

Adriana was making tea over a small kitchenette. It was a strangely tranquil act, made bizarre by her tall frame and muscle. Here was a Spartan, out of armor, doing something so . . . *normal.*

She handed a steaming cup of water to Melody, then a cherry-colored container with a selection of teas in it. "You know already," Adriana said. "You just called us Gray Team. Your answer is there."

Later on, the tea still hot in her stomach, Melody lay looking at the ceiling of her own cabin. No matter how hard she tried, she still couldn't fall asleep.

Twenty minutes to slipstream transit.

Commander Yarick returned to the briefing room and shut the door. Someone moved in the dark at one of the desks at the back. Yarick quickly turned the lights on.

"Admiral Osman," he said, startled. "I didn't realize you were on board."

Where the hell *had* she come from? His heart pounded despite his forced casual tone. He desperately wanted to sit down in case his legs gave out. The Commander-in-Chief of the Office of Naval Intelligence sat right in front of him when she was supposed to be light-years away on Earth.

"I came in via prowler to take a look at Carrow, Commander. I wanted to see it firsthand. I'm actually on my way somewhere else: there's another storm brewing." She didn't get up. Just watched him with slightly narrowed eyes for a moment, then: "Gray Team encountered this Forerunner weapon, the Sharquoi. We almost lost a planet here because of those things, Commander. We could have ended up with them on Earth thanks to one disgruntled Jiralhanae chieftain."

"Gray Team acted quickly. We were lucky to have Spartans on the ground," Yarick said.

"*Lucky*, were we?" Admiral Osman raised an eyebrow. "Someone told the Sangheili where to find their lifeboat. Yes, that was very fortunate. Someone trained the envoy how to free them. Some would call that *more* than just simple luck."

Yarick gaped at her for a moment. "Of course, Admiral."

"Why don't you tell me about your meeting with them." She looked down at a notification from a viewscreen built into the desk and swiped at it.

"We issued the proposal, the one you approved. They said they have demands. Admiral, if they don't bite, we both know they're not the only team that did black ops against Covenant targets during the war. I could offer an alternate choice for the specialized group we're trying to build. One that would likely . . . integrate better. And be more affordable."

The admiral looked at Yarick as if he were an idiot. "They're Spartans, Commander. They will be taking the pardon and joining the team, even if they are negotiating a little with us. And yes, they'll never fully integrate into this new team; I agree with your report. But that's precisely why I want them to be out there. They don't trust others outside their circle, and that means they're exactly the kind of soldiers I want on this team, right next to our allies. Especially in the event that our allies ever decide not to be friendly anymore. We'll have eyes and ears right there. And weapons, should the situation require it."

"Admiral, they want a prowler," Yarick protested.

Yarick had never seen the admiral smile before. "Okay. So give them one. And new armor while they're at it."

"Admiral," Yarick nodded curtly. One prowler for Gray Team it was, then. Apparently if Gray Team wanted a fast, armored and stealth capable UNSC starship they were going to get it. He'd have to go looking through his notes for Adriana's very long list of Covenant weapons.

"Lastly," the admiral continued. "What about the Sharquoi? Did the Havok really take everything out, or have your scans from orbit been able to pick up anything left over?"

"We have our Surakan contacts in place with all governmental science agencies down on the ground. Their scans and ours from orbit don't indicate anything made it. But we will need to continue keeping an eye out for any that might have escaped into the desert. Otherwise, yes, I'd say we're clean."

Admiral Osman nodded. "Good."

Yarick let out a deep breath. "Admiral, what about Azikiwe?"

"Azikiwe doesn't know it yet, but she will be spending a lot more time with the Sangheili. She'll be one of our formal envoys to the Swords of Sanghelios as we create this new team."

Now that's interesting, Yarick thought. "Should I know about this other threat? The 'storm' you mentioned?"

"No, we've got others handling it. Your job is simple, Commander. Gray Team needs to be sharp and ready as soon as possible."

Admiral Osman stood up. "Things are about to get more interesting, and I'm going to need every last Spartan out there in the dark to protect us."

ACKNOWLEDGMENTS

Big thanks to my family, who put up with me during the year I worked on this book. Cal, Thalia, thanks for your patience. Double thanks to my wife, Emily, who sent me away twice to stay with friends or hole up in a hotel so I could really focus on the book.

Thanks also to Charlie Finlay and Rae Carson for letting me bunker down with them under a deadline so I could change my surroundings to somewhere warm while I wrote.

Thanks to my agent, Barry Goldblatt, for making sure everything went smoothly.

Thanks to Ed Schlesinger and the team at Gallery Books for bringing another fun Halo story to audiences.

And super big thanks to Jeremy Patenaude and Tiffany O'Brien, as well as everyone else at 343 Industries who wanted to see more of Gray Team. Jeremy was responsible for a lot of great ideas and was available at any moment to help answer questions I had.

ABOUT THE AUTHOR

Called "violent, poetic and compulsively readable" by *Maclean's*, science fiction author Tobias S. Buckell is a *New York Times* bestselling writer born in the Caribbean. He grew up in Grenada and spent time in the British and U.S. Virgin Islands, and these places influence much of his work.

His Xenowealth series begins with *Crystal Rain*. Along with other stand-alone novels and his more than fifty stories, Tobias has been translated into eighteen different languages. He has been nominated for such awards as the Hugo, Nebula, Prometheus, and John W. Campbell Award for Best New Science Fiction Author. His latest original novel is *Hurricane Fever*, a follow-up to the successful *Arctic Rising*, which NPR says will "give you the shivers."

He currently lives in Bluffton, Ohio, with his wife, twin daughters, and a pair of dogs. He can be found online at www.Tobias Buckell.com.

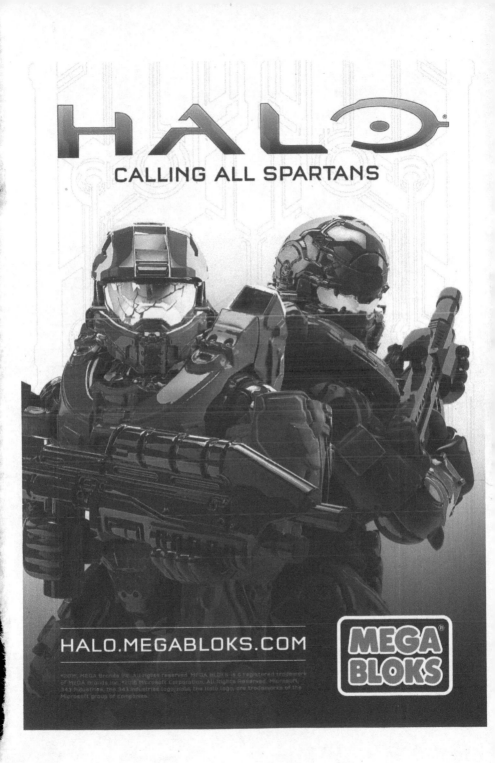